Praise for the Chronicles of Kaya

'This beautiful fantasy novel not only delivers surprises, suspense, a magical but dark world and great action, but also a moving and powerful exploration of love, loss and second chances.' *Sophie Masson*

'To enter this world, you must prepare to have your heart and soul and imagination invaded and overmastered. The series demands it and you would be a fool to resist. There will be laughter and sorrow and fear, but you will emerge richer than you entered.' *Isobelle Carmody*

'Highly recommended.' *Stephanie Gunn*

'Between the nail-biting scenes and the sexual tension, I had a lot of trouble putting this book down.' *Angelya*, Tea in the Treetops

'Full of action, magic, love, war, loss and friendship, definitely a must read.' *Paola Emilia*

'No matter what I say, or how much I try to explain, some of you will just never understand that this isn't just a book. It is an all-encompassing feeling that has stormed into my life and I'm not sure if I'll ever be the same. They called this book "a sweeping romantic fantasy". How aptly described. It swept me off my feet and swept the air out of my lungs.' *Morgana's Book Extravaganza*

'I can't recommend this book highly enough.' *Kathylill*

'That was the craziest ride I've been on for a while and I'm exhausted. Someone fetch me my Valium and a tumbler of gin! Not only is it full of bad-assery, but it's also heartbreakingly sad and full of eloquent expressions of love, suffering and the human condition.' *The Urban Book Thief*

'This book may very well be one of my favorite books of the year.' *Rireading Books Blogspot*

'Every fan of the Graceling Trilogy will swoon over this book.' *Patrycja*

'Charlotte McConaghy is a brilliant writer, she easily captivates you with her words and makes you laugh with her characters as well as cry.' *Kenzie,* Chasing My Extraordinary

'The Chronicles of Kaya is a MUST read for all the fantasy lovers. It has everything to be your next favourite series, so please go and give it a try, you won't regret it!' *Azahara Arenas,* Living in Our Own Story

'Wow – that is what comes to mind when I think of this book.' *M Pollard*

'You. Guys. This series. What in the hell have I even gotten myself into. I just innocently started Avery about a week ago and now here I am, suddenly done with the entirely trilogy. I legitimately feel like I have had part of my heart ripped out and crushed but I'm also feeling so in love. These characters and their journeys have quickly and easily become embedded in my heart and will never leave. I honestly can't wait until I can re-read them all again.' *Arielle Reads*

'Full of action, magic, love, war, loss and friendship, definitely a must read.' *Paola Emilia*

'This book was beautiful. Romantic. Real. Heart-wrenching and happy and tear-your-heart-out-madness and then just lovely.' *Rachel Carter*

CHARLOTTE McCONAGHY

THE CHRONICLES OF KAYA

ISADORA

BOOK THREE

BANTAM

SYDNEY AUCKLAND TORONTO NEW YORK LONDON

A Bantam book
Published by Penguin Random House Australia Pty Ltd
Level 3, 100 Pacific Highway, North Sydney NSW 2060
www.penguin.com.au

Penguin
Random House
Australia

First published by Random Romance in 2016
This edition published by Bantam in 2017

Addresses for the Penguin Random House group of companies can be found at global.penguinrandomhouse.com/offices.

National Library of Australia
Cataloguing-in-Publication entry

McConaghy, Charlotte, author
Isadora/Charlotte McConaghy

ISBN 978 0 14378 469 2 (paperback)

Series: McConaghy, Charlotte. Chronicles of Kaya; 3

Romance fiction
Fantasy fiction
Man–woman relationships – Fiction

Cover image © Aleshyn_Andrei/Shutterstock Images
Cover design by Isabel Keeley-Reid and Cathie Glassby
Map by Xou Creative
Internal design and typesetting by Midland Typesetters, Australia
Printed in Australia by Griffin Press, an accredited ISO AS/NZS 14001:2004
Environmental Management System printer

For the romantics

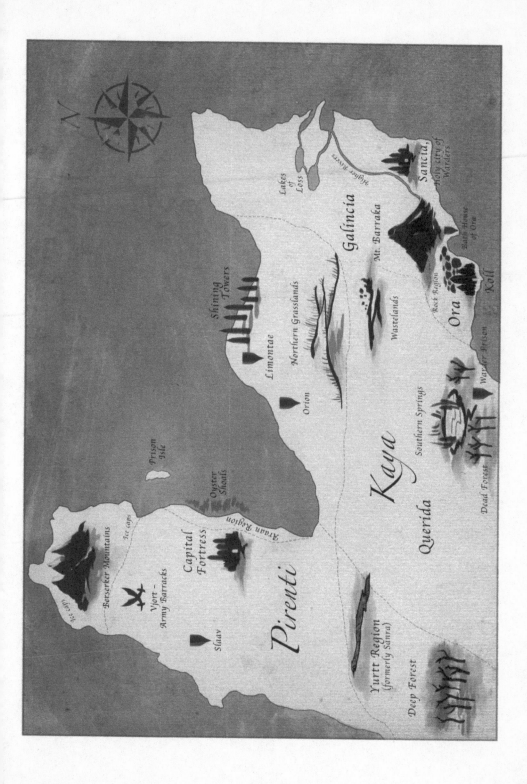

'There is a land of the living and a land of the dead and the bridge is love, the only survival, the only meaning.'

—Thornton Wilder, *The Bridge of San Luis Rey*

PROLOGUE

The world is made of numbers. I see every one of them. I *feel* every one. Some numbers fit inside others, some form patterns, some are breakable and others aren't. Numbers are infinite and counting makes sense of the noise, the buzzing of feelings that gets inside me and makes it hard to breathe. People's hearts flutter, their minds whirl and their hum saturates me. They forget how much they feel, but I never do.

I can count anything.

The number of steps from the top of Limontae's cliff to the sand of the beach: 581. The number of lemons Alexi puts in his famous spiced cod: 5. The number of freckles on Finn's nose and cheeks: 112. The times Jonah frowns each day: 9. How many times he smiles: 64. The centimeters between Thorne's feet and the top of his head: 199. The centimeters from one of his stretched fingertips to the other: 210.

The number of times Isadora has looked past me without seeing me: 0. The number of times she has ignored me: 0.

I have 1 family with a dozen members, and 2 very mad parents. I had 1 pegasis before he died, with 4 spots on his hind legs and 3 on his breast.

There are plenty of things to count, see?

What I'm counting at this very moment is the number of minutes I've been sitting in this prison cell, waiting for the world to die.

There is 1 moon in the sky and she's slim. There are 6 metal bars blocking her face. There have been 13 screams from beyond the window.

Something metallic rattles and I spin to face the bars of the cell door. There is 1 woman standing behind it, and she's using 1 key to unlock 2 padlocks.

'Shh,' she bids me and I realise I have been counting very fast out loud, so I close my mouth and count inside.

The door is open now. She gestures for me to hurry, but I don't move.

'Come, boy,' she urges. 'I won't hurt you.'

'You're the Viper.'

To which she replies, 'I've shed my skin. Would that you could, too, Penn. It might see you through this nightmare.'

But I don't need another skin. I just need more time.

I'm 43 minutes and 4 seconds late as I sprint away from that prison cell in the bowels of the world. And during those 43 minutes my friends could have been killed 43 times over. Maybe more. How many seconds does it take to die? If they are dead it will be my fault, my burden to bear. Because it's my 2 parents who will have struck the killing blows.

Chapter 1

Falco

Once I had a ma and da. I had two older brothers and one little sister. They had names and spirits, souls and smiles, words and thoughts and breaths and *lives*. I was loved. Drenched in love, a luxurious, absurd embarrassment of it.

Now all I had was a mask I should have been able to remove. And dreams.

In these dreams lived a girl with wings of snowy plumage and eyes filled with blood. I couldn't escape her and often woke with the certainty that I was choking on her feathers.

I could feel her circling. Most would look at me now and know I wasn't worth the bother of putting down. But she'd always been different. For the Sparrow, the only question of my death was when.

Isadora

I woke with his name on my lips and it burned. The lingering taste, as always, turned my mouth to ash.

Half a dozen warm, sleeping bodies were nestled around me, snoring quietly. I rolled over and stared at the ceiling. For the first week or so I'd been acutely uncomfortable with their nearness – with the communal nature of life here. But this morning, as the sun prepared to rise beyond the windows and the walls, I felt a moment of gratitude that I was not, for once, alone.

Rising from the too-hot flood of blankets and limbs, I crept out into the small back courtyard.

I wasn't the first. Only yesterday he had mended that stool, not with his magic, but with his hands, and now there he sat. I drew near, waiting for him to notice me in the dark.

'Did your dreams wake you again?' Jonah of Limontae asked, turning from his silent vigil of the dawn sky. When I didn't reply, he said, 'They woke me.'

'I'm sorry.'

'Don't be. It's just that you say his name all night, every night.'

I swallowed the shame at this mention of the curse on my soul.

'Why?'

'Hatred.'

'Yes, but why?'

I met Jonah's green eyes. 'He left us here.'

And there was truth in that. Sancia was now under warder reign, its citizens living under curfews, punishments and the fear of imprisonment. With no way in or out people were starving, dying of infections, their homes destroyed and freedoms stolen. No escape and no end in sight. All bequeathed us when the Emperor of Kaya turned tail and ran, leaving his people to be conquered by the Mad Ones, Dren and Galia, whose ugly souls were warped by magic and cruelty.

'We'll get out of here,' Jonah said with a certainty I didn't share. 'Finn and Thorne are coming.' Which was what he said every night and every morning and every time anyone asked him. But it had been months and Finn and Thorne had not come. We had no way to tell if they were even receiving the messages we smuggled out.

'What do you believe in, Iz?' he asked me softly as he often did, always trying to make sense of the battle raging in his head. I hadn't answered and didn't intend to. Instead, I watched the moon. Jonah was prone to sentimentality, but it was foreign to me.

'Why do you have so few words?' He sounded frustrated now.

I sat beside him on the bench, unsure how to offer him anything but this small gesture.

'I believe in the madness of magic,' he murmured. 'Dren and Galia are wicked to their core. But at least I understand the nature of their madness – they've been corrupted by the very same thing that courses

4

through my veins. It's the other one I don't understand. The Sparrow. I think he must be a monster to have set his life to destroying things without the madness of magic to blame.' Jonah turned his eyes to me and said, 'It'll get him, too, eventually. It's magic that will be the end of us all.'

★

Here was what I believed.

That you were either the hunter or the hunted. The butcher or the meat. The caged or the free.

And that four of my daggers had the names of their targets writ into the sharp edges of their blades. The Mad Ones, Dren and Galia.

Falco of Sancia.

And the name I hated most. Isadora the Sparrow.

★

My body ached as it did each time I had night-walked. I went through my stretches slowly and methodically, working the muscles and easing the tension. My neck always ached the most, and it took some concentration to knead the knots from it. When I was done I nodded at Penn and we left the small house, checking the street to either side. We kept to the shadows as we made our way to the marketplace.

I wore a hooded cloak so my hair and skin wouldn't be remembered. My hands strayed unconsciously beneath it to check each of my daggers, even though it had been years since the six weapons had left their places on my body – aside from when I used them. I couldn't even stand to remove them when I slept or washed. The cool touch of metal against my skin had a calming effect. But then again, everything had a calming effect on me.

The marketplace had long since died and now all that remained was its skeleton. The first time I'd witnessed it, nearly a year ago at Falco and Quillane's national tournament, it was abuzz with life. I'd been wandering, wanting quiet and solitude, when instead I'd come across this explosion of sound and mess and something had stayed my feet. For the first time I'd let myself explore tastes unlike

5

any I'd experienced – little morsels of sweet and savoury delights, dripping in crystallised sugar or spice. I gazed at gems and jewels of sparkling beauty, carved wooden trinkets and jewellery, leatherwork fine enough for royalty. I listened to instruments I couldn't name and ran my fingers over endless, glorious weaponry. The knives were the finest I'd seen, but I hadn't purchased any – mine had been forged specially, their weight an extension of my body.

Now Penn and I entered a grey, drab parody of a marketplace. Few stalls remained, and these were for ration distribution. Warders guarded them, watching as Kayan folk lined up for what little food had been afforded by their new rulers.

Penn and I waited our turn. My eyes scanned the proceedings, looking for the face of my soldier. The girl, whose name I didn't know, worked for the Sparrow and thought I did too. I spotted her exchanging chits for food. These chits could only be earned by turning in weapons, medicinal supplies, any belongings, or by working for the palace. If you worked you'd find yourself cleaning streets – collecting the dead bodies and human waste – or serving the palace. This last duty paid a great deal more and was reserved for the beautiful. The Mad Ones did not abide ugliness.

When Penn and I reached the front of the line we handed over our chits. To earn them, each night I pillaged abandoned houses for anything I could trade. I stole from the dead and felt no remorse. It was the living who suffered now.

The girl took our chits without looking at me and turned to gather the small packages of grains and oats. All other supplies had been cut off when movement within the country was forbidden and the roads to the agricultural areas closed. Grains and oats came in at the behest of Dren and Galia, but there was only so much and it was never enough. Inns and taverns had shut their doors, bakeries had closed and fishermen were forbidden to unmoor their vessels from the docks.

With an inconspicuous glance at the warders on either side of her, the girl handed us the packages, four in exchange for four chits. Underneath the bundle was a small scroll of parchment, hidden in her hand. I slipped it inside my tunic and nodded my thanks.

'Lower your hood,' one of the warders said abruptly. He was the shorter of the two, but it was difficult to distinguish him in any other way.

I didn't move.

'Sire, I'd warn against it,' Penn spoke for me. 'She has a birth defect, and might scare the children.' There was indeed a family behind us, a mother and her three children gazing at us curiously.

The warder flicked his hand impatiently and my hood flew back to reveal the truth of me, hideous as it was. Born without pigment in my hair or skin, I was as pale as a snowflake, as colourless as a wisp of cloud. Except for my eyes. They were the only parts of me with a visible hue: the deep crimson of vein's blood. They had shifted from this shade but once in my life.

One of the children gasped aloud. Another started to cry. But the third, I saw, smiled with rapt fascination even as his mother pulled him away from me.

'She won't hurt you!' Penn assured them.

I returned my eyes to the warders. One of them looked bored enough with the world to drift off to sleep right there. But the one who'd spoken had a lip curled in disgust. I'd come to expect it from warders, although it never failed to strike me as odd, given they too were sapped of colour. I supposed it was different: they'd once had brown hair, or eyes that shifted to brilliant azure. In warders there was always the memory of colour, but in me there was not even a whisper.

'What *are* you?'

I raised my chin. Not a good idea, as it would turn out. But even if I rarely felt much else, I did feel hatred, and it was too often an unwieldy beast.

'Answer, demon,' he ordered.

Demon. A memory brutalised me, but I pushed it back inside its box and locked it tight at the bottom of my mind.

'She's just a girl,' Penn said quickly. 'Born differently to you or me, but a girl.'

'I'll have the answer from the demon,' the warder said. He wasn't as small as Penn or me, of course, but small nonetheless. He bore it poorly, the weight of being so small in both body and spirit. It made him cruel.

7

Calmly, I placed my packages on top of Penn's and told him with my eyes to leave the square. He shook his head, but I darted a second, firmer look at the exit and he acquiesced. Calmly, I straightened. Calmly, I squared my shoulders and met the warder's faded eyes. And, calmly, I spat in his face.

Oh, boy. The fury that manifested in the alley was a living, throbbing thing. The sheer force of his anger sliced a sudden crack of lightning into the road beneath my feet and the force sent me flying back. Right before I hit the wall I went limp to lessen the impact. It still hurt. A lot.

I straightened myself slowly out of a crumpled heap in time to see Penn shepherding people from the markets. The warder stormed towards me. A second bolt of lightning struck a stall to his side; the material of its roof went up in flames and then his magic pummelled me into the wall, pinning me there. Pain flooded every muscle and bone, every nerve ending. I thought my teeth would shatter, my eardrums burst.

'*What are you?*' he snarled, too close to my face. 'Why is your mind blank? You are no warder to block my powers, so why can't I see anything?'

Because there was nothing. There was a body and a purpose and nothing else.

'Speak or die, demon!'

He intensified the pain and I closed my eyes. The lake of liquid calm spread through my mind.

For twelve years I lived in a cage. Suspended over a chasm haunted by monsters. And when finally I escaped it, I stumbled through the forest and came upon a vast, still lake. Its silver surface was calm until I waded into it. But even then it seemed to close around me and I had the clearest sense that nothing could disturb it. With a single breath I sank below to where the scraping claws and bars of my cage didn't exist anymore. Here I knew a quiet that moved inside me, taking root in my mind and soul. I became the lake, and it me.

Now, in the marketplace, I let it soothe the pain and allay the hatred until I became nothing but the reflective glass of its surface, protecting the truth of what lay beneath.

The warder grunted in outrage and his eyes held their intent to kill.

'That's enough,' a flat voice said.

The small warder lowered his hands immediately, ceasing the hail of pressure on my body. I sagged to my knees, trembling so badly it was a miracle I didn't lose consciousness.

Approaching was a second warder, a woman tall and physically strong, far stronger than this male. She'd once had red hair, but it was now streaked through with white. 'You've made your point,' she told the man. 'Killing in anger is beneath a warder.'

'She was insubordinate.'

'I will punish her. You are too emotionally disturbed.'

The male warder looked like he wanted to argue, but she clearly outranked him so he strode away. I forced myself to stand; my body felt like it had been taken apart and sewed clumsily back together. The female appraised me carefully, probably probing my mind like the man had tried to. 'I am Gwendolyn.'

Interesting. This was the Viper, Galia's right hand. A first tier warder and very powerful. She was on my list, after Lutius, head warder of Kaya.

'What's your name, girl?'

I said nothing.

'Are you mute?'

I inclined my head subtly. Let her think I was. Words were precious and powerful, and hadn't nearly been earned by her.

'Wretched creature,' she murmured, and her voice held vague, weary pity.

I could have smiled then. She was amusing, this woman and her magic, that small man and his.

'I find myself reluctant to punish you,' Gwendolyn mused. When you rarely spoke people deemed you stupid as well as silent, and said things in your presence they wouldn't otherwise. 'I had a daughter born with a lame leg,' the Viper continued in the same detached voice. She had a shrewd look in her eyes and I suspected she was trying to manipulate me somehow. 'Her father drowned her.'

We stared at each other. I let my eyebrows narrow coldly. She wanted anger. Empathy. Pity. I would give her nothing but contempt: for not having stopped him.

Gwendolyn shook her head suddenly, breaking our shared trance. She sighed and waved her hand. 'Away with you. Keep the hood raised in future.'

I walked from the alley, focused on keeping my footsteps straight. Waves of ache made my spine feel brittle. At the street corner I found the small male warder. He motioned for me to stop and I braced myself for another attack. 'If you weren't so freakish, you might be appealing, demon,' he told me with a chuckle. And then he backhanded me hard across the cheek.

'Simple physical pain is often more brutal than anything rendered with the mind, I've found.' He smiled and made way for me. 'Go on then.'

As I walked past him I met his eyes and gave him six words: 'I'll find you in the dark.'

*

Penn was waiting for me nearby and thankfully didn't say anything as we walked home. Well, nothing to me. He counted urgently under his breath, trying to soothe himself with the numbers.

The house was a long way from the palace in a small, rundown neighbourhood. We'd boarded up the windows and doors and were careful not to let anyone follow us home. Bands of hoarders had taken to killing and robbing any who strayed into their paths.

After scaling the wall of the back alley, Penn and I went into the kitchen to unload our food rations.

There were nine of us living here, including the baby. I had come somewhere in the middle of the party, having lost Jonah and Penn on that fateful night of the invasion. I'd only found them by following rumours and searching house by house. They were holed up here with the owners of the house, Elias and Sara, and their baby daughter Eve. Jonah had been deathly ill that night, having jumped the three of us from Pirenti to reach the palace in time to warn Falco of Lutius' betrayal. Somehow Penn had managed to get him out of that crumbling building. They'd travelled through the night until they could go no further, and when they collapsed in the street, Elias – a scribe for the university – had seen them from the window and run out to help.

In the following days warders raided homes and placed wards on doors and windows to detect magic used in private residences. A great deal was destroyed, many killed. Riots began, but warder magic cut the revolt down with mass slaughter.

Jonah managed to save a woman called Glynn from being trampled in the street. I came next, and then Penn found the brothers Wesley and Anders, who had been beaten to within an inch of their lives for daring to stop the warders entering their home. Their sister was killed that night and the grisly young blacksmiths recovered fast from their beating, keen for blood.

Sara entered the kitchen while we unpacked rations. She took one look at my face and cursed loudly. 'With me, now.'

I obeyed reluctantly, and after catching sight of me Jonah tagged along. 'What happened?'

'A warder attacked her,' Penn informed them. 'A warder attacked her. A warder attacked her.'

'Penn, don't lock on,' Sara said distractedly, but he kept saying it anyway. She sat me on one of the beds and started applying cream to my cheek, eye and lip. I was sure it looked worse because of my skin, but I didn't bother saying so because she'd only keep fussing. Sara took pleasure in fussing.

'I got what you asked for,' Jonah told me. 'Though after this you'll have to delay the plan at least a week. It might change your skin and hair, but it won't cover bruises this bad.'

I nodded, but there'd be no delaying anything. I reached under my tunic and removed the scroll the market girl had smuggled. An invitation to work in the palace.

'Are you sure . . .?' Jonah asked nervously. 'I still don't think it's a good idea, being so close to them.'

'Hush,' Sara told him. 'She's made up her mind. And I can always cover her bruises.' At the thought of this, Sara smiled a glorious smile – the kind of smile given by people who loved easily – and then she reached out to touch my cheek in the casual way people who think touch is normal do. I forced myself not to flinch as she considered how

11

best to work her magic. She wore amazing, strange face paint each day. It was the thing I liked best about her – that even during such danger she didn't wish to blend in – but I was also nervous about what she might do to my already-strange face.

For now, Sara used some kind of salve to coax my split cheek and lip to heal more quickly, then set me free. 'I told you last time to watch your mouth,' she admonished me, then realised what she'd said and laughed. If I'd been the laughing type, I might have too. She knew just as well as I did that the reason I kept getting beaten up by warders was for my *lack* of mouth, so to speak.

Once she'd bustled out, Jonah asked, 'Want to try it now?'

I nodded, so he retreated to find his stolen goods.

Penn walked past the doorway, muttering under his breath. 'A warder attacked her. A warder attacked her.' Inwardly, I sighed. There was nothing to do but wait it out.

Jonah and I made our way to the washroom and I sat on the side of the tub. He showed me the small glass pots. 'This one is for hair, this one for skin. I can't do anything about your eyes, though.' He opened the pots and made as if to start applying them.

'I'll do it,' I forestalled.

Jonah looked at me, softening. He was very slender, a little bit pretty. His eyelashes were long, his blond hair growing out and his lips were shaped like a perfect love-heart.

I could feel that he still wanted more than friendship from me. There was some kind of affection living in his touches, but no sign of the same thing in mine. I was too far away from it all, incapable of anything of the sort.

I didn't think of the other one. I never thought of him, or the throbbing unease at the base of my spine, or the dual hearts beating against the cage of my ribs.

'You're not going back out tonight, are you?' Jonah asked as he handed me the pots of dye.

I didn't answer.

'Iz . . . I go to sleep every night thinking I'll wake to find you dead.'

There was nothing I could say to that, so he left me alone in the washroom.

I undressed and steeled myself to stand before the mirror. I hated my reflection, but this would require a careful eye. With steady hands I lathered the ointment over my skin and into every inch of me. It was an arduous task and I took my time to make sure there were no streaks. Then I washed my hands and started working the powder through my white hair.

When I was done I looked at myself for a full minute, counting the seconds and forcing myself to stay. It would take some hours for the effect to be visible. So until then a bloody-eyed snow-creature would stare back at me. She was unusual, certainly. Was she monstrous? I wasn't sure.

But perhaps that was because I knew the truth: the real monstrosity lived on the inside.

Chapter 2

Falco

'No. Again.'

Inwardly, I sighed. Inwardly, I said, *Shove the blasted training up your enormous Pirenti backside.* Outwardly, I made no reaction at all. I was a picture of dispassionate calm.

A trickle of laughter cut through the afternoon and I looked over at Finn lounging along the top of the battlement. 'Ambrose, he just said you have an enormous Pirenti backside.'

'I did *not* say that,' I replied, folding my arms petulantly. 'The witch snuck inside my head and stole thoughts that do not belong to her.'

Finn laughed again. They all did, actually. 'This is fast becoming my favourite activity,' she admitted.

Thorne sat next to her, his back iron-straight as always, stiff alongside his small, lazily sprawled wife. His massive white Alsatian, Howl, sat attentively between his legs, Thorne's fingers perpetually threaded through the dog's fur. Finn's fingers, on the other hand, were perpetually touching her husband in some way, and now traced idly along the back of his neck. I was distracted by the thought of how those fingers would feel on *my* skin, and hoped she didn't catch that one.

Ambrose remained standing to watch the proceedings, growing more impatient by the minute. Fair enough, I supposed. He'd been trying to teach me for months, to no avail. Opposite me stood Osric. The only first tier warder in all of Kaya. Except he wasn't anymore. He was the only *legal* first tier warder.

'Focus!' the King of Pirenti ordered me in that deep booming voice of his, the one that scared birds from the trees in the forest below.

'Shall I point out that yelling at me is not helping clear my mind?'

Ambrose's glare was so displeased I would not have been surprised had he used that ludicrously large axe of his as a pike for my head. I turned back to Osric, trying to ignore the endless laughter of bloody Finn of Limontae, gods-cursed bane of my existence.

'Oh, come now, I'm not the bane of your existence,' she murmured. 'And if I am, then you lead a very sad existence indeed, Emperor Feckless.'

'Muzzle your dog!' I snapped at Thorne, who smiled placidly at me.

'I think that's the nastiest thing you've ever said about me,' Finn sniffed. 'Or Howl. Either way, I'm offended.'

'If you are all so feeble-minded as to think I don't have better things to be doing with my time, then I'm done,' Ambrose said, striding for the stairs.

'Wait!' I called. 'Sorry, sorry. I'll focus, I promise.'

Ambrose paused, giving me one more chance. 'Go!' he barked at Osric. Who smiled that quicksilver smile and sent a huge blast of energy straight into my body. I didn't even have time to pretend I was clearing my mind of all thoughts – I sailed back through the air and slammed into the stone battlement. The air was knocked from my chest with a *whoomph*. I coughed and spluttered, rolling onto all fours and trying to drag in a breath.

Howl padded over to sniff at me, then kindly licked my face.

A human knelt before me, larger than life. The King of Pirenti with his huge knuckles and huge arms and huge shoulders. How was he so huge? How were they *all* so huge up here? *It's almost grotesque*, I told my poor emasculated self.

'Falco,' Ambrose said in his honey-voice, the singer's voice. 'You will never kill a warder.'

I struggled into a sitting position.

'I don't say that to wound you,' he added, 'but to prepare you. There is far too much going on in that head of yours for you to ever be impenetrable to their powers. So just don't try.'

'What do you suppose I do then?'

And that was when he smiled, and the normal Ambrose returned to the roof. 'Just hide behind me, kid. My head's empty enough to protect you.'

Which sent the rest of them into fits of laughter. Even I cracked a smile, but had to be careful to maintain an air of wounded pettiness: the act was hardest to maintain around people who constantly made me laugh.

Ambrose helped me to my feet and headed off to do kingly things. I staggered over to my friends. 'Forgive me,' Osric said gently, reaching to pat me condescendingly on the head. 'But you did ask me to do this.'

'*I'd* be happy to do it,' Finn offered with a wicked glint in her eye.

'You're not coming anywhere near me,' I warned her. 'And you know it's still illegal for you to be using your magic, so your Emperor would be well within his rights to punish every count of mindreading.'

Finn flung her arms around my neck and gave a dramatic swoon. 'Forgive me, oh mighty Emperor! Please don't punish me!'

'You think you're being cute, but you're not.' I couldn't curb the twitch of my lips.

Finn smiled a real smile and kissed me on the cheek. Then told a big fat lie. 'You're right. I'll be more careful.' She beckoned to her husband as she headed for the stairs, whistling to him like a dog and slapping her thigh. 'Here, boy.'

Thorne made a face and she made one back, then both their mouths split into smiles. His was the kind only he could offer – an expression infinitely more gentle than anything else that existed under the sky of this world. 'Give me a moment.'

Finn nodded, dragging Osric from the roof with a rude comment about the lack of finesse in his teaching methods.

I was left alone with Thorne and Howl. We looked out over the oyster farms of Pirenti, which glistened like silver teeth in the distance. The prince placed a thick, meaty hand on my shoulder. 'What's going on with you, brother?'

I sat down against the balustrade, needing to not be touched, to have no one look at the pitiful mess of me. Howl rested his head in my lap, knowing. He always knew.

Here was how it seemed to work. I couldn't block a physical blow from a warder. I couldn't stop them from controlling my body or coercing me to believe I was sensing what they wanted me to. But I could block them from reading the truth. Finn and Osric read my surface thoughts. They did not read anything deeper. They didn't see any of the real truths, any of the things I kept hidden. I had training from a lifetime of deceit; no matter how powerful they might be, they would never know what I didn't wish them to know without, as Finn put it, smashing my mind to pieces.

But Thorne – he was different. The berserker in him could *smell* what lay beneath the surface, just as his dog could, and I had absolutely no power over that. 'What are you getting?' I asked him.

He tilted his head and drew a long breath through his nose. 'The usual things. Frustration. Amusement. Desire for my wife.'

My head whipped towards him.

Thorne smiled a little, just a little. 'Don't worry. I've scented that on you since the day you met her.'

'How is that consolation?'

'What's new,' he murmured, 'as of the last six months, is the despair.'

Howl chose that moment to give a slight whimper in my lap.

'Despair is the worst scent there is,' Thorne added softly. 'It's thick and rancid, my friend. It smells like death.'

I watched a swallow dip through the sky above us, its melancholy path beautiful. I was an absence. Where there had once stood a man there was now a hole. The cut-out shape where a person had been.

'I understand. The subjugation of your people. The usurping of your reign.' He took another breath, another smell of me, and this time it unnerved me. I fought the urge to move away. 'But it's more than that,' Thorne concluded. 'It smells . . . intimate. More intimate. I don't know how else to describe it.'

I stood up to force some space between us.

'Falco, must we play this guessing game? Won't you just tell me?'

'It's nothing.'

'The rest still think you feckless, but I have never believed the ruse.'

'*Leave it.*' I strode for the stairs, then forcibly drew myself to a halt. *Don't*, I warned myself. *You have never had friends before. Not true ones.*

17

Don't push him away now. It was a battle every day not to hide from the people in my life. A battle to show them pieces of the truth, as many as I could stand to give away. Because whenever I tried a voice whispered my deepest fear — that it would be impossible to show any pieces of truth when *there were none.* That Emperor Feckless was a mask, and beneath him was nothing. Perhaps the bones of a child that had long since been picked clean by life's vultures.

I faced Thorne once more. I was fifteen years older than him, but he stood more than a head taller, was at least double my width. He had a harsh, blunt face, with hair shaved short enough for his scalp to be visible. He wore a huge cloak, but unlike his kin, he did not wear fur. He never wore animal fur, and I was one of the few people who understood that it was because he felt so animal himself. Something dark and strange had happened to him in the north, and he had returned King of the berserkers. A brutal, bloody fate for a man to carry, especially when he was barely more than a child. Now Thorne spent most nights roaming the forest, pulled by the weight of an anvil to be wild and free and alone. And yet still he managed to stand here, present, painfully refined and caring more for his friends and family than anything.

'Forgive me.'

'There's no need,' he replied simply. 'I worry for you.'

'And I love you for it, brother.' I smiled. 'But all I need is a night on the drink and a couple of women to share my bed. You have divine ones, you know.'

'Women?'

'Aye. Or at least *new* ones. I was growing bored of bedding Kayans who all look and taste the same.'

He gave me an impatient look, but I grinned. Because that was all that was left. Grinning and lying, or turning to dust.

★

I spent the evening in the armoury with my two favourite people. While I used seed oil to treat the wooden slats, my team members painted flowers and other embarrassing things onto the undersides of the huge wings.

'Sigh,' I said, instead of sighing.

'What now?' Ella asked me.

'He doesn't like the pictures,' Sadie explained with a roll of her eyes.

'How could he not like moths?'

'Or spiderwebs?' She flicked paint at me.

'Watch it! This shirt was expensive.' I flicked paint back and before long it was an all-out paint war, the three of us diving behind counters and lurching out to splash vermilion at each other. I got splattered way more than either of them, which they were happy to point out.

'Just you wait,' I warned. 'When you least expect it, I'll destroy you and all you hold dear.'

'Lovely.'

We all whipped around to see Ava standing in the doorway, looking unimpressed. 'Hate to interrupt the ruthless attack on my offspring, but you need to come with me, Falco. Now.'

'We're otherwise occupied, darling.' I waved her away.

'Now,' she repeated, in that very 'Ava' way of hers.

I shared a bewildered look with the eight-year-old twins, who shrugged. 'You'd better do it,' Sadie commented.

'I'll be back,' I warned.

'No, it's bedtime,' Ava told them. 'Upstairs for washing, please.'

'Oh, *Ma*,' they whinged together.

I followed Ava into the corridor. 'What's going on?'

'A messenger has arrived.'

'So?'

'From Sancia.'

My heart lurched, but I gave no sign of it. Ava and I hurried up the winding steps to the tenth floor and entered the war room. At its center was a beautiful wooden table, large enough to seat at least a score of people. Around the walls were maps of Kaya and Pirenti, as well as maps of the Kayan cities of Sancia and Limontae that we'd been using over the last few months.

Ava and I were the last to arrive. Ambrose, Thorne, Finn, Osric and Roselyn were already there, waiting for me in their usual seats. There was also a very sweaty boy of about twelve standing nervously to the side.

I went to him. 'Are you well, lad?'

He nodded, bowing low. 'You're His Highness?'

I nodded.

'Beg your pardon for the intrusion.'

'Not at all. You've run the length of the world, by the smell of you.' I made one of my routine expressions of distaste to the others, who weren't impressed by it.

The boy procured a scruffy looking piece of parchment from his pocket. 'I'm sorry to the rest of you, but I had orders to give this to the Emperor of Kaya, and none but him.'

'Who did it come from?'

'I don't know, Sire. A girl.'

'Can you describe her?'

A look of fear passed his eyes. 'She was . . . soulless. Damned.'

The words caused a strange ache in my chest. 'White hair? Red eyes?'

The boy nodded.

'Did she say anything?'

'Only that I was to get this to you, or she'd haunt me the rest of my days.'

I almost smiled.

'Can you tell us anything more about what's going on in the city?' Ava asked him. 'How did you get out?'

'Secret tunnels, Majesty,' he explained. 'The city's still overrun. It's bad. Not much food or clean water, bodies piling up and causing disease. But . . . someone's been . . . killing the warders, Sire.'

We stared at him. 'Who?'

He shrugged.

'*How?*'

'Dunno, Majesty. But every morning the city wakes to find one of them dead and laid out in the town square. There's always something carved into their foreheads.'

I swallowed. 'What?'

'A sparrow, Sire.'

★

After sending the child to be seen by a physician, I sat down at the table with the parchment.

'It's from Isadora,' Finn exclaimed. 'She's alive!'

Heart pounding, I uncurled the note. '*Emperor Feckless,*' I read aloud, curbing my embarrassment. Of course she'd addressed it so. '*If it be your will, we kindly request that you deign to send aid.*'

'Wow,' Ava commented. 'Someone does *not* like you.'

'*As stated in the previous letters, Sancia is under warder reign. But there are those on the inside who have formed a resistance. We seek a sign, any sign, that we have allies on the outside. That we have not been forgotten. We would like to know if our Emperor has any regard for us at all.*' I stopped. 'That's it.'

Finn snatched it from my hand. 'It's Jonah's handwriting!'

We sat in silence for a moment, considering the note.

'Several things,' Ambrose surmised. 'Isadora and Jonah are both alive, or were when the message was sent. There are secret tunnels in and out of the city. And someone is assassinating warders in the name of the Sparrow.'

'Could it *be* the Sparrow?' Ava asked.

'It's possible.' Osric shrugged. 'We have no idea who he is – he could have been in the city when it was overtaken.'

'What about these tunnels?' Thorne asked. 'We can use them to get in.'

'Did you know about them?' Finn asked me.

'I did.'

'Then why didn't you tell us?'

'I suppose it must have slipped my mind.'

They stared at me.

'You're kidding, right?' Finn said. 'What's wrong with you? People in that city are dying.'

I shrugged. I hadn't forgotten the tunnels. I simply hadn't mentioned them because they were dangerous. Most had collapsed before I left and several had been found by the warders on the night they took Kaya, so I assumed the rest were also discovered and guarded. Not easy to keep things hidden in a city full of warders.

'According to the boy, there's at least one in use,' Ambrose said.

'Unless this is a trap set by Dren and Galia,' Ava pointed out. 'How many knew of the tunnels, Fal?'

'Me. Quillane.' My voice hitched over her name. 'And probably every warder in that city.'

And Isadora, apparently.

'I knew,' Osric admitted. 'I assumed they'd have been long since discovered by the Mad Ones.'

'So who told the boy?' Finn asked. 'It could be a trap. Except that doesn't make sense, because how would he know to describe Isadora? There's no way in the Gods' world that she would be working for Dren and Galia.'

'Unless she was being manipulated by them,' Ava said. 'They have the power to do that, if they wish.'

'Isadora might have found the tunnel,' Thorne said. 'She's always been capable of more than one might expect.'

As they talked themselves painfully in circles I melted to a puddle of guilt for not sharing the truth I knew. Isadora, rebel Sparrow of the South, was my bondmate. She knew of the tunnels because she'd spied on me to discover them, and then used them to find her way to kill me. There was something far too intimate about divulging that, and I felt a peculiar repulsion at the thought of discussing anything about this without first speaking to her. That loyalty was surely misplaced – *these* were the people who deserved my loyalty, not my greatest enemy. Still, no words came from my mouth. The truth of my bonding wouldn't fit with any of my masks. Perhaps it was another mask in itself, one I didn't know how to wear.

'So if she wasn't being controlled and she found it herself,' Thorne hedged, 'why didn't Isadora send the message to Finn and me? She doesn't know Falco. Doesn't know where he is, if he's alive, where his loyalties lie . . .'

'Do my loyalties not lie with Kaya?' I asked.

Thorne met my eyes. 'What I mean to say, brother, is that you have a difficult reputation in Kaya. Isadora does not know you to be capable of helping her. But she knows Finn and me, and she knows we'll try to get her out. So why send the message to you alone?'

There was a slightly awkward silence at the mention of my reputation. I'd earned worse.

'It's a good question,' Ambrose agreed. 'You never met the girl, Falco?'

I shook my head.

'What if she's allied with the Sparrow?' Ava wondered. 'The message was derisive, at best. Perhaps she's aiming to wound an Emperor she doesn't believe in.'

'It's not enough of a reason to waste her only message out of the city,' Finn said. 'This is her one chance at seeking aid. Why waste it on an insult?'

'So she thinks Falco can help her,' Ambrose said.

I could hear their doubt, and found myself taking shelter behind it.

'There are very few who can kill a warder,' a voice said softly, and we all turned to look at Roselyn, with her auburn hair and porcelain skin. 'So how could this Sparrow have murdered several, unless he has magic of his own?'

In the silence that followed my eyes met Roselyn's and found her as eerily unreadable as ever. The woman somehow knew too much and too little at the same time. In her hands was a spool of wool and she went back to her knitting as if she had not made the most astute point so far this evening. Under her breath she counted her stitches, touching each one with her index finger.

'Marry me, Roselyn,' I implored for the eighth time, and for the eighth time she blushed and smiled and didn't look at me. 'Gods, have mercy on me. One of these days you'll say yes.'

'If you're quite finished,' Ava interrupted witheringly.

'What kind of man is ever finished seducing a beautiful woman?' I asked, earning a few impatient eye-rolls.

'However the killer is achieving his kills, we should see this as an opportunity,' Ava said. 'If the Sparrow is killing warders, then he's potentially on our side. We may be able to broach a temporary alliance.'

'No,' Osric said with a flash of his eyes. 'Never. He is traitorous, murdering scum.'

There was a short silence.

'Say what you really think, Os,' Finn muttered.

'Either way,' Thorne said, 'we gather our forces and move south.'

'War,' Finn said, and for once she didn't look flippant or reckless. She looked scared as she met her husband's eyes. 'You're talking about waging another war on Kaya.'

'Not Kaya,' he replied. 'The warders who seek to take what does not belong to them.'

They turned as one to look at me. Expecting something. Perhaps an impassioned speech about how I would take back what was mine, and welcome Pirenti aid in doing so. Instead, I asked, 'You think I know anything about war?' I shook my head and stood, scraping my chair back loudly. 'This is too tense for me. I'm going for a drink.'

'This isn't the time, Falco –'

'It's always the time for royalty,' I laughed. As I left their disappointment was palpable, but so familiar it felt safe.

I remembered vividly the fury I had felt that night, when Lutius had betrayed me and let the warders invade Sancia. I remembered the hatred I'd been filled with and the accompanying need to cast off all pretense, to fight for revenge and justice and power and respect. I had drawn my swords and screamed his name, and I would have fought him then and there – until something very, very different found me.

All of that was gone now, that fury and hatred. Everything was gone, and the more they expected of me the worse it would be for them when I failed to deliver.

★

After an ocean of ale I wound up in bed, staring at the ceiling. I could feel wingbeats inside my ribcages. I could feel *her*. Assassin, murderess, children's nightmare.

My Sparrow.

I remembered hearing her. That day. Or hearing something – footsteps. I remembered thinking to myself: *He's here. The Sparrow.* I remembered thinking it was fitting, now that Quillane was dead, for me to either die or kill. There was a pit of grief in my chest as I kissed my Empress on her cold lips. This slain person had been my someday, the beginning and end to every plan, every ruse, the reason to keep going. I had forged the mask, but Quillane had been the reason I wore it each day.

And that was when I saw it.

A wraith. Some kind of monster, something not human at all, too pale by far, too colourless. And who dared to be colourless in this world, this world ruled by the shades in eyes and souls? Who had ever dared but *me*? Me, whose eyes did not change, had shifted but twice since the day I was born?

My same shiftless eyes travelled over the creature and a sucking riptide took hold of my soul, dragging me into the unknown, the infinite, the absolute beauty of the void to which I had been blind.

She was not colourless after all. She had eyes of bloodiest crimson and she looked at me with them and –

– and I was aware for the first time of the complete savagery of life, the tearing hands and teeth against my skin, the perfection of fate and the *strength* of the world. Here, in her, the *strength*. I understood it immediately: the iron force of her will, the impossibility of it. The detachment she had from anything mortal – she was too cold by half for mortality.

Inwardly I sank to my knees before her, dwarfed. A slave to her for the rest of my days as I had never been to anyone. She made sense of my existence. As we bonded she let loose the fury that lay dormant in my heart, she gave power to my impotence. My eyes had shifted three times in my life. Once to gold on that night, with her. And twice before, twice when they had turned the bloodiest crimson. Isadora's shade of red.

Without her near I shrivelled and returned to dust.

Tonight I tried to form a thought, unsure how it worked, this bond. I formed it as hard and as clear as I could.

I'm coming for you, little Sparrow.

To have her or kill her, I didn't know. But either way the message remained the same. And that was when I was jerked from consciousness with a wrench on my guts and balls and lungs and dragged into a different plane of existence.

ISADORA

I took my place on the floor of the living room, surrounded by sleeping bodies. Jonah was outside on watch, but Penn lay to one side of me, Wesley to the other. I stared at the ceiling and let my mind calm into that place it inhabited during sleep. I would need focus.

The dream arrived with a tingling, sinister brush of my skin. Things blurred and warped. They became a cage of forged iron, swinging very gently over a precipice. I could hear the slight creak of the chain suspending me. And I could hear the faint shuffle of things below. I didn't know what that sound meant, not yet. I knew I had space to stand because I was small, but no space to walk or run. Space to curl in sleep and food that was raw and dead and never enough.

I was crying, sobbing. Wordlessly *begging* the men at the edge of the chasm. They were watching me, and there were two of them. They were so pale, as fair as me, and I thought they were surely here to help me. I knew only the cage, and that I must escape it.

But when one of them spoke he called me demon. 'Stay where you belong, demon,' he said. 'Guard your precipice.'

Demon, demon, demon. I'd heard the word before but this was the first time I'd been old enough to understand it.

I stopped begging then because it was suddenly clear that they were not here to help me. They'd put me here. And I would never beg again.

No.

No.

This is not now. In the house in Sancia I twisted one of my knives from its hilt and sliced it through the flesh of my thigh. My consciousness was reeled back from the cage and I returned to this room and this time with a brutal *whoosh* and a bloom of blood.

This was how I did it. Pain, and dreaming. Knowing the precise moment my knife was needed to tether me to my body. It was the trick no one else had learnt; it was how I alone killed warders. Lucid dreaming.

I'd first learnt to control my dreams while in the cage. I chose where they took me and how I could spend my sleeping hours. When I escaped I began to sleepwalk through the forest in this same lucid state, and after some years I could control that, too. So that now, as I stood within the dream realm, my body stood in the waking world. My body moved while my mind dreamt; I was a reflection of myself, a lake-still reflection.

I moved from the house and into the dark; I was invisible to magic, no matter how powerful the warder. Lucid dreaming was naught but a trick of the mind – it blanketed me in a state between dreaming and waking, the plane that magic did not inhabit. But I stayed silently to the shadows because, though impervious to magic, I was still in my body and could be spotted by eyes.

It was strange, this dreaming land. Nothing was quite as it looked when awake. Things had a less defined edge. Colours bled into each other, were more vibrant. Objects moved at unusual speeds, and I was often in danger of seeing things that weren't real. I had gone a little mad with the strangeness of it when I first discovered the ability as a child. I had dreamed myself beyond that cage and it had been so seductive that I had struggled more each day to return to reality. Eventually I nearly wasted away, having spent too long sleeping. But this, I understood, was what it meant to enter the subterranean realms.

The small warder who'd hit me today was on watch duty atop the city wall, as I'd hoped. In my dream state I approached him. He didn't hear or see me, intent on the grassy hills beyond the city. The sky above him was full of burning shooting stars, thousands of them. Things too beautiful to believe were always part of the dream.

My hands moved to my knives, drawing two. They were liquid in my fingertips. I could have killed the warder in a painless, fearless instant. But I didn't. I let my footsteps make a sound and watched him whirl to face me. A look of disbelief crossed him, chased by confusion. He didn't recognise me. Not with my altered skin and hair.

'Who are you?'

I licked my lips. They felt too dry, like I had swallowed a gallon of seawater.

'You're in breach of the curfew –' He stopped, sensing something. They could always sense something terrible. A truth about the human race: we always knew when we were about to die. When all possibilities and future paths ceased. When the culmination of who we were and what we had achieved came to pass.

Or perhaps that was me being whimsical.

He saw the knives then, and moved his hands. Whatever wave of energy he'd sent at me was impotent. He tried again, this time probably seeking to reach inside my mind. He failed.

I decided to speak. That was how cruel my hatred had become. A thousand glittering raindrops fell free of my mouth. 'Found you.'

He frowned as recognition dawned upon him. 'The demon child.'

'Why do you follow them?' I asked. It was a trick. A way to take advantage of this last moment of life, when people felt so vastly vulnerable, so desirous of connection or meaning that they would answer anything, reveal any truth, give up any piece of themselves. A strange subterranean realm of its own.

The warder shook his head, shaken and pale. He didn't understand what was happening, and yet he did. 'They have power that dwarfs the rest of us. They freed me from the prison.'

I felt prickles against my spine and darted a glance over my shoulder to see that there were needles injecting themselves into each of my vertebrae. *Not real.*

I always gave them words, in the end, these poor dying victims. Because I was taking everything from them. More than everything. I was taking the possibility of *anything.* Which meant they deserved something from me. 'You chose wrong,' I told the warder softly. 'Serving the Mad Ones has brought you death.'

And the small man, with his small body and his small soul, straightened his shoulders and became bigger than I imagined him to be. 'Better death, than that prison,' he told me simply.

So I nodded and killed him with two blades through his neck. Stars exploded from the wounds. He slumped to the ground and bled over the stone, his blood tiny waves in an ocean. I watched. I always watched, right until the end. Even though hundreds of sparrow wings brushed against my face to remind me of the desolation of my soul. To remind me of beauty in the same moment they reminded me of my lack of it.

Demon. Guard your precipice.

I knelt and used the same knife to cut a sparrow into his forehead. The skin there was delicate. Most of the blood had already left through his neck. There was not much of a mess, and I managed not to stain my hands.

That was when it happened.

I'm coming for you, little Sparrow.

The words tugged me sideways into the very thing I had spent the last six months trying to avoid. I was yanked violently from crouching over the dead warder to find myself standing in what I could only assume was Falco of Sancia's dream.

Huge feathers brushed against us, buffeting us upon the stone walls of whatever place we stood within. They were both gentle and rough.

'Sparrow,' Falco said, and it echoed eerily.

He fought through the feathers, reaching me and pressing me to the wall. He was all long pale hair and sharp lines and painfully glittering eyes. He was all . . . He was *all*. 'I'm coming for you, little Sparrow,' he said again, and then a rose bloomed from his mouth. The wings of the birds pressed at us; I felt their soft force on every inch of my skin.

No.

With all the strength of my will I wrenched myself from the dream and back into my body, the feel of his fingertips against mine tingling even after I'd gone.

★

I woke beside a dead body. I lurched upright, not breathing, unable to suck air into my exhausted lungs. My head and neck ached. Reality was brutal. Here everything looked blunt and ugly and normal. There was just a body, dead and carved, no burning stars or oceans. The city wall was empty and I was awake and nothing but a murderess.

I ran. All the way home, keeping silent, keeping invisible. Darting over rooftops and sliding down fences. Over the back wall and into the courtyard. I couldn't help the trembling of my knees, the way my breath was rattling.

I'm coming for you.

I couldn't have this. I would not.

It was Penn who found me, in the end. Penn, who didn't expect me to talk like everyone else always did. He sat beside me and when he took my hand in the dark I knew, somehow, that he understood exactly what it felt like under the surface of the lake. He gave me peace, just a glimpse of it, and I loved him for it.

★

The world made its monsters. Humans forged them with care and dedication. Twenty-six years ago I was born and in the twelve years that followed I was created – forged with care and dedication, into a monster.

And what was it that determined one to be monstrous?

Simple. It was hate.

When the Emperor of Kaya came for me, what would he find but that?

CHAPTER 3

FALCO

Thorne moved ahead of me, swifter and more silent despite being twice my size. I followed, allowing myself to drop back a few paces and watch the ground for any signs of disturbance in the underbrush.

We were tracking reindeer and the pack wasn't too far ahead. I had no tracking skills, but Thorne could smell them from miles away so it hardly mattered. Watching him was most of the experience for me. He melded with the forest, with the earth. He was animal, here in the wild.

He crested a rise and flattened himself to the ground. I approached loudly on my belly and crawled clumsily to his side. In a valley below was the herd of reindeer, grazing happily. I drew my bow and arrow, but Thorne reached to stop me.

'What do you plan on doing with *that*?' he asked.

'Look impressive.'

'Is it the animals you're trying to impress, brother?'

'It's you, Thorney, always you.'

He snorted and settled in to simply watch the deer. I relaxed beside him and there were long minutes of silence.

'Your thoughts are so loud they're likely to scare the herd away,' Thorne commented.

'So you're a warder now, are you? What is it with everyone in this damned place wanting to spy on what's in my head?'

Thorne just smiled.

'What would you do?' I asked him.

He considered silently. 'Go.'

'Even if it's a trap?'

'Yes.'

'They won't want me to go. They want me to do something, but they don't want it to be anything I could stuff up.'

He turned to me, my young friend, and said, 'Are you, or are you not, the Emperor of Kaya?'

I met his eyes. 'And what are those words but a title?'

He shook his head. 'Make them more. Give your people someone to believe in. I know you can, I just don't know why you choose not to.'

As I rose to my feet the beasts below sensed my movement and fled, but I didn't care as I walked angrily down the hill.

The trees were dense, making it impossible to see the sky. I wasn't sure how I knew. How I suddenly . . . sensed. But I did. There was a shift in the nature of the air, in my lungs, my heart, my ears and nose. I knew her with every sense, felt her with all of me.

A huge breath filled my lungs and I saw her.

First it was her thick dark hooves, and then her long, glorious wings. Her nose was slender and inquisitive as it poked down through the canopy. She descended in slow, dreamy arcs, gracefully finding a path through the trees and letting the sunlight catch the glistening snowy plumage of her wings. Some maddening part of me could feel her intent, her pride, her desire to please me, just as I could feel every one of her heartbeats, and the muscles in her flanks, and the wind in her feathers.

I walked without hesitation to her side and ran my hand over hair that was as dark as her deep, liquid eyes. She stamped her hoof, tossed her mane and took a snorting breath. The warmth of it made my skin prickle with delight. I could see fierce adrenalin coursing through her powerful muscles – she was a wild creature, not born to be tamed or ridden. But when she nuzzled her face into my side I felt it. Our bond.

The threads of our souls reached out and intertwined.

I pressed my face to hers, breathing in her warm scent. It was not like the bond I shared with Isadora – this one held no death within it, only life. Only love. In its tender touch I was remade.

'You're just in time,' I whispered.

Thorne put his arm around my shoulders as we watched her launch up into the sky and fly away, her black tail trailing behind like a dark comet. 'Why didn't you ride her?'

'She has more important things to do.'

'What will you name her?'

'Radha.' Thorne wouldn't understand, but I added, 'Quill would have loved that.'

Then I grabbed his arm and pulled him at a run towards the fortress. 'Come on, Thorney. Alert the messengers – the ladies of Kaya should beware! Their handsome scoundrel of an Emperor is returning to them.'

Thorne covered his laugh with a cough. 'Their idiotic Emperor.' But he added, 'Good man.'

★

I lay on the floor of Ella and Sadie's room, looking at the moths plastered over their ceiling. 'This fixation definitely means something psychological.'

'Don't change the subject. You're lying,' Sadie said. She was draped on the top of her wardrobe as usual, which I always found impressive given I could see no reasonable way of her getting up there. Her fingers brushed against the ceiling, and I was sure she was watching the moths just as I was.

Ella was on her bed, drawing quietly. She had become less interested in the insects than her sister, which I found curious.

'What do you think I'm lying about?'

'The reason.'

'You think it sounds false that an Emperor would want to free his people?'

'No,' Ella answered for her sister. Having a conversation with them meant interchanging constantly. 'But *you* sound false.'

'I want you to keep working on the wings,' I told them, a lump forming in my throat.

'You must love someone there more than you love us,' Sadie said, her voice floating down from the ceiling.

'No,' I managed, and then I was crying. Abruptly, ludicrously. Meeting my pegasis had ripped something open within me, something that had too many raw nerve endings. 'I don't want to leave you.' I played a role with the twins too, but it was one that felt truer than most.

Ella wriggled from her bed to my side and Sadie swung down to drape herself over me, and in their arms I couldn't help it – I wept like a child.

'You're a chrysalis,' Ella whispered, 'about to be reborn.'

I hoped she was right.

'Oh dear.'

We looked up to see Finn in the doorway. She smiled gently and I abruptly felt light as a feather and utterly, blissfully carefree. Ella and Sadie jumped to their feet and twirled ecstatically around the room, taking pieces of cloth to act as wings and brushing them sweetly over my face. I laughed softly, the bubble of joy lifting me to my feet.

'What are you doing?' I asked Finn, realising she must have been manipulating this feeling for us.

'It's just a moment,' she murmured. 'A moment without burden.'

'You can do that?'

'Seems so.'

I wanted to touch her. Wanted to kiss her lips and her face and her eyelids and her breasts. I wanted to hold her and fuck her and *have* her.

She tilted her head and I felt normalcy return, and with it that heavy weight. A breath left me, knowing she must have heard most of those thoughts. 'Forgive me.'

'Not your fault.' Then she turned those yellow eyes to me and said, 'Falco, I'm coming with you to Kaya.'

THORNE

'No. Please don't.'

She looked at me, my wife, and didn't need to say that she had to. I could feel it. I also knew I couldn't go with her, and that was a brute force to my chest. The wild called, but this woman called much louder.

'You won't be here either,' she reminded me. 'We both know you intend to go north.'

It was true. I had to go back for my berserkers and I couldn't take Finn with me. The thought of her waiting here for me, however, was far more pleasant than the thought of her creeping into the most dangerous city in the world. Her warder powers grew each day and I had no idea how she expected to hide them from Dren and Galia. But I didn't say any of that, because her brother was trapped in Sancia, and that meant she was going.

Finn climbed onto my lap and, lowered her lips to mine. Our breath mingled, heartbeats fell into time. Her yellow hair brushed my face.

'How long will you love me?' she asked against my mouth.

'Always.'

'And how long will you live when I die?'

I swallowed, felt my heart break. 'As long as I can.'

She whispered while kissing me: 'I'll come back to you. We will see each other again, Thorne, I promise.'

AVA

Who would imagine life after death would be so rich?

My husband paced back and forwards, fury and fear given full reign in his mighty northern form. The girls were in bed, but at this rate he would wake them. I didn't mind – if they woke it meant more time with them.

'This is idiocy,' Ambrose said. 'You would truly risk it? Risk all that we have on a suicide mission?'

I watched him, letting his barrage of fear wash over me. I did this all the time – let the sight of him or the girls wash over me and envelop me in the sweet disbelief of joy. It had taken me many years to come to terms with what I was feeling and to accept it as my right, instead of pushing it away as though I was not worthy of it, or as though its power lay only in taunting me before its disappearance. Joy, now, was so commonplace that it was actually rather ludicrous. Life after death had become an embarrassment of riches.

I understood that even if, in some horrendous twist of fate, it did disappear – all this love – I was still better for having had it in the first place. Just as I was better for having loved and lost my Avery.

I smiled and spoke to him now. My first mate, the one whose life had been cut so tragically short. *How impossible is this husband of mine.*

And in my heart Avery smiled in return and said, as he had done before, *How boldly he loves, petal. Who has ever loved so boldly as Ambrose of Pirenti?*

Together we watched Ambrose pace our living room and rage at me for the thing that might part us forever, if we were unlucky. For this terrible knowledge that I must go with my cousin to help him seize back our country. Falco would be useless on his own. And I trusted Ambrose to take care of our children, who meant more to me than anything.

The King of Pirenti stopped suddenly in the middle of the room. His words fell away. And like some kind of phantom had passed through him, he shook his head and started laughing at himself, and at us. He laughed a lot, my husband.

I crossed to him. He was so much taller than me, so I looked up at those wide lips, at the pale eyes and the scarred face. It was not as scarred as my own – no face ever was – but he certainly bore the marks of many attacks.

'These scars,' I murmured, running my fingers over them. 'Do you know what I once thought about scars?'

'What?'

'I thought they were ugly.'

My husband smiled his smile, the one that I was certain I had loved before I even loved him. 'How foolish you were, pretty boy.'

I kissed him. My hands undressed him but I didn't let him do the same to me. I wanted to see him, and made him lie on the rug before the fire. I looked at him carefully, every inch of him. I touched each of his scars in turn – there were so many I felt momentarily dwarfed by this thing that he did, this constant defense of the life he repeatedly made himself worthy of. I saw and touched him every day – it was too easy to forget how brutal these moments had been, when they'd come for him because of me, because I represented a weakness.

'Each one of these,' I said, sitting atop him, 'is proof of how strong you are.'

Ambrose frowned. He knew me too well. Knew this was the build to something brutal, because he didn't need to be told how strong he was, and I'd never tried before. But I held his eyes now. 'Any scars to come are as bearable as any of these.'

He sat up slowly, reaching to move his hands through my hair and against my cheeks. He knew what I meant: the scar I might leave were I to die. Softly, so softly, he said, 'How foolish you are, pretty boy.'

And it was then that the ache built inside my chest to the point where it spilled out of my eyes in salty tears that slid onto my cheeks and his, and onto our lips as they pressed together.

★

Later we both crept into the girls' room and slid into bed with them, one with each.

'Ma . . .' Ella complained at the intrusion, but then she curled against me, her fingers clutching my neck. I saw Sadie nestle into her father's arms as he stroked her hair.

This was it, then. An ugly part of me reached back and understood that the grief I'd felt upon losing my first bondmate would be nothing to how I'd feel if I lost these three people. It would be nothing. Even leaving them . . . even this. How could I have imagined the trauma of children? Of a family? What right had I to such joy? Was this the moment when fate stole it back?

Ambrose's eyes found mine in the dark. We looked at each other and our gazes shifted to gold. I decided then that fate would be what I made it. And my fate was to return to my family, no matter what stood in my way.

Chapter 4

Falco

It was four of us, in the end: Ava, Queen of Pirenti; Finn of Limontae; Osric, first-tier warder of Kaya; and me, Emperor Feckless. None of them trusted me to go alone, and I was actually rather grateful for the company. We rode south towards the border, our packs filled with supplies.

'If I wasn't the only one evolved enough to bond with a pegasis we could have made much better time,' Ava pointed out.

'Booo,' Finn exclaimed. 'From now on, no rubbing our privileges in each other's faces. And I'm looking at the royals in the group.'

Ava grinned. 'It's not a privilege.'

'Whatever! I don't have a flying horse, so kindly shut it!'

Travelling with Finn was clearly going to be a challenge.

The farewell had been painful. Watching Ella and Sadie wave from the wall was a gut-punch, but I'd looked over at my cousin and seen her eyes turn a perfect clear blue, and I'd known my pain at leaving them was as nothing to their mother's.

It took us several days to travel south to the border. Crossing into Kaya was where it would get dangerous, for no one could know who we were. I wouldn't be recognised, because if anyone had ever glimpsed me it was from a distance and with half my face covered. Osric looked every inch the warder, which could help us but also draw unnecessary attention. Finn wasn't recognisable as anyone important, which she'd taken great offence to when I pointed it out. But the terrible wolf scar on Ava's cheek marked her clearly as the Queen of Pirenti. She had to wear a scarf over the bottom half of her face, which was another unusual touch that would draw attention to our group.

Ava and I rode in a small carriage driven by Osric, while Finn preferred to flank us on a horse. I could hear her chatting away to Osric up front, though the warder gave no sign he was listening to her.

'. . . and I didn't think I'd miss it as much as I do. Da makes this delicious spicy dish with it and you just die, you *die* when you taste it. You'd die, Os. Do you eat fish? Do you eat anything? Or do you just exist on a diet of droll boredom? What's your favourite food? Where did you grow up? When did you become a warder? Do you know people trapped in the city? Am I talking to myself? Should I use my invisibility for good or evil?'

I couldn't help laughing.

Ava smiled. 'One guess who does the talking in that marriage.'

'Poor Thorne,' I agreed.

'I heard that,' Finn said through the window.

'Go ride further ahead so I don't have to listen to you prattling on.'

'Someone's in a bad mood,' she commented, then kicked her mount forward.

Ava shot me a look.

'What?'

'You're always so rude to her.'

'She doesn't care. She knows I'm playing.'

'Are you in love with her?'

'*What?*' I blinked. 'Of course not.'

'You're sure doing a good job of acting like you are.'

I groaned, resting my head in my hands as though this was embarrassing to me, when actually it was exactly what I'd been angling for. What was all too real was the fact that the slow jostle and bump of the carriage was making me nauseous. I would have preferred to be on a horse.

Ava was waiting for an answer. Over the last six months I'd made my feelings for Finn clear whilst also managing to seem contrite about them. It helped me look reprehensible if Emperor Feckless lusted over his best friend's wife. Honestly, I didn't know what all the lies were for anymore, except to build a web of armour against the entire world's gaze. Funny, I supposed, that this lie also happened to be true.

'I'm not in love with her,' I told Ava. 'But I . . . When I met her, I took off her blindfold because I thought I was going to bond with her, and I wanted to.' I didn't have to fake how pitiful that sounded.

Ava's mouth fell open. '*Sword.*'

'You sound like your husband,' I said. 'In any case she bonded with a man who became my best friend. And that's *fine*. I suppose there are just . . . lingering thoughts. Or something.'

Or perhaps, you moron, you're allowing *there to be lingering thoughts because frankly you'd like to distract yourself from the far bigger romantic problem looming in your near future.*

'How did you bridge the distance?' I asked my cousin abruptly. 'Between you and a man who was your enemy?'

Ava thought about it, putting her boots up on the seat beside me and reclining. 'No one *has* to be your enemy. It's a choice.'

'The things he'd done to you . . .'

'Ambrose did nothing to me but love me,' she said firmly, her eyes challenging me to argue by sliding to a burnt-umber shade.

I let it go, sensing this was a touchy subject even after all these years. 'Will you seek out your parents when we pass through?'

Her gaze found the trees outside the window. 'Orion isn't on the way.'

Ava's mother, Pria, had been my mother's older sister. They'd grown up together in Limontae until one of them married an Emperor and the other bonded to a fisherman. Pria had moved away to live with her mate in Orion, while my ma moved into the palace with Da, a man she'd been permitted to marry purely because she *hadn't* bonded with him. When my family was slaughtered, all ties were cut with Pria to keep her family safe from attack.

Ava's family still regarded her as a traitor for marrying a Pirenti soldier. Pria had refused to meet her grandchildren, and that had been the final straw for Ava. She'd stopped trying to have any kind of relationship with her parents, though I was fairly sure she occasionally visited her brothers.

'We can detour,' I replied. 'To see if they're safe.'

'There isn't time,' she said.

I understood. She'd cast them out. They belonged to the life of a woman she no longer was. 'You dressed as a boy when you first came here, didn't you?'

She nodded.

'Why?'

'So I wouldn't be treated the way women often are by men who are cruel and violent.'

I too watched the trees outside the carriage, thinking about the unfairness of that. She'd donned a mask of her own, a very good one that no one could see through – not even her mate.

'It . . . grew difficult,' she admitted after a while.

'How so?'

'Telling the difference between that boy and the real me. It warped me.'

'So what's the real you?'

'This,' she said, tracing her finger over her wolf scar. 'This,' she said, gesturing to her whole self. 'Exactly what you see.'

I was wracked with a wave of envy. She was exactly what she seemed; she was proud of being exactly what she seemed and, best of all, she had *known* what she was in the first place.

'We're about to cross through,' I heard Finn call, cantering her horse back to our side. 'I can feel the wards.'

I climbed out of the carriage and looked around. On the road ahead a sign had been erected.

'*The Emperor Dren and Empress Galia welcome you to Kaya,*' Finn read aloud. '*All with Pirenti blood may turn back now or suffer dire consequences.* How cheery.'

'What are the wards?' I asked.

'Rudimentary,' Osric muttered with a roll of his eyes. 'Pirenti blood will alert the nearest warders to its entry. There'll no doubt be a check-point nearby that houses low tier warders who keep the wards up. They'd come and kill us if we were foreigners.'

'Are you sure there aren't any other wards?'

Rather than responding, Osric flicked the reins and drove the carriage through the border. I had time to swing onto the back as it rolled past. Finn followed, and inside the boundary we paused again.

'Huh,' Osric said, sounding bored. 'Guess there was another ward.'

'What?'

'To detect anyone with soul magic.'

We stared at him. 'So . . .'

'So they're on their way to kill us.'

My mouth fell open.

There was a trickle of laughter from Finn. 'At least his laziness is consistent.'

'I ought to kill you myself, idiot,' I snapped as the carriage hurtled forwards.

Osric shrugged. 'It's not as though we wouldn't have crossed had we known. The whole border's probably warded.'

That was true.

We needed to get off the main road and even though the carriage offered us valuable anonymity, it was slowing us down. 'Dump it,' Ava decided, though it felt a shame to lose it so soon. Osric untethered the horses.

'Ride with me, Ava,' Finn offered, reaching a hand down to her.

'No need.' The Queen sheathed her sword at her waist and slung her bow and arrows over her back. She put her fingers in her mouth and gave a loud whistle. It wasn't long before her pegasis, Migliori, careened through the air and came to a thunderous landing.

He whinnied and lowered his front legs so Ava could swing gracefully onto his back. She whispered in the horse's ear as he exploded back into the sky. 'Follow me,' she called, riding fast and high.

If we hadn't been in such a rush I might have taken pleasure in the glorious sight, but as it was I had to grab my twin swords, my pack, and swing quickly onto the third horse. Osric, Finn and I plunged off the road and into a denser part of the forest. It was hard to see Ava here, but every now and then she whistled down to us so we'd know which direction to take.

'Why are we running?' Osric asked at one point.

'Because when someone hunts you, it's best not to be caught,' Finn answered archly. 'It's kind of concerning to me that you don't find that obvious, Os.'

We emerged at a gallop onto a stretch of plains; the grass was high enough to reach my knees atop the horse. I slowed her, not wanting her to lose her footing.

'Three behind and five ahead,' Osric warned calmly, dismounting.

'What are you doing?' I demanded, letting a panicked edge into my voice.

He looked at Finn and smiled. When Osric smiled, it meant trouble was afoot. 'What's not obvious to me,' he said, 'is why the hunters would run from the prey.' And with that he walked deep into the grass.

Finn and I shared a look, and then three warders arrived at our backs.

I angled my horse to face them.

'Throw down your weapons,' the female warder at the front of the trio ordered. 'You've been detected to be harbouring illegal soul magic.'

'It's not as though we can unload it at the door,' Finn pointed out.

Ava soared down on her horse and let fly an arrow. She used one of those huge Pirenti longbows, and was famous for being the only woman who'd ever been able to wield one. If you were shot with one of those arrows, you died, no question. But the warder lifted her hand and the arrow fell uselessly out of the sky.

It didn't matter. One by one the three warders before us went stiff and dropped to the ground. I stared at them, confused, until Osric waded through the grass, his skin tinged with an unearthly blue and eyes so white they'd lost both their irises and pupils. The air was prickling so badly that all the hair on my body stood on end.

'Stop, Osric!' Finn shouted at him. Osric walked closer to the warders. Each second that passed drained them of more colour and life, as though he was sapping their very souls.

'Stop!' Finn yelled again, and dismounted so she could shove him to the ground.

Osric blinked and his eyes returned to normal. 'What?'

'You don't have to kill them!'

'Of course I do.'

I dismounted and walked to the bodies, checking them.

'Are they?' Finn asked.

I nodded.

She rounded on Osric. 'So now we just murder our way through the country?'

'They're warders,' he spat. 'And warders in Kaya are loyal to the Mad Ones, otherwise they'd be in prison or dead. So not only will I kill any I come across, I will make it my business to seek out and slaughter as many as I can find.'

Finn looked pale and furious as she stared at him.

'Easy,' I warned them both. 'Take a breath.'

'Finn,' he pressed, lowering his voice, 'they're killing more innocent people by the day. They're twisted with power and too dangerous to let live.'

'What if they could be . . .?'

'Rehabilitated?' He snorted.

'Saved.'

'Listen to me carefully,' Osric bid her. 'Once the power has twisted you, there is no going back. It's why we must be *so* careful with it. And why I allowed myself to be outranked by less powerful warders. I curb the pull, the seduction, every day.'

Finn took a breath, relaxing her aggressive stance. Her eyes moved to the three dead bodies. 'I think today it bested you.'

Osric shook his head and mounted up, riding ahead.

Finn and I looked at each other.

'Don't be too hard on him,' I murmured. 'If we survive to tell the tale, this will be a time in Kaya that will live as the most ruinous in our history. Osric carries the great shame of his kin deep within him.'

Just as I carried the shame of having allowed it all to come to pass.

As we passed the three bodies I reached out to take Finn's hand. She wasn't nearly as unshakable as she let on.

ISADORA

I walked into the kitchen and stopped as every damned member of the household stared at me.

'*Gods above,*' Elias said.

'She's so pretty,' Anders said.

'Beautiful!' Sara agreed.

'More than beautiful,' Wesley said with a *wink*.

Jonah was staring wide-eyed at me, the heat of his desire like a furnace. Thank Gods for Penn, the only one who didn't seem dumbstruck.

The powder and ointment I applied last night had deepened my hair to a honey colour and my skin to a sun-kissed bronze. Sara had done my makeup to cover the bruising on my face, and had also blackened my eyelashes and coloured my lips red to match my eyes. The whole effect was utterly bizarre, and I'd stared at myself in the mirror this morning for a good twenty minutes.

'The only question they might ask you,' Anders said from where he was kneading dough at the counter, 'is "Why haven't you been working here the whole time?"'

'Be *careful*,' Elias warned me. 'If they ask you a question, answer it.'

Apparently they all thought me simple-minded. I headed out.

'Iz,' Jonah called, hurrying after me to the back door. 'Your knives. They'll search you.'

I hesitated, realising he was right. A sick feeling flooded my stomach as I carefully removed each of the blades and left them to him.

'You'll be okay,' he laughed. 'I'll look after them.'

He thought it amusing. I strode for the wall and climbed over.

'Iz?' I heard him call, but I was already down the street.

For the first time in my life I didn't need to hide what I looked like. Nobody stared, or if they did it was with an entirely different look in their eyes. No warders stopped just to taunt me.

I made it to the palace and handed over my work chit. The two guards looked me up and down and nodded me through to the next part of my registration. Here I was strip-searched by two female servants; it was humiliating for everyone involved and I let the lake of calm settle upon me, shutting out anything and everything that could ruffle it. They garbed me in a white dress, sleeveless and cut low between my breasts. I might as well have been naked. My hair was left out and I was given no shoes. The two girls didn't talk to me or to each other, and they looked terrified the entire time.

As I was ushered into the next area two male servants were also brought in from adjacent chambers. They had been given only a pair

45

of white linen breeches to wear – no shirt or shoes, and it occurred to me how deliberately degrading this all was. Both men were extremely handsome, with muscled, brown bodies, but both looked like they'd rather be anywhere else.

Three warders entered and one moved to each of us. My warder ran his eyes over me, studying carefully. 'What's wrong with you?'

I took a breath and inwardly sent a silent apology to Penn for what I was about to do. 'Ma said to tell you,' I said slowly, clearly, 'that my mind is simpler. My mind is simpler. My mind is simpler. My –'

'This one's cracked in the head,' he told his companions impatiently.

They looked me over. 'She doesn't have to open her mouth when she's that beautiful,' one of them said. 'They'll want her.'

My warder smirked and ushered me forward. The men stepped in after me and we were taken straight to the kitchens. The staff here were abuzz, preparing food and drink as though for a mighty banquet.

'You!' A grey-haired man addressed me. 'Take this in.'

I blinked and was handed a tray of drinks. Really? It was nine o'clock in the morning. And take it where?

There were other similarly dressed girls carrying trays through a door, so I followed them. I found myself entering a vast chamber, its roof held aloft on thick marble pillars. Its center was a long rectangular pool of glistening water, languishing within which was a tangle of naked bodies. I had to force myself not to double take as they kissed and made love without a care for who might watch. Around the pool were tables covered in absurdly decadent foods and scattered around the room were softly-playing musicians. At the end, reclined on thrones to watch it all, were Dren and Galia.

I had to refrain from rolling my eyes. It was so disappointingly clichéd. If I were mad and had all the power in the world I'd at least use it to do something interesting.

The only things that piqued my curiosity were the birds: there had to be at least a hundred kept in cages suspended from the ceiling. They sang prettily, or chirped and squawked to get out. I ached to set every one of them free.

We carried our trays to the Mad Ones, who waved us away without a glance. I followed the other girls to a long sideboard where we placed our goods and then apparently had to wait in case any of it was wanted.

I took the opportunity to study the fraudulent rulers, coldly thrilled to be so close to them. If only I had my knives the world would very quickly be a different place. Both had sparkling silver hair and wore crowns made of finely spun gold thread. Dren was small in stature, with a hooked nose and heavy eyebrows. Even indoors, in this sauna of human flesh, he wore a heavy gold cloak. Galia's hair was long, but exactly the same shade as her husband's. She wore a jewel-encrusted gown that covered every inch of skin except her face. And when I looked at that face I felt a rip inside my heart, because she was Penn – she was a female version of Penn.

As I watched Galia she sat forward, concentrating on the people in the pool. She shook her head in frustration. 'More.'

The minute she spoke, several servants who'd been lined around the walls removed their clothes and climbed into the pool. And just started . . . touching each other.

Dread thundered through me. My skin felt warm with horror and bile rose in the back of my throat. If they told me to get in that pool I would die first. Or kill them.

'You.' Dren's cold voice struck through the room. Everyone froze, fearful that he was addressing them. 'Red eyes,' he said more softly, and he was looking straight at me.

I had no idea what I should do, so I walked over to bow before him.

'Who are you?'

'Isadora, Sire.'

'Where are you from?'

'Limontae.'

'Why is your mind closed?'

I wasn't sure what to say. I didn't think my little act from before would work on this man – his eyes were alarmingly shrewd.

'Very well,' he said. 'I shall smash through whatever barriers these are and take the answers for myself.'

47

'Please,' said a voice. There was a soft gasp from someone in the pool. I looked to see that the word had been spoken by one of the men who'd entered with me. He'd stepped forward and was bowing his head respectfully. Those large shoulders of his, I was surprised to see, had whip scars on them. It was a wonder he'd been allowed in. 'She isn't well in the mind, Sire,' he was saying to Dren. 'Born with a defect.'

'Ah,' Dren sighed. 'Poor pet.'

Pet?

'And who are you?' Galia asked him.

'Ryan, Sire.'

'You weren't given permission to speak.'

'Forgive me. But I wasn't sure the girl was able to speak for herself.'

'You can sit by me here, pet,' Dren cooed at me. 'You're nice enough to look at, at least.'

'No,' Galia interrupted. Good. I didn't want to go anywhere near that sycophant. But then she said, 'I want what's between them. Take her.'

I looked around, no idea what was going on. Ryan swallowed and took my hand. I forced myself not to rip my skin from his, the touch abhorrent.

'Wait –' I said.

'Shh,' he whispered. 'Trust me.'

My heart hammered as he led me to the pool. The pool I now saw was filled with something that was definitely not water. It smelled odd, and looked too thick. Was it . . . drugging the swimmers? They all looked so dazed.

Dren and Galia were taking something from them. Some kind of energy. Were they empaths? I understood now, better than I ever had, why they were called the Mad Ones. Draining the energy from slaves forced to have public sex was some truly twisted lunacy.

Ryan took his clothes off. I went rigid.

'She certainly doesn't want it,' Dren chuckled. 'Poor pet.'

'Show her what we do to those who don't want it,' Galia said.

Dren flicked his wrist and the servant closest to him was ripped apart. Pieces of his body fell in a heap on the marble and blood seeped over the floor.

A dark fury found my heart.

This was it, then. I didn't have my knives. I couldn't kill them before they could destroy me. And if I wanted to kill them, someday, then I had to live long enough. Which left me one option.

All of it – this room, these people, the pool, Ryan and the Mad Ones – it all went into a box that was locked tight and shoved to the bottom of the lake. Above it, a long way above it, was the glittering reflective surface. All anyone would see.

Ryan removed my dress and pulled me into the pool. 'I'm so sorry,' he whispered. 'I won't hurt you.'

It didn't matter. I was calm. Because I knew about humiliation. I knew about being treated as an animal. This was a different kind of cage, but it was a cage nonetheless, and I knew all about cages.

FALCO

It hit me without warning.

Her fear. True, gut-wrenching fear. And more than that. Worse than that. Humiliation. Skin-crawling humiliation. It hit me so powerfully that I was nauseated.

My horse felt the unnatural shift in my emotions and spooked. She reared, toppling me. I hit the ground and rolled over to retch onto the grass.

'Falco!'

But I couldn't help it – a scream of fury left me as I smashed my fist into the ground. Whoever was making her feel this way would die an ugly death.

ISADORA

That night when I returned home it was to find everyone in the living room.

'How was it?'

'What happened?'

'What was it like?'

I stared at them, not knowing what to say.

'What did you have to do?' Jonah asked me.

'Nothing. Serve drinks.'

'Oh. That's good.'

I turned for the bathroom.

'Did you learn anything?' Elias asked.

I swallowed and shook my head.

'So you're going back tomorrow.'

This time I hesitated longer before shaking my head.

'Why not?'

A breath of air left my lungs. I locked myself in the washroom and climbed into the empty bathtub. Jonah banged on the door for what felt an age, and I hated him for it. I considered leaving them all. Why was I here? I could steal out of this city and return to my people in the forest. I didn't need to be here, surrounded by pretty, normal, privileged people who had an abundance of love and intimacy and couldn't give me a single moment to myself.

I stayed in the bath the whole night through. I didn't sleep. I didn't go sleepwalking or thieving. And I didn't go back to the palace in the morning.

The next time I went back to that place it would be to destroy it.

*

I hadn't spoken a word to anyone in three days when it happened. I hadn't left them, either, which had surprised me. I pondered why as I stood in the courtyard on guard duty. There were several missing bricks in the back wall, through which you could see the alleyway. But the movement I spotted wasn't through the hole, it was above in the sky. A flash of moonlit white.

I peered up and as I understood my heart ruptured.

The pegasis flew out of the inky night and landed in the courtyard, though her white wings were almost too wide. The creature's body was as dark as the sky above and she pressed her forehead into my hand. Her brown eyes saw all the way through me and loved me despite everything. How terrible for her.

I stroked her silky nose. My heart was full of our bond.

But.

Radha. I felt the name rather than heard it. And the dizzying, silky, sweet love fell from my heart. This was a creature bound to the two of us, connected by the two of us. And she had been named after a woman I murdered. I couldn't do it; I didn't deserve her.

'Forgive me,' I whispered to the pegasis. But she didn't leave, instead she tried to get closer, gave a soft whinny and nuzzled into my side. So I said, 'I don't want you.' And as I turned my back on her I heard her finally take flight. She flew away and I was alone again.

A monster indeed.

CHAPTER 5

THORNE

The stables reeked. I usually avoided them, the smell not unpleasant, but overwhelming. The earth, the dust, the hay, the horse sweat and shit, and rust and leather, and even the stink of the creatures when they felt pleasure or hunger or fear or anxiety – it was all too much to take at once. But I couldn't avoid it this morning because I'd heard a concerning rumour. Breathing through my mouth, I entered the stone-and-timber building and made my way quickly to the stalls at the end. Howl padded alongside, panting after our run in the forest.

Ambrose was brushing his stallion down; the creature was still and calm until he scented me, giving a nervous snort and stamping his hoof. 'Easy,' the King soothed him, glancing at me.

Ella and Sadie were in stalls on either side, brushing down their palomino ponies under their da's instruction.

'Hey, get out from behind her,' Ambrose ordered and Sadie quickly moved away from her pony's back hooves. 'You know better.'

'I was just brushing her tail.'

'You do that from behind the stall wall. El, come on – get a move on, please. We're not going anywhere until this is done.'

Ella had given up brushing and was threading her fingers through her pony's mane while she hummed sweetly, lost in some distant imagining. She ignored her da; Ava was the disciplinarian and everyone in the family knew it. Ambrose sighed and moved to finish brushing his daughter's pony for her.

'I'm not doing this for you on the road,' he warned.

So it was true. 'Am, no,' I groaned.

The King grinned cheerfully at me. 'Don't you mean *"I'm so excited to have you along, uncle."?*'

'I need to move quickly.'

'Which is exactly why we'll be riding.' He winked at me. 'It'll be a family trip, kid. The girls haven't had a proper winter solstice yet. Don't disappoint them.'

'Also Da said you shouldn't be left to your solitude or you might turn even stranger than you already are,' Sadie informed me.

I looked at Ambrose. He gave a happy nod. 'I did say that.'

I sighed. My uncle knew I grew more introspective by the day without Finn here to draw me out, but I meant to go north into the ice – the cruellest, loneliest place in the world, and to survive there I would need to be as strong in my solitude as I had ever been. Much as I loved my family, they were going to get ditched long before we reached the ice.

★

By midday we were on the road. Ambrose and his twins rode their horses and Ma drove a carriage carrying our belongings, inside of which the girls could rest when they needed to. Howl and I jogged alongside – horses and I didn't do well together, not since I'd returned from the ice mountain. We kept a good pace, but even so Ambrose managed to sing every inch of the way. Ella and Sadie occasionally joined in, harmonising perfectly, but they were more interested in making up stories to tell each other.

I listened half-heartedly, concentrating instead on the smells to ensure no danger lurked. It was highly unlikely anyone would be stupid enough to attack a royal party containing both King and Prince, but if someone did decide to challenge us, violence was inevitable and I didn't want Sadie, Ella or Roselyn to witness it. Plus there were always bandits on the road, ignorant enough to attack without checking who we were.

I watched Ambrose stop singing to listen as Avery's name came up in Ella and Sadie's story – he was always at least one of the characters in the tales they concocted.

'It was Avery's job to creep into the fortress and steal the dragon-heart blade.'

'No, he should be guarding it.'

The twins argued about his role for a minute, then turned to Ambrose. 'Da, tell her Avery would be the thief. He was cheeky like that.'

Ambrose smiled crookedly. 'You're probably right, but why do you say that?'

'Because you are,' Sadie replied.

'What do you mean?'

'He must have been like you, don't you think? For Ma to have loved you both?'

Ambrose considered this, scratching his cheek. 'I suppose it's a fair assumption, but you're forgetting something.'

'What?' the girls asked in unison.

'The ability of the heart to love different things,' he explained. 'Your ma's a complicated woman – don't you think she could love opposites?'

Identical frown lines formed between Ella and Sadie's eyebrows.

'For example,' Ambrose went on, 'are you two exactly the same as each other?'

They shook their heads adamantly.

'That's right. El, you're far quieter than your sister, aren't you? And Sade, you're more curious. El's stubborn, and Sadie constantly changes her mind about everything.'

They nodded, then glanced at each other and giggled.

'And have you ever thought Ma could love one of you but not the other?'

'Don't be stupid, Da,' Sadie laughed.

Ambrose shrugged, having made his point. Then his face lit up. 'We're nearly there! You're going to *love* this. Race you!' He raced his girls towards the lavender fields, more of a child then either one of them.

I smiled as I watched. My eyes met Ma's and she was smiling too, though always sadly. I turned my eyes to the forest looming beside us, and there he was. My da, watching silently. A monster of a man corded with muscle and covered in ink.

It was one of the reasons I plunged into the wilderness each day – because he was always there waiting for me.

*

We spent hours in the lavender fields. Ambrose, his daughters and my dog played within the sea of lilac flowers, running and dancing and singing. '*It smells like Ma!*' one of the girls squealed in delight while Howl barked his glee. Roselyn and I sat to the edge, relaxing in the afternoon sun. I was getting too much pleasure watching their play to be concerned about the wasted travel time. I thought, inevitably, of Finn – of how much she would love this, and how worried I was for her.

'She'll be well,' Ma said softly, interpreting my thoughts. 'Who better to look out for her than Ava and Osric?'

'And Falco,' I agreed.

Ma raised a sceptical eyebrow and I couldn't help smiling. She was very rarely impatient with people, almost *never* disliked anyone, but something about the Emperor of Kaya got under her skin. Perhaps it was his repeated marriage proposals.

'You have a crush on him,' I guessed with a grin.

She blushed bright pink and her eyes widened. 'Don't be absurd, darling.'

I laughed heartily. 'Oh, Ma. Your face.'

'What's so funny?' Sadie demanded as she, Ella and Ambrose arrived, panting, at a sprint. All three had lavender threaded through their hair and flushed pink cheeks.

'Just teasing Ma about her crush on Falco,' I said with a wink.

'Thorne!' she protested.

The twins exploded into excited laughter; Falco was undoubtedly their favourite person in the world.

Ambrose grinned slowly. 'Well, he's unattached, Rose. And sweet as sugar on you.'

'*And* my wife,' I couldn't help muttering.

'And possibly every other woman in Pirenti,' Ambrose added.

Roselyn rose calmly and waded into the field of lavender. As she disappeared behind its curtain I shared a look with my uncle. Ambrose sighed and there were no words between us, only an understanding of all that was lost.

I followed Ma as she wandered through the stalks, running her fingers idly over them, perhaps silently counting them. She was worlds away.

'Sorry, Ma,' I murmured.

In the light of the setting sun her hair was a brilliant, burning shade, and I could see that her eyes were full.

'We know you don't have a crush.'

She swallowed, struggling with words. 'It feels . . . disloyal. Even to joke.'

Twenty years later, and still. I pulled her into my arms and held her tight. She was such a slight, delicate thing. I stroked her hair gently. 'I'm an insensitive fool. But don't you think he would have wanted you to find some happiness without him?'

Ma pulled away and looked up into my face. 'That's not how it works,' she replied simply, then returned to the others. I followed in time to see Ella and Sadie present her with a garland of flowers. My mother looked incredibly beautiful in the golden light as she knelt to accept the crown wreathed in lilac blooms. A strange fey queen, or something equally ephemeral. Something *fragile*.

★

That night we slept in a travellers' inn but Howl and I crept out to sweep the forest and keep watch. The air grew cold and my cheeks felt frozen. It was nothing compared to how low the temperature would drop as we ventured further north, and I wondered where Ambrose would draw the line – Ella and Sadie would be in danger even in Vjort. Any closer to the ice and they'd perish.

'The cold is in their blood,' a deep, scratchy voice spoke. 'To endure it will forge their strength.'

I looked at my da, standing in the shadows. My chest and arms were filling out now to rival his, but I would never match his outlandish height. 'And how far is too far to push them?'

He shrugged. 'Ambrose knows the answer to that.'

'Are you always watching us?'

He didn't answer. His breath made clouds just as mine did and he seemed equally as substantial – there was nothing ghostly about him.

'Are you real, Da?' I pressed, a strange urgency in my heart. 'Or am I mad?'

He met my eyes; his glowed incredibly blue in the moonlight. Ma often said we shared the same eyes – I wondered if mine looked as his did now, or if Da's were different because they held the frost of the otherworld within them.

'What does it matter,' he asked me, 'as long as I am with you?'

And I supposed he was right.

Howl chose that moment to lift his muzzle towards the moon and give a long, mournful bay, like a wolf in the night.

AVA

'Alright, step forwards, please.'

Osric, Finn and Falco stepped towards me as though they'd just been asked to witness the executions of their bondmates.

'*Must* we?' Finn sighed.

'I'm concerned for the Emperor's life,' Osric said drolly, with a sideways glance at said Emperor's flimsy grip on the deadly weapon. He had a point.

'It's not up for discussion.'

They knew why this was happening. Not one of them had even the slightest ability to protect themselves without magic – or in Falco's case even *with* magic. So we were having a sword lesson.

And with the sun on our faces, the stream trickling to our right and the heady smell of lemons from the orchard we stood within, what could be nicer?

I reconsidered as Falco slashed his beautiful sword in a playful arc at Finn's head and nearly chopped her ear off.

'Careful!' she roared.

'Whoops. Sorry.'

'Do *not* swing your blade at a friend!' I instructed and he flashed me a sheepish grimace.

'I was just playing.'

'Well *don't*.'

I rubbed my eyes and thought back to my first lessons at the academy. I'd followed Avery to Limontae – the first time I'd ever left the tiny village I'd grown up in – overwhelmed with excitement at the bustling new world before me. It had all moved quickly from then: I'd ranked top in my combat training classes and been recruited by Gidion to join a small force of soldiers being trained for a particularly difficult mission. I'd felt proud to have been chosen alongside Avery; I was thrilled to be given responsibility for the first time in my spoilt young life. I didn't know then that it was to be a suicide mission, or that it would change the course of my days forever. Avery probably knew. He was much smarter than I'd been.

A lifetime ago. And though I felt a twinge of guilt for thinking it, that same old excitement was making its way into my bones again. To be beyond the walls of the fortress without the heavy weight of my crown and title, to even vacate my duties – dare I say it – as a mother. It reminded me of the woman I'd once been, the fighter. My hands tingled with the feel of my weapon, my muscles made to wield it.

'Swords up,' I ordered.

They held out their swords.

'Firmer, Falco. Why's your wrist flopping like that?'

'I normally have people with firm wrists to hold things for me.'

Finn snorted with laughter and Osric looked skyward as though for divine intervention.

'Is it your intention to get skewered by the first street brat who spies you as an easy mark?' I demanded. 'Sancia – *if* we miraculously make it inside – will be dangerous not only because of the warders, but because anyone could attack you at any moment. So concentrate.'

We managed to get through about half an hour of clumsy movements. Osric clearly paid no attention to any instructions, and Finn's blatant lack of respect for combat of any kind meant she didn't take it seriously. Falco nearly killed himself a dozen times because he was extremely poor at it; when I asked them to raise their swords to block a downward strike at their heads, he lifted his blade so fast it went flying from his hand, and when he was meant to be working on his footwork he tripped and nearly impaled himself as we all screamed. He turned to see the sword a hair's breadth from his eye and smiled disarmingly at his own good fortune.

'I think that's about enough of that,' I said. 'Gods help me.'

We packed up and went on our way, and I didn't feel quite so excited anymore. In fact I felt rather nervous at their cumulative vulnerability: I'd have been better off with Ella and Sadie as back up.

FALCO

We made our way to a town called Glenvale that was small enough – I hoped – not to be monitored by warders. It didn't make strategic sense for the warders to spread themselves too thin, so I was betting on certain areas being left to their own meager resources. There was a single inn here, and we were keen for a bed after two weeks of making do on the ground. This journey was the first time in my life I'd slept anywhere other than a palace or fortress, which was now evident in my sore muscles.

How amazing to walk into the inn and look everyone in the face. In the eyes. Without a gods-cursed blindfold. Strange to see so many expressions at once, on so many unguarded faces.

'So do you just wear those swords for decoration?' Finn asked me around a mouthful of damper.

The four of us were in a corner table, trying to mind our own business even as Osric was receiving some seriously dodgy looks.

'I beg your pardon?' I replied, hoping she'd get the message and stop talking with her mouth full.

'You clearly can't use them,' she said, mouth even fuller than the first time. A piece of bread sprayed onto the table and I stared at it. She grinned and I realised she'd done it on purpose after hearing my thought.

'You're such a brat.'

'I thought you liked that about me.'

'I don't like anything about you.'

'What a liar.'

'Now, now, children,' Osric sighed, bored as usual.

'She's needling me,' I said. 'As always.'

'Only because you've been acting like a big pile of poo this whole time!' Finn said.

'I see the mature part of the evening has begun,' Ava commented.

I couldn't help it – I burst out laughing. The others followed suit until even Osric gave a reluctant chuckle.

I threw a piece of damper at Finn's head.

'Infantile.' She grinned. 'Why *are* you so miserable, anyway? Ava and I are the ones who've left our husbands but we don't mope around all day long.'

'I don't mope! And just because you're married doesn't mean you have the monopoly on misery.' I met her eyes. 'I hear you, though. And I'm sorry.'

Finn's smile grew gentle. I'm glad she didn't question me further about the swords. I wore them because they were the only things I owned that had belonged to my father. They meant more to me than every other possession. And who knew – by some miracle I might actually need them one of these days.

The thought of my father left me even more depressed than I'd been a moment ago, and that wouldn't do. 'In fact,' I announced, forging through it with bullish determination in the only way I knew how, 'it's time for a celebration!'

I climbed up onto the table, managing to knock several things over at once.

'What are you *doing*?' Ava hissed.

'Attention, please!' I boomed, draping the familiar cloak of Feckless about me. 'In accordance to the new laws of our most knowing rulers, we should all be heading to our beds in time for curfew!'

There were shouts and grunts of outrage from the room crowded with patrons. Someone threw a mug at my head and I could have ducked, but instead I let it clip me painfully on the ear. 'If you're quite done,' I shouted, rubbing my head. Finn was giggling into her ale, enjoying the embarrassing spectacle, while Ava looked ready to murder me.

'What I say to the new rulers is this: They can shove their curfew up their backsides! Tonight's ale is on me!'

A huge cheer went up and I grinned, enjoying it. 'And all women should feel encouraged to show their appreciation as explicitly as they please,' I added, earning a swell of laughter.

I skolled the rest of my mug and jumped down.

'You never cease to amaze me,' Ava snapped. 'We're meant to be avoiding attention.'

I ignored Ava and turned to the other woman at our table. 'Finn of Limontae. I believe you like to have fun, do you not?'

'I do indeed.'

'Then dance with me, and don't be shy about it.'

She took my hand and I swept her into the middle of the floor. We danced wildly and obnoxiously, laughing and twirling and drinking as much as we could. Finn had a hunger inside her that could never be sated and a wildness of spirit that sought risk – I'd recognised it the second I spotted her in that tournament arena. It was exactly what I wanted right now – to live loudly enough to drown out all the things I missed.

''Scuse me.'

I twirled Finn to a stop and faced the tavern owner who'd addressed me.

'Could I speak with one of you in private?'

I followed him into his small office behind the bar. 'What can I do for you?'

'I don't mean to be rude, but it's the man you're travelling with,' he hedged.

'I know he makes everyone nervous, and I apologise for it. He's not with the Mad Ones.'

'Well, that'd be easier to believe if I didn't know that all of them are with them. If you get what I mean. He's scaring my other patrons. And the lady with her face covered . . . that ain't helping things. It makes them nervous. Plus you and the lass are doing an alright job disrupting the peace and quiet most folk come to my inn for.'

I nodded. 'Forgive me. We'll move on. Thank you for being kind about it.' I handed him a purse of coins that nearly made him faint.

'No, sire! I couldn't possibly! Not after pushing you on!'

'Please. Take it. I appreciate what you're doing here, making a safe haven where people can escape the warders. I won't forget it.'

'Thank you,' he breathed, his cheeks bright pink.

I smiled and headed back to my table. 'Looks like the dream's over, friends. You, my magical comrade, are too pretty for them. Ava's too sweet, and Finn and I are too boring. Let's go.'

They didn't complain, simply finished their drinks and followed me outside. At least we'd had a nice warm meal and a couple of dances. We rounded the corner to the stables.

Figures moved and there was a scuffle of shoes against cobblestone. Before I could see what was happening in the dark, three men had taken hold of Osric, one of whom had a dagger pressed against his throat.

'Don't!' Finn warned quickly, and it took me a moment to realise she was speaking to Osric, not the men.

Before I could make any response of my own, several more men appeared behind us, blocking any retreat. 'Men who shout and brag about their defiance while traveling with a monster,' one of the men addressed me, 'are either fools drunk on their own audacity, or spies.'

The men moved in more tightly around us, and I could see the glint of their weapons.

'I'm no spy.'

'Then you're a drunken fool and this warder is the spy. Either way, we can't have you leaving.'

'You truly think you could stop us?' Osric asked mildly.

There was an uneasy shuffle of feet. 'Warder filth,' one of them spat. 'What business do ordinary folk have with his kind?'

'Is he coercing you?' a third man asked. 'Are you under his influence?'

'No,' Ava replied firmly to curb the joke she could see begging to leave my tongue.

'Then you ought to be ashamed.' He gestured and I heard the men move to take hold of us.

'Finn,' I said.

She nodded once and with barely more than a blink she dropped the men to their knees. They scrabbled for the ground, swaying oddly.

'What are you doing to them?' I asked curiously.

'Just a teensy earthquake. Tweaked their balance and perception.'

My eyebrows arched, impressed. Abruptly the men regained their footing and sprinted away as fast as they could.

'Os!' Finn snapped. 'I had it.'

'Wasting time with silly tricks.' He rolled his eyes.

'What'd you do?' I asked him.

'He coerced them,' Finn answered.

'How is that different from what you did to them?'

'I didn't go inside their heads and insert a direct order. That's mind control and it's vile.' She shook her head.

'You're just jealous because you can't do it yet,' Osric said with a wink.

'We wouldn't have had to do anything if it weren't for Falco's gormless behaviour in the tavern,' Ava pointed out.

I shrugged it off. 'Bit of excitement. No harm done.'

'Can you try to act like a normal human being from now on?'

'I can *try*.'

They stared at me, and something in my expression made Osric and Finn dissolve into giggles.

★

As we walked our horses back to the road I said to Osric, 'We're going to have to do something about the way you look, my man.'

'How about this?' He shimmered before my eyes and I was suddenly looking at a black-haired, green-eyed man.

'Wow!' Finn exclaimed, applauding him. 'Can you make yourself look like anything?'

He shrugged, feigning disinterest.

'Why didn't you do that earlier?' I asked.

'Because it takes magic, and they'll sense it.'

'Well, won't they sense it now?'

I was ignored.

'Can you make yourself look like a dog?' Finn pressed. 'A seagull? A slug?'

'What are you *talking* about?' I asked her.

'What? He could walk right into the city. What about a scantily-clad woman carrying a big tray of food? They'd let you straight in.'

'You're an idiot,' Osric muttered. 'I just said they'd notice the magic.'

'How about making yourself look like a nicer person?' she asked sweetly. 'Because that would be a real talent.'

'Give it a *rest*,' Ava snapped from up ahead. 'The three of you are worse than my bickering eight year olds and you're annoying me.'

We shut up and followed her.

★

By daybreak a week later we'd reached the rocky coast that would make way for the seaside city of Sancia. We'd had a dozen encounters with warders on the journey, each of which had been resolved with Osric's particular kind of justice, much to Finn's disgust. Now we stood at the base of a dizzying rock cliff, the violent sea smashing into the coast below our feet.

There were many tunnels into the palace and I'd seen with my own eyes that several of them had collapsed while others were discovered on the night of the warder takeover. Which left one that the Mad Ones *might* not know about, because I was fairly sure *no one* knew about it. Only me, and apparently Isadora. It was cut high into this rock face and almost impossible to access: it would be a risk to reach it and a risk to follow it.

My da had showed me this tunnel when I was five years old. We'd been on a boat, my two brothers and me, and he'd pointed it out to us from the sea, saying it was only ever to be used in times of direst need. Which meant that I had, of course, snuck straight into it at the first possible opportunity. The smack I got in punishment stung so badly I had decided to forget about the tunnel. Now I only had a hazy memory of where it emerged, but that was better than nothing.

'If only Thorne were here,' Finn sighed. 'He's so good at climbing. Or just, like, holding people up while they climb. Actually, he's terrified of heights so he'd probably be a dangerous hazard. Still. If only he were here.'

'Snore,' Osric muttered.

'Don't pout,' she said. 'We all know you have a crush on him.'

Osric didn't deny it, which made Finn laugh.

'Strongest to weakest,' Ava interrupted. Taking a length of rope we'd acquired at the last town, she uncoiled it and prepared to tie us together.

'Physically? Or by climbing ability?' I asked.

'Best climber goes at the top. Strongest goes last in case anyone falls and needs to be caught.'

'That's going to be a problem,' Finn said. 'Because Falco is definitely the weakest climber and he's also not very strong.'

'Please don't concern yourself with tact,' I said.

'Sorry. It's true though.'

I thought about arguing – shouldn't I tell them I could climb? Or at least offer to go last, where I could take their weight? I had to have some sort of mental derangement because, instead of those simple statements, what came out of my mouth was: 'Finn first, then Ava, me and Osric at the end. Happy? The weakling in skill and body will be safely in the middle where he can't cause a fatal accident.'

What is wrong with you.

'Aw, Fal,' Finn smiled. 'We're just trying to protect you from yourself.'

'How generous.'

We got into place.

'One thing,' Osric said before we began. 'From this point, no magic. They'd definitely feel it.'

'So if one of us falls –' Finn started.

'If it looks like one will dislodge the rest, we cut the rope and keep going,' Ava said. 'The mission is paramount.'

There was silence.

'De–pressing. Let's go.' Finn started scampering up the rocks and we had to yell at her to slow down.

'How in gods' names did that little messenger boy get down here on his own?' Ava wondered at about the halfway point, as the sun reached its apex above. I almost didn't hear her over the wind and the noise of everyone panting. The pack on my back, which had been laughably light hours earlier, was now suspiciously filled with lead.

'Little can mean agile,' Finn said cheerfully. She was perched on a precipice, waiting for us to scale our way up to her. 'You're doing surprisingly well, Fal,' she added.

I rolled my eyes.

'No, seriously.'

'Thank you. And thanks for the condescending surprise, too.'

We stopped on the ledge to take a water break. There was enough room for us all to sit with our legs dangling over the edge. The view was magnificent from here, and seemed endless. Way out to sea I could see the horizon, blue on blue. Seagulls flew by our heads, squawking loudly, and the waves below were a rolling tumult of sound. If we fell from this height without magic it would be an instant goodnight.

'Have I ever told you the story of the sea god and his bride?' Finn asked.

'No,' Ava answered.

'Wanna hear it?'

'No,' Osric answered while Ava and I said, 'Yes.'

Finn shot Osric a smug look and then launched into it, the cadences of her voice altering to become melodic. With every word she painted I felt myself slip further into the story.

'One of the Vanir, Njörðr, was god of the sea and ancient beyond most of his kind. For all the millennia of his existence he had desired above all the salt of the ocean – he cared for naught else. But he was lonely, his only contact being with his age-old enemy, the war god himself. Far to the north, in the snow that never melted, was the ice goddess, Skaði. She had a cold soul, and was fierce beyond reckoning. Seeking revenge for her slain father, Skaði strayed south to the pantheon of the gods and demanded that she be allowed a husband of her choice in redress for her loss. Thinking to choose Baldur, the largest and most brutal of gods – and so the only one she thought might survive in the north – Skaði searched for him in their midst. But instead she came upon Njörðr and was struck by an inexplicable love for him, and he for her. The two married, a more splendid wedding than any that had come before. But then it came time to decide where the couple would live. First they spent nine nights in the foreboding fortress of ice belonging to Skaði. That time, for Njörðr, was a nightmare. The call of the wolves chilled him to his core, a horror compared to the beloved swan calls from whence he came. Next the pair spent nine nights in the sunny, seaside ship harbour belonging to the sea god, but for Skaði those days were loathsome – the screeching of the seabirds aggravated her to distraction, while the heat grew unbearable.'

Finn paused, and I felt myself leaning in a little to hear the end.

'Heartbroken, the sea god and his ice goddess came to a terrible realisation: they were each a creature of their own world, and each too desirous of what they knew to ever give it up. Their love, it seemed, was not strong enough to broach the distance between them and so they parted ways, returning alone to their homes. But they made each other a vow: every nine hundred years they would meet in the middle, in the land both warm and cold, with both swans and wolves, and there they would spend nine nights together. And so it was that for every second of those waiting days they would long for the time when they might meet again.'

We sat in silence once she was finished. I felt transported and melancholy.

'Cheery,' Osric commented. Finn reached to rough the warder's hair affectionately. He ducked his head to hide a smile.

'You have a gift,' Ava said.

Finn shrugged. A shy smile tugged at her lips and she looked down at her hands. It was such a sweet moment that I felt an ache in my chest for her. She had no idea how painfully true her story felt to me now, thinking of my own ice goddess and the worlds stretching between us. Although knowing Finn, maybe she did. Her stories always had strange relevance, which I suspected was due to her subtle empath ability and a hefty dose of intuition.

I turned my eyes to the horizon and my mind to how much I wanted to know what was out there. I thought of Ella calling me a chrysalis. I thought of what lay waiting for me in the city above. I didn't know how any of those things fitted together in the one life.

'Come on, we're nearly there,' I said softly, and we rose to continue.

*

We'd only been climbing for half an hour when we reached a huge hole in the rock face. It was too big to avoid, so we had to scale it, which meant climbing upside down on a stretch of horizontal rock. Finn had no trouble. Ava and I did alright, going slowly and following Finn's instructions about where to place our hands and feet. Then it was Osric's turn.

He reached the top section and stopped entirely, sweating badly. It was the lack of magic, I knew, that was freaking him out. He'd never had to rely on his body without it. 'Stop embarrassing yourself, Os!' I called down to him. 'Even I did it!'

He nodded. And slipped, falling from the cliff and jerking the rope taut. His entire body weight pulled against the three of us. As we all scrabbled for a hold Finn screamed at the sudden jerk.

'Cut it!' Osric shouted, hanging mid-air with no way to reach the wall.

'Don't move!' I ordered the women. I took a breath and dragged myself two paces up the cliff, taking the weight of the rope so that neither Ava nor Finn would be dislodged. They were already trembling with the effort, and I could see Ava reaching for her knife.

The rope around my waist was cutting me in half as I took all of Osric's weight to myself. Ava and Finn peered down, suddenly free. 'Falco! What are you doing?'

'I've got him,' I grunted. 'Pull yourself up, mate.'

'Cut the rope,' Ava ordered me, trying to pass me her knife. I ignored her, looking down at Osric. He was flailing about, unable to right himself. My fingers on the rock were trembling dangerously. If I fell too, there was no way Ava and Finn could hold us both. They'd have to cut us free.

It was funny, what I thought about then. Or perhaps it wasn't funny at all. Perhaps it was obvious. I thought of Isadora tumbling with me to the base of those rocks, her body smashing with mine into a million pieces.

I took hold of that image, held it close to my heart, and I breathed it deep into me. I would don a disguise I had never worn before, a new one that actually asked something of me, required me to be not less but more.

'Cut it!' Osric shouted.

That wasn't happening. I took one hand off the wall.

Finn screamed.

I reached down, the left side of my body shrieking in agony, to take hold of the rope beneath my waist.

Osric had drawn his own knife.

I met his eyes. 'Don't you dare.'

'I must.'

'Sheath the blade. On your Emperor's order.'

He faltered. And as he hesitated, I used my right arm to start pulling the much larger man up, inch by painstaking inch.

Sparrow's wings brushed against my face. I felt a trembling through my body; it screamed at me, this was beyond its capability. But I let the wings lift me, lift my arm until Osric was close enough to reach for the rock face and take his own weight.

I sagged against the cliff, breathing hard. My body was spent. The roaring tide receded from my heart.

I'm coming for you, little Sparrow.

★

We found the tunnel eventually, in a far up rock ledge smaller than the shelf we'd rested on earlier. This one had no shelter against the shrieking wind and the four of us had to struggle with the iron door set into the rock to get it open, almost losing our footing in the tight space. Dust burst out into our faces and we coughed until it cleared. The dark hole wound its way into the cliff. It would steadily ascend until it reached the aerie in which sat Sancia.

Osric took hold of my arm to forestall me. 'I must thank you, Majesty.'

'Don't start calling me that now!'

'It's your title. You have earned it.'

I frowned. 'I just pulled a man up a rope. That's not earning anything.'

'Why didn't you cut me free, Falco?'

I shrugged. 'Don't get carried away – it just didn't occur to me.'

Osric smiled. 'That's what makes you a true Emperor, Majesty.'

CHAPTER 6

ISADORA

The palace was readying itself for a banquet. Which meant Dren and Galia were busy preparing themselves in their private chambers, and hadn't yet begun to whore the servants out for their own pleasure. The banquet was being whispered about throughout the city, so I'd steeled myself to return and take advantage of the opportunity. One last time, I swore. This was the last time I'd have to come here.

I walked through halls I'd first walked six months ago, on my way to kill a different Empress, a different Emperor. That night felt heavy in my mind now, as I followed the same route to reach the same room. I'd failed to kill Falco then, but I would not fail in my efforts tonight.

It was Penn who'd given me the courage to come back, in the end. The night my pegasis had come to find me, Penn had been watching from the window. He'd found me outside, alone in the moonlight.

'Why send her away?'

'It's too dangerous for her here.'

We watched the crescent moon together.

'I don't believe you,' he said eventually. 'I had a pegasis once and I never would have sent him away.'

'What happened to him?'

'My parents killed him.'

I licked my lips. 'Would you let that happen again? Or would you send him away to save him?'

He cocked his head, thinking about the dilemma. 'Yeah. I guess. To save him.'

I put my arm around him. His was the only touch I wasn't bothered by.

'They hurt you, didn't they?' Penn asked. 'They tried to take something from you.'

I managed to nod, just a jerk of my head.

'But they didn't take anything.'

In the moonlight I peered down at his face. 'How . . .' I cleared my throat. 'How do you know?'

'They didn't take anything, and they won't take anything. Because they can't.'

I leant my head on his and took a long, trembling breath. *They can't.*

So here I was. In preparation for the banquet I'd been working in the palace for the past week. I knew the layout perfectly, had memorised all the work shifts, though I couldn't predict who would be here on which day. I knew that on those nights when they participated in their particular fetishes, Dren and Galia would ready themselves beforehand in their chambers for several hours. So that was where I went, laden with a tray of delicacies and sweet honey-wine.

They knew me now. They hadn't put me in the pool after that first day, but kept me by their thrones as their *poor pet*, the perfect spot from which to witness their depravities. They killed people each day, on whims. They forced servants naked into the pool, drugged them to be more amorous. It was about desire, I learned, but also about making those around them feel degraded, particularly the beautiful. Dren and Galia loved and desired beauty, but took just as much pleasure in marring it, ruining and humiliating it.

I saw Ryan again each day, the man with whom I'd been forced into the pool. I couldn't bear to look at him, too ashamed. He was kind, though. He was always very kind, and I knew he had a large soul. I just couldn't let the kindness of that soul be pulled into the maelstrom of what I had to do, so for his safety, as well as for my own shame, I hadn't once spared him a glance.

Tonight the Mad Ones had invited their inner circle of warders to dine with them. Which was why I'd hidden after my shift and was now heading towards their bedchamber, despite not having been summoned. Staying to the wall as servants were ordered, I entered the

71

royal chamber to a moment of acute disorientation. There was where we had stood, he and I. My bondmate. There was where I had shed tears, *tears*, and there was where his lips had touched mine.

'It's pet!' a voice said, slicing through my memory and the fluttering of my heart. I looked up to see Dren. It was probably not such a bad thing that he'd caught me staring sightlessly at empty air. I was mentally defective, after all. I placed the tray on the sideboard and bowed.

He threw his slipper onto the balcony. 'Fetch!'

I hesitated. Did he actually want me to *fetch*? This man was going to know a world of pain when I was done with him. I toddled out to the balcony and got his bloody slipper, maintaining a look of dumb obedience. It certainly wasn't the worst thing I'd endured for such an end.

'Bring me a drink,' Galia called, so I dropped the slipper at Dren's feet like a good little dog and took his wife a drink. She was sitting before her mirror, gazing at her beauty. 'Are you good with hair, pet?'

Definitely not. I shrugged.

'Go on. Try your best.'

I picked up the brush and started raking it through her hair, surprised by its brittle feel, the texture so straw-like it seemed as though it would break off in my hands.

Galia laughed a little, her cold eyes watching me in the mirror. 'The task bewilders her,' she told Dren. There was a hairpin on the dresser. I imagined how easy it would be to jab it into her neck and watch the blood drain from her cruel face.

Galia moved her hand and I felt myself fly into the air. My entire body hung suspended in the middle of the room, incapacitated. Had she heard my thought? Galia spun me slowly so she could look at me from every angle. Fury bloomed bloody in my heart.

'I don't trust her,' Galia murmured.

'She's dull as a mule.'

But Galia wasn't convinced. She watched my blank face. Moved closer and ran her hand over my foot. Inside, I screamed. Inside, I broke that hand for daring to touch me. Outwardly, I was blank. Galia moved her fingers slowly up my leg, under my dress.

Then, thankfully, she grew bored. With a shake of her head she muttered, 'Maybe you're right. That agitation from the first day is gone. She feels like nothing.'

'So why bother?'

Galia let me fall to the ground and I landed so heavily both my ankles rolled and I crashed awkwardly onto my hands and knees.

'Out,' she ordered, enjoying the dog game her husband had started.

I began to rise.

'Uh, uh, uh,' she scolded. 'On your hands and knees, poor pet.'

So I *crawled* from the room, imagining the brutal ways I would torture her before her end.

Once out of sight, I moved into the antechamber. Following it around, I managed to slip inside the dressing alcove, from which I could see snatches of the Mad Ones in their room. It would be some time yet before they left for the banquet. I had plenty of opportunity, and settled in to make myself comfortable enough to sleep.

Their voices were soft, but I could hear them well enough. 'They're not as frightened as they should be,' Galia said. 'It's why the resistance is forming.'

'Why should it concern us? They have no power.'

'Hate is power enough. Hate overcomes fear every time.'

I couldn't help peering through the slats to get a look at them. Galia remained before the mirror to undress. In public, she and her husband were always covered from neck to toe, and now, as she dropped her robe to the floor, I saw why. Galia's naked body was hideous. Her skin was discoloured as though every inch was bruised or . . . rotting. She peered at herself, letting the ward she'd pulled over her face disappear to reveal the truth. Her flawless skin and eyes became sallow and sunken as the illusion fell away, wrinkled almost to the point of desiccation.

My eyes widened in shock and then I felt a slow smile curve my lips.

'So we must deepen their fear,' Dren was saying, no doubt as rotten as his foul wife under the heavy robes. 'Either way, he cannot hurt us.'

'And what do you make of the bodies?' Galia snapped, studying herself. I reminded myself to breathe. I now knew their secret – the power was not only making them mad, but also destroying them slowly from the inside.

'One a day!' Dren argued. 'One a day is nothing to us.'

'One a day is one more than should be possible. Who is killing them in his name, and *how the fuck are they doing it*?'

'Could it be him?'

'We've read them all. The Sparrow isn't here. No one knows anything about him. And yet.'

I smiled. It was amusing how everyone in the world assumed I was a man.

'What else amuses you?'

I froze. Because that voice had come from right beside me.

Skin crawling, I turned slowly. There, standing in the small, shadowy alcove hidden between walls were two people.

Quillane, Empress of Kaya, and her mate, Radha. Both dead.

I searched my mind, wondering if I had accidentally slipped into the dream realm where things were not as they should be.

'You're very much awake,' Quillane said. Her silky black hair swayed gently, cut along the line of her sharp jaw. She truly was beautiful.

'Do you know why we're here?' Radha asked. She was the opposite of her mate, a wheat-coloured creature of hard lines and thin lips. She had fought well the night I killed her. She'd been clever, I remembered now, blowing out the flame of light and facing me in the dark. Blind in one eye and knowing well how to fight without sight. It hadn't mattered.

I didn't speak to either of them. I couldn't afford to give them that power over me. I let their presence settle. I accepted my ghosts as penance. I had never expected to pass through this life without having to pay a heavy price.

Their presence changed nothing. They knew it and I knew it.

They watched me and I watched them and none of us blinked, and at some point I must have fallen asleep. Because I was abruptly not here in this alcove, but in Radha's room, slicing my blade into her heart and telling her I was sorry as her sweet, sweet eyes lost their glitter with a final shift to gold.

Pain. *Quick*.

I dug my fingernails into my palms hard enough to draw blood. It yanked me back in, harnessed me, and I rose, feeling the shift and blur in everything. The dead bondmates were gone. Asleep, I walked from the alcove and back into the chamber, only to find that too much time had passed and the Mad Ones were also gone.

Though the walls of the hallways bled thick drops of blue-red blood, I walked through them until I found a staircase and then on until I reached the kitchen. There were knives here. The cooks and servants darted me glances but they knew my face by now and shooed me away without concern. I ignored them and their warped dream appearances, and it was so easy to slip two knives covertly into the folds of my skirts and lift a tray of drinks to carry with me.

Now the walls of the corridors were made of twisting vines. Tiny rosebuds bloomed in them, fragrant and heady, alongside razor-sharp thorns.

Servants passed me, not sparing me a glance. Why should they? I was the slow-witted pet. I aimed for the dining hall where the Mad Ones enjoyed their banquet with Lutius and Gwendolyn. I would take them all tonight. But before I reached them I had to pass through a room filled with dragonflies.

The gossamer wings flickered and parted before my eyes, revealing what waited in this chamber. Twelve warders. Torturing a girl with magic.

A dozen men, and I had only two knives.

Impossible.

But the girl screamed, her agony bursting into the air as a thousand flapping crows. The birds shrieked and cawed, their wings filling the air above the group like a dreadful cloud. They set my heart to thundering, set it to certainty. There was no way on this earth that I could turn back now, impossible as venturing forward may be. No way that I could let the girl continue to be harmed.

FALCO

In the tunnel I stopped. Something wasn't right. My heart was beating too fast and my skin was tingling. Were there *dragonflies* darting around my head? What – no, there were no dragonflies in the tunnel. I was going mad.

'Falco?' Finn asked from up ahead. They stopped to look back at me.

We had been walking so long. Too long in this dark, dank tunnel.

'It can't be much further,' Ava consoled me, thinking I was anxious about the confines. But I couldn't care less about the tunnel. It had disappeared.

I could feel her. And a deep, approaching dark. 'I think . . .' I whispered. 'Oh, *fuck*.' And blitzed past them, running faster than I ever had.

ISADORA

A dozen men with two knives. Very well. I would find a way.

But even dreaming, I felt the task settle upon me with concern. The dragonflies had shifting wings of gossamer and so beautiful were they, as they flew between the heavy dark of crows' wings, that it was painful to drag my eyes from them. The roof was a veritable chaos of flying creatures. But on the ground was something else entirely.

On the ground were twelve men and a girl. One small girl, weeping.

Warders were different to men. I had an advantage, and it was simply that they wouldn't know how to proceed when their magic didn't work. Twelve normal men with only two knives would be too many, because they would react with physical urgency and that innate human need to survive, to use fists and elbows and feet and guts and balls and the fight fight *fight* of life.

But these were barely men anymore. They knew the lofty unreality of magic. They knew a detachment from base urges and primal, animal instinct. They knew nothing of fists or fight.

That girl on the floor knew animal instinct. She knew fists and fight. She screamed again, but this time in fury, and she lashed out at the warder even though she knew it would provoke him into sending a terrible bolt of pain into her arching spine.

It was in her courage that I found mine. I took a breath and began.

Speed. That was what I'd need. Before they understood I had already taken out two, raising the blades and slicing them through two throats. For the next I slid low, slashing through the artery in his thigh, and twisted back up to stab a fourth in the guts. I leapt onto a table and used the momentum to plunge my knife down into the skull of another. The blade was far blunter than I was used to, and it got wedged in bone.

There was shouting now. Flinging impotent hands at me but I was still moving, wrenching the knife free and plunging it into the heart of a sixth. One of the warders ran at me, trying to pull me off his comrade, but he was clumsy and weak. I allowed him to haul me free, and as he tumbled back I jammed the blades down into his guts.

Kicking out at another warder who came at me, I flipped myself back over the body beneath, using the momentum to cut my knives up through the throat of my attacker.

I turned to the rest of the room. Someone screamed for help. 'Destroy her!' another snarled. I ran at him first, spinning to cut his throat, then another, and another. And for the last warder, who even now stood over the girl as if she was his possession, I threw my dagger through the air and embedded it in his heart.

As the room fell still I stopped to catch my breath.

It was a mistake, stopping. Looking. Letting adrenalin settle. Because a great, woozy sense of horror struck me, even though it never struck while I still dreamt. No, the horror usually waited for me in the waking realm. But here the crows dived at me, screeching their attack. I could feel them raking through my skin, tearing off pieces of me. I curled into a ball and squeezed my eyes shut, willing it away, all of it, including everything I was.

*

'Wake up!'

No. The nightmare of waking.

A voice split my ears and I lurched into consciousness. Above me was an unfamiliar face. The girl who'd been tortured, shaking me. 'Please, wake up! We have to go! They're coming!'

I struggled to rise, saw the desolation around me and stopped, paralysed.

'Please,' the girl wept frantically. 'Please get up. We have to go. People are coming, I can hear them.'

'Go,' I told her.

'Not without you. I won't go without you.'

But the bodies and the blood. Something had changed. I couldn't look away. I could always look away only I couldn't, not now. I had to stay here with the dead, my dead.

She sobbed, climbing to her feet. 'What's your name?'

My eyes darted up to the ceiling. There had been wings. Now there were none.

'*Your name!*'

'Isadora.'

'I'll find you,' the girl vowed, and fled.

Alone, I leant over and vomited onto the marble. I didn't understand – I had seen worse, I had imagined and done worse, but my body was revolting. It had had enough. I couldn't leave this room, I'd never deserve to. I'd stay here in this nightmare forever, trapped with them, with all the lives I'd stolen –

No. Don't. Don't go there.

Slowly, very slowly, I stood.

Around me was a sea of blood; it seeped towards my feet and for some mindless reason I didn't move. I just let it reach me and lap languidly over my skin. It licked my feet as it already did my hands until I wore red socks and red gloves.

That was when I heard footsteps approaching along the marble corridor. The girl had been right. They were coming. *The butcher or the meat*, I screamed inwardly. *You can't be the meat. You can't.*

Please, I begged myself. *Don't give up now.*

Ten seconds, if that, to place my actions and the violence inside a very small box and move it to the bottom of the lake. Ten seconds to do that, and to draw the two kitchen knives. No time to escape – no possible way out of this. Which meant whoever entered through that door would have to die. Because I *had* to get to the Mad Ones, *I had to.* Ten seconds to do all of that, but I couldn't. I couldn't. Nothing was fitting in any boxes, and no locks were strong enough.

Eight, nine, ten, and the footsteps arrived. A person exploded into the room and stopped. Shadows obscured them and for a disorienting moment I couldn't see properly, didn't recognise who had come.

78

Then he shifted, and I saw – he was here.

A great, woozy disbelief and a pounding panic and a heart *beat beat beating* – how could I not have felt him sooner? Because of the violence, that was why. The bond did not live in the same space as this kind of violence.

His long golden hair was tied back, his glittering eyes shadowed and his boots muddy. I started to cry. Because I had done too much, had become too monstrous for my own heart to bear. And yet here he was, as strange as any dream.

Falco crossed the bloodied tableau in an instant. He put his hands on my face and he held it and looked into me and even though I was crying he still managed to keep me inside his eyes. I shook my head desperately, whispering, 'You're too late, I already did it, I didn't stop.'

But he said, 'No more. Put it in its box and lock it.'

'The box is too small for this.'

'Make it bigger.'

'The lock is too weak.'

'Make it stronger.'

'I can't.'

'Then I will do it for you.'

I stared at him. His face was so close, his breath on my lips.

'It's done,' Falco said softly. 'All of this is small and over. We have to leave now.'

And so that was how the boxes became big enough and the locks strong enough. That was how all of this went to where it couldn't touch me. That was how I straightened my shoulders and turned myself to stone. How I emptied my mind spirit heart and remembered all too clearly that I hated this man almost as much as I hated myself.

I nodded once, and we moved for the door.

Someone was darting down the hall and I could hardly believe my eyes as I recognised her. Finn of Limontae spotted me and closed the gap between us, taking me into her arms. I stiffened, unsure of what to do. Her skin on mine was unbearable. But some part of me wanted so badly to give way to it, to allow it – this affection of hers, this strength and generosity and caring. That was not, however, the monster that had been forged.

Finn stood back, searching my face. She wore none of her usual scorn or sarcasm. 'You look weird,' she said. Whether she meant the look of my hair and skin, or the look of my soul, I didn't know.

I licked my lips, stepping away from her. There was too much blood on my hands.

'Jonah and Penn?' she asked urgently. 'Are they alive?'

I nodded, and she sagged against me once more.

'Come on,' Falco said.

He was right – we had no time for talk. A guard ran towards us along the hall; I spun and slammed my fist into his jaw, knocking him unconscious. He fell and we continued on. I didn't look at either of my companions. I didn't care what they thought. There were boxes and I was a gods-damned soldier in this war.

'Izzy, we have to –'

I threw my knife, hilt first, into the temple of the next guard who ran at us, then crossed to reclaim it from beside her unconscious body. Glancing over my shoulder, I saw Falco take Finn's hand and draw her forwards. My eyes moved to where his skin touched hers. Such ease he had in touching another human being. I turned and continued on.

'Where are we going?' I heard Falco ask Finn. Their familiarity was clear; it was there in their voices and clasped hands.

'Os is waiting for us on the roof,' she answered. Going to the roof would be infantile. I shook my head, stalking forwards.

'Izzy, there's a plan, we have to go to the roof,' Finn pressed. 'We have a warder who's meeting us . . .'

A balloon of hatred in my chest, my throat, moving up into my mouth, curling my lip.

'Not with them,' Falco told me. 'With us.'

Us. An amused breath left me. *Us.* 'I'm here to kill the Mad Ones.'

'The palace is in chaos. You'll never get to them now,' Falco told me. 'Either you come with us and our man gets us out, or we go with you and try to get out your way. We don't separate.'

My hackles rose. We would separate if I wanted us to separate. I could lose them in a breath. But I looked at Finn's face and knew that even if I did disappear, she would follow. And my way had us plunging into the bowels of the palace and hoping for enough luck to fight our way out. It had been a suicide mission, after all. Which meant Falco died. And Finn of Limontae. Finn, who I – surprisingly, abruptly – cared for.

So I followed them to the roof.

A man stood there, his hair a faded black, his eyes a faded green. Perhaps he looked a little like me. All I knew was that he looked like a warder, and I hated him. There was a woman, too, half her face covered.

The warder's eyes took me in. 'Hands,' he ordered.

People were mounting the stairs – I could hear them. The door crashed open, just as we grabbed each other's hands and –

Whoosh.

I slammed into the earth, my ankles and knees buckling. My spine hit hard ground and I felt the air ripped from my lungs. Nausea followed, a great roiling mess of it through my guts. All my energy was gone and I realised the warder filth had stolen it.

Swallowing quickly, I forced myself upright even as the world spun around me. The warder and Finn were already standing, unaffected. The other woman struggled to sit and Falco was curled into a ball, but straightened as I watched. I felt his heartbeat in my chest, then forced it into a box. Whatever had happened between us in that death room upstairs was irrelevant. I had to distance myself from it, from the dangerous intensity of it.

I peered around dizzily. We were not in the palace anymore. We were in an alley near the markets. It was a rough, violent area.

'Where are we?' Finn asked.

'I don't know where I brought us,' the warder said wearily. 'Too many people . . .'

'Where's safe?' Falco asked me.

I didn't meet his eyes. 'Nowhere at night.' He and I were keeping as far from each other as we could. The thought of his skin touching mine again caused a revolt in my chest, as it must have in his.

Carefully I led them out into the streets. We crept along several, staying to the edges, the shadows, though there was hardly any light left. I could get myself home easily enough but I couldn't get four

others through the city without being spotted, so we needed somewhere to hide until daybreak.

'A tavern?' Falco whispered.

And be detected within moments by the warder spies? I shook my
head and led them to a stable. The warder calmed the horses within
so they wouldn't make a sound; not with magic, but with a gentle
touch and a soft voice. We crouched low in an empty stall at the
very back.

'This is Osric,' Finn said of the warder.

I glanced at him, then away.

'And this is Isadora,' she went on. 'I'd say she's usually friendlier, but
it would be a big fat lie. Izzy, you seem to have already met Falco. You
know – *Emperor* Falco. And this is Queen Ava of Pirenti.'

My eyebrows arched and I looked at the woman as she removed her
scarf to show me the terrible scar on her face. The brand of a howling
wolf. The ugliness of it was beautiful. I inclined my head to her and
she did the same to me.

But I was still covered in blood – too ashamed to be comfortable
under their gaze. I busied myself checking the stalls for any sign of
surveillance. The windows were locked, as was the door, and we were
far enough from the palace that –

'I'll know of any approaches,' Osric told me.

Turning my eyes to his, I met them coldly for a long moment. Then
I continued my check on the stables.

'She doesn't mean to be rude,' I heard Finn say.

That was when Falco spoke. 'She might mean to be. She might be
entitled to be.'

A chill moved over my skin. I didn't like that he'd stood up for
me. I thought of feckless, beautiful royals, untrustworthy warders and
amorous laughing cliffside girls. I thought of home, my forest and its
deformed inhabitants, silent and cast-off like me. I didn't belong here,
or anywhere near it.

'Osric is with us,' Finn snapped. 'You'd have Isadora treat him like
those morons in Glenvale did?'

'She can treat him however she likes,' Falco replied. 'He's a big
boy – I'm sure he can handle it.'

I walked back to the stall and sat facing the door. I had no interest in their argument. Clasping my hands over my knees, I settled in to keep watch.

'Shifts,' Ava said softly. 'Isadora will go first, clearly. She will wake Falco in an hour. I'll wake Finn, who will wake me. Then we leave.'

'What about me?' Osric asked.

'You need more rest. Sleep the night through.'

If I was so inclined I might have pointed out that a warder would be useless from here on in, because any use of his powers would be a beacon to the Mad Ones; I was not, so I stayed quiet and kept watch. Let the precious warder have his precious sleep. The moment he and I were alone, I would gut him.

As Finn, Osric and Ava slept soundly, I felt Falco watching me from the other side of the stall. There was a deep, thrilling panic in my breast. I tried not to look at him but it was like being dragged against the strongest current in the ocean. The urge to touch him was like nothing I had experienced.

Obviously he hadn't told them about us, or about me. For some reason they had no idea I was the Sparrow (was he embarrassed of being bonded to me?). What did he expect would come of this? That we'd now be allies against the Mad Ones? Or simply pretend to be, until we could kill each other?

'Are you alright?' His voice cut through my thoughts.

I didn't answer.

'You don't look well. Let me take your watch.'

That didn't even deserve acknowledgement.

'Who are you? Where do you come from?'

I stared resolutely at the door.

'It's whispered that you were born in Sanra.'

This time I looked at him. 'Don't you mean Yurtt?'

'Then it's true. It makes sense. That you'd be angry.'

Did he even understand what anger was?

'I do,' he said.

I glanced at him, realised he'd responded to my unspoken thought and recoiled. My fingers went to my knives, then felt their absence with cold vulnerability.

83

He raised his hands quickly. 'Easy.'

'Stay out of my head.'

'I didn't mean to. I can't control it.'

'Do you hear everything?'

'No.'

My heart thundered in my chest. Not even *warders* could read what was in my mind, and yet this man could. And if he could hear some of my thoughts, why could I hear none of his?

'I felt it all,' Falco said softly. 'When I was in the tunnel and you were in that room. I felt what you felt and I know, Isadora.'

I tried to breathe. Found myself unable to look away from his eyes. 'What do you know?'

'What it does to you.'

Suddenly it all surged up through my chest and my heart and into my mouth. 'So then what?' I demanded, a lump in my throat. Gods, the words that fell free were as shocking to me as anything had ever been. 'You think I want any of this? You think I like the violence I'm capable of? I didn't ask for it – there's no other way. I didn't want to be born like this, into this. But what am I meant to do? Let them win? Let them ruin the helpless? I'm capable of stopping them when there are so many who aren't, who are hurt over and over again, and I can make it stop, so doesn't that mean that I have to?'

Falco crossed the stall to my side swifter than a breath. 'Yes. But you don't have to do it alone anymore. I'm here now.'

I let out a laugh that sounded more like a sob. Turned away from him. 'You? You're a joke. Just as this thing between us is a joke.'

'Isa—'

'You *left* us here, to this nightmare.'

My words let the air out of the world. He closed his eyes, resting his head on the wall behind us. Long minutes ticked by as I stared at the stall door and Falco kept his eyes closed.

But then he murmured, 'How are you killing them?'

I looked at his face. With his eyes closed I could better focus on the shape of his features, the narrow delicacy of his sharp cheekbones, the heavy brow and square jaw. He looked just as everyone thought an Emperor should look – an expertly sculpted example of perfection. The golden ones. That damned royal blood of his. Beauty bred beauty, after all. How they would love him in the palace now. What sick pleasure Dren and Galia would derive from his loveliness. A lock of his long golden hair had come loose and I fought the urge to reach over and brush it behind his ear.

That was the moth being drawn to the flickering flame, only to be destroyed by the heat. That was the nasty tug of this unnatural warder's bond. The seductive, deadly trap.

Softly I said, 'You don't get to have all of my secrets, Emperor Feckless.'

Chapter 7

I woke the others in the cool quiet of predawn. I hadn't slept, and neither had Isadora. We'd kept watch together in stubborn silence, allowing the others to rest. As the sun began to rise we made our way through grey streets, moving quickly. If we were stopped we were to say that Osric was escorting us home after shifts at the palace.

It felt remarkable to be moving through my home city without a blindfold or a dozen guards, but I was disturbed at its decline. Buildings were abandoned and crumbling, waste lay in gutters and I could smell the heavy scent of death. It felt too much to solve, a task far too big for the kind of person I was. Quill would have known exactly what to do, but I felt dwarfed.

I watched Isadora as we travelled. I couldn't help watching her. There was an ugly tint in her hair and on her skin, but despite that . . . She moved with a slow, dreamlike grace, unlike anyone else I knew. The tilt of her neck was almost gentle, the slenderness of her tiny fingers elegant. Everything was calm and deliberate; she was extraordinarily lissome and I found her almost unbearably lovely to watch. Which was what made the blood staining her hands and feet such a dichotomy, the twelve dead bodies in the palace such a brutal contradiction.

I noticed a flow of people and asked Isadora where they'd be going at such an early hour. Her enormous red eyes watched the bodies turn up a side street. 'Temple.'

'Let's go,' I said.

'It's illegal.'

My head whipped back to her. 'Why?'

It was Osric who answered. 'All that should be worshipped is the soul magic, and the wielders of the soul magic. The old gods are heretic now, I would imagine.'

I led them to follow the families who crept through the grey predawn. It was dangerous, but my curiosity was an undeniable force.

'Os will be trouble,' Finn pointed out, handing him a sash to wrap around his head. At least it would hide his hair. She then removed her cloak and draped it over Isadora's bloodied and torn dress. Isadora buried her smeared hands inside the pockets – she'd been unable to clean them properly.

The temple was disguised as a closed fabrics shop. Two men guarded its entrance, sitting on upturned crates and casually smoking pipes. As we drew near their eyes fixed on us with wariness. 'What business?' one of them asked. He had a yellow braid hanging on either side of his face, and a thick blond beard.

'Prayer,' I replied.

'Haven't seen you before.'

'I only just learned you were here.'

He studied me carefully. 'Where would you die?'

For a moment I was confused, and then I recalled summer nights thirty years ago spent on rocky seashores with my ma, and the stories she would tell me about the old ways. She had believed deeply, so I would don her cloak as I entered this place; in temple I would be as pious as she'd ever been.

'At sea,' I murmured, 'that the goddess Rian might claim me.'

The man reached for my hand, clasping it tight. His was a large, firm grip, and it moved me, somehow, as did the look in his eyes. His eyes. To have eyes look upon me without a blindfold, without fear – it was an intimacy I was unaccustomed to, and it thrilled me. 'What's your name?' I asked.

'Coll of Orion.'

Ava cleared her throat. 'Do you know of your home's fate?'

Coll met her violet eyes through the gap in her scarf. 'Aye, and it is a sad one, I'm afraid. One of the first towns to be destroyed.'

I reached for Ava just as her legs wobbled. Caught her as she steadied herself, saw the grief in her eyes. I wanted to tell her I was sorry, so desperately sorry, but I couldn't find my voice. It was the second man who spoke: Coll's companion, who remained sitting on his crate. 'The feathered cloak will wrap them in her embrace and protect them now. She'll carry them to the bottom of the ocean. You have only to believe and it will be so.'

We stared at him but he didn't look up, intent on his pipe.

'Follow the stairs to the bottom,' Coll said, and we made our way into the small, dusty shop. Behind the counter there was a trapdoor in the floor, which was lifted to reveal stairs. They led down into the ground, where it grew cold. Our footsteps echoed as we descended steadily.

The feathered cloak. It lodged itself in my mind.

Beneath the ground was a basement in which dozens of people were sitting on the floor in prayer. At the farthest end of the room was a plinth, and on it an ancient-looking piece of driftwood, intricately carved and twisted. So beautiful it stole my breath. I moved slowly through the sitting bodies until I reached it. In the early days of the world, from the sea had come dark, curled pieces of salt-drenched driftwood. These had been imbued with life by a trio of old gods, and as such had been the first humans to walk from the ocean and onto land. Or so some believed. Others used to believe it was the warders who came first, and gave life to the rest of us. Pirenti believed in an entirely different origin story: one of ancient ice and fires, of men forged in iron just as the Holy Sword had been, of women uncurling from deep within the earth. But here, we believed in sea and salt.

The feeling I had then – standing before the wood and surrounded by Kayans who worshipped such ancient stories – was of an immense connection to something flesh and blood. There was no magic down here, only earth, only life.

I swallowed and looked up to see Isadora watching me. I couldn't read the expression in her eyes, but they did not move from me even when I met them. I wanted to know how she felt about the feathered cloak and the driftwood. About the old gods and the soul magic. About anything, *everything*. I knew nothing about her except the way her heart felt when it beat, and try as I might I couldn't control when

I heard her thoughts. In this moment she was silent. Everything was silent. Then I realised *that* was what I was hearing from her: a deep, undeniable quiet.

The tolling of a bell broke into my thoughts, startling everyone in the room.

'Raid!' a voice screamed, and every person in the basement went scrabbling up the stairs. My companions and I waited and then followed the terrified crowd back up to the shop. Coll and his friend were ushering people out.

'Get on,' he urged.

'What's happened?'

'Warders on their way.'

I heard it then, a second distant bell, tolling to alert the temple to an approach. 'You'll flee too?'

'Run!' he snapped.

We sprinted up the street and rounded a corner but something about the look in his eyes stalled me. I peered back, spotting the fabric shop in the distance. The two men were still smoking in front of it when four warders arrived.

'Fal, come on,' Finn pleaded.

But they weren't moving. Coll and his friend. I could see it coming and hurled myself back towards them, drawing my two swords. I barely got two paces before Ava, Osric and Finn tackled me to the ground and literally dragged me back around the corner.

'Get off!' I hissed. 'They'll be killed!'

'You run out there, they'll read you in a second and then the Mad Ones will know you're here!' Osric snapped.

'It's not worth their lives!'

'It is, Falco! Of course it is!'

But I could not abide that. I would not allow any more deaths for me and my fucking secrets. Not of men who believed in the same things as my ma.

It went through my mind in the flash of a moment, less than a moment – how I would lay my friends flat on their backs, turn that corner, cross that street and use my two swords to destroy those corrupt warders. I saw it all; it would be easy.

But in that moment, less than a moment, I heard the grunts of pain and knew I was too late. I saw the two dead bodies. The warders disappearing down the steps of the shop to destroy the temple and its precious symbol of defiance.

I turned back to my company. They were staring at me, pale and concerned. Except Isadora, who watched me with something completely different, turned from me with something brutally like scorn.

The fury in my chest made it hard to breathe, but breathe I did, long and slow. *Don't blame them, they were protecting you.* But a dark thing in me wanted them punished, wanted them to understand who I was and the kind of power I could wield.

That wasn't true though, was it? Power only lay in the opinions of others, and if no one obeyed my orders then I had no power. Perhaps they would have obeyed me if I'd been honest with them, but instead I had lied and lied and lied those men into their graves. I walked down the street, needing air and space and none of their gods-damned faces staring at me like that, with *pity*. The endless cursed pity of being Emperor fucking Feckless.

'Fal—' Finn started.

'Do not follow me,' I ordered her coldly and she fell back. Rounding another corner, I stood in the empty street and rested my forehead against the wall of a house. *Breathe.*

Coll's handshake tingled in my palm. His eyes. His friend's words. The driftwood and the prayers and all those bodies pressed in together. It crystallised me, activated something within. For the space between heartbeats Quill was here with me and I wanted only to make her proud, to be the kind of person she could have faith in. As I'd never been for her while she lived.

As my pulse settled once more I put it all in boxes, just as I had seen Isadora do. Locked away the things that, if left free, would weigh too heavily. And perhaps shutting things in boxes would allow them to rot and fester deep within, but it was better that than letting one single piece of them stop us from walking on. There was no time to slow or stop, not now, not when people were dying.

I returned to my friends and gestured for Isadora to lead us home. No one asked me anything. It only took another twenty minutes to reach our destination and we walked it in silence. Entering a back alley, we snuck behind several buildings and then scaled the wall of a courtyard. Finn was first over, tearing inside the house.

'Jonah!'

I landed and followed her in time to see the young man fling himself from a sleeping roll on the ground. The twins collided with each other, and Finn was sobbing wildly and then Penn was there and she was kissing him over and over and the three of them collapsed to the floor, hugging each other so tight, utterly heedless of the fact that they were squashing people who'd been sleeping on the floor and who were now quickly disentangling themselves.

'I knew you'd come,' Jonah was saying over and over.

I turned my eyes to the other people in the room. All half-asleep and blinking drowsily at us.

'Iz?' a man asked, eyeing us nervously. 'Who's this?'

'Gods, girl!' a woman exclaimed at the sight of Isadora. 'What's *happened*? You look a sight! Are you wounded?'

Jonah finally caught sight of Isadora and frantically took her blood-stained hands in his. 'Did they hurt you? What did you do? Are you alright?'

I frowned, then saw Isadora uncomfortably remove her hands from his. 'I failed.'

'Who *are* you?' a man asked me.

'And why is there a warder in my house?' the woman demanded. There was a rustle of unease, and I saw one of the big fellas reach for a sword sheathed in its scabbard.

'Easy,' I told him.

'I grow weary of this.' Osric sighed. 'I would die before I lifted one finger in an effort to help the vile false rulers of this graveyard.'

Silence followed that, until the child started to cry and I saw the woman take her baby from the room.

'You sent word, asking for aid,' Ava said into the silence. 'We have come to help.'

'I've told you of Finn, my sister,' Jonah explained. 'And . . .' Looking my way, he hastily lowered his eyes and then sank to the floor. His friends watched in confusion.

I frowned wishing the anonymity could last. 'My name is Falco. I was once Emperor of Kaya.'

There were gasps and a general ruckus of bodies flattening themselves to the floor, eyes squeezing shut.

'You remain Emperor of Kaya,' Osric said.

Finn peered down at the prostrate people, then looked at me. 'Should *I* bow?'

'Please stand,' I told them. 'You need not bow or avert your eyes.'

'But . . . why, Majesty?' the woman of the house asked from the doorway, eyes still closed.

I couldn't help glancing at Isadora, which was a mistake. 'I can hardly be dethroned for bonding if I have no throne to lose.' Once my eyes had strayed to her I had a very hard time dragging them away.

'But, Majesty . . .'

'Please,' I murmured, forcibly trying to wrest control of myself. Something prickled in the air between our bodies, something painful. 'I am a guest in your home,' I managed to tell the others. 'You will honour me enough if you offer us shelter while we take stock of the situation.'

They rose, still looking unsure. Their knowledge of the law was so deeply ingrained that looking upon me was terrifying – long before my reign people were killed for meeting the unguarded eyes of an Emperor.

I introduced Ava and when she removed her scarf we had to go through the whole thing again as they dived once more to the floor. I worked hard to make sure I didn't forget anyone's name. By the end of the introductions, during which not one of them had looked me in the eye, it was clear how desperate they were for help – or even a scrap of hope.

Soon it was time for the workers to earn their food chits. They were all, including Penn, working as street cleaners, which was apparently a nice name for a job that entailed entering homes to remove dead bodies or waste and taking it all to a pit. I felt sick to my stomach upon hearing this, and a weary headache started at the base of my skull.

Sara stayed home to look after the baby, along with Isadora, Jonah and my party. While the twins stood in the kitchen, talking a mile a minute at each other, I noticed Isadora sneak away to the washroom. I'd been very careful to stay as far from her as possible, but I'd known every second that she was near, she was *here*, she was in the corner of my eye, something I couldn't look directly at for fear of being blinded. Now that she was leaving that space, my space, I couldn't stand it. It wasn't so much a decision to follow her, but an inevitability. I ignored the question in Ava's eyes.

I didn't knock. Insanity wielded my limbs and banished all clarity and there couldn't be a closed door between us. Isadora whirled to see me, wrenching the dress she'd half-removed back over her legs. 'What are you *doing*? Get out!'

'I'm sorry. I just . . .' I was having trouble breathing. My face felt flushed, feverish; my eyes were struggling to focus. There was too much horror here and I didn't know how I was supposed to fix any of it and it plagued my thoughts but I *still* couldn't stop looking at her and thinking about her and wanting to touch her and how sickening that felt in my guts –

'Falco,' she said softly.

'I can't take this. It's been one night and it's already sending me mad. Your nearness . . . and I can't touch you . . . It doesn't feel right.'

She swallowed. Met my eyes. There was an impossible, glittering, burning thing between us, connecting us, tugging my heart to hers and all I wanted was for our skin to touch. I wanted to run the bath for her and undress her from that filthy white dress, to wash her skin of the blood, and all that tint that made her look unlike herself.

I saw her forcibly don a cloak of calm. I wanted to rip her free of it, of all that fucking *calm*. But then, what did I wear, if not a dozen cloaks all too similar?

Amidst the bodies of twelve dead warders there'd been a crack in the calm. She'd been right on the edge of a mighty precipice, and I would never forget the terror she couldn't hide from me.

It's not real, she thought now, unafraid, and I caught it, the gentle whisper of her mind inside mine. I nodded. She was right. Of course she was right. She was able to see through the illusion, even when I wasn't.

I went to the door and it was as though I had to step out of my body to get there. 'Why did you do that to yourself?'

She frowned.

'Your hair and skin.'

A funny expression passed her gaze and I realised it was bitterness. 'To be beautiful.'

My eyes widened. 'It's not beautiful. It's false.'

She smiled. The first smile I'd seen her give. It was rare and sweet and slow, like the gently falling leaves of autumn. 'And this from the master of disguise himself,' she murmured, amused and a little mocking. But her eyes shifted to brilliant, glittering gold, and mine followed.

A groan left me and I hauled myself from the washroom, slamming the door behind me. I kept my eyes squeezed shut as I rested my forehead on the door. My fists clenched painfully: I could feel her on the other side.

Shift, I bid my eyes. But I could feel them and they were still so gold.

'Falco?' Ava's voice came out of the darkness.

I didn't look at her, couldn't let her see the truth.

'Be careful,' she murmured. 'Your flights of fancy will hurt her.'

A weary smile found my lips and I looked at my cousin, eyes normal once more. 'I'm always careful.'

But it was abruptly, painfully, clear how little anyone in this world knew me. Clear, also, how little they knew Isadora the Sparrow, if anyone thought she was capable of being hurt by flights of fancy.

ISADORA

I sent him from the bathroom because he was Emperor of our nation and he hadn't freed Sanra from its subjugation – even in twenty years of peace, he had been too weak to do this simplest of things and change the lives of thousands. I sent him out because he'd fled this city when it was overrun with warders and left his people here to struggle alone. Because he and I had been born enemies, and I'd spent most of my life seeking a way to kill him. Because he had always been a coward, in every sense of the word.

I sent him from the bathroom because of all these things.

And none.

Together in the confined space I imagined his hands on my body. I imagined fingers and lips and eyelids and heartbeats, and the two of us diving below the lake's surface to discover what lay beneath, as mysterious to me as it was to him. It was a cruel kind of magic that sent those thoughts into my head and my skin, it was a maddening kind of magic. But it wasn't why I sent him away.

The real reason was simple. It was shame.

I had murdered the woman Falco loved. And it had been a love that was true. Not a farce, not forced upon him, but chosen freely. For that my punishment would be this: the Emperor of Kaya would be the first and only soul in all the world to hate his bondmate.

It was a lucky thing, I supposed, that I had the ability to hate him even more. As I went to the bath and scrubbed my body clean of the blood and the colouring potions, I pulled that hatred around me like the feathered cloak of the goddess, protective and strong. It would be my armour, just like the cloak I wore for calm.

The only problem with this plan – with this garment I'd fashioned – was that small moment of defiance. Of selflessness. As he'd prepared to rush down that street and face those warders outside the temple, I'd seen again the undeniable truth I'd first glimpsed on the night we bonded: Falco was no coward.

AVA

I remained out of the way as the chaos of night meal began. With eleven adults and a baby in one very small house, it was a shambles. Falco had announced that our party would find our own food, as we had yet to contribute to the ration chits by working. This was met with a scoff and a giggle, and then completely ignored.

'The Emperor comes to dinner and expects us not to feed him.' Elias grinned with a shake of his head. 'Sit down, Majesty. You can help us with the food problem tomorrow.'

We ate heavy damper and drank water. If Falco was unused to the simplicity of such food, he was graceful enough to hide it, praising the cooks with a flamboyant extravagance that made them laugh.

After I'd witnessed him following Isadora into the washroom this morning, I watched my cousin with the tiny pale creature, the albino we'd met in the palace. She was a strange thing, mostly silent, extremely solemn. I couldn't read a single expression on her face or in her unchanging blood-eyes. But I could see that he and she watched each other when they thought no one would notice.

As everyone bedded down for the night, squashed wherever there was floor space, I noticed Finn was nowhere to be seen. Falco and I were given the baby's room, in which had been placed two cots. It was easier to accept the offer than to make everyone uncomfortable with our presence. I didn't retire yet, but wandered outside to look for Finn.

Her twin, Jonah, was on watch duty, and pointed to the roof. 'She likes to be up high,' he said with a shrug. I nodded – I knew well of Finn's love of rooftops. As I passed him I stole a look at the boy who was so much like his sister. It made me think, inevitably, of my own twin children, and all the things inside me tightened unbearably.

I scaled the outside of the building, grappling with the vines. I'd well and truly had enough of climbing by the time I reached the top. Finn was sitting on the flat roof, legs dangling over the edge. She flashed me a smile as I perched beside her, but neither of us spoke for a time.

'It's physical pain,' she murmured with a laugh of disbelief. Missing her bondmate. 'I don't think I was prepared for it.'

'There's no way to be.'

'Are you able to speak with Ambrose?'

I shook my head. Some bonded couples could communicate mentally. There was no way to predict who would be able to and who wouldn't. It seemed random, though some believed it was a skill that could be learned. 'I could with Avery, but not with Ambrose. You?'

'No. Not at this distance. But I can feel him still. I can feel him missing me as I miss him. It feels sort of . . . *cruel*, to have twice the pain.'

'Do you ever consider ending it? Breaking your bond?' She and Thorne had discovered that the ability lay in his blood, her magic and their bond, but we hadn't told anyone yet – there would be widespread chaos when the Kayan people found out, and they had more than enough to deal with at the moment.

Finn shook her head vehemently. 'I'd rather die.'

I lay back against the roof and watched the stars. On a whim, I asked, 'Have Falco and Isadora met before?'

'Just last night in the palace. Why?'

'How did he recognise her as a friend then? And vice versa?'

I could almost hear Finn frowning. 'I don't know. I didn't think about it. What are you . . .?'

'It just occurred to me as curious, is all. Him sprinting into the palace and stumbling upon a girl covered in blood.'

'I'm sorry to say that Isadora being covered in blood doesn't particularly surprise me. And Falco was helping her.'

'But how did he *know*?'

'He . . . I don't know.'

'How do you know her?'

'We met her last year on our way to the tournament.'

'How?'

'She helped us, one night when Thorne went beast. She's saved my life many times, Ava. She's a friend.'

I shrugged and nodded. But a suspicious thing inside me was bidding me to be wary.

Finn lay back beside me. 'Do you think he can do it? Free us?'

'Do you?'

'He can't fight, can't use magic and nobody listens to what he says because it's mostly idiotic. So the answer should be easy. But . . .' Finn paused. 'I'm not so sure.'

'Perhaps his age is finally catching up to him.'

'Or maybe he was never what he seemed.'

'What do you mean?'

She shrugged. 'I'm not sure. It's just . . . when he and I first met I touched his skin, and I felt this sort of throbbing, dark, *ancient* thing. And I just . . .' She shook her head. 'I guess it didn't feel like something that would belong in a feckless wimp.'

We pondered for a while, and eventually I murmured, 'People wear many faces. I think our Emperor holds more secrets than we might imagine.'

I thought of Isadora and knew the same to be true of her. Which was exactly why I was going to keep an eye on her.

Snow crunched underfoot as I jogged. Ella and Sadie were riding inside the carriage with Ma, while Ambrose had taken over driving. Snow-covered hills sloped before us, kissed by sparkling sunlight. To our right snaked a river, its surface coated in a fine layer of ice. Howl had run ahead to scout the way, following the scent of a winter hare as it scampered into a rabbit's warren. He growled at the mouth of it for a few moments, then gave up and loped cheerfully through the snow to my side.

'Spar at lunch?' I asked Ambrose.

He smiled crookedly. 'Or we could play at some dice instead. Talk a little.'

I frowned, surprised. It was the first time I could ever recall the king turning down a wrestle. 'Are you well, uncle?' I asked.

Ambrose chuckled. 'Aye, boy. Lately I just grow bored of fighting.'

My eyebrows arched but I didn't press the matter. It was a curious thing to say, and I wondered where it came from. Growing bored of a thing that kept you and your family alive seemed dangerous to me.

Ambrose called a halt so he could water the horses by the river while we had something to eat. I poked my head into the back of the carriage. 'Alright in here, ladies?' Ma was braiding Ella's hair while Sadie read aloud to them from a book. Cushions and swathes of fur lined every surface for warmth and comfort. 'It's very cosy in here.'

'It's hot,' Ella replied wanly. I caught a look at her cheeks and saw how flushed she was, then reached in to touch the girl's forehead.

'She's really warm, Ma.'

Ma nodded, giving me a pointed look to say no more. 'Some fresh air is all she needs.'

'I'm reading to make her feel better,' Sadie informed me.

Ma finished braiding Ella's hair up off her sweaty neck. I helped them climb out and watched as Ella sighed in relief at the frigid air on her skin.

'Sword, it's freezing!' Sadie exclaimed.

I laid out a quilt for them to sit on to have their midday meal. Ma fed Ella a drink with herbs of some kind, and I had no doubt it would break the poor little one's fever.

I walked over to where Ambrose crouched by the river, capturing water in our canteens. 'Ella has a fever. Ma's taking care of it but we need to reach Norvjisk by nightfall.'

Ambrose passed me the canteens to finish while he went to his daughter. 'Are you not feeling well, darling?'

'She was just hot. She's fine now,' Sadie said protectively.

Abruptly, Howl starting barking and I shot to my feet, peering ahead.

'Howl!' Sadie called sternly.

His bark deepened, signalling danger. I was running before anyone had a chance to respond, already drawing my axe from my back. Over a crest in the road was another travelling party. They'd paused before the barking dog, peering beyond him to spot my approach. The sun was behind me, making it difficult for them to see, while I could observe them well. Five in all, three young women and two men, all mounted on weary horses. And all Kayan, by the looks of their size and colouring.

'Greetings,' one of the women called.

I lifted a hand, but remained a fair distance. Something about Howl's unease was creeping into my own bones. He didn't mistrust people as a rule, so their scent was disturbing him. In fact, I'd caught a whiff of something rotten too.

'Greetings. What brings you to these parts?'

'We're on route to the fortress,' the same woman replied. She was the oldest and had her blond hair tied into several braids. 'We've heard Kayans are welcome there.'

'They are,' I agreed. 'But how did you come to be north of the fortress?'

'We got lost,' one of the men answered bluntly. He wasn't scared of me – none of them were, which was interesting. It was also interesting that they seemed to be lying. The road from Kaya was clear and straightforward, and led directly to the fortress.

'We didn't travel the road,' the Kayan woman told me as if she had read my thoughts. 'We were much further south when we made for Pirenti. We were forced to go through Yurtt.'

All that was south of Yurtt was deep forest and the warder prison. I glanced behind me, but Ambrose and Rose had remained out of sight with the girls. 'What business do you have here?' I asked.

'None we wish to share with a stranger,' the man said.

Howl growled low in his throat, sensing the tension. I took a deep breath through my nose, wanting to understand where my unease was stemming from. And then I had it. 'You're warders.' Not finished their training, by the looks of them – their hair and eyes still held their colour, and the scent of their magic was subtle.

'No,' the woman said quickly, and now I caught a whiff of wafting fear. 'Not yet, and not . . . not like the others.'

'I'll ask you once more, before my patience runs out. What are five warders in training doing on a road in the north of Pirenti?'

'We're on a quest for our Empress.'

'Which Empress would that be? The rightful one was slain.'

'She sent us before Kaya's fall. We would finish what we were asked to do.'

Dread filled my guts and I gripped my axe tighter. 'What quest?'

'To find the end to the bond.'

So this was another of the groups who'd made it through Falco and Quillane's tournament last year. I forced myself to remain calm, even to give them a smile. 'A noble quest, then. Can I offer you aid?'

They glanced at each other. The three women dismounted their horses, but the men stayed atop theirs.

Before Finn had discovered that I wielded the power to end the bond through our connection and her soul magic, we had believed that the bond's end would come from twin faces born of both lands – presumably the royal princesses. If these warders possessed the same clues, then they would almost certainly have come to the same assumption. Which meant they were after the twins. I prayed Ambrose would keep them out of sight.

'What draws you to the fortress?' I pressed, keeping my tone light.

'Information,' the man said.

'We would speak to the King, and ask permission to meet his daughters,' the woman agreed. 'Do you have any knowledge of him? Most say he is a reasonable man.'

It was true then. They were after Ella and Sadie.

Abruptly my da was standing beside me. Voice flat, he said, 'Kill them. Kill them all, right now.'

I swallowed, my heart beating quickly. To the warders I said, 'He is a reasonable man, less so when it comes to his children.'

'We bring no threat,' the man said, but I could smell the lie. They'd do whatever they believed necessary to use the princesses.

My beast and I grew hot; the flames of threat, danger, fury, *kill*. But could I kill five innocent young people seeking the very thing I myself had searched for six months ago? Aside from the moral question, would I even be *able* to? They were warders, after all, and there were five of them.

'Whelps,' Da growled. 'Children. Easy.'

I drew an uncertain breath, then heard approaching hoofbeats. Ambrose arrived on his stallion, regal with the sun silhouetting him from behind. 'Weapon down,' he ordered me. To the warders he said, 'The world has changed. Your quest is void. Go home.'

'We take orders from Falco of Kaya now,' the woman said.

'And your other masters? The traitors and murderers and corrupt usurpers? Do you do as they say?'

'Never,' the man burst out.

'Falco of Kaya is in no place to give you orders, but if he were, he would order you from this path.'

'And what would you know, Pirenti pig?' one of the other women snarled, one who had been silent until now. She was little more than a child, with pale-orange hair.

Ambrose looked at her in surprise. 'The animosity between our peoples is over. You might heed that tongue.'

'We've wasted enough time,' the orange-haired girl said to her companions. She gave off a different scent to the others – hers was of rage and violence and desire. And *magic*, as she sent a mighty burst of wind our way. Neither of us was quick enough to react to the surprise attack. I was thrown from my feet, while Ambrose's horse hit the ground heavily and rolled on top of him with a wild whinny.

Howl stood guard over me, growling savagely as I rose and raised my axe. But Ambrose roared, 'Weapon down!'

He heaved the huge horse off him, then calmly help the creature up, smacking it gently on the rump until it lurched to its feet. Unhurriedly, he soothed its unsettled snorts and finally looked at the orange-haired girl. 'I will not fight you. But I'll warn you not to do that again. You're lucky my horse didn't break a leg.'

She smiled a little, moving for another attack. 'Get out of my way, brute.'

'Kill her,' my father snarled.

He was right. I moved to intercept her.

'Stand *down*!' Ambrose ordered me. But I couldn't. They posed a threat to my family so they had to die.

Confirming it, one of the male warders hissed, 'The princesses are here! Ahead and unguarded!'

The flames of violence flickered closer. 'Unguarded?' I repeated softly. The warder's eyes flew to meet mine, and *there* was his fear.

'Thorne,' Ambrose said, '*you will stand down*.'

Was he mad? What was possessing him to allow them free reign over his children? I shook my head, watching as even now the orange-haired girl angled around us. Howl moved to meet her, barking ferociously and darting in to snap at her feet. She waved her hand and he went tumbling backwards. My heart seized, but he quickly shook himself off.

'Stay where you are,' Ambrose snarled at the girl, but she ignored him. This was getting out of hand.

Kill her, my beast, my da and my own mind whispered at once.

And I would have. I knew that, within. But I never got the chance, for down from the ridge to our left came a host of riders galloping at breakneck pace. More arrived from the road ahead and behind, circling us. Unmistakably Pirenti, soldiers from the Vjort barracks, a score of them. And before Ambrose could give any orders, the soldiers sent the bolts from their longbows straight into the young Kayans' chests, slaughtering them. No warning, no fuss.

I blinked, my mind clearing now the threat had passed. And I saw that not all five were dead after all. The orange-haired girl had been left alive, but there were twenty arrows trained on her heart. She was staring in shock at the bodies of her companions.

'The girl's death is yours, Majesty,' a soldier said.

Ambrose looked at the four corpses on the ground. His eyes went to the girl, and then to the soldiers on their horses. 'Did I tell you to kill these people?'

'They attacked you,' the soldier replied. It was obvious.

I watched my uncle's face and for the first time in my life he felt very distant from me. His behaviour this afternoon was bewildering.

'The girl remains alive and captive,' the King said. 'Secure her with sleep. We move north.'

'Curse you all,' she snarled, and lifted her hand towards Ambrose.

In less than a blink an arrow shot straight through her palm, ripping a brutal scream from her mouth. She sank to her knees to cradle her bloody hand. The archer dismounted and took hold of her head and neck in a sleeper hold. She slumped against him and he lifted her unceremoniously onto the back of his horse.

'Your name?' Ambrose asked him.

'Fain of Vjort, Majesty.'

'The next time you harm a captive without my instruction, you will be punished.'

Fain squinted in confusion, but nodded.

Ambrose turned to the soldier in charge. 'Hirðmenn Erik of Norvjisk,' he said. 'What brings you so far south?'

I studied the man curiously, having heard of him. The title of hirðmenn was not necessarily about rank – it named this man a royal bodyguard, one of the deadliest and most respected warriors in the country. There were only three hirðmenn in Pirenti today. Once there had been dozens, but my father had dismissed or killed most of them, stating publicly that any king or prince who needed bodyguards was no true leader of Pirenti. Ambrose kept the three remaining hirðmenn north in Vjort to maintain the barracks and to protect the Jarl in charge of the walled city. I'd met the other two but not this one, this Erik, whose eccentricities were infamous. All of his kind were bred to be painfully loyal, but Erik the most; if Ambrose ordered him to take his own life, he would be dead before the last word of the command left his mouth.

'Orders from Jarl Sigurd. Patrol group.'

Ambrose frowned and mounted his horse. I knew for a fact that the king's soldiers patrolled this area, so there was no need for Vjort men to come so far south. Which meant something strange was going on.

'You'll travel with us back to Vjort,' he said, 'but leave two to bury the slain.'

If Erik found the order strange, he didn't let on. It was practice to leave the bodies of enemies for the wolves in offering to the gods. Ambrose was making it clear that Kayans were no longer our enemies, even if warders still were.

I followed him back to the carriage, where we found Ella and Sadie battering Roselyn with questions about what was going on. Neither of them seemed remotely frightened.

'We have a new escort,' Ambrose told them, 'but stay inside until I tell you otherwise. Are you feeling better, darling?'

Ella nodded.

'Her fever's broken,' Rose said.

'Excellent.' Ambrose gave both twins a kiss, then gave Rose one as well, making her smile in surprise.

As our much larger party rode forth over the snow-dusted road, I took a moment to squat beside Howl, who made a pleased sound and nuzzled his face into my hand. 'Good boy,' I told him softly. 'You did very well.'

I turned my gaze to the soldiers digging graves. The four dead warders looked very young, still carelessly arranged as they had fallen. In the wake of my retreating bloodlust the violence seemed repulsive, and I thought I understood why Ambrose had wanted to avoid this. But surely risking the lives of his children was no way to do that?

Da paced the road back and forth, his long fur cloak sweeping behind him. He looked grim as he gazed at the bodies. He shook his head, spat on the ground. 'And to think,' he said to me, 'you're married to one.'

*

We made camp once the girls had fallen asleep within the carriage. Wind howled through the hills around us and there was little cover. Ambrose and I sat with Erik at our own small fire, nestled beneath a

104

single rocky incline. The King called for Rose to join us; she peered nervously at the nearby soldiers but sat nonetheless. I passed her a mug of warm spiced ale, which she clasped between cold hands. Her eyes immediately drifted up to the sky and her expression turned to one I knew well – the one that meant her mind had vanished from this mortal plane and travelled somewhere lovelier by far. As a child I'd been desperate to understand where she went, but she'd never been able to share it and eventually I'd given up asking.

'What were you really doing so far south?' Ambrose asked the hirðmenn, pulling my attention.

Erik mostly kept his eyes lowered from his King's, I'd noticed. His forehead and cheeks had been tattooed to mark him as both a servant of the King and as unfathomably dangerous; these were the marks of the warriors of old, those forged the same day as the Holy Sword.

'Orders from the Jarl,' Erik replied. 'But not a patrol, as I said before the others, Majesty.'

'Then what?'

'A supply run.'

Ambrose frowned. 'Traders and merchants take supplies north each week.'

'It is a different kind of trade that the Jarl works in.'

My uncle and I shared a glance. 'Tell me, Erik – unless you have been ordered not to?'

Erik met the King's gaze now, looked him right in the eyes. 'I'll take no orders but yours, Majesty. Jarl Sigurd has been trading in people.'

A queasy horror clenched my stomach. Ma went stiff beside me. And on Ambrose's face there was dark fury. The audacity of this Jarl was disturbing.

'He's a twisted kind of man,' Erik added softly. 'We in the north all take a little pleasure from violence, but not a lot, never a lot. The Jarl is seeking more and more, always more. He sells the stolen men and women to the lonely soldiers, to do with as they will.'

Ambrose stood abruptly and walked alone into the night. I watched him disappear into the darkness, then turned back to Erik. 'How long since Jarl Sigurd took his place in Vjort?'

'Only a pair of years, and a world of whispers, Majesty.'

'Whispers?'

'Of Sigurd's master and his weak lungs that had never yet been weak, and of drowning in his blood on a night dark with no moon.'

I blinked. 'You think it was foul play?'

'I've no thoughts either way, Majesty.' Erik shrugged. 'Not for rumours.'

'Ribweed makes a fine poison for the lungs,' Roselyn said softly, looking at the hirðmenn.

Erik gave her an appraising look through the flames of the fire. 'Aye, that it does, Lady. That it does.' He had a peculiar, rhythmic way of speaking, almost like reciting poetry. He lowered his head to my mother and added, 'Forgive this talk of dark deeds and death. The night is more beautiful for your flame-hair and I've the honour of meeting you both.'

'And you,' I replied faintly. 'From where do you come?'

'From the north-west coast, as far north as a man may survive in the wilds.' He smiled. 'Though not nearly as far north as His Highness can wander.'

I was still reeling from the information he'd imparted, but I managed to give him a crooked smile in return for what he believed was a compliment.

'My family live in a rock castle on the edge of sea and ice. We grow to manhood with tales of the wolves under the mountain and the ancient souls who bear those wolf-hearts within their own.'

Roselyn's soft voice lifted in response, and I noticed, abstractly, how similarly they used their words. 'The late King Thorne spoke of this tale. Wolf souls within human bodies and human souls within wolf bodies. He said it was both gift and curse to be not one thing nor two things, but caught in between.'

Erik gazed at Ma, and I saw a shift in his eyes, something completely undeniable and just as unnamable. 'My Lady, he was wise then, your husband.'

And this about a man who had killed almost all of Erik's kind for offering him their lives in protection. Ma felt it, too, the generosity of the words. Whatever intimacy the conversation held was becoming too much for her, because she dropped her eyes and excused herself. Erik's gaze followed her until she disappeared inside the carriage. Despite myself, I looked around for Da, expecting to find him listening to the conversation, but he was nowhere to be seen.

'Sleep, Erik,' I said. 'We have a long day's travel ahead, and you'll be sorely needed when we get to Vjort.'

Erik inclined his head while I rose to follow the path I had watched my uncle tread into the night. I could smell him, smell his travel clothes and dirty, sweaty skin. I could also smell his grief and his rage and his fear. He had climbed to the top of the ridge and was looking down over the camp, at the small lights of the campfires flickering within an expanse of black. The wind was brutal, whipping against my uncovered face, but Ambrose seemed unbothered by it.

As I joined him I realised that Da had not been with me at the fire because he stood here beside Ambrose, and the sight of the two brothers together caused a disruption in my heart. It made me think, not for the first time, that he must truly be here watching over us, not only in my mind. But that was my yearning given voice.

Sword, what Ambrose wouldn't *give* to be able to see his older brother standing with him, keeping him company in the cold. Or even just to know he was here. I couldn't tell him, though, without revealing my own particular brand of madness.

We stood in silence before Ambrose broke through with sudden, desperate words. 'I can't kill anymore, Thorne. I can't.'

'I thought that once too –'

'No. Not to survive. Not even to protect. I just can't.'

Fear made me colder. 'There are twenty men down there who've seen you attacked by a Kayan child. And those twenty will tell twenty more the minute we reach Vjort.'

Ambrose shook his head. Didn't speak a while. 'A warder once told me I was weak of heart. Perhaps I am.'

What a ludicrous notion. I didn't know what to say, couldn't think of the right words.

'All I know is that I don't recognise the man I once was. I must set the example if I wish for change. I cannot kill anymore.'

'Tell him he has to,' Da said.

But I didn't, I couldn't. It felt too bruising to force someone into a smaller, sicker box than they could fit within. Instead I placed my hand on Ambrose's shoulder and said simply, 'I'm yours to command.'

Because we both knew that Vjort would be brutal, bloody and violent. And we both knew that I had become more of those things than Ambrose ever was.

Da and I shared a look, and to my words or my thoughts he nodded with a grim sort of acceptance.

Chapter 8

Isadora

I was settling to sleep when I saw Falco creep from his room and then from the house. I watched him speak to Jonah in the courtyard and climb over the wall. Grabbing my cloak, I followed quickly.

'Did he say where he's going?' I asked Jonah.

'What are you doing up? You don't have watch duty until dawn – Iz!'

I scaled the wall and landed silently on the other side. Falco was moving north, and he was fast. And surprisingly silent. I kept up with him but remained a good distance behind, stalking him through the shadows of the city. I wasn't sure why, I simply knew I didn't trust him.

Since I hadn't had time to fall asleep, warders would have power over the two of us. Which made this a more dangerous night outing than usual. Falco wore his two swords, but it was commonly known that he couldn't use them, and weapons were no good against soul magic anyway.

He slipped into an alley with a dead end and I wondered what in gods' names he thought he was doing. I crept around the corner and ran smack into him. My knife was out without conscious decision, pressed tightly against his kidney. It had been a long time since someone had got the drop on me.

'Well, well,' Falco said.

My jaw clenched as I fought the urge to slice him open. Not yet. Not until after I destroyed the Mad Ones. But this postponement didn't mean that a dark part of me didn't want to spill his blood right here and now, didn't *crave* it, even.

With my knife still pressed against him, Falco leaned in close, murmuring, 'Aren't we looking ghoulish tonight, little Sparrow?'

I recoiled, my lip curling in anger.

Falco smiled. 'Come on then.' He led me out of the alley and east towards the sea. Though it grated that he'd discovered my presence and then ordered me along like his obedient servant, I smoothed my feelings away and focused – distractions in the night could get you killed, and I now had an idiot to protect as well as myself.

We wound our way expertly through side streets and tunnels, over rooftops and behind abandoned buildings. I was surprised at how well he knew the city, particularly in such heavy dark. The man hadn't entered it without a blindfold in twenty-five years. An image of the ten-year-old orphan he'd been when they crowned him pushed its way into my mind. But that thought was uncomfortable, so I pushed it straight back out.

As I realised what we were nearing, I stopped. Falco glanced back at me and continued on. I hesitated. The fool was going to get us caught. Cursing him, I ran to catch up and found him breaking into the bell tower. He'd drawn a knife from somewhere on his person and was running its tip around the edge of a window. Carefully, he pushed the whole pane of glass in and caught it before it broke. Then he climbed inside and waited for me before replacing the piece of glass.

We took the stairs to the top – hundreds of steps that curled at least seven stories high. The ancient bronze bell was even bigger up close than it looked from the ground. The ropes that would toll it were thick and heavy, and the thought of using them to fill the world with noise was repulsive to me. Falco moved around the bell and stopped at the tower's eastern balcony. I did the same, and we gazed into the warder stronghold below.

It was huge – Sancia was the holy city of warders after all. This was where they came to train in their magic, from age thirteen right through to twenty. The stronghold – or, as they preferred to call it, 'the temple' – had at least a dozen different buildings and was guarded by warders who walked the perimeter at all hours. I could imagine that the wards they'd set up around it would be considerable, just as at the palace. This was the only vantage in the whole city from which to see inside the temple walls, and in their arrogance they kept not one guard up here with the bell.

Falco removed a small piece of parchment and a stick of charcoal from his pocket. He settled in to watch, and began marking things down. I snuck a look and saw the marks represented the number of guards and how often they appeared. He was making a schedule of their movements. He also sketched the layout and added in detail he must have already known.

My first thought was that this was a fool's errand. No matter how well he knew the movements of the warders, he would never get inside without magic – more than his single warder Osric could possess. But that thought faded quickly. He was actually trying to *do* something, even if it was hopeless.

I too surveyed the movements below, soon reaching over to touch the drawing of the east wall to indicate a warder's movement. Falco marked it down without taking his eyes from the temple.

And this was how we spent the night. He watched the right and I watched the left, and as I informed him of what I spotted, he marked it down. We didn't speak and we didn't look at each other. I was agitated to pain by his nearness but we didn't touch. Of course we didn't.

An hour or so before dawn he put the parchment away. 'How do you kill them?'

I didn't answer.

'Fine. They'll be here to ring the bell soon.'

So we descended the stairs and climbed back out the window. As our footsteps sounded softly in the night, he took a surprising turn.

'One more stop,' he said. 'You don't need to come with me.'

I looked at him.

'Truly – I don't think you would enjoy it. It's nothing to do with . . . anything important.'

When I made no move to turn home he shrugged and led the way once more. As we walked he seemed to want to distract himself, for he asked, 'What news from within the palace? How are they managing things?'

I didn't have to tell him, but it seemed pointless to keep quiet. Sharing my knowledge wouldn't hinder my plans. So I explained in short words what it was like under Dren and Galia's reign – the humiliation of the servants, the energy they stole from the living creatures around them, their concern for what the 'rebels' within the city were planning. Falco remained silent throughout, but I could feel the anger rolling off him in waves. I finished by telling him the secret I had uncovered: 'They clothe their bodies and faces with magic because they don't want anyone to know the truth of their decay.'

'The power eats at them,' Falco said. 'This is good news. They'll not last indefinitely.'

'I plan to kill them long before their power runs out.'

He glanced at me, but didn't ask how I planned to do it. Instead he said, 'How did you come to be in the palace?'

'Working as a servant.'

'And they didn't read your true intentions?'

I shook my head.

'Why?'

'They can't.'

He considered this. 'What of Penn?'

'I don't think they're aware of his presence here. If they are, they don't care, or they're planning something more subtle.'

'How does he feel about them?'

I hesitated. 'He doesn't speak of them. But he understands. And I believe he's ashamed.'

'Is he frightened of them?'

I didn't like where that question was leading, so I shrugged.

It took us only five blocks to reach Falco's second destination. He squatted behind some dying bushes and peered at the building down the end of the street. It was the royal tomb. My heart picked up speed as I crouched beside him. There were four guards at its entrance, all human soldiers.

'We're too close to the warder temple for this,' I whispered.

He ignored me. Fine then. I drew two of my daggers.

'I don't want them dead,' Falco forestalled.

'They work for Dren and Galia.'

'I don't want them dead.'

I sighed, sheathing the weapons. It would be dangerous to leave them alive. But I found myself relieved not to have to kill them. I stood from the bushes and walked towards the guards, Falco right behind me.

They straightened at our approach, dressed in leather body armour and brandishing spears. 'It's after curfew,' one of them pointed out stupidly.

I took him down first. One kick to the groin forced him down and I caught his spear before it hit the stone. I cracked it over his head and then swung it back into the second guard's throat. The third came at me and our spears snapped together – too loudly. I swept for his legs, jabbed the fourth soldier in the chest to wind him, turned back to the third and whacked him on the head, then finished off the fourth with a second jab to the temple. I set the spear down and glanced at Falco, who was watching with comically wide eyes.

The tomb was locked, but I had pins in my cloak pocket that made short work of the padlock. I didn't know how he'd imagined getting inside on his own. We crept down the steps to the underground crypt, to where the world disappeared into pitch black.

'Take hold of my cloak,' Falco murmured. I remembered he was used to moving without sight and clasped the fabric of his cloak, careful not to brush any part of his body. I was uncomfortable with such vulnerability but thankfully he soon found a wall-torch. I heard him strike a piece of flint and then the crypt was illuminated. We both looked around. Stone graves lined the walls, what had to be dozens of them. Names had been carved into the slabs. The Emperors and Empresses of Kaya, dating back hundreds of years. Falco's royal blood-line. It was hard not to be awed by it, by the passing of time and the power in these graves.

Falco made his way to the very end of the crypt and stopped before five slabs of rock. I felt it then, the wings of sparrows flapping against my skin and hair, flickering in the candlelight. They were in my heart, too, and I felt more frightened than I ever had. I couldn't walk over there and see them, the names of his slaughtered family. I couldn't allow them to be real because they would make him real. They had the power to turn him from a privileged, sculpted specimen into a damaged and lonely man.

I watched him place his hands on the stone, stroking it gently, tracing his fingers around the edges of each of the five graves. I watched him press his cheek against their names. I saw the tenderness in his touch, and the sadness in the bowing of his shoulders.

And then I turned and left the crypt.

FALCO

I stayed with my family as long as I could afford, aching to stay always. My memories of them grew so faint that I felt a savage loss each time I tried to conjure their faces and failed. It had been six months since I'd been to visit them, a very long six months, when normally I went each morning. Every visit I ran through the stories of them, recounting them so I couldn't forget, so they wouldn't slip away. But each day the stories felt more and more like they were being recited instead of remembered.

This morning I whispered to them, telling them all I could. I told Ma, with my cheek pressed to her name, of the driftwood and the temple, finding that it unlocked new memories from all those years ago, several I thought I'd lost. Then I told them Finn's story about the sea god and snow goddess, thinking of my own snow goddess as I did. I was unable to give voice to her, to the reality of Isadora, but I was sure that even thinking of her in this place, here with my family, was a kind of sharing. They would sense that it was too complicated to explain but just being here eased something in my chest. Helped me, in a way, to come to terms with the bond.

I rose some time later, kissing them all in turn. I slowly made my way out of the tomb, though it hurt to leave them.

Isadora was waiting outside, a guard to replace the ones she'd knocked unconscious. We looked at each other for a moment. The light was changing, shifting towards dawn. She looked unearthly in it, her ashen skin glowing.

'You never found them, did you?' she asked me. 'The people who did that?'

I shook my head.

'I would have hunted them until my last breath.'

'I chose another way.'

There was a question in her eyes. As we made our way back through the streets I ordered my thoughts. And I decided, for the first time, to be honest with someone. 'Do you know of the blade fish?'

She shook her head.

'It's small and slow, and unable to hunt its food. So it lies on the sea floor and lets its scales shimmer iridescent. This beauty is like a flame to a moth. It attracts dangerous creatures, who circle it slowly. The blade fish lies very still, an easy, harmless target. As the predator attacks, the blade fish turns its fins to reveal the serrated edges hiding beneath. These make quick work of the predators and the blade fish eats their remains.' I ran my hand ruefully through my hair. 'I owe that damn fish twenty-five pointless years of lying in wait and flashing my iridescent scales.'

I saw a line form between her eyebrows as she considered my words. 'You wanted them to come back for you.'

'Aye, but they never came. Only you did.'

Her gaze flicked to mine. But a noise to our left drifted through the quiet morning, and Isadora froze. Running footsteps approached. A shouted voice – *Take south, enter every building!*

Fuck. The warders had discovered the unconscious bodies at the crypt. The full implication of this hit me in a rush: the warders could have plucked the look of Isadora from the guards' minds. They would identify us the moment they spotted us. I should have let her kill the guards. Or not gone into the temple at all. My heartache may have destroyed us.

Isadora grabbed my arm and wrenched me into an empty tavern. All the chairs and tables were broken or upturned and the kitchen had been ransacked, but she sprinted up the stairs and into one of the loft guest rooms. I helped her drag a chest of drawers in front of the door, though what good that would do was beyond me. We should have been getting away from here, not holing up to be caught.

'How easy is it for you to fall asleep?' she asked me.

'I beg your pardon?'

'Lie down and go to sleep.'

I nearly laughed. But she was actually reclining on the bed and closing her eyes. 'What in gods names are you *doing*?'

'Do you want to know how I kill warders?'

This was lunacy. But she *was* the only one in Kaya who'd figured out how to kill the monsters. With a groan of disbelief, I lay down on the bed opposite hers. My mind was racing and there was no way I was about to nod off.

'Concentrate on your breathing,' she murmured. 'Slow it right down, as far as you can. Move your mind through every inch of your body and focus on the feel of it, on every muscle, every organ, every inch of skin. Imagine all of it slowing right down. Then imagine your mind is a still lake, and nothing can disturb its surface.'

I did as she was telling me, concentrating hard. *Slow*, I bid myself. Let everything be slow and still. I could feel myself relaxing, growing weary. It helped that I had been awake for over two days straight and was honestly exhausted. My body was heavy and sluggish, my mind was the lake.

The lake was . . . it was here. I stood before it, transfixed by its beauty. It stretched as far as I could see and its surface was sunlit glass. A ripple moved at its center, and then a small, pale hand emerged, fingertips first. The arm slid out, moving as if from between strips of silk. A creamy shoulder slipped free, shrugging from the water's cloak.

A face emerged, turned up to the sky, blinking drops of water from her white eyelashes, drops that fell up into the air above. Her neck tilted, rising long and slim. Her breasts, small and white like the rest of her body as it slid up, falling up, up out of the lake, up like gravity was pulling her towards the sky.

When her hips and legs had come loose, when all of her had fallen from the water, her feet rested upon its surface, which was glasslike once more. Isadora turned her head and those red eyes locked onto me. I wanted to step in and meet her. Wanted to wade out to her, but my feet wouldn't move.

So she came to me, drawing a knife from beneath her skin.

I dared not move.

116

She came so slowly, it seemed to take an age. Snow began to fall. Flakes rested in her hair, on her nose, her lips, her eyelashes. I'd never seen anything so beautiful. At last Isadora reached me. She said, 'Don't wake up,' and then she cut me open with her dagger.

Pain broke through and I took a gasping breath, wrenching my eyes open. She was still there, but now she was clothed and we were in the attic room of the tavern once more.

Except . . . except that it was still snowing. Inside.

'Don't wake up,' she said, but urgently now. Her eyes were so gold. Disoriented, I looked down to see that she had cut open my collarbone.

I climbed unsteadily to my feet, peering around in wonder.

'It's working,' she breathed.

'What is this?'

'The dream realm.'

'You brought me?'

She nodded. 'Warder powers can't touch us here.'

'*How*? How did you bring me here?'

'It's pain. Pain to tether the body between realms. And our bond that let me tug you through the fold. We should hurry.'

'Are we . . . where are we?'

'Your body is in the real world. You can control it from the dream realm but things will be strange. Not as they appear when you wake. I can guide you through, but be certain not to let go of my hand.' She met my eyes. 'If you let go, Falco, I don't think I'll be able to keep you here, and they'll kill you.'

'I won't let go.'

She pulled me to the door but I was suddenly drunk on her, on the snowflakes and her perfect skin, on the silken locks of long, white hair, on her scent and the impossible way she moved –

'Falco!'

I shook my head, stunned. 'You're so beautiful.'

'Concentrate,' she urged. 'Stay present.'

I helped her shove the chest out of the way; it weighed a thousand tonnes. We hurried down steps slippery with ice to find a warder charging through the door of the tavern, blasting it into a splinter heap.

I reached for my sword.

'No,' Isadora said, throwing a dagger made of light into the warder's unprotected heart. 'Leave the weapon. Just hold onto me.'

As we walked past the body she snatched her dagger free, releasing a burning slice of sunlight from the wound in the man's chest. I tried to breathe. Tried to stay present. But it was so tempting to follow that light up –

She spoke my name, tethering me again. Into the early morning street we plunged. It was heavy with fog, so heavy I could hardly see my hand before my face.

'Stop!' came a voice, and there before us emerged four warders. In the dream realm their skin looked bruised and sallow, their eyes hollow pits of black.

Out flew her daggers. It turned the men to dust.

I felt an ache in my chest and lead weights in my feet. I couldn't move forward, no matter how hard I tried. I was anchored to the earth beneath this road, and beneath that to the sea, way down below. I sank to my knees, listening for that sunken water. It was whispering in my ears, its waves crashing endlessly and growing so loud I could hear nothing else. I was sinking into it, swallowed by it –

Pain sliced through my face and I looked up, tethered once more. Isadora was gazing at me, and my blood dripped from her blade. 'Concentrate,' she said. 'We're almost free.'

The warders were all dead. As she collected her knives from their bodies I was overcome by the violence. I had never taken a life. Not the life of an animal, not the life of a human, not the life of a warder. Isadora's kills were likely too many to number. She was so distant from me then that the string tying our hearts together was pulled taut, stretched to the point of breaking. We ran with it stretching further and further, the distance opening up until we were on opposite sides of an infinite abyss.

The sun rose golden, on fire, crackling and spitting flames upon us. My hand went limp in hers.

'Don't,' she said, feeling my intent to let her go. 'Not yet. We're not there yet.'

But it was burning.

'Please,' she begged, 'there are more coming. I can't protect you if you let go.'

'You're the only one I've ever needed protection from.'

She looked into my golden eyes. 'Falco. Don't let go.'

So I didn't. I held tight and we escaped past another dozen. We sprinted through streets, took sharp turns, doubled back to make sure we weren't being followed and finally made it home. My feet sank into the stones; it was difficult to move. But together we climbed the wall, still holding hands, and we walked past a staring Glynn, still holding hands, and we went inside to the bathroom, still holding hands.

Even now we didn't let go, and I no longer knew why, and my heart was thundering.

'You're safe,' Isadora said, as though worried I might be scared, and it was gone suddenly, the abyss, the distance, even the rope. The rope was gone: our hearts no longer needed it; our hearts were one. I understood it all. The death and the blood and the violence she endured was not born of desire or cruelty, but shouldered as a burden by someone strong enough to bear it. I understood she would kill again, to protect those who could not protect themselves. She would keep killing until there was no war, until we were free. And I understood, finally, how the necessity had turned to a sickness in her heart, a kind of madness.

I lifted my free hand to her cheek, her jaw, her neck, threading it through her hair. She turned her face into it, squeezing her eyes shut as her lips brushed my palm. 'Don't.'

'It's only a dream,' I whispered, lowering my face.

'Then don't wake up.'

Our lips met and the world was filled with falling feathers, falling like snow, brushing our skin and our hair and our mouths. They wrapped us in their embrace and pressed our bodies closer until I felt the length of her along the length of me, tasted her lips and her tongue, kissed her eyelids and cheeks and neck. My mouth discovered that her skin had been sprinkled in a fine sheen of salt. As though she had just stepped from the sea. As though she was of the sea. A slippery creature of the dark depths. Or, no, perhaps it wasn't salt, but snow. She was of the mountains, the ice, the winter. She was wild as wolves and just as fierce. I couldn't get enough, couldn't get close enough. I wanted more of her; I wanted all of her.

'Falco.'

I blinked and she was gone. Where she'd been there was only absence. The bathroom was normal. The strange, beautiful colours had gone. There was no salt or snow on her skin, no feathers falling through the ceiling. She simply looked at me from the other side of the room – our hands were no longer entwined.

'I lost you for a moment,' Isadora told me softly.

'Am I awake?'

She nodded.

I breathed out heavily. My head was spinning and my body felt too . . . real. It was heavy and clumsy, and I didn't know if we had really kissed like that, as though we'd die if we ever stopped. I didn't know if she had tingled in my hands like she was made to fit there, or if she'd clutched at me as though I was her only home. But I knew I could not ask her. If I'd only dreamt it, she would be horrified to know.

'Sleep now,' she said. 'You won't dream this time.'

I stumbled to the baby's room, sinking onto my cot. Ava had already risen so I was alone, gazing at a mobile made of hanging driftwood. As my eyes fell shut I felt ancient with weariness, and a deep, dreamless sleep took hold of me.

ISADORA

I slept until midday, and with waking came the realisation that I could no longer leave the house, unless I wanted to be recognised. Nor could I return to the palace to work, in case I'd been identified as the killer of the dozen warders. In truth, I felt sick at the thought of returning there anyway.

Being cooped up inside was a struggle. The others had gone to work – Finn went with them today, so that left Osric and Ava, whom I didn't particularly want to speak to, and Falco, who was still sleeping. I helped Sara in the kitchen for a while but fidgeted so much that I nearly ruined a loaf of bread, and was banished. I tried spending time with the baby, but she was too uncomfortable around me for either of us to enjoy it. Next I turned to reading, but sitting still for extended periods of time was difficult: it always reminded me of the cage.

So I settled on target practice in the courtyard.

In the familiar throw and release I gratefully felt calm return. The blade edges were my focus, sharp and precise. I couldn't allow fear to keep me from the palace, I couldn't allow Falco's arrival to distract me from what I was doing here. It might be time, I thought, to leave this house and these people to their plans and their Emperor, and find a base of my own somewhere.

I spun a dagger in my fingertips and hurled it swiftly at the wooden bench on the other side of the courtyard. I wasn't concentrating, though, and saw the figure too late. He'd moved to sit on the bench when my back was turned, and I couldn't catch the blade before it was flung free of my fingertips. I blinked and it was already landing –

In Falco's hands. He had *caught* it between his palms, seconds before it embedded itself in his chest. The air left my lungs completely.

'I surrender,' he said, turning the knife lazily in his grip.

'How did you do that?'

He blinked, realising what he'd done and dropping the blade as though it were a poisonous spider. 'Lucky catch, I guess.'

My eyes narrowed. He sat in full sun, its glare making it difficult for me to properly see his face.

Did he think me an idiot?

'No, I don't think you an idiot. But don't you ever stop?' he murmured, still half asleep.

I threw three more daggers and they *thunked* into the wood around his body, close enough to shave off a fine layer of hairs. He didn't flinch or try to catch them this time, calling my bluff.

'Aim's getting lazy,' he pointed out, wrenching the knives free. 'Or were you *playing* with me, little Sparrow? I'd be shocked and appalled to discover there was anything like *mischief* under that scowl.'

I stalked over and held out my hand.

'Why thank you,' he murmured, reaching for it with his own. I wrenched my palm away just before his skin touched mine and he grinned, amused. If he thought I was going to play this game with him, he was mistaken. I snatched the knives and turned away to restore them to their sheaths.

'Are you any good with other weapons? I know you're pretty mean with a spear, but how about a sword?'

I shrugged.

'How did you learn to do it?' he asked more firmly, the real question he'd come outside to pose. 'The sleepwalking or whatever it was.'

I didn't answer.

'Is it magic?'

'No.'

'Then can you teach me to do it on my own?'

Maybe, but I certainly didn't plan to.

'You don't say much, do you?'

I didn't bother looking at him as I strode back inside. The sun was setting and I needed to prepare.

Under cover of night I searched the city for a good place to hole up and spent hours picking the right one. In the end I only discovered the small house because a desire to see the ocean took me right to the cliff's edge. The house was perched on a steep incline in an area that had been completely abandoned in the first wave of attacks. This cliff was dangerously close to the warder temple, but they wouldn't notice the sound of my mind. Plus they didn't patrol this area because, despite it being unwalled, there was no way to reach the ocean below without being dashed on the rocks.

The house had an open front with a balcony protruding over the cliff. It was simple, with one bedroom, an open kitchen and a skylight in the roof of the living room. I walked around it, looking at the abandoned possessions of the young couple who had lived here. A portrait had been slashed through, and there was a thick layer of dust over every surface. I wondered if they'd fled this place to find safer ground, or if they were dead. Carefully, I turned the painting to face away, then gathered the personal items and trinkets into a chest of drawers where I wouldn't have to see them. They were too sad to gaze upon every day.

I snuck home to spend the rest of my last night with Penn. I gently woke him from the fray of sleeping bodies and the two of us went outside to join Finn on watch duty. I didn't wake Jonah, though I did feel a twinge of guilt as I passed his sleeping form. I couldn't endure his eyes on me, begging me for words and answers.

We found Finn on the roof. 'Where have you been?' she asked me as Penn and I took spots on either side of her.

'Patrolling.'

'The warders are patrolling. We're supposed to be hiding.'

I cracked my knuckles, thinking about that. Sometimes it scared me how vulnerable Finn of Limontae allowed herself to be. She didn't seem to understand that she needed to protect herself, that the world was a disturbingly violent place and she couldn't just will it to be as gentle as she wished. This concern was probably the only reason I spoke, shooting her a glance in the dark. 'Survival means becoming the hunter, not the prey.'

'Funny. Osric – the warder you're apparently mortally opposed to – said almost the exact same thing on the journey here.'

My mouth closed. I was done with that conversation.

'You two have been with him this whole time,' Finn said. 'So what's going on with Jonah?'

'What do you mean?' Penn asked her.

'He seems lost. And I don't . . . it's weird not to have that instinctive connection to him anymore.'

'He hates the magic in his veins,' Penn said. 'Hates it. Hates it.' I watched as he clenched his jaw and wilfully stopped his repetition. I was impressed: I'd never seen him try that before. 'But he doesn't know how to turn it off.'

'He can't,' she muttered. 'And he shouldn't hate it. He mustn't allow it that power over him.'

'Talk to him,' Penn said. 'He hasn't been right without you.'

'I'm glad he had you two,' she replied, then flashed me a sly look. 'He seems very attached.'

'He loves Isadora,' Penn agreed as though it was the most obvious, normal thing in the world. Panic struck me. I could see him struggling and failing to contain himself. 'He loves Isadora. He loves Isadora. He loves –'

'Penn, *please*!' I exclaimed.

He fell silent, but I could see his hands fidgeting badly.

'Relax,' Finn said, reaching to ruffle his hair. But he was agitated and recoiled from her touch. Penn fled, swinging himself from the roof with the grace of a monkey.

Guilt was hot in my stomach. I rubbed my eyes wearily. 'Jonah doesn't.' He couldn't possibly. He didn't even know me.

'You don't need to fear it,' Finn said.

My jaw clenched and she fell silent.

There was a question I needed to ask her and I'd been gathering my courage since she arrived.

'When you went north,' I hesitated, 'did you find it? A way to break the bond?'

'Oh!' Finn exclaimed. 'Forgive me, I should have told you.'

I swallowed. *Please.*

'It's Thorne,' she said. 'He has the power to end the bond in his blood, just as the ability will be in the blood of his children. And it doesn't have to be all or nothing – he can break individual bonds. At least we think he can, anyway. We haven't tried it yet.'

I let out a rushed breath of relief. There was a means after all. But he was too far away for it to happen any time in the near future. So for now I'd have to settle on removing myself from Falco's presence.

'I'm going to start sleeping elsewhere.'

'Why? Izzy, don't do this now. Don't pull away.' When I didn't reply she reached for my hand. 'You're family. We don't separate.'

Calmly I withdrew my hand from hers. I wasn't family. I might wish I could be, but if they had any idea what I was, they wouldn't want to be within miles of me.

The sound of someone climbing the wall interrupted us and we looked over to see Jonah. 'My turn on watch,' he explained helplessly when he saw our expressions.

Finn looked like she wanted to say more, but refrained. We both headed for the edge of the roof, but Jonah stopped me.

'Iz. Can we talk a moment?'

It was the last thing I felt like, but guilt stayed my feet. Finn disappeared and I stood awkwardly, not looking at Jonah.

'Are you okay?'

I nodded.

'You've been distant lately. More so than usual. I guess I thought . . . I thought that the two of us had come to understand each other.'

I looked at him with no idea what he was talking about.

'You were thawing. Opening up. We were connecting. I *know* we were. Now you feel a thousand miles away again.'

Something in me turned sad. For his need. For my inability to fill it. For whatever he imagined lived between us.

I sat on the edge of the roof, trying to discover words that might ease his pain but finding none. I couldn't possibly know how I might have felt had I not bonded to someone else. I didn't know if affection might have grown between Jonah and me. Perhaps it would have. Perhaps it would have been real. More likely I would have forbidden its existence in favour of my revenge. In the end, there was no life in which I could give him what he wanted. I'd never possessed it.

'Why is this so hard for you?' he asked, taking my hand. He assumed so much.

I urged myself to stay seated, to find kindness. 'You don't know what I am, Jonah.'

'Of course I do.' He leaned in and I realised with alarm that he was about to kiss me.

'I hate to interrupt.' A cold voice sliced through the moment just as I recoiled. We both turned to see Falco's head emerging from the vines. 'My turn on watch.'

'I just started,' Jonah said. 'I'll stay.'

'Get inside the house, kid,' Falco ordered, and there was steel in his voice.

Jonah was irritated. 'Come on,' he murmured, pulling me up by the hand.

'I'll stay a moment.'

'No,' Falco said flatly without looking at me. 'You go too.'

Fury kindled inside me. 'Leave, Jonah,' I all but spat.

He frowned, confused. 'Fine.'

Once he was gone I whirled to face Falco, who was standing on the very edge of the roof, arms folded. I imagined pushing him off. 'You don't give me orders.'

'No? And why is that?' I couldn't see his face, but I could hear the disdain in his voice. 'Because you're a rebel leader intent on disrupting my reign and killing me? Remind me why I haven't imprisoned you as a dangerous criminal yet.'

'Because you don't have a prison, nor do you have any power,' I snarled. Gods, how did he get under my skin so badly? I drew a deep breath, trying to calm myself.

'That's it, shut it all out,' he muttered. 'Wouldn't want you to feel anything, would we?'

'Grow up.'

'I'm not the one messing around with a poor child who has no idea who you really are.'

I flushed pink. 'It's no business of yours what I do with anyone.'

He laughed coldly. 'Oh, really?'

'There's an end to this bond,' I snapped.

'Yes, and he's a thousand leagues north.'

'You *knew*?'

'Of course I knew.'

White-hot rage threaded my veins. I wanted to kill him. Desperately. How could he not have said anything? 'Is this a game to you?'

'On the contrary,' Falco replied, facing me. Shadows obscured his face and for a moment he seemed like someone else entirely. 'It's my whole life. It's my death. It's my fate to shoulder as I must, not something to cower before.'

I *hated* him. My fingers twitched towards my knives.

He saw it and rolled his eyes. 'Go on then. It's always the knives.'

I climbed back into the courtyard. But as I lay down at the edge of the sleeping bodies I knew there was no way I would sleep. I stared at the ceiling and dreaded the moment he would return and walk past me. Even the sight of him made me sick to my stomach, even the thought. Because the desire to climb back onto the roof and hurt him somehow was more intense than any desire I had ever known – except the desire to touch him.

FALCO

I watched the sun rise over my city, and I watched the horizon. My heart beat painfully; my thoughts were too erratic to pin down.

I imagined flight, and out and *away*. I imagined chasing that horizon for all the days of my life, no matter where it led me.

It was my rumbling stomach that finally made me descend into the house. This constant hunger played tricks on my mind. I was so unused to it, had never gone hungry a day in my life. Everyone was rising but I couldn't see Isadora and for once I was glad. On my way to the kitchen I passed Elias and Sara's bedroom, and though I didn't mean to, I heard their voices clearly.

'. . . and then what – just hope?'

'What else are we meant to do?'

'I don't know, but I don't think we're putting our hope in the right thing. He's a *coward*, El. He's impotent.'

My heart lurched and I went to sit at the kitchen table, barely aware of the people around me. Glynn placed a bowl of oats before me and I thanked her faintly. What was I *doing* here? I needed a plan. I needed to not be constantly wrapped up in the ache of having a mate who hated me.

Isadora walked past and I felt the lurching tug. My thoughts were wrenched from anything important and settled instead upon our argument last night.

'You two,' I addressed Ava and Finn, who were sitting on the kitchen bench. 'What do you think of ending the bond?' I was watching Isadora and saw her shoulders tense.

'Why?' Finn asked, ever contrary.

'Humour me.'

'Well I don't want to end mine.' She shrugged. 'But then again, I happen to be bonded to the best person in the world, so it's different for me.'

I smiled. She wasn't wrong. 'What about you, Ava? Knowing what it costs you, and what you stand to lose, would you end yours?'

She shook her head.

'Elias and Sara?' I turned to where the couple was leaning in the doorway.

'No,' they said at once.

'Why not?'

The married couple glanced at each other. 'Why would we?'

'Fate bonds you for a reason,' Finn said.

'There's no such thing as fate,' Isadora said softly, and everyone in the room turned to her, surprised she'd spoken.

'How can you say that?' I demanded. 'It's proven every time a life is entwined with another.'

She met my eyes. 'What you're describing is magic.'

'Is that not a coward's way to look at it? If fate is real, then should we not have the strength to endure ours?'

Softly she asked, eyes flashing, 'Would you have us lie before it and surrender, Majesty?' The slow tilt of her head was bird-like. The raising of her chin. She spoke clearly, her voice a deep seductive calm. 'I shall choose my own fate.'

My spirit bucked against it, denied its pull. It wanted not calm but anger. 'The very *nature* of fate is that it is not ours to determine!'

'Easy, you two!' Finn interjected. 'The kitchen is about to spontaneously combust.'

There was a charged silence as Isadora and I held our tongues.

'No offence, Iz,' Finn went on, 'but I thought as you do before I bonded. I couldn't understand, but now I do: the bond reflects the choice of your soul. It knows you better than you know yourself. You'll see one day.'

Elias and Sara nodded emphatically.

Isadora's lip curled into a smile. The red of her eyes seemed to deepen somehow, shifting only the slightest towards black. It startled me, drew me deeper. I could feel myself slipping, my edges blurring. The truth was becoming harder to deny by the second.

Before anyone could say more she walked from the kitchen, her gait so graceful it was more like a glide. Her usual response to emotion: to walk away from it. I stood so fast my chair clattered to the ground, startling everyone.

'Sorry,' I muttered, reaching to right it.

I knew they watched as I hurried after Isadora – I didn't care what they thought or what they knew. I was feverish. She was closing the door to the bathroom when I shoved it back open and shut myself in with her.

'What are we arguing about?' she asked me. 'There is poison in our veins and neither of us wants it there.'

My heart thumped and the words died on my lips. Why *was* I so angry with her? The sight of her on the roof, holding Jonah's hand . . . a complete impossibility. But worse, so much worse, was what she'd said. She wanted to break our bond. That's where the fury was coming from, and the knowledge hit me woozily.

My own foolishness felt as vast as the ocean. *Of course* she wanted to break it. What right did I have to be shocked by that? *I* should want the same.

'The night you and I met, we sought each other's deaths,' Isadora reminded me, her voice low. My eyes fell to her lips; they hardly moved when she spoke and as such she pronounced her words strangely. I hadn't noticed until now, but it suddenly seemed like a clue to all her secrets, the treasure trove of them in her center.

'Nothing has changed,' she went on. 'The second you and I break our bond, this stalemate is over, fated or no.' She stopped. She always seemed surprised when words came from her mouth, as if she sometimes forgot she had the ability to speak at all. My eyes went to the rise and fall of her chest. I could feel her heart thundering and I wanted to get at it, wanted to hold it in my hands.

'Is that what frightens you so?' she asked, even more softly. 'That I'll kill you?'

I leaned in close, could feel her breath against my lips, the heat of her skin on mine. It was intoxication, it was a shot of adrenalin to my heart. I murmured, '*You could try.*'

Cold laughter fled her lips. But her disbelief didn't bother me, because I could see behind it to the doubt in her eyes.

I left her in the bathroom – this tiny bathroom where everything seemed to pass between us – knowing with painful certainty that she was wrong. I didn't fear for my life when our bond ended. I simply didn't want it to end. Every version of me wanted Isadora, *all* of her, to be mine until the day we both died. And the only way to ensure that was to do the impossible: I had to make her want the same thing before she realised that Finn could break our bond even without her husband's presence.

AVA

'What in gods names is going on?' Finn asked in the absence of Falco and Isadora. No one had an answer.

Until Glynn said, awkwardly, 'I saw them holding hands the other night.'

'*What?*' Jonah exclaimed.

'Holding hands?' Finn repeated, confused.

Glynn nodded. 'They'd been out all night. And they were acting strangely. They didn't look at me, but passed like phantoms in the night.'

'But . . . but they hate each other!' Jonah protested. Poor kid.

I left my mouth shut. I'd assumed Falco had begun some sort of affair with Isadora, but after that display I was no longer so sure. There was something different in my cousin. Something he could not be careless with.

'There's an explanation to this,' Jonah snapped. 'She *hates* him.'

Wisely, no one replied.

'I'm going to find out,' Finn announced, following the arguing pair.

'It's none of your business,' I called after her.

'Never stopped me before.'

It was Penn who caught my attention; I turned in time to see the amused smile at his lips. I liked him better than the rest of them combined.

ISADORA

When I finally felt calm enough to emerge from the bathroom I was met with the sight of Falco and Finn sitting together in his room. I froze long enough to see it all – the closeness of their bodies, the way their heads were turned in together, the soft urgency of their voices, the touch she so easily bestowed upon his hands.

I thought I might vomit.

Had Finn not been in love with Thorne the last time I saw her? Had she not been giddy with it? Six months had passed – perhaps during that time she had changed her mind and fallen for the Emperor instead. I hadn't thought her so fickle, but I could certainly feel something in Falco, a stirring as he sat so close with her.

I wanted to tear my own skin off to reach this vile thing in my center. I wanted to claw it out, strip it from me. It *had* to stop. He looked up, straight at me. He could feel it, I realised. He knew, and he said quickly, 'Finn and Thorne are bonded.'

And there was no smugness, no satisfaction or victory. There was nothing but understanding, and it hit me like a tidal wave.

My humiliation was a brand as I left the house, lifting the hood of my cloak. I wouldn't go back again. Because how *dare* he be a better man than any knew? How dare he be *good*? How would I ever manage to hate him if he was good?

When I reached my little cliff house I paced its wooden floors and I draped the lake upon me because I had to find perspective on all of this. I had to clarify my priorities.

My concern was and would always be the forgotten souls in the forest of my escape. *My* people – those loyal to the Sparrow, who had spent their entire lives being abused or ignored. It was for them that I would end the power of the warders, for them that I would at least try.

But what had always been most important? I knew the answer well, though it shamed me to name it even to myself. It was vengeance. For the cage, for the brutality of the world, for the simple fact that some were born without fortune of any kind while others wasted the abundance they lucked upon. So I made a vow with myself, because it was the only way I would get through this. I'd continue with my plan to assassinate the Mad Ones and help free the Kayan citizens. But the next time I saw Falco of Sancia would be the day I killed him, regardless of what I had already achieved, regardless of whether or not it would also kill me.

CHAPTER 9

THORNE

We travelled without rest for days, stopping only to take a short detour through the Misty Valley because it was a rite of passage for youths to visit the ancient tombs. Ambrose, Rose and I took the girls down into the valley of limestone, to where slabs of rock had been mounted atop each other to signal the burial of someone beloved. Erik trailed behind, always on the watch for threats so I could relax. Over the rock was a fine sheen of frost or, in some spots, ice, so we moved slowly and with careful tread.

'This tomb is thousands of years old,' Ambrose told his daughters as we reached the largest in the valley. 'It's older than any other building or structure still standing today.'

'Who did it belong to?' Sadie asked.

'We don't know – the words engraved here have long since been eroded by the weather. But we know it was a burial tomb because of its shape, and we know how far it dates back because it has been marked on maps that span as long as we've recorded our history.'

I could really feel it, standing here in the Misty Valley – the incredible lightness and heaviness of the turning of the world.

'One day when your mother and I are gone, Thorne will be King of Pirenti. If, gods forbid, something happens to him and he has not yet produced an heir, one or both of you will rule this nation.'

Ella and Sadie nodded earnestly – they knew this well, and already took it very seriously.

'My da brought my brother and I here when we were boys, and

he said that one of us would rule and the other would not, but that it would be equally important for both of us to understand the Valley.'

I felt a pang, thinking of Da and Ambrose here as little boys, with Ambrose's father Rourke, the man they'd both idolised and adored. I thought, too, of the day Ambrose had brought me here as a young boy, and how awed I'd been. Now, to his daughters, Ambrose spoke the same words his father had told him, and which he had gone on to tell me. I hoped, as I listened a second time, that I would get to say them to children of my own.

'Run your fingers over this stone and think about the interminable, immeasurable nature of time,' Ambrose told Ella and Sadie. 'I want you to consider this earth, this land, and our place here on it – and to think about both the impermanence of humankind and the lasting effect we have on the world. Our duty will always be to respect and protect the land, to understand our lives here as short, but meaningful, to respect our ancestors and to know that we can have a powerful effect on the things around us. Consider, too, whether you believe it falls to us, as leaders, to understand these things a little more than most – do you believe the burden of time sits a little heavier upon us? Or do you believe all humans are the same in the face of eternity?' He looked at both of his daughters and they stared back, unblinking. 'Either way, there's history in these rocks, in this valley. Connect with it and the immeasurability of time will become less frightening, I promise.'

We left the twins to spend time pondering and exploring the tomb. We walked a short distance away, staying close enough that we could still see them in the fog. A light drizzle fell on our faces, freezing cold and sharp like pins.

'I met your father Rourke once, Majesty,' Erik told Ambrose as the four of us huddled close, breathing warmth onto our cold hands.

'Truly?' Ambrose asked, surprised.

'Aye. When I was a lad, he spent some time on our winding stretch of coast and stayed in our twisty old castle.'

I smiled a little, both at what he was saying and at the rhythmic way he said it. In the short time I'd known him it had become clear that Erik had a calming effect on those around him, and I liked him very much.

'The ocean there is rough and full of glaciers and impossible to swim. The cliffs are steep and deadly. But Rourke spoke of boats, and of rowing out into that rough sea that he might seek and find distant shores. He spoke of not wanting to waste the life he had been given, to take it full and devour it, and he spoke of carrying his wee son with him as he did all of this. He was, in my opinion, Majesty, a great man. A true one.'

I watched Ambrose swallow. After a few long moments he cleared his throat and said, 'Thank you, Erik.'

I thought again of what Ambrose was going through. The terrible ache of questioning himself and the life he led. The dilemma of feeling one thing and needing to be another.

A very distant rumbling began in the earth, starting as next to nothing and then growing so that I could feel it in the soles of my feet, through my boots and inching up into all of my muscles. 'Here we go!' I announced with a grin.

Ambrose gave an excited whoop and bolted over to his daughters. 'They're coming – quickly!'

I swept my mother into my arms and carried her, laughing, deeper into the valley floor. Popping her down in front of me, I held her shoulders and chuckled with her as Ella and Sadie scrambled raucously to the front of the group. We stood in single file behind them.

'Are you sure you don't want me to stand first in case?' Erik asked.

'No, my friend,' Ambrose grinned. 'This is a rite of passage even more important than the tomb!'

Adrenalin throbbed through my veins as with every second the rumbling vibrations grew. The first time I'd done this, at ten, I'd been petrified and ready to wet myself. Ambrose had laughed uproariously then, too. The excited girls were far braver than me.

'Don't move,' I warned Ma. Behind me I could hear Erik fiddling with his axe. 'You won't need that,' I told him. And then to Howl, at my feet, 'Stay very still, boy.' Howl looked up at me, motionless.

And then they were upon us. A herd of wild horses, thundering through the valley and emerging out of the grey fog; they were ghostly, eerie, almost spectral and utterly beautiful. Their powerful, fast gallop angled straight at us. Sadie squealed and Ambrose roared with elation, and then the horses split down the middle and flowed around us with incredible grace. A great *whoosh* pushed against us from both sides, the sound of their hooves drowning everything else in the world. They were so close I could have touched them. White and black and all shades of grey flashed past me, their scents washing through my nose and making me heady.

And just like that they were gone again, thundering into the mist as quickly as they had come. The earth slowly stopped trembling, the frost resettled and the fog closed like a curtain around us. We exploded into cheers and laughter, falling against each other in sheer excitement. Howl barked with glee, having instinctively known not to spook the horses. Ella and Sadie were rapt and flushed. The courage it took a child to face down the approaching herd was legendary – boys had to do it as they neared manhood, and if they ran instead of remaining still they were ridiculed for years. I'd never been so proud, watching my cousins chatter hysterically in its wake.

We climbed our way out of the valley and regrouped, pushing on towards Vjort. I watched Ma fuss over Ella when she refused to don her cloak, claiming to be hot. Sadie, by contrast, couldn't cease her teeth chattering, and was shooed back inside the carriage.

'Some blood runs colder than others,' Erik commented blithely.

Rose frowned, watching Ella ride her pony forwards to flank her father. The girl's long dark hair trailed behind her just as the pony's tail did, before both were swallowed by the fog.

My eyes caught on a flash of orange. The warder girl's hair, where she slept over the saddle of Fain's horse. We had to keep putting her to sleep, for fear she'd wake and use her magic to harm us, but the longer she slept the worse it would be for her health. I couldn't help feeling concerned.

'Is there something you can give her for nourishment?' I asked Ma.

'I have a sedative that would addle her magic when she woke, but might let her take food and water.'

'You'd risk your own safety for her?' Erik asked, looking between Ma and I.

I shrugged. Ambrose wanted her alive, so she was alive. No need to torture the poor creature.

We stopped to water the horses late in the afternoon. Ma had the drink made up, and Erik insisted on being the one to rouse the warder and feed it to her. Ambrose and I moved in close, blocking her view of anything else. Erik's large, tattooed hands were surprisingly gentle as he tilted her chin up. She moaned as she woke, and before she'd had a chance to open her eyes Erik was trickling the draught into her mouth and running his fingers over her throat as he would to a dog. The girl drank, then coughed and lurched upright on the cold road.

'Easy, lass,' Erik coaxed softly.

Her eyelids flew open and her gaze found me. I watched the irises shift to a brilliant sky blue, a glorious shade beneath her pale orange hair and eyelashes. They were unearthly in the fog, and too bright. I scented her magic once more, and her ferocity, but the drink was already taking effect. Her pupils dilated and her mouth went a little slack.

'Let me go, pigs,' she tried. And then, 'Where are my friends? Where's Ben?'

'Dead,' Erik said.

A moan left her and with a mighty effort she lifted her hand to send some sort of power at us. Nothing happened.

'What's your name?' Ambrose asked.

'Curse you.'

Erik took the girl's throat in his hand and squeezed gently. 'Answer His Majesty.'

'Don't hurt her!' We all looked to see Ella and Sadie watching worriedly. 'Don't hurt her,' Sadie repeated.

Erik dropped his hand quickly.

'Get back in the carriage,' Ambrose ordered his daughters. 'This isn't for you to see.' Softening, he added, 'She won't be harmed.'

Rose shepherded the girls away.

'Forgive me,' Erik said, retreating.

Ambrose called for the group to get moving once more. On a whim, I lifted the warder girl onto the carriage seat and sat beside her, taking the reins to drive. She sagged against the wood, not quite sleeping, not quite awake. I flicked the reins and we clattered forward, flanked by the soldiers on their mounts.

'You alright?' I asked.

'Feels quite nice actually.' She sighed.

'What's your name?'

'Maisy.'

'I'm Thorne.'

'Know who you are . . . prince. You're the liar.'

'Take some bread,' I bid her, finding some in one of the packs and passing it over.

'The second this poison wears off, I'm going to kill you,' she said clearly. 'For Ben.'

I breathed out, watching the road ahead. In the end I just said, 'Alright.' Because she had as much right as any to want to avenge the person she loved.

★

We entered Vjort after nightfall. Snow was falling, as was usual in this walled, stone city. Maisy was asleep again, but Ella and Sadie were wide awake at the sight of the army barracks. We rode straight for the castle on the other side of town, passing the square in which I had executed my first soldiers for attacking Isadora, Jonah and Penn. I shivered as we rode by, but not from cold. We passed by the tiny temple where Finn and I were married, and I missed her with such acuteness that it felt there was something seriously wrong inside my body. I had promised to show Ma the temple, and to redo the ceremony with our families present, but I was starting to think this was not the kind of place in which we should marry twice.

I could scent Ambrose's urgency from the back of the group and knew he was desperate to put a stop to Jarl Sigurd's crimes. What struck me as we entered the castle was how very *relieved* the staff were to greet us. I shared a concerned look with Ambrose as one of the women burst into tears and insisted on bowing four times. Things here were obviously worse than we'd imagined. Apparently Sigurd had moved into the royal chambers, even though tradition dictated they be left empty for Royal visits. The housekeeper was mortified to convey this bit of information.

'No bother,' Ambrose assured him. 'We'll take any rooms you have ready and warmed.'

Once Ella and Sadie were settled into their beds with Rose reading them a story to calm them, Ambrose, Erik and I gathered in the castle war-room. The first thing Ambrose did was search through desks and drawers, looking for any proof of Sigurd's actions. According to the housekeeper he went out most nights to enjoy himself at the largest tavern – Iceheart's – and wouldn't be home until close to dawn.

When Ambrose didn't find anything, he asked Erik to write down the names of the men in league with Sigurd – those helping him with the trade, those supporting it or funding it. Erik explained that he could not read or write, so he spoke the names and I took them down for him. It seemed there was a group of about six high-ranking soldiers who helped run the human trafficking trade for Sigurd.

'Find him and report back,' Ambrose told the hirðmenn. 'Tell him the truth – that we intercepted you, so you weren't able to complete your task. Say nothing of what we know – I want him ignorant of why we're here, and I want him to think you're still loyal to him.'

'I was never loyal to him, Majesty. I was loyal to the last orders you gave me, which were to serve Jarl Sigurd and so serve him I did.'

Ambrose smiled. 'I know, Erik. I'm grateful to you. Go now, and report back of Sigurd's whereabouts as soon as you're able.'

Erik bowed and headed out.

'How do you want to play this?' I asked my uncle when we were alone.

He sat on the carved wooden chair, leaning back so he could place his booted feet lazily on the desk. His eyes were very pale in the flickering candlelight. 'One way or another,' he said, 'this ends tonight.'

FALCO

'Keep low,' I whispered. Ava, Osric and Finn ducked to creep forwards. On the other side of the wall was a host of warder guards. If they heard or sensed us, we were dead.

The idea had occurred to me as I tossed and turned in bed last night. No matter how tired I felt, I never seemed able to sleep. I thought of Quillane, endlessly, and Isadora, inevitably. I'd also been contemplating how difficult it would be to sneak back into the royal tomb to visit

138

my family. A bad idea, since my desire to be close to them had already nearly seen us killed.

My thoughts turned to Isadora in the crypt, the fear in her eyes as she'd watched me with the graves. I wondered for the millionth time what had damaged her so badly. My thoughts shifted to something else. Something I'd seen every time I went to the tomb but of which I had taken very little notice. In the corner was a small drainage grate, which no doubt led to the sea. And that was how the idea occurred. If I couldn't get people out through the tunnel in the palace, then I would make my own tunnel.

Ava, Osric, Finn and I now made it past the warders and hurried down a street that wound its way around the curve of a rocky hill. We were nearing the cliff's edge, and the smell of the ocean was heavy with salt and seaweed. An eastern wind rose up, pressing my long hair behind me. It whipped Ava's face-scarf off and away, and she wasn't quick enough to catch it.

'How brazen,' Finn commented, reaching for her belt sash and passing it to the Queen. 'Cover your shame, woman.'

It made Ava smile as she wrapped the sash over her cheeks and mouth.

We descended a steep hill and came to the old fish markets. It was deserted at this time of night, but I imagined it was just as empty during the day since Dren and Galia had banned all fishing boats from embarking.

'What are we looking for?' Ava asked.

'Any building set into or under the ground,' I answered. We moved quickly, checking each building – it worked in our favour that most were abandoned.

I caught sight of Finn watching me. 'What?'

'Nothing.' But the worry in her eyes reminded me all too clearly of our conversation the other morning after Isadora and I had fought in the kitchen.

Finn had followed me into my room, uninvited as usual. 'What's going on? And don't you lie to me, Falco.'

I sighed, resting my face in my hands. 'Leave it be, Finn, for once in your life.'

'There's a whole lot of talk going on about you and Isadora, and that's my business because she's my friend, and you're my friend, and you happen to be extremely important to me, and also because my brother is in love with her.'

I snorted. 'He is not.'

'How would you know?'

'He doesn't know her.'

'Neither do you!' she exclaimed. Silence reigned as she watched me, bewildered. Finally Finn sighed, sitting beside me and taking my hands. 'I know how you treat women,' she told me carefully. 'Everyone does. If there is something between you and Izzy, you should end it before she gets hurt.'

'Why is everyone so sure it would be her who got hurt?'

Finn rolled her eyes. 'Please.'

Shame heated the back of my neck and I couldn't look at her. 'There's nothing between us,' I said. 'She hates me.'

'Good.'

I couldn't help smiling, meeting her yellow eyes. 'Where did you come from?' I asked her softly. 'Why did you come to me that night we met?'

'Because the Emperor ordered me to.'

'You didn't know, did you? You didn't know for sure.' I searched her gaze, then pressed her: 'You thought maybe we'd bond.'

Her yellow eyes shifted deep lilac. 'I played with the idea. Teased it between my fingertips. But only as a way to hurt Thorne.'

I shook my head. 'You weren't sure, when you came to my room. I know you weren't.'

'What difference does it make?'

'I just need to know that what I felt was real.'

Finn gazed at me and her eyes shifted yet again to a deep blue. She leant forwards, seeming to understand my fear or my unease or whatever it was that had overcome me. 'I thought maybe. I wanted you, certainly. I wanted your reputation for being out of control and reckless, because I . . . well, because I'm me. But do you know the moment I knew you and I weren't for each other?'

I swallowed. 'When?'

'Not when our eyes met, and we didn't bond. But when our skin touched for the first time. When I felt the true heart of you, and knew it to be very beautiful, but not forged as half of mine.'

And if it was forged as half of someone who didn't want it?

That was when I'd felt a great rush of *shock-horror-rage-hurt* and looked up to see Isadora watching us. My pulse lurched. 'Finn and Thorne are bonded,' I'd blurted. She'd left and I hadn't seen her in two days and every minute since I'd felt sick.

'Over here,' Osric now called softly, and we hurried to his side. He was prying open the door of a warehouse. 'It will have an underground room to store fish in cool temperatures.'

Inside it was dark, so Finn scrounged around until she found a lamp. We spotted the steps and followed them down into the coolroom, which was full of rank, rotting fish. 'Holy *gods*,' Finn exclaimed, eyes watering. 'Lucky Thorne isn't here or he'd keel over dead at such a stench.'

'Look for a small grid in the ground,' I said, hiding my nose inside my shirt collar.

'Here,' Ava said a few moments later. I crouched over it, using my blade to jimmy the metal covering off while Finn held the lamp aloft to give me light. It was exactly what I'd hoped to find – a hole disappearing into darkness below.

'What is it?' Finn asked.

'A drainage system.'

'But the water can just drain over the cliffs. We have gutters and drainpipes for that.'

'The buildings underground need drainage too, or the moisture would seep into the rocks and erode them, eventually crumbling the whole city into the sea. This little tunnel will dip down into the earth and lead to the bottom of the cliff.'

'Which would be great if anything larger than a mouse could fit down it.'

I flashed her a grin. 'That's why we'll need diggers.'

They all stared at me. Finn said, 'I thought you were meant to be useless.'

I had a very bad feeling about this. Ambrose refused to listen to me. He wanted to deal in words and the power of his reputation. He wanted a different way of things. But if he could not *show* his strength and punish with his own two hands, it was likely we were walking into a great bloody mess. Two men against gods only knew how many. If he refused to fight, then I'd suggested he at least wait until trusted soldiers were collected from the fortress. But he wouldn't wait that long.

Erik had reported Sigurd was taking his pleasure at Iceheart's Tavern, and he'd warned us that it was not a pretty sight tonight. An auction was being held.

Ambrose took Erik by the back of the head and held him firm. 'I have a charge for you, more important than any other. Guard Lady Roselyn and my daughters from harm. If something happens to me, I want you to get them out. Go straight for my fortress and don't stop, not for anything.'

Erik bowed his head solemnly. 'No harm will come to them under my charge, Majesty. That I vow upon my life, and my forefathers before me.'

'Thank you, my friend.'

Ambrose, Howl and I stole out into the cold night, the coldest it had yet been. We walked in silence to Iceheart's, our feet soft on the cobblestones, and it was only when we turned a corner and saw the tavern at the end of the street that Ambrose spoke.

'The same goes for you, Thorne. If something happens to me, you go for the girls. You get them out, no matter what. Don't spare me a thought.'

'If you know how dangerous this is, why do you insist on such haste?'

Ambrose took my shoulder in his huge hand. 'Listen to me. You don't need me to tell you the answer to that. The ice did not change you so much that you no longer see the necessity of stopping this atrocity.' He leant closer, holding my eyes. 'There are women being *sold* in my land. *I will not have it.* Now are you my prince and my second, or are you not?'

I drew myself up, frost encrusting my heart. 'I am.'

'Then set free the beast.'

A thrill trembled down my spine: he needed no freeing, he'd been free since the day I became King of the Ice. He was me and I him.

'Good lad,' my father told me from within the shadows. 'Your King is right – a threat is met without hesitation, only fury. Find yours now or die.' His teeth flashed as he smiled, and it was the smile of the wildest wolf in all the world. It was the smile of the King of the Underworld as he draped himself in the skins of the dead. It was the smile of a berserker.

Together we followed Ambrose into Iceheart's. Howl stayed close to my side, on the ready. The tavern was full to bursting and loud. The din was created by at least a hundred men, all crowded onto tables and against the bar, filling the staircases on either side of the room and draped over the top floor railings. Within a small circle was a row of women, manacled to each other at ankles. And watching over, perched lazily on the bar, was a delighted Jarl Sigurd.

That was when it found me, my fury. It erupted through my veins, cold like the ice mountain itself. I wanted blood and the feel of bones breaking beneath my fists; I wanted to kill.

The women were young, battered and bruised and hollow-eyed with fear. Ambrose's urgency became mine – this needed to end *now*. No one had noticed us yet so we stood by the door, surveying the proceedings to understand what was going on. Sigurd called for a girl to be brought forwards. The prisoner on the end was unlocked from the line and tugged into the ring.

I watched her face crumple with fear, but then she looked back at the girls she'd been chained to, at one in particular, the youngest. This young one wore such an expression of defiance as she nodded at her companion that the girl straightened, her face calmed and she turned to meet her judgment with pure, simple courage. It humbled me; beauty could be hidden within the ugliest of all things.

Bidding began with men shouting numbers. The highest price was reached and the winner entered the ring to claim his purchase. He didn't take her far, choosing to sit and watch the rest of the auction with his prize on his lap.

Instead of choosing the next girl in line, Sigurd pointed at the youngest, the most defiant. 'Her,' he said softly. 'I'll take her for myself.'

The second she was unchained the girl struck out at the soldier holding her, taking him in the eye and then smashing her knee into his groin. He doubled over in pain and she spat on him before she was overcome by another two soldiers.

Sigurd smiled at her spirit; I could see in his eyes the desire to break it.

'I think I've seen enough,' said a deep voice. The King of Pirenti stepped into the ring. There was an awkward hush as most recognised him and whispered to those who didn't.

Jarl Sigurd didn't climb down from the bar. Instead his smile widened and he spread his hands. 'Welcome, King Ambrose! It's been too long since your last visit! Come, enjoy the nightlife of Vjort with us.'

Ambrose didn't waste a moment in play. His voice was flat as he said, 'Jarl Sigurd, for crimes against humanity, you are stripped of your rank, title and honour, and will spend the remainder of your days in prison on the Isle. Enter into our custody by your own will, or be forced into it. Each and every person you have illegally stolen and sold will be freed and anyone guilty of purchasing will also be put in prison. I'm sickened by the lot of you, and ashamed to name you men of mine. This vileness ends now.'

A rustle of sound moved through the soldiers. I listened closely and took a deep breath to gauge how they felt about this; a mix of fear, anger and resentment. The girls were wary.

Sigurd gazed at Ambrose, no surprise evident on his face. He was a handsome man, with blond hair and beard, finer in build than most in this room. No doubt more dangerous than all.

'Here's the problem with that, Majesty,' he said delicately. 'In your absence – during which we can only imagine you've enjoyed playing host to your Kayan whores and piss-whelps, inviting them into our lands and groveling at their feet like the good little cocksucker you are – we here in the north have been taking what is rightfully ours. That being: whatever we want. As Pirenti men have done and will do for all the days of this world.'

A cheer went up in the tavern and I knew then that we were dead. Unless I curbed it now and challenged this scum before –

'Do you know what they whisper of you, Ambrose?' Sigurd addressed him insultingly without title. 'That you are immortal. Impossible to kill, like one of the gods themselves. But I'm no man to be frightened of myth or superstition. I was born to kill gods.'

Now – I had to do it now before he got any further. I pushed forwards but the throng was heavy and –

He was already booming, 'I, Jarl Sigurd of the ancient barracks of Vjort, son of Jarl Seth, formally challenge you, King Ambrose of Pirenti, son of a disgraced traitor, brother of a slaughtered slaughterman, husband of a boy-bitch enemy, for your throne.'

I would kill him. Tear his limbs from his body and listen to his screams. I pushed through the men before me, scattering them; they were small and weak, all cowards, the lot of them. '*You will die for such insults,*' I snarled, and at my side Howl let out a ferocious snarl.

Sigurd smiled again, looking me up and down. 'Well, if it isn't the princeling of the ice. Too cowardly to train here at Vjort with us, like all hard men. Too cowardly to leave the care of his addled mother, too cowardly to go anywhere but south into the sunny ease of enemy lands and marry a girl whose vile warder magic is more powerful than he.'

Was he trying to get himself killed? The insults were spewing forth as though he thought they made him stronger, when they only made him small.

'You don't stop, do you?' Ambrose asked calmly. How was he so calm? My fury filled the whole tavern, a living breathing roaring that made the walls swell and threaten to burst. Ambrose put a hand on my shoulder and I tethered myself to it, breathing deeply.

To Sigurd he said, 'I don't accept your challenge.'

Confusion rippled through the crowd, and for the first time Sigurd looked thrown. 'You have to,' he argued. 'It's law.'

'No longer. I've seen enough proof in the last ten minutes to warrant your death, but I'm shaping a new country, where killing is not the answer to everything.'

'I've *challenged* you – if you wish to defend your throne then fight me, or give it up like the coward you are.'

'Whether or not you can beat me in a fight does not mean you have earned my throne. *I* have earned my throne, by creating more peace and prosperity in this land than any ruler before me. I have earned it by working for it, by respecting it, and by giving my life to this nation. I will not fight you for something that is beyond your petty power to obtain.'

There was an intake of breath. Ambrose looked so strong, standing without fear, only conviction, passion, disdain. He was a giant.

But Sigurd's words were insidious and deceptive; he had the power of swaying weak minds. 'Your so-called King thinks so little of his people and his land that he spits in the face of tradition. A god indeed. He is the lowest form of coward. Kill him.'

'Don't move!' I roared. 'His Majesty is a greater man than any here, but I am not. I will fight you, Sigurd, if it's violence you seek.'

'I didn't challenge you, Princeling.'

'I am berserker King of the Ice Mountain,' I told him softly. 'My enemies will use my title before they die.'

Sigurd bristled and I saw a flash of fear in his eyes. The tavern was abuzz with excitement. I'd lost their scents – there were too many and they'd blurred into a heavy rank odour.

'No one is dying tonight,' Ambrose's voice cut through the noise. 'Anyone who uses violence in this room is a criminal and a traitor to his nation. *Do not fall below your honour for such a weak man.*'

Confusion again, I could smell confusion. Disbelief. And rage. These were men of Vjort, after all. They knew violence. They knew strength of a very different kind to the one Ambrose was displaying. And they didn't like him undermining what they knew in their hearts to be true: that men fought for power with the strength they possessed, and that only the strong survived.

'Kill him!' Sigurd screamed, and this time they came at us.

A hundred men, at least. Brutal, bloodthirsty men. Most of them trained if not by Ambrose himself then by my father, who could not be beaten. We would die here.

I thought of Finn as I drew my axe and swung it straight through the skull of a man running at me. I thought of Finn with every blow and strike and slash and block I executed, killing the soldiers one after another. Howl was beside me, tearing savagely into throats and thighs, spilling blood with wild courage. But we could not keep it up – there were too many and they crowded too close, hindering my range of movement.

'Thorne!' a voice shouted over the din, and that was when I looked up to see that Ambrose was not fighting. He was amid a sea of attackers, with Sigurd at their head, enduring blow after blow as they beat him to death.

My heart broke and a desperate sound left my throat. *Why was he not fighting?*

'Do what you promised me!' Ambrose yelled before Sigurd's fist slammed into his cheek, shattering it.

He sank to one knee, then rose again as the butt of an axe swung into his guts.

'Fight!' I screamed at him. 'Ambrose, *please* fight!'

'*Your promise!*' he roared.

Sword, no. Unruly panic in my chest. Disbelief. How could he ask me to leave him? I couldn't. I couldn't possibly.

'You can,' said someone at my elbow as I smashed my axe into a man's throat. My father. Motionless within the madness. 'Do as he says,' Thorne told me. '*Get to the girls.*'

And with them both bidding me the same thing my resolve broke, the walls gave way, and I fought a path to the door.

'Cowards!' I heard Sigurd yell as I burst outside. 'See how the Prince flees and the King cowers?'

A few men followed but I hacked them down. My last sight of Ambrose, over the heads of his swarming enemies, was of him nodding to me in gratitude. And then he was hammered so hard in the head that he hit the ground and disappeared from my view.

A desperate sob left me. Howl gave a mournful bay; he didn't understand what we were doing. There was blood through his white fur and he moved with a limp. How could I do this? How could I ever leave? How would it be possible not to drown in this wretched guilt?

Ambrose.

'Move!' Da urged. 'The children!'

So I turned and I sprinted towards the castle, my lungs floundering with grief and an endless, endless self-loathing.

There were soldiers guarding the castle when I arrived, men who had not been here an hour ago. Horror made me nauseous as I sprinted up the steps and swung my axe through four men. Smashing the locks on the door, I was inside and charging through the corridors within minutes. Servants fled but I found one cowering by a window.

'Where is my family?'

She wept, clutching at my feet. 'They came for them.'

'Who did?'

'The Jarl's men.'

'*Where are they?*'

'I don't know, Highness! They were in their rooms!'

I ran up four flights of stairs and arrived at Ella and Sadie's chamber, only to find the door wide and the corpses of six soldiers scattered in the hallway. The twins and my mother were nowhere to be found.

A terrible sound left my mouth and I slammed my fist into the stone wall, smearing blood. My legs gave out and I sank to my knees, sobbing wretchedly. Howl whimpered and tried to lick my face but I pushed him away.

The voice came again. This voice that plagued me, haunted me, wouldn't leave me for one single second. Was he my conscience? A ghost?

Was he the worst part of me, or the best?

He said, 'No son of mine weeps when his family must be found. Rise to your feet, and follow their scent.'

So I rose to my feet. I drew a deep breath through my nose. And I started tracking.

Chapter 10

Roselyn

I used to make wishes. Little wishes and large, wishes for each moment of the day and a great many moments that didn't yet exist. But no longer. Wishes were a fool's hope, and I'd learned long ago they didn't help anyone. I didn't count much either, not like I once had. It didn't have the same effect on me, just a whispered linking together of things that served no purpose once linked.

People still talked about me, but it was no longer to cruelly comment on my strangeness or my oddities – now they whispered with concern, with pity, wondering how I could still be so lost and what they could do to shift this melancholic cloud I lived beneath.

I didn't mean to be sad. It wasn't a choice. I felt terrible when someone's energy was spent worrying for me. But I couldn't change it, couldn't cast it off.

It was simple. I loved him so, and he was gone.

When the soldiers came for me I thought, for one single, brief moment in time: *at last.*

But the thought that came after stayed much longer, would stay for always, for all the beats of my heart, however long they might last.

This thought was just as simple, as all the things in my life were. I thought: *the girls.*

*

I read to them for hours tonight; they were unsettled, their little hearts beating fast in their little chests. They'd never been so far north, and nor had I. It was a strange, masculine place, an ugly place for all its lovely old architecture. Within Vjort's walls there was a restless aggression, a heavy kind of energy. I found myself thinking of these men who were born and raised here, bound for the life of a soldier, fed into the army with no say, no choice, no awareness that there should even be a choice. They must lead very lonely lives, very small lives, within these walls. Or perhaps I was simply judging what I didn't understand.

Sadie wanted the tale of the wind nymphs, but unusually Ella disagreed – she was mostly inclined to allow her sister the choice in these things. Tonight she asked to hear the tale of the marriage of the ice goddess to the sea god, so her sister shrugged and nodded.

'Finn's told us before,' Sadie said. 'It's a good one.'

I flipped through the book and found the right page, then read to them of ice and sea, and the distance between lovers from different worlds. When I finished, Sadie said, 'The book doesn't tell it like Finn does. When she speaks of the screaming of the wind and the gulls you can really hear them, like they're in your head, and when she describes the snow on the fir trees you feel cold! Truly.'

Ella peered out the window at the naked tree branches that scraped their sharp fingers against the glass. She wanted to get out as much as they wanted to get in.

'Finn has a silver tongue,' I murmured to Sadie. 'Sleep now.'

In truth I was worried about Ella, about the fever that kept coming and going with no understandable cause. Each time I beat it down, it returned. Her cheeks were flushed and warm when I felt them once more, so I gave her more of the cooling draught.

'Could you tell us of King Thorne?' she asked me suddenly.

I frowned, surprised by the queer urgency in her voice. 'It's late, darling.'

'Did he love the cold?'

I thought about it, nodding. 'A little. I think perhaps he loved that it had no hold over him like it did others.'

'Ella loves the cold,' Sadie said solemnly. 'More than normal.'

'She's a Pirenti child,' I replied. 'It's in her blood.'

'But I've no berserker in me,' Ella argued. 'Not like Thorne and Thorne.'

'That's true.'

'So it doesn't make sense.'

I stroked her hair off her forehead, considering. 'I think that what anyone is and is not doesn't have much to do with sense. We just are. Inexplicably.'

She sighed and threw off her covers. 'I want Ma.'

'And Falco,' Sadie added.

'I know you do, darlings. It won't be too much longer before you see them.'

'Where's Da?' Sadie asked.

'He went out with Thorne to work. He'll be home soon.'

'Can we have the window open?' Ella asked.

'Absolutely not. You'll freeze.'

She sighed again – she was getting very good at sighing – then rolled over and shut her eyes. Sadie kissed me on the cheek and I doused the lamps, closing their door behind me. Turning in the dark, I got a fright at finding Erik waiting in the shadows of the corridor.

'My Lady,' he said softly.

I inclined my head. In this light I couldn't make out the tattoos on either side of his skull, around his ears where the hair had been shaved short. The rest he left long and braided. I couldn't see his eyes, either, but I knew they were a dark, dark brown, almost black and sometimes frighteningly bottomless.

'You're very good with them,' Erik said. 'Some are born mothers.'

'I'm not their mother,' I explained quickly, embarrassed to be thought of as Ambrose's partner by this strange man.

'I know you aren't,' he said, and I could hear the smile in his voice.

'Oh. Forgive me.'

'I only meant . . .' He paused, and it was almost as though I could hear the echo of his deep, melodic voice throughout the silent hallway. 'I have heard stories of you, Lady Roselyn.'

Oh no. I felt myself shrink in preparation for a blow.

But he said, 'Stories of the woman from the coast of oysters who spends her life helping people, and raising her boy to be the kind of gentle that shifts the world. It sounds like a beautiful life you've led. A life that means something.'

I swallowed, overwhelmed. Because it was and it did, and I'd never heard it spoken so.

'I will watch over you tonight, my lady,' Erik told me gently. 'You and the little ladies.'

He opened my door for me, then bowed his head before shutting it between us. I undressed and pulled on my nightgown quickly, shivering in the cold. Rushing into bed, I drew the covers over my head and cocooned myself in a dark little nest. I listened to the screaming of the wind through the trees and thought of the way Finn did indeed describe it into life.

I was lifted by this wind, picked up and carried into the sky. I was danced and thrown about, somersaulted and caterwauled like a winged creature, one designed not for earth but for flight. I stayed here in the sky for such a long time that I forgot what body I truly inhabited, I forgot which body made a prison for my soul.

But without warning I was reeled back into it, into my flesh, bound by a sudden and impossibly powerful knowing. My mother would have called this a black knowing, a premonition. She would have kept it secret for fear of being branded a witch. But the knowing would only have stayed and buried deeper, just as it was doing to me now.

My son was in danger.

I didn't wish for him – to wish would condemn him to fool's hope. To wish would make it never come true. But I sent him silent prayers and thoughts, and I tried very hard to settle my heart back in its place and cast out the ugly foreboding.

A noise from beyond the window drifted up. Hurried male voices and the clang of steel. I threw off my covers and peered out. In the courtyard below I could see soldiers. And then came the sound of them inside the castle.

This was Ambrose's castle, in a city of our nation – we were among friends, and there was no need to fear anything. And yet the presence of those men felt wrong in some way I couldn't name, the sounds they made felt wrong. I donned a robe and padded to the door. In the hallway I didn't spot Erik until he returned from the stairwell at the end with a sharp, 'Back to your room, lady!'

'The girls,' I breathed, ignoring him and heading for their room.

They were both still in their beds and looked at me curiously. 'All's well,' I said.

'No matter what happens, stay in the room,' Erik bid me, making my heart stutter.

'What is it?'

'I fear Sigurd's men may have come to detain you. Lock the door, barricade it and don't open it, not even to me.'

With cold terror turning my stomach to liquid I locked the door.

'What's going on?' Sadie asked.

'Shhh.' It was freezing in their room as I moved between their beds, reaching to stroke both their foreheads.

'Aunt Rose,' Sadie demanded. 'What is it?'

'I'm not sure, darling. Erik thinks there may be some danger, but we're very safe in here.' I remembered his instruction and moved to push the dresser in front of the door. The girls ran to help me, and together we got the heavy wood in place. I didn't think there was much that could break through such heavy locks and barricades, but for safe measure I also lifted one of the side tables on top of the dresser.

The noises intensified, footsteps and voices. I heard Erik's muffled voice say, 'No one enters.'

A scuffle, the sounds of pain, of weapons clanging, bodies hitting walls and floors. I didn't know what was going on, but my heart was racing, a cold sweat breaking out on my forehead.

It occurred to me suddenly that they would get in, no matter how well we'd barricaded the doors. Eventually someone would get in. Looking around swiftly, I noted the large wardrobe and gathered the girls into it. 'In here. Don't come out for anything. Close your eyes, block your ears and count to one thousand, do you understand?'

Ella nodded but tears welled in Sadie's eyes.

'Don't cry,' I bid her. 'You must be silent. All will be well.'

'But you – you have to hide too.'

'I'll be fine, darling, I promise.'

I closed the doors on them and turned back to the room, thinking quickly. The beds. I moved to push them together, but they were heavy and it hurt my back. When they were as close as I could get them, I threw the bedcovers over, making the twin beds appear like a larger single. Then I crawled into one side and kept my eyes trained on the door.

More noises in the hallway, the constant sounds of fighting. Which meant he was still alive out there, still defending our door.

My teeth were chattering and I felt so cold. *Fear*, I told myself. *You must be stronger than it.* But this was too cold. This wasn't normal. As I looked up and saw the window ajar, recalling Ella's desperate desire to have it open, terror struck. Because the branches of that tree were jerking as though someone was climbing it.

Move move move I screamed at myself. But I was frozen.

And then he was at the window, swinging it wide, unhindered by the lock and jumping heavily into the room. He was a large man, fat through the belly but broad in the shoulders.

I sat up, placing my feet flat on the cold stone floor.

'Where are they?' he asked me. 'The princesses.'

I didn't answer.

'*Where?*' He took two strides and smacked me across the face.

Wincing, I drew a deep breath. 'This is my room. They were put in another down the hall.'

He looked at the bed, glanced around, seemed to believe me. I prayed with everything I had that the girls would remain silent in the wardrobe. 'What's your name?'

'Roselyn.'

'Then it's true.' He sounded as though he couldn't quite believe it. 'The wife of the slaughterman really is in Vjort. What could have possessed you to be so stupid?'

A hammering came at the door. 'My lady?' Erik's voice called. 'Roselyn!'

My teeth started chattering.

'Have you any idea how much we hated him?' the soldier asked me. 'Do you know how many fathers and sons and brothers he killed?' He shook his head and that was when I saw his eyes go to the wardrobe.

Panic struck, and I knew what I must do to distract him. I knew, too, what the words would cost me. But I also knew that if there was going to be violence here tonight, then I would do what I must to ensure it was not bestowed upon the children in my charge. I stood suddenly, movement enough to draw his gaze back to me, and then I spoke very clearly, channeling the cool disdain I'd seen in Ava: to protect her children, I would become as much of her as I could. 'All of them weak men, foolish and ambitious enough to challenge him. They deserved no other fate.'

It was a beacon for his fury. He leant close and I caught sight of a red beard and rotten teeth. His breath stank awfully of rum. 'From whatever bloodied underworld he is condemned to, the slaughterman will watch this.'

The man shoved me back on the bed and ripped my nightdress up. His hands pinned my arms and throat painfully, then one hand moved to undo his breeches.

'Roselyn!' My name was being screamed over and over again from behind that door – perhaps he heard the man's voice within, or perhaps he could simply tell something was wrong. Either way Erik wasn't getting through in time. I had barricaded us in too well. I had no illusions as to my ability to fight, and none for any mercy that might live in this creature atop me – I was a woman and he wanted to debase me.

And so.

I moved my eyes to the window, to the long scraping tree branches, and I counted all the ones I could see. I counted softly under my breath until it unnerved him and he mashed his meaty hand over my mouth, and then I counted silently in my mind. I let the numbers reach out and cloak me in their calm; I let the numbers protect me as I came to understand what true violence was.

I understood, too, how to be more than it. It was, after all, a small price to pay to stop him from finding the children in the wardrobe.

*

Once upon a time I said to my husband, 'I thought humans were different to animals.'

And he replied, he who understood such things, '*So did I. But I think we were both wrong.*'

*

When it was over the soldier straightened, retied his breeches and started shoving the dresser from the door.

I pulled my nightgown over my legs, tightened my robe and wiped the blood from my lips. *Scrape scrape* went the branches against the glass, seeking always to get in. *Thump thump* went the beat of my sluggish heart, seeking to get out.

The door was unlocked and crashed open under the force of Erik's hammering blows. The red-bearded soldier had his sword ready and sliced it down upon Erik as he bowled in. With impossibly fast instincts the hirðmenn dropped low to avoid the blade and swept his axe through the calf of the soldier. A scream rent the air, and as Erik rose he smashed the end of his axe into the soldier's skull. I looked away so I wouldn't have to see any more of it. Not one single second more of it.

I will have no more violence in my life. More foolish words spoken to my husband. There seemed no end to my naivety.

'My Lady?' I heard Erik pant.

But I didn't look at him. One thing mattered only. I went to the wardrobe and opened it to find Ella and Sadie huddled on the floor in each other's arms, eyes firmly shut. The sight of them nearly undid me, but we were far from safe yet. I helped them climb out, soothing them with murmurs. They emerged, wide-eyed and shaken. Both were staring at me and it was clear they knew something bad had happened. I gave them a reassuring nod, and asked Erik, 'How do we get out of here?'

'More will be coming,' he breathed, and I could hear an alarming wheezing in his lungs. 'We cannot go through the castle.'

'The window,' Ella said and I knew she was right – if someone could enter through the window then we could escape through it.

But Erik had slumped to the ground and was struggling to breathe. I pulled open his tunic and undershirt to see that his chest was bruised and swollen.

'What's wrong with him?' Sadie asked, her panicked voice pitched high.

'His lung has been punctured,' I replied. 'Lock that door and find me something sharp.'

Sadie went for the door while Ella dashed to search through drawers until she found a letter opener. 'Will this do?'

'Yes, quickly.' My kit was in my room, but I couldn't risk going for it. Not when there were more soldiers coming.

'Go,' Erik wheezed. 'Forget this.'

I ignored him and took the letter opener, using my fingers to feel between his ribs for the right spot.

'Roselyn,' he gasped, struggling terribly to get air.

'Hush.'

'Forgive me,' he uttered, and there were tears in his eyes and I knew that he knew, he *knew* and he was looking at me with such pain that I couldn't bear it, and I had to drop my gaze to the task.

I pressed the tip of the letter opener to his flesh.

'Rose,' Sadie whispered, kneeling on his other side. 'You're crying.'

I lifted a hand to discover my cheek was wet. Impatiently, I dashed the tears away and swallowed.

Above the rib. It had to be just above, for below there were nerves and an artery, which would kill him if I hit it. I made a small incision – my tool wasn't sharp enough and made a mess, but I managed to get it in and turn it sideways so air could fill Erik's lung. How fragile, this flesh.

He took a mighty gasp that rushed so quickly to his head that he passed out. Oh gods. I covered the incision and then tried to rouse him, but he was out cold, probably from a concussion received earlier. I glanced at the girls, unsure of what to do.

'He was protecting us,' Ella said. 'He comes.'

I nodded. But how? I couldn't carry him – certainly not out a window. I was no good at solving problems of this nature.

'We'll use the sheets!' Sadie exclaimed. 'Like the cinder girl in the story – she ties bed sheets to the window and climbs down them.'

'He can't climb down anything,' Ella pointed out.

'No, I mean we'll wrap him in one and use others to lower him down.'

I let out a breath. 'Clever girl.'

We hurried to strip the beds and tie the linen together. We wrapped Erik – a rolled up sheet beneath his arms and around his waist – then slid him to the window. Even with three of us we couldn't lift him, so Ella climbed out onto the sill and hooked one of the sheets over a thick branch. This we attached to Erik's harness so we could heave him up and over. The girls both gave a squeal as he swung, suspended over the drop.

Footsteps and voices approached along the corridor.

I started lowering Erik, wedging my feet against the wall and wrapping the sheets around my palms so I wouldn't drop him. The soldiers in the hallway were storming through the rooms on either side of us and hammering on our door – they'd be inside soon. I quickened my pace, arms trembling with fatigue.

Ella and Sadie both scampered easily down the tree branches until they'd reached the ground. They waved at me, motioning to lower him further but there was no more sheet. The lock on the door was about to give out. I made a choice, and dropped him.

Then I leapt onto the tree branch, turning to close the window behind me so the soldiers might not realise at once how we'd escaped. I edged my way down, terrified of falling and counting loud and fast in my mind to make it stop, to banish this poisonous fear –

The scent of rum on his breath was still in my nose. I was saturated in it.

I finally made it to the ground, where panic and adrenalin helped me drag Erik behind some trees. 'Don't worry, he's still alive,' Sadie assured me and I sagged in relief. My body hurt and I'd been too panicked to think of grabbing cloaks or shoes for us. *Foolish, foolish woman*, I cursed myself. It would be my fault when we froze to death.

I shrugged out of my robe and tore it into strips, which I wrapped around Ella and Sadie's feet. Ella protested that she didn't need it, but I replied that now wasn't the time to argue. The rest of the material I wrapped around their heads and shoulders.

I had to find us somewhere safe, somewhere warm. To hide and wait for Thorne and Ambrose. *Where were they? Why had they not yet come?* I hardly knew Vjort; I had been through its streets but once this evening, inside a carriage. The same carriage would now offer at least a little shelter and anonymity. And the only place I knew about was – 'The temple,' I murmured. Finn had told me about it a thousand times. 'Our carriage is in the stables. We'll use it to find the temple.'

We crept through the castle grounds, slowly dragging Erik along as quietly as we could. My feet were numb from cold and my hands had turned blue. I kept having to clench my jaw to stop my teeth from chattering ferociously. If only Erik would wake.

The carriage was at the far end of the stables and after I'd painstakingly harnessed our horse I used some of the carriage's upholstery to drape around me like a cloak. I would need it to hide my hair colour, and as relief against the frigid air. I was frightened I'd gotten too cold, that the chill would never leave my bones. This was how you died in the north: by forgetting for a single second, by lowering your guard and allowing the freeze to slip inside.

The sound of my beating heart seemed to drown out even the racket of the wooden wheels against the cobblestones as I drove the carriage. My mind wanted away, to hide from all of this, to simply distract itself and flee into the safety of imagination. My body wanted warmth and rest, badly. Or, failing that, to be forgotten entirely. Discarded like a snake's skin and left behind, used up. But I had not earned those things yet. There would be no stopping or slowing. My body no longer had anything to do with me, except as a means of protecting the children. *I must get them to safety.* That was what life meant. That was what it was for.

It sounds like a beautiful life you've led. It sounds like it means something.

Erik was right when he said that. My life did mean something: it meant the love of my son, and of these two girls. It meant more than anything any man could do to me. For the first time in my life I felt an iron fist take hold of my heart. I felt the steel of the Sword curl around my spine and straighten it.

It was close to dawn by the time we reached the temple. We'd been hiding and searching and evading for hours. I'd lied my way past those who stopped our carriage to question us – and I had never lied so well. Before tonight, I'd barely known how. Necessity was motivation for anything. I staggered from the carriage to find the twins still wide-awake and overwrought – but profoundly courageous. Erik was thankfully still breathing. Inside the temple it was cold and empty. But we called out and were soon met by an old couple who'd risen from their beds in the cottage attached to the main building. I explained who we were and they were so kind – just as Finn had described them – that I felt my soul swept out in a tide of weariness.

They took us into the basement, where they said no one would think to look for us. They gave us blankets and water and promised they would hide us as long as we needed. But I knew we could only stay so long – if my son didn't come for us here, then something was very wrong and I would have to get the girls out of the city myself. The old man – I had already forgotten his name in my delirium – helped me get Erik inside. We covered him and I checked him once more, determining that he would either wake or he wouldn't and there wasn't any more I could do for him. A spirit had to fight to survive, had to want it very much.

Once the girls were wrapped up with warming bricks for their poor little feet, I sank to the ground nearby. It was mere moments before they both moved to lie on either side of me, tightening their arms around me.

I struggled against tears. For their sweetness and their courage. For their strength.

'You're safe,' I whispered to them in the dark. Dawn was not far, but we wouldn't know it down here – there was neither door nor window, only a dusty trapdoor beneath a rug.

The longest night of my life. The coldest. But not the worst. No, it was not the worst.

'Of course we are,' Sadie replied.

And Ella said, 'We're with you, Aunt Rose.'

Chapter 11

ISADORA

I spent time in the shadows, listening to snatches of conversations, until I was sure the Mad Ones had no suspects for the Palace Massacre, as it was being called. Which meant I was safe to return to the palace. I couldn't face it now though – I'd go tomorrow. Tonight I would tint my hair and body, and try to leave my mind behind. I'd failed in everything I'd attempted so far, but I wouldn't fail again.

The way home took me through the abandoned cliff streets, past dead or dying trees and empty houses with salt-rimmed windows. It was dark and silent; I felt like the only creature left alive in this whole, desolate place. It wouldn't be the case for much longer. The last attempt I made on Dren and Galia would surely see me dead, too: it seemed naive to hope I'd escape the palace a third time.

As storm clouds rolled in from the sea and snatches of lightning lit the dark, I wondered what was in store for my soul. I didn't believe, as most did, in the Gods. I didn't believe in an underworld or a kingdom of endless glory, as the Pirenti folk did. I wasn't sure what would become of me beyond providing food for worms. Justice should exist in this world, in our flesh and bones. Or perhaps that was simply my hope, because if there was an underworld waiting for us then surely a woman such as I would find herself condemned to its very lowest pit.

I was imagining this when I felt him.

I stopped walking. A tingling, thumping, throbbing.

No. Not tonight.

His heartbeat drew near, hunting me.

I was so close.

Fear spiked my blood, that animal urge to run, fight, kill. I closed my eyes, seeking calm. Perhaps after he died I would live long enough to return to the palace. Would I have the strength for that? There were half-walkers who did, but was it the love they felt that kept them alive?

I would soon find out. Falco was coming for me, and I'd made a vow.

FALCO

For two weeks we'd been working in the fish storage building to widen the drainage hole. The tunnel grew each day, but I knew we were running out of time. As Finn had pointed out on about eight thousand occasions, she and Osric could have blasted through the rock if only they'd been able to use their magic. This comment aggravated the diggers, to say the least, who toiled day and night.

I didn't help them. They believed it was because I didn't want to dirty my hands or bend my back. I let them believe that, easier than explaining the truth: I had been spending my days and nights clearing the dead bodies. Carrying them one after the other from their homes to their burial because I couldn't bear for a single one to go to ground without a prayer whispered for its soul. For two weeks I lived among the dead, carried their bodies with trembling hands and tried to take the burden of their passing upon myself. I kissed their hands and I loved them and, because I couldn't return them to the sea, I imagined the Goddess wrapping them in her feathered cloak and delivering them to its depths for me.

I didn't move the bodies of the warders with the tiny birds cut into their foreheads. Not because I didn't pity these twisted men and women, but because their gruesome presence bolstered the hope and the fury of my remaining people. Loyalties were shifting, from a dethroned Emperor who'd left them to a rebellious Sparrow who fought.

When my back ached too much to continue I went home for the night to wash the smell of death off my skin. Ava and Osric sat at the kitchen table, drinking whisky after a long day of digging. 'The tunnel is nearly finished,' Ava said. Dirt streaked her face and hands.

'Well done,' I said, sinking into a chair beside them.

'Where have you been?' Os asked.

'Just walking.' I looked at Ava. 'If we smuggle people out, could you receive refugees?'

'Of course,' she replied. 'I'm more concerned about getting such a group safely to Pirenti.'

'Sounds like a job for the mighty Pirenti army.' I unrolled a map of the two countries.

'Where did that come from?' Ava asked.

I shrugged. 'I drew it.' My finger traced the expanse of land, from Sancia to the safety of the Pirenti border. 'It's a long way. Do you think they can manage it?'

She met my eyes. 'Pirenti warriors have been fighting Kayan warders for centuries. If anyone can make the distance safely, it is them.'

I nodded. I didn't point out that they'd also been dying in battles against warders for centuries. 'Will they come, if we ask?'

Her eyebrows arched. 'If their King would like to remain married to his wife, they will come. What of the other cities?'

'Limontae is under warder dominion,' Osric said. 'And we know nothing of the southern regions.'

'Sancia is our priority,' I said. 'We must focus on evacuating people from under the shadow of Dren and Galia's power. I won't attack and turn this city into a battleground while it is filled with innocent lives.'

'And us? What do we do while the women and children flee?' Osric asked.

'We find a way into that palace to kill the Mad Ones.'

He shook his head. 'Impossible. There are too many within those walls, their magic too powerful. They know the trace I left when I jumped us from the palace and would destroy us the moment I tried to enter.'

'It doesn't matter,' I said. 'I know someone who can kill them.' Before they could question me I cleared my throat. 'I need you both to promise me something.'

Two gazes remained unblinking, one a rich violet, the other a milky, streaky green.

'If I die, I need you to carry this plan to its completion, or do whatever you must to free Kaya.'

'You're not going to die,' Osric snapped.

'I may. So promise.'

'Of course,' Ava said.

'And then?' Osric asked, frustrated. 'Who rules Kaya then? It certainly can't be left to the bloodthirsty hands of the Sparrow.'

'My only living relative inherits the throne,' I said, looking at Ava. Her eyes flashed sky blue. Her thoughts were obvious: ruling here meant leaving her husband and splitting up her family.

'I cannot rule two nations.'

'No,' I agreed, 'you cannot. So I'll try my best to not die.'

Finn traipsed into the kitchen and leant mindlessly against the bench, clearly dead on her feet.

'Are you alright?' Ava asked.

'Mmph,' she replied, or something to that effect, running a dirty hand through her dirty hair.

'Have you seen Isadora?' I asked. Finn shook her head. 'Do you know where she is?' Another head shake. 'You wouldn't keep it from me?'

Finn sighed. 'When you come to know Isadora, you'll understand that no one truly knows Isadora. She comes and goes as she pleases like a wraith in the night. I haven't a clue how she spends her time and if I were you I wouldn't hope to find out.'

I would find out, and soon. The pounding urgency to see my mate had been growing by the day, and I no longer had any desire to ignore it, even if it was pulling me swiftly to my death.

ISADORA

I deliberately maintained a steady pace home. Blood rushed in my ears; I could taste rust in my mouth.

I went straight to the balcony to watch the wild ocean. With my face to the wind, tiny drops of rain spattered my eyelids and lips, and the scent of its approach filled my nose. My favourite smell, I realised. I had never thought to have favourites before - had never taken the time to think about what gave me pleasure. But here it was, my favourite smell: rain. This was not the thought of someone hardening herself to kill a man.

I gripped the edge of the wooden railing with knuckles turned white. Waves crashed below, black as tar and far more savage. I pictured my pale body falling to smash against those rocks; churning ferociously beneath the surface, no way out or up or free.

Stop it.

My mind and heart were not under my control, but they had to be, now more than ever. I needed pain, like in the dreams. Pain to tether me to reality. The dagger on my wrist lay flat against my skin until I turned its edge to my flesh. Blood bloomed and the pain was white hot. It vanquished both the falling image and the pleasure of the rain. I walked inside, away from the smell and the sight. Pleasure was too weakening. Hatred too raw, and too close to love. So do it with detachment. He wouldn't be long; I could feel him approaching.

My hands traced the knives strapped to my body. Perhaps they would feel the hatred and the pleasure, while I felt nothing. Perhaps they would kill him, instead of me.

He was so close now. *He doesn't have power over you,* I told myself, *screamed* at myself. *This bond has no power – you will give it none.*

The door banged open and there he stood.

Instinct demanded I close my eyes, keep them shut until I died. But I believed in the butcher or the meat, the hunter or the prey, so I forced them open and refused to blink. I gazed at him with all the fire of twelve years' torture, with the bars of a cage and the bones of sparrows, and a wasted life, a wasted heart, a useless endless sea of waste.

He was an outline in the doorway, lit from behind by the flash of lightning. How often he was obscured, how rarely I saw his face. It was so easy to mistake him for someone else. But maybe that was my fault instead of his, my eyes that looked at him and so often saw a stranger. I *would* look at him now, honestly and unburdened by indecision. I would *see* him: it was my last chance.

In the dark, he was still like cut stone. His outline was tall and fine, with both elegance and boorishness in his limbs; a tongue that could be both the sharpest and the most foolish; fingertips filled with grace one moment, clumsiness the next. He was every contradiction and my mind was deciding how I would kill him as my eyes traced up – just as they had on that first night – to his face.

There was a rumour started once that Emperor Feckless had eyes of crystal. No one knew from where it had come. Some claimed it was started by a servant who'd glimpsed him without his blindfold. Others said it was a fanciful lie. Either way, it became myth. I had wondered, years ago on a night slept in the forest, how someone could possibly have eyes of crystal. I listened to all the rumours of him – he filled my mind night and day – and this one had sounded so foolish, so whimsical. I'd never had room for whimsy, and I'd imagined watching the life fade from his hidden eyes, no matter their colour.

Now as I looked at them I understood. They were otherworldly in their strangeness. Translucent, almost. Glittering with a thousand colours like the refracted light of, yes, a crystal. They belonged to a face that was made to wear masks, hundreds of them. A face that molded to each one, takings its shape, just as his eyes held no colour and all colours, so that he would always be nothing and everything. He was a trick of the light, a glimpse of a shadow from the corner of an eye. He was as insubstantial as a passing phantom, as sweet as the most ephemeral whisper.

He was temptation in its purest, simplest form.

Falco, fallen Emperor of Kaya, said, 'You think you can will it not to be.'

I held still near the window except for the twitching of my fingers towards my knives. Dead in less than a second. The left thigh dagger through his throat. As easy as taking a breath, as slipping free the blindfold.

'But no will is as strong as that.'

My jaw clenched. I was ablaze with endless fury. Who was he to decide what strength I possessed? I straightened my shoulders, defiance in every muscle. *Use it. Use this rage.*

'How will you do it?' he asked. His eyes darted over my body. 'The dagger at your thigh? Or the one at your ribs? Where will you send it? Through my throat? My eye? Into my heart?'

Something caught in my chest. No one spotted my daggers. No one had ever, and I had taken pains to ensure he never saw where I placed them.

'I won't stop you,' he murmured. 'Even if I wanted to, I doubt I could.'

Falco moved restlessly to the cabinet, procured an old bottle of brandy and some dusty glasses. He poured two, left one for me on the windowsill, then made his way back to the door. He downed his glass and let it fall, empty, to the floor. The soft *thud* seemed to echo around the room. My eyes were adjusting in the dark to make out all the lines of his face.

'Maybe I'm lying,' Falco said. 'Perhaps I would stop you. But I'm not sure either one of us could have expected the reason. Not before . . .' He smiled wryly, almost perversely, and dropped his eyes from me.

Did people who were raised in the palace truly enjoy all this point-less talk? It occurred to me that he was donning this formality as a cloak – just as I wore my cloak of calm. Perhaps it was the only way he could endure this.

Falco licked his lips; they must taste of brandy, sweet and burning. 'I'm not as fond of the idea of your death as I once was,' he said. It fell into a silent, airless room. He cleared his throat and tried again, more simply. 'I won't let you die, Isadora. I couldn't bear it.'

I wondered which version of him was speaking, which of the dozens of men who stood before me couldn't bear the thought of my death. Which had been weak enough to fall victim to the bond, or had they all?

It didn't matter. None of them would have to endure my death.

'No words, little Sparrow,' Falco murmured. 'Never any words. I don't deserve any, I suppose. I can't hear your thoughts now, either. Only silence.' He paused, and then an edge of desperation crept into his voice. 'I'd give anything to understand the silence.'

I swallowed and it ached. I didn't know how to speak. I had never learnt a single word but he had so many, hundreds and thousands of them. He knew so well how he might use them to manipulate.

'You plan to kill me,' Falco said. 'But I came for something else.'

I shook my head, helplessly frustrated. *Kill him*, I begged myself.

The vulnerability left Falco's face. Instead a blunt thing formed his features. 'I wanted you to know. We're digging a tunnel. I will send for Pirenti and they'll march south to meet the people we smuggle from the city.' His voice dropped. 'When everyone is safe I will turn Dren and Galia to dust and memory. I will scorch them from this earth for the pain they've caused. I vow it on my life. If you'll help me, my quarrel with the Sparrow will be held in abeyance until Kaya is free. Then she may formally rally for a throne without my interference and the people may vote her into power – and you will have what you always wanted, without the bloodshed. Neither of us needs to die.'

Did he think it was power I wanted? I only wanted freedom. From magic, and pain, and from him.

He couldn't see that offering me an alliance was asking me to freely enter a prison. So why did his words fill me with such treacherous longing? A sound left me, one of panic. The magic of the bond was seducing me to crawl blindly back into my cage.

'Isadora –' He started towards me but I threw a dagger that pinned his shirt to the wall. He stopped. Blood bloomed through his sliced tunic.

I had another blade drawn and raised in warning.

The pain in his shoulder found its way into mine. I felt it so clearly, as though I were the one who'd been wounded.

'Alright,' Falco said and there was an ocean of weariness in his colourless eyes.

Before I knew it my second dagger was flying through the air. It *thunked* into the wood of the wall directly beside his other shoulder, catching and pinning the fabric of his tunic. Buying more time. I didn't have enough time.

Falco looked down at the dagger, then calmly removed it and let it fall to the floor. I threw another and this one took him through the flesh of his thigh, through the flesh of my thigh. My fourth dagger sliced through a piece of his ear, a piece of mine. I watched blood trickle down his cheek.

I drew a fifth dagger and we both knew it would be the last.

A moment passed between us, an infinite moment. We stood before the endless dark. The endless, cold, oceanic dark. No longer was he a distant name in my mind's eye, but a man. A brave and cowardly man, a selfless and selfish, foolish and clever, cruel and *kind* man. A creature of a thousand faces, and right now all of them were gazing inside me.

He broke the silence: 'It's alright. If you have to.' And I could see in those clear eyes that it really *was* alright, if I had to.

Tears slipped onto my cheeks. 'How could you?' I whispered, the first words I'd spoken. The dagger dropped with a clatter to the floor. I became a fool of fate once more - perhaps she had always known I didn't stand a chance. Perhaps everything in the world had known I would lower that dagger, except me. My heart split down the middle and opened wide. Here I was, and here he was, and I couldn't fight it anymore.

With my eyes squeezed shut I heard him move and then I felt him. His hands on my body. The length of me pulled against the length of him. He felt enormous and too-hot; his smell overcame me, his skin rubbed mine raw. A sound left my mouth, an animal sound, one of pain and hunger but then his mouth was upon mine, swallowing it, swallowing all of me, my entire soul.

'Isadora,' he whispered against my lips, 'no one is strong enough to fight against this tide.'

And wasn't that the joke of it. That I had honestly thought I would be. Salt spilled from my eyes as he stole my clothes from me, and my skin from me, and he stole my body and my life and my soul and everything *everything*.

His mouth tasted my breasts and ribs and hips. I drew his tunic over his head and saw the wounds I'd inflicted. His blood smeared my fingers as I touched the broken skin at his shoulders, his ear, his thigh.

Something reared awake in me, something roaring aloud with horror. I shoved him away and held my hands out between us, held them so he could see the red of his blood staining them.

'This is what I am. *This.*'

'No, it isn't.'

'I'm death. I'll be the death of you,' I said, agonised.

Falco smiled. 'You're the life of me.'

He knocked my hands out of the way and held me to the glass of the windows. His eyes shifted to gold, still crystal, and I felt sad for him, sad that he should be bound to such a creature of ugliness, when his heart was so beautiful.

I traced his face tenderly, hardly able to believe myself capable of such gentleness. A spell indeed. He seemed as astonished as I was, and there was a moment then, as we looked into each other's eyes, a moment in which my heart spoke and his heard it. *All of me*, it said silently. Falco closed his eyes as though the words hurt, and then he kissed me so deeply. His lips tasted of brandy after all – they were sweet and he was sweet and it wasn't anything like what I had expected from this poisonous thing between us. It wasn't twisted or toxic – it was love. His large, slender hands were on my jaw, my throat, my breasts, they were at my hips, pulling them against his, they were lifting me and pressing me to him and all the while I was diving into the lake, destroying its calm, its glass surface. There was no lake inside me now, only a roiling, violent ocean.

'Iz,' he murmured, as he pulled down every barrier, every defense, built me a new world of intimacy and held me within it. I couldn't escape as he pressed inside me and we moved together, for once I could not look away, and I was dying aching living *living*. It was everything, all at once, and it was the loss of everything; it was knowing, finally, how it felt to have someone inside my body and inside my heart; it was closeness, the closeness of him, of his shape and his skin and his mouth and his eyes – what a *miracle*, the fact of him – and then with a mighty wonderful rush of fire it was over.

I breathed quickly as he held me. Our hearts pounded in time, each as stunned as the other. His hand was against my spine, the other cradling my head. My mouth rested on the sweaty skin of his shoulder and the taste of him was sweet and salty. Slowly the burning became too much, too scorching; it was hollowing out my insides like a husk. I disentangled myself from his lean, strong body and hurried to dress.

Falco remained where he was, naked and staring at me. I could feel it but I couldn't look back at him, terrified of what might happen if I did.

'Come home with me,' he said. 'Come home and we'll work it out together, all of it. We don't have to be parted anymore.'

A new life splintered away from mine and ran its course alongside. I saw this second life in all its details and truths. I would become his Empress or his bride, or simply his lover. We would touch and kiss and make love with this same delirium, a delirium that would never fade, never, because it was magic of the maddest, cruelest kind. We might find some way to fight the warders together. We might take back Kaya. Maybe we would rule the nation together, from the throne he'd been given before he could have possibly been worthy of it.

Maybe, in this second life, we would have children and a family, as the fates had created us to do. Maybe we would be in love, and happy.

But here was what I knew: it would be a lie. It would scrape us raw from the inside out because none of it, not a single moment of it, would have been by our choice. This fantasy had never been mine; I was not the creature in that imaginary life. That creature had not been born in a cage.

I turned away from him and felt his hand along my spine like a brand. I needed this to end, to be ruined, and for his hate to return to the cabin. In his hate would I find my armour. Protection from the simple truth that I loved him.

'I killed her,' I said. 'I killed your Empress and her lover, the night we met. I murdered them with the daggers I planned to use on you.'

With the absence of his hand, my back was cold.

I heard him dress. Heard him walk to the door. I couldn't bear to look at him, only listened to the sounds of his movement, his body, the rustle of his clothing. But as he stopped at the door, I forced myself to turn.

Raw grief lay in his face. But something else, too, something more difficult. A brutal kind of disappointment. It was a rotting sickness within me.

'War,' I said flatly. An explanation, of sorts. The only hint of regret I would admit to.

'What war?' he asked, holding so desperately to his composure. 'There was no war.'

'You waged war on your people when you forgot about them. I gave you fair warning – *years* of it – that I would strike back. And if you were too foolish or too arrogant to acknowledge that and prepare yourself for it, then you truly are Emperor Feckless.'

He remained silent a long while. 'Did you come to the palace to kill me because you knew I couldn't put up a fight? Because I was an easy target?'

171

This was a fate he had reaped for himself, and I owed him the truth. I nodded.

Something crossed his gaze. Something bitter. 'How did you know about Radha?'

I licked my lips and tasted his brandy on them. 'You followed the Empress. My spies followed you. You discovered the tunnel to Radha's sleeping quarters, so they discovered the tunnel. I knew that killing the unprotected mate of the Empress would also kill Quillane, and this would weaken you for my attack.'

I watched this tear through him, this terrible truth. That he was responsible in more ways than one for the deaths of Quillane and Radha. I felt his poisonous pain in my veins, his airless grief in my lungs.

'But you knew I had no hope of fighting you, or protecting myself. So why did you need to weaken me?'

I tried to draw breath. *The truth, all of it.* There was no point if it was not all of it. 'I wanted to torment you before you died. That is . . . it's the nature of the kind of thing I was. *Am.*'

Emperor Falco stared at me a long time, and then finally he turned for the door. 'I may have been Feckless, but what need does Kaya have of a ruler so cold and merciless she would slaughter innocent women?'

What need indeed.

He left me, as I'd known he would when he learned the truth. We were enemies, born to reap each other's deaths. The second life running alongside mine faded and fell away, rotten petals on an old bloom. My chest ached with shame. For the lives I had taken, but also for something else. Shame for having a soul that surrendered to the tide.

CHAPTER 12

AVA

I stood at the back door and watched the storm rage. Behind me Finn, Jonah, Penn and Osric played dice on the living room floor. Candlelight flickered, casting long shadows.

'Your mind is an open book,' Osric addressed Finn lazily.

'I have nothing to hide, Os,' she answered. 'Read away.'

'My point was that you need to work harder on your shield.'

I listened vaguely to the two of them bicker, my mind many miles north with my daughters. They would be asleep by now, if their da was behaving. I ached at the thought of him putting them to bed. How many more nights would I miss if I had to rule Kaya? Being parted from them permanently or separating the three of us from Ambrose was equally unendurable.

My mind turned to my cousin and his strange behaviour. I'd watched Falco lose weight over the last fortnight. He was giving most of his food rations to the others, but while that was a generous gesture he was coupling it with taciturn moods and shifts in temper that made the household worry. The already rampant scepticism about his character was thriving.

Apparently Finn was thinking similarly, because I heard her ask, 'Can you read Falco the way you read me, Os?'

I turned to look over at where they were playing.

Osric shook his head. 'I would never presume to.'

'Why are you so loyal to him?' Jonah bit out.

'Because he deserves it,' Osric replied.

'*Why?*'

'Courage.'

'What courage?' Jonah snapped. I felt my eyebrows arch in surprise at his venom.

'Don't speak of what you don't understand, boy,' Osric said.

Jonah shook his head, pushing his pebbles into the circle to bet.

'Big spender,' Finn said.

'Big spender, you're a soul bender,' Penn sang loudly, making us grin.

'I'm fairly certain you could make anything a rhyme,' Finn told him.

'I'm sure you're right, given enough time,' Penn sang, and Finn applauded him before glancing back at Osric. 'Maybe you ought to presume, Os. Because he's acting batty.'

'Falco has a natural shield. I'd have to break through it and it would ruin his mind.'

'I hear his thoughts all the time,' she said.

'Surface thoughts. You don't hear anything of what's going on beneath.'

'Slippery bastard,' Jonah muttered.

The room went silent as we stared at him.

'Have a care what you say about the Emperor of this nation, to whom you owe your fealty,' I said coldly. 'Especially when you sit within earshot of those who are loyal to him.'

The boy blushed bright red and lowered his eyes. 'Forgive me. I didn't mean it.'

Lightning flashed through the dark sky above. *They're only children,* I reminded myself. But I felt surrounded by them, and I wanted my husband. He would cut through it all in that way of his, with that smile of his. He'd have understood what was wrong with Falco at a glance – Ambrose understood people better than anyone I knew.

Osric appeared beside me and we watched the sky. 'I could help you unlock it.'

It had become apparent to me, on a prison isle twenty years ago, that I would have made a good warder if I'd been trained as a child, for I had the ability to manipulate the soul energy. Because I'd never practised, the power lay dormant inside me. I knew Osric had been training Finn in her soul magic for the last six months and she'd flourished under his tutelage, though you wouldn't know it for all their arguing.

'I've seen what it does,' I told Osric. 'Best it stays locked.'

The warder nodded. I took the moment to study him out of the corner of my eye. Here was a man who had more power in his grasp than anyone I had ever known. A true giant. The only legal first-tier warder. They were rare because that much power rotted the mind; bearers of first-tier magic eventually had to be imprisoned before they hurt people. Which meant that this man had a far stronger mind than most, to withstand that rot. It was inevitable, though, and I wondered how he felt about such a fate.

'I try not to think about it,' he murmured. Then flashed a rueful smile.

'We're very lucky to have you,' I told him.

His smile turned almost . . . *shy*. 'You think me strong, Majesty, but you should know this: no strength equals what it takes to survive the death of a bondmate. And that is truth, not flattery.'

I smiled.

'I could connect you to your husband,' he offered abruptly. 'Through your bond. Just for a few moments.'

The force of that slammed into me. 'Wouldn't they sense it?'

'If we were quick, perhaps not.'

The brief moment of hope died as I looked at the children behind me. 'No,' I murmured. 'I won't risk their safety. Ambrose wouldn't want to either. We'll have to send word to him the old-fashioned way.'

That was when a body dropped over the wall in a movement so lithe it was acrobatic. The cloaked figure melted through the rain. I reached for my sword - I didn't know *anyone* who moved like that.

But in a flash of lightning I saw his face and confusion stalled my hand. It was Falco who pushed inside, lowering his hood. And something was very wrong. Because his eyes – eyes that never shifted, not ever – were the leeched white of hatred.

'Falco,' I started.

But he was looking past me at Finn, Jonah and Penn. 'You're her friends. Bring her home. She's at a house on the cliff in the northern quarter. Tell her we'll make an end to this tonight.'

They stared at him, uncomprehending.

'Are you alrigh-' Finn tried.

'*Go,*' Falco ordered and then vanished into his room.

Finn looked to me for guidance and I nodded. 'Be careful, and be safe. I think it's important.'

When they'd armed themselves and disappeared into the night, I turned to share a pensive look with Osric. 'Did you catch any thoughts?'

'Nothing.'

'This doesn't feel good.'

While we waited the rest of the household returned home from the tunnel, drenched to the bone and desperate for hot tea. As they bustled about I remained at the window, watching the courtyard.

It was nearing dawn when they came. There were, thankfully, four of them. Isadora entered last and removed her soaked cloak to reveal a bone-deep stiffness in her usually graceful gait, a bleak detachment in her scarlet eyes. She was a walking corpse.

I looked swiftly to Finn, who was visibly sick with worry. She shook her head as if to say she had no idea what any of this was about. Penn was agitated, staying as far from Isadora as he could. Jonah fussed over her, but she didn't speak a word. He guided her to the lounge and sat beside her holding her hand, though I doubted she was aware of it. Her eyes were fixed on the closed door of Falco's room, trancelike.

The rest of the household pottered about preparing for bed. 'What's wrong?' Sara asked, peering at us. 'Has something happened?'

Before anyone could answer, Falco emerged from his room and strode into the small space. He took one look at where Isadora sat, her hand in Jonah's, and it couldn't be clearer that he'd simply had enough. He was abruptly a man made of skin and bones and fury.

Into the silence his presence had created, Falco said, '*Take your hands from my mate before I remove them from your body.*'

ISADORA

A bolt of shock struck the room. I realised belatedly that Jonah was holding my hand and I wrenched it free. I couldn't believe I hadn't felt his touch – I was now repulsed by it.

I willed Falco to remain calm, but he looked far from it.

After he left me I had stood by the window for a long time. When I could stand it no longer I turned to look at Quillane and Radha. I waited for them to tell me, and they waited for me to ask. But I had spent twelve years without saying a word – I could outwait even my ghosts.

'It's your will that makes it this way,' the dead Empress of Kaya said eventually.

'You will not receive forgiveness unless you ask for it,' her dead bondmate agreed.

'Why would I ever ask for something I don't deserve?'

Before they could answer, Finn, Jonah and Penn found me. They said that Falco had demanded we end it tonight. I was confused, wondering if he meant for us to die. I followed in a daze. I thought only of seeing him again, of being near him, of his touch, his kiss, his eyes . . .

Now, in his presence, I was limerent, sick with love, *mad* with it. My soul threw itself over and over at the cage of my body, desperate to get at him, to have him.

'*Take your hands from my mate before I remove them from your body.*'

A hush of disbelief fell over the room. I felt their eyes on me.

'Finn,' Falco said coldly – this was the cold mask, the detached one. It was thin, though, and didn't hide his fury well. 'You will break the bond between Isadora and me tonight.'

'*What?*'

No one explained. I certainly couldn't. Didn't we need Thorne to break the bond? Confusion was drowning me. Had I not prayed for this?

'Gods above,' Sara whispered.

'What bond?' Jonah demanded.

Finn shook her head. 'No, I couldn't –'

'An order,' Falco said flatly. 'I know you possess the capability.'

So he'd lied to me. But why? Had he not wanted to end our bond? That thought was horrifying – it opened up a thousand other questions and possibilities and realities, all of which I had destroyed when I told him the truth.

'Wait,' Ava said quickly. 'You don't know what you're asking. You can't break the bond willingly. It will destroy you.'

He was immovable.

'Falco,' the Queen of Pirenti persisted desperately, 'don't do this. If the two of you are mated, then it is *right*!'

'Right?' he asked, looking at me for the first time. His beautiful eyes were white and swords through my chest. 'I cannot be bound to this woman for the rest of my days,' he said. 'She is too cruel for my heart to forgive.'

I couldn't help it – tears spilled down my cheeks.

'Falco!' Finn gasped.

'He's right,' I said. 'I am. You must end it.'

Ava moved between us and I had never seen her look so fierce. 'Do not rush into this. You will regret it. Give it time. *Please.*'

'It's been six months,' Falco said flatly. 'And enough. I've had enough. Finn, do it.'

Finn shook her head in horror. 'I can't. It's not right. It's *clearly* not right. Not like this, with the two of you so – Izzy doesn't *want* it, and I won't force her –'

'I do,' I lied. 'I do want it.' What was *wrong* with me that I had to lie? Of course I should want it! But there was a frenzied thing inside me screaming *no no no*.

'Why?' Ava demanded. 'Tell us why.'

Falco stared at me. My heart flailed, wingless. Just as I was about to tell them everything – everything and be damned – he snapped, 'The rulers of Kaya can't be bonded – it makes us too easy to kill. If the Mad Ones were to find out . . .'

Even here, even *now* he was generous enough to lie for me. I didn't think anyone would believe it though.

'So this is about safety?' Ava asked sceptically. 'I never thought you were *this* much of a coward, Falco.'

Falco just shook his head – he was past caring what they thought of him.

Jonah was stiff beside me and I could see his hands trembling. I was too far away to care. I managed to get to my feet. 'What do you need?' I asked Finn.

She shook her head, rubbing her eyes. Couldn't gather her thoughts. Said eventually, 'For one of you to die.'

AVA

An overwhelming urgency had taken root in me. This was wrong. I could feel it in every cell of my body.

I followed Falco, Isadora and Finn into the small bedchamber. Osric had busied himself cloaking the house against detection. It would take a lot of power to ensure no warders felt what was about to take place. I closed the door to buy some privacy.

The bondmates weren't looking at each other. I had never witnessed mates acting this way. The bond shut out all else, made you crave touch and closeness and connection. But they'd been fighting the love between them with every inch of willpower they possessed, and *why*? What could possibly motivate such a brutal, pointless fight?

'One of you must die in order for the bond to break,' Finn said. 'I will bring you back using the necromancy powers my ma left me.'

'The bond doesn't break even in death,' I snapped.

'That's true, but Thorne's blood, through our bond, will give me the power to break it.'

I shook my head. It was heinous.

'I will die,' Falco said.

Isadora smiled this wretched, empty smile, and simply said, 'Don't.' Hidden within the fluidity of her muscles I saw a stiffness, something that ached deep inside her as she lay on the bed. She had aged a thousand years in the span of a heartbeat. Falco watched like he might argue or change his mind, but didn't.

Stop them, Avery urged me from within my frantically beating pulse. He knew exactly what this would do. 'Wait,' I tried again.

'Leave the room, Ava,' Falco said tonelessly. I'd never seen him like this. It was frightening.

'You *must* hear me. You don't understand what you're doing. The bond makes you infinitely stronger than you are on your own. To end it now is . . . is like intentionally wounding yourself before a battle. We need you both strong, not lame.'

179

'We're no good to anyone like this,' Falco said faintly, like he was barely listening.

I ran my hands through my hair, not knowing what more I could do. Could I knock them both unconscious? It would be better to hit Finn and incapacitate her.

'Jonah!' Finn shouted suddenly.

Her brother pushed in immediately, looking pale.

'Contain the Queen.'

'*What?*' I gasped. And then felt my body freeze. I was locked, couldn't move a muscle, could only watch. Jonah's warder magic had bound me to witness this nightmare. Finn gave me a look that said it all – that she was sorry, but she would respect their choice. What no one but a half-walker could understand was that if they truly knew what they were doing, they would *never* choose it freely.

'Are you sure you can bring her back?' Jonah asked his sister nervously.

The girl hesitated. It was clear she had no idea. 'Of course.'

I wanted to close my eyes in horror but couldn't.

'How . . .' Finn cleared her throat. 'How do you want to do it?'

Isadora slipped a blade from the sleeve of her tunic. She held it out to Falco.

'No.' He shook his head vehemently. 'I won't.'

'You will, or no one will,' she said.

Their eyes met and I watched it. I watched this indefinable thing pass between them, like truth or infinity or death, and larger than all three. Their eyes shifted gold and I felt a sound leave me. There were tears streaming down my face, but I was lost in the look they shared. It was a parting look, a farewell, an immense sea of farewells. They would march blindly into the cold dark together, no matter how foolish it turned out to be, and I would be forced to watch because not even my eyelids would obey me.

'I'm sorry,' Isadora said softly.

Falco's face twisted with pain and he broke the look, reaching for the knife.

A surge of denial flooded me and I felt the magic freezing my muscles, got my mind's fingernails into its edges deep enough to *drag* it down, down until it freed my mouth and I could cry in one last effort, *'It's not warder magic! The bond – it's love!'*

But they weren't listening.

Falco pressed the tip of the knife over Isadora's heart.

'Not through the breastplate,' she told him gently. 'Here, and slide quickly up into the heart.' She guided the knife to her ribs and angled it correctly, her fingers lingering on his. He nodded once. His hands were steady.

'Are you ready?' he asked Finn.

The warder girl closed her eyes, breathed deeply and nodded.

'Are *you* ready?' Falco asked his mate, his voice growing tender.

Isadora murmured, 'Fate's fools no longer.'

Falco's anger disappeared as though stripped from him – for a moment he flickered in the light, discarding something or drawing something on, and I could have sworn I was witnessing the appearance of an utterly new person, a man none of us had yet met. He gentled with a breath into something stronger than iron and as he pressed his lips sweetly to Isadora's, Falco slid the knife with one swift movement up into his bondmate's heart.

Chapter 13

Isadora

It is a stripping away of everything to nothing. It is a void and an infinite brutal shrieking within this void. It is pressure and weight and squeezing *squeezing*, pounding into small tiny nothing *gone*.

His hands are ripped from mine in a great *whoosh* and I scrabble desperately for them in the black but they are swept away. He is lost from me and I'll stay here forever in this screaming void, alone.

But

As I am ripped back up into life, it is worse: it is everything in my body rupturing into endless *endless* agony.

And no more of him.

Falco

It is torment. Absolute fucking torment.

And worse, indescribably worse: the absence of her.

Ava

As the knife found its home, Isadora coughed and blood spluttered from her mouth and onto Falco's. As she died he dropped to his knees with a haggard, airless gasp.

I looked to Finn, whose eyes were completely glazed over, her skin glowing a bruised blue as she worked her magic. We all knew the moment she severed the bond – Falco let out a hideous scream and slumped unconscious to the ground.

'Let me go!' I snarled at Jonah, who belatedly freed me.

I rushed to my cousin and tried to rouse him, but he was very far gone, circling death himself. I was certain that if Isadora had died and stayed dead, Falco would have passed almost instantaneously. An extraordinary thing, given it usually took at least days for a half-walker to waste away. As it was, only Finn now stood in defense of the loss of them both. The young warder's spine arched and her fingers curled unnaturally as she *wrenched* at her hold on Isadora's life. 'Sword help me,' Finn gasped, groaning and trembling until with a final pull, Isadora lurched back to life. I watched her face as she blinked to get her bearings. It took her a moment, hair and eyes wild, and then she saw Falco on the ground, and a terrible cry tore from her: '*Is he dead?*'

'No!' I assured her. 'Unconscious only.'

Isadora curled into herself as though her severed soul was trying to claw its way out of her. Finn slid wearily onto the bed and held her, cradling the hysterically sobbing woman. She looked to me, horrified, not knowing what to do.

I ran from the room. 'Sara!'

The woman stood immediately. 'What's going *on*?'

Isadora's sobs were tearing through the whole house. Everyone looked terrified. 'Have you got a sedative?'

'I can make something.'

'Do it now. Make it strong.'

'*Help!*' Finn screamed from the bedroom. I raced back to find her desperately trying to hold Isadora's wrists to the bed. In both the woman's hands were knives and she was flailing savagely.

'She's trying to kill herself!' Finn gasped as I launched myself onto the bed and pinned Isadora.

'Hurry up with the sedative!' I shouted. 'And get Osric in here *now*!'

My gods, she was a strong little thing. I was almost bucked from her. 'Get your whole weight on this arm,' I instructed Finn, and then I took Isadora firmly by the throat, forcing her head still.

'Look at me,' I ordered her. '*Isadora*. This will pass!' A lie, probably.

Her eyes were awfully dilated and shifting a thousand colours a moment. Scarlet azure lime ebony steel aubergine rust violet white. The speed made them look almost crystalline. Like Falco's, I realised with an ache. 'Make it stop,' she wept. 'Make it stop.'

'I will,' I promised. 'I will.'

We were not made to endure this, we humans. This was why we died when our mates did – as a mercy. This was why the bond pulled the other half of us into death instead of severing – *as a mercy*. This pain she was feeling was beyond what I had known, because my bond with Avery had never been broken. This was a pain unlike any human had endured, and we had no way to predict what it would do to either of them.

Sara hastened in with the sedative.

'Drink this and it will stop,' I promised Isadora, and the poor girl finally stopped struggling. The daggers fell from her fingers as she reached urgently for the liquid. It took thirty seconds for her eyelids to droop. Her weeping ceased and she drifted into a heavy sleep.

I sagged in relief, resting my forehead against her sleeping one. What force had such power over us? From whence had it come, and could it be fought? Was it *meant* to be fought? I thought I'd known it well, I thought I'd understood, but I wasn't sure that was true anymore. If any mortal in this world understood the bond, it was this wrecked woman and that ruined man.

'Ava,' Finn said, her throat thick with tears. 'What have I done?'

I carefully removed all the knives from her body in case she woke too soon, then disentangled myself from the bed. I didn't want to leave her, this tiny sleeping figure of white and red, this child I had hardly spoken two words to and had spent the last days being suspicious of. I couldn't bear to leave her alone with her pain. But that was when Osric skidded inside, looking frantic in a way he never did. 'The power – it was so much more than I thought. It decimated the shield. *They're coming for us.*'

One frozen moment of horror was all I allowed myself. Then I started moving. 'Finn, get everyone outside immediately – they bring nothing but weapons. Osric, help me find stretchers for Falco and Isadora.'

'No need,' Wes said as he and Anders arrived in the hallway. Anders grabbed Isadora, who was tiny in his arms, and placed her over his shoulder, while Wes hurried to lift Falco. I armed myself and we shepherded the terrified group into the courtyard. Thankfully Eve was asleep in her mother's arms, and I prayed the baby wouldn't wake.

'They're moments away,' Osric warned.

'Which direction?'

'All!'

I thought quickly. 'You're with me. Finn – get everyone south-east to the tunnel, swift as you can.'

'Ava –'

'Just do it.'

I pulled Osric with me and we climbed over the wall to the alley. 'Start using some of that power of yours, first-tier,' I told him, 'and make it impressive.'

Understanding passed through his eyes before they rolled back in his head and he began to glow. I led him out onto the main street and stopped in full view of the approaching warders. They sent a bolt of energy at us, but it was blocked by the iron force of Osric's shield. The warders on the other side of the house would hopefully come straight to it, feeling the draw of its unexpected power.

A striking woman with faded-red hair stood at their front. 'How long do you think you can deny us, Osric?' she asked as more warders appeared behind us, boxing us in.

'As long as I must, Viper,' he snarled.

So this was Gwendolyn. She was a first-tier, and right hand to the Mad Ones. She had been named the Viper because they sent her to annihilate any threat. None saw her coming and none survived her.

But it seemed there were first-tier warders and there were *first-tier warders*. Osric gave a roar and sent Gwendolyn flying through the air with a mighty burst of power.

'Touch my skin,' he ordered me quickly. I grabbed his arm and as we moved into the throng of warders I felt the pressure in the air that meant his shield had enveloped me. The bodies around us threw their wards again and again; there was a woozy kind of shimmer to the air, a swelling of the moon above. One or two of them tried to attack us physically, but I ran them through with my sword. An oversight, not to train the apprentices to use their bodies as well as their minds.

Osric seemed to be pinning Gwendolyn to the ground even as he was maintaining our shield. I could see sweat trickling into his eyes. The strength it must have been taking to keep her impotent and immobile; we reached the fallen warder and I met her eyes. I couldn't help it – I winked at her as we passed.

'Get to the house!' I heard Gwendolyn order her warders, and knew we'd have a few minutes to get away. It concerned me that she sent none after us, but perhaps she thought Osric would kill them.

To be safe he dropped his magic so they couldn't follow it, and we pressed ourselves into a hard sprint through the city. I made us pause and hide a dozen times to ensure we weren't being followed before we cut across to intercept Finn's group on its way to the tunnel. They'd hardly made any progress and were all huddled under a shop's eave not far from the house. 'Why aren't you moving?'

Finn's head whipped around to spot me. 'We can't find Penn!'

My heart fell.

'He hid when Izzy started screaming,' Jonah said. 'He can't handle that much feeling.'

'Gods curse it,' Osric muttered.

I caught Elias' eye. 'Get everyone to the tunnel. We'll follow.' He nodded and most of the group hurried off. 'Jonah, go with them in case they need protection.' Though what he would do against more than one warder I had no idea.

'I'm not leaving Penn.'

'Now,' I snapped, and whatever he heard in my voice must have alarmed him enough to obey. I had no patience for those who didn't follow orders in a crisis.

Finn, Osric and I started creeping back towards the house. I was scrabbling desperately to come up with some kind of plan. There was no way the warders wouldn't find him in there. We crouched a block from the courtyard, looking at each other for inspiration. 'Have you enough energy left to shield yourself again?' I asked Osric, but he shook his head.

'Not against Gwendolyn.'

Damn it.

'We have to *hurry*,' Finn whispered.

'Let me think.' But in my heart I was coming to one conclusion. We could not risk losing multiple people on a suicide mission to save one, when there was every chance he was already dead.

A tragedy, one Finn might never forgive me for.

Footsteps sounded in the night and we all turned to see Isadora – who only moments ago had been deeply unconscious – moving through the shadows.

'What in gods names?'

She didn't look at us, nor did she react as Finn pulled her to a halt. Her face was blank and slack, her eyes empty. 'Izzy?' Finn waved her hand in front of Isadora's face but the girl didn't react at all.

'I think she's . . . *sleepwalking*,' Finn whispered. 'Isn't she?'

Isadora's unblinking eyes noticed us for the first time. When she spoke her voice was lazy and lilting, as though she could barely get the words out. 'I'll get him,' was all she muttered, and then she pulled herself from Finn's grip and went for the wall. I grabbed for her but she was too quick, climbing up and over with the economic agility of a cat.

Finn passed a trembling hand over her eyes. 'I think I'm gonna be sick.'

'There's a chance she may yet be alright,' Osric said, deep in thought. 'If she was sleepwalking . . .' He scratched his chin absently.

'What?' I asked.

'Not sure. But warders can't enter dreams.'

'What does it matter? There are still too many!' Finn exclaimed. 'Way too many. Falco would *never* let her go in there alone.' She shook her head furiously and rose out of her crouch. 'I have power. I'm going.'

I pulled her roughly back down.

'Not enough, kid,' Osric told her. 'There are at least thirty of them.'

It came down to the same decision again. Finn was pleading with me to help. To *do* something. I was meant to be able to fix things but my hands were trembling with a wretched powerlessness. This was beyond me. If we followed them in, the three of us would die.

And perhaps I would have made that choice earlier tonight, before Falco did what he did. Perhaps I would have chosen not to let them die alone, perhaps it would have been enough to die fighting for friends. But now I had no idea what the Emperor of Kaya would ever be capable of again, and if this country had no ruler, and no heir, no one

187

who even knew of our plan, it would crumble to dust. Which meant I couldn't afford to let the three of us die.

Isadora and Penn were on their own.

ISADORA

I should have known.

But madness had taken over my limbs and all I wanted was an end to it. So I drank the sleeping draught given to me by the Queen of Pirenti. She had no idea what she'd condemned me to, could have no way to know. But I should have.

Sleep was quick – it was a strong potion. Then came the pain. Pain to tether me to awareness – and there was *so much* pain. It would trap me here in this ravaged body, here in this realm of nightmares, lucid and knowing it, *feeling* it.

It was the void. The nightmare had sent me straight back to the screaming void. I had to get out. I had to find a way to get out. I had to, right now, right now now *now*. But the pain was everywhere. It wasn't part of my body it was just everything and I couldn't breathe or find my way up and I didn't know which direction up was or even if up existed in this madness, I had to get out right now, right –

'Isadora.'

The screaming went quiet. Everything went quiet and there he stood in the cold dark of it.

He wasn't the real Falco. The real Falco didn't look at me like that, with love in his crystal eyes. This was Falco as I dreamed him in my most secret of hearts. I was about to speak when he pressed a finger to his lips to quiet me. That's how I heard the words.

We can't find Penn. He's hiding.

A second stretched into an eternity and then

Falco bridged the space between us and whispered into my ear, 'Don't wake up.'

Pain sheathed through my head, a very different kind of pain. Much sharper, more pointed. I was in my body once more, and I was not in the void but being carried in someone's arms through the normal dark of the city at night, and I was still asleep.

Don't go, I whispered in my heart, but he was already gone.

'Shit,' the person in whose arms I lay muttered. 'Sorry, little one.' It was Anders, and he reached to wipe the blood from where he'd knocked my scalp against a wall. The moment he caught sight of my open eyes his hand jerked away and he set me down. 'Isadora?'

They couldn't find Penn. So within the dream realm I turned and forced my body to move, to work. It was almost impossible; the pain allowed it, but so too did it make it difficult. I was a skeleton under water, barely in control. This was how it would feel to be a ghost, I imagined. How it must feel for Quillane and Radha.

It only came to me very slowly that Finn was in front of me and halting my path. *I'll get him*, I promised her. I thought I promised her, but perhaps not.

Concentrate now, I willed myself. *You must concentrate.* I had no weapons. Somewhere in the chaos they'd gone from my body. I was climbing into a house *full* of warders. And my muscles carried a thousand lead weights, the entire volume of the ocean was in my heart, and I was missing him and missing him and –

They had Penn in the living room.

He looked petrified as I crept through the courtyard. I could see his heart through his chest, glowing with blood and throbbing throbbing throbbing. Perhaps this was how Penn saw all hearts, perhaps this was how he felt them, as I could feel his now. The roof of the house creaked and then with a rumble it detached entirely, flying up and away into a clear night sky filled with stars. I wanted to go with it. Wanted to take Penn in my arms and carry him up, up until we couldn't see the ground any longer –

Concentrate.

At least a score of warders stood around him, waiting for their orders, while Gwendolyn the Viper crouched and spoke to him. '. . . did they go?' Her voice drifted to me as I drew closer. 'It's no good. His mind's blank. We'll take him to the palace.'

'No,' I murmured.

Because. The hunter or the hunted.

They whirled to see me, hands flying impotently.

'Run, Penn!' I roared, flinging myself into the fray. Several grabbed at him, but I attacked them first, my blows as heavy and sharp as I could make them. Penn stumbled to the ground and I pulled him against my side, using one arm to drag him through the chaos of arms and legs hitting and batting at me.

'Stop her!' the Viper was ordering again and again but they couldn't, they wouldn't, not ever. I would drag him forever, I would never let go.

I felt arms wrench me back so I lashed out with an elbow and took the warder in the face. The coward dropped me and I swung wildly at anything I could reach, anything that was in my way or pulling me back, and always I was *hauling* Penn's struggling body towards the door. I felt a chunk of my hair ripped out and fingernails raked at my neck, drawing blood, but I was already bleeding and it didn't matter because we were here, we'd made it. I shoved Penn roughly into the courtyard and turned back to block the way.

'Izzy,' he sobbed, 'come *on*.'

'Run,' I told him, and then I fought, properly now, going for eyes and testicles and throats, anywhere that would drop them quickly.

They were too many, of course. They were always going to be too many. Even with weapons, even with full control of my body, it would have been so. One too many blows to the head and they overpowered me, pinning my struggling body to the ground. I looked to see that Penn was gone, he'd made it away. Hopefully the warders rushing after him wouldn't be quick enough to catch up.

I allowed myself to stop. A life for a life, then. A tainted life for an innocent one. An unfair trade, really. And too easy. Far too easy.

'You surprise me, demon child,' Gwendolyn said. 'And I'm not easily surprised. What are you? Why are you invisible to our wards?'

I spat in her face.

She wiped her cheek. 'Take her to the palace.'

It's alright, it's alright. This was your plan all along. I just had to stay asleep long enough to get free and find a weapon. But I knew, even as I thought it, that the sleeping draught would not keep working forever, not in this kind of danger. I would wake sooner or later, and they'd be able to kill me with their magic.

And so as I watched the falling stars in a sky made of dreams, I thought of my end, this approaching return to the screaming void. I thought of the bowels of the underworld and the strange beauty of the dream realm, which I would never again visit beyond tonight. But I wondered, as they carried me south to the palace, what the breaths in my lungs or the beats in my heart or even the most beautiful fantasms I could dream up were worth without him, without Falco of Sancia.

Chapter 13

Thorne

The timing was not ideal.

The moment Finn's power and pain hit me full force in the chest, the moment she broke the bond between two souls using the energy of my own and caused me to collapse to the ground, happened to be the exact moment I was trying to kill Sigurd of Vjort.

Falco

I woke in the dark to the smell of death and rot. I felt raw. Lacerated. Weak beyond belief.

'Thank gods,' a voice said and my eyes adjusted to a yellow gaze staring down at me. Finn helped me sit; my muscles were as stiff as if they'd never been used. We were in the cool room above the tunnel. The whole group was huddled around, waiting for me to wake.

A spike of severe nausea took me and I leant over to retch violently. Pain was a shock behind my eyes and down my neck. It took some moments to gather myself well enough to look up. Finn had tears in her eyes and Jonah was pacing, and Ava looked shadowed with regret. Penn was counting and counting and counting and –

'Where is she?' I asked.

I couldn't feel her. It hit me, the absence. I was shivering with a bone-deep cold and I knew I *knew* that this wasn't right, it wasn't natural. The absence was the most *wrong* thing I'd ever felt.

'You're in shock,' Sara said, wrapping me in a cloak that could never help with the kind of cold I was.

'*Where?*'

'They took her!' Penn burst out. 'They took her! They took her! They took her!' It was a *wail*, a mourning cry, barely intelligible but persistent like a heartbeat.

'The warders felt Finn break the bond and came for us,' Ava said. 'We escaped, but Penn was left behind. Isadora went back for him. She was . . .'

'She got Penn out, but there must have been too many to face on her own,' Osric finished.

'They took her.' Penn's voice had fallen to a whisper.

I closed my eyes. Through the maddening emptiness and the jagged shards of my soul, I needed to find some kind of clarity.

Too many to face on her own. Which meant many. The warders had Isadora at the palace. She would wake, if she hadn't already. If she wasn't dead. When she did they would make her reveal all. The tunnel, our plan, her identity and my presence. Everything. How did I feel about this? I searched for an answer. Angry. I felt angry. With her, with them, with myself. With the whole gods-cursed world. I felt barely human, a creature made of fury. But at least, I realised, I no longer felt chained to a murderess.

I looked at my cousin. 'Start evacuating as many as you can tonight.'

'And you?'

'I'm going after Isadora.'

There was a lot of arguing then. *It was far too dangerous, it was a suicide mission, someone else should go but who should it be, who had the best chance, etcetera, etcetera, etcetera.* I barely listened. Instead, I made plans.

'Falco.' Ava's voice eventually cut through my thoughts. Finn and Jonah were arguing about something and Penn was still counting tiredly, while most of the others had already started the long journey through the tunnel. 'This is why you broke the bond,' the Queen told me. 'So you wouldn't *have* to save her. Her death will not cause yours.'

She was baiting me to see if I'd admit I felt something for her. That I wanted to go after Isadora because of our connection. But I didn't, and I wouldn't. 'She knows too much,' I replied.

'So let someone else go. Let Osric. He might be able to shield against their power.' Which was obviously bullshit. If Osric could shield against every palace warder at the same time, including Dren and Galia, he would have told me by now and we wouldn't have a problem to begin with. But instead of calling out the lie, I simply asked, 'All magic aside, can Osric fight? Because he will need to. That place is swarming with soldiers proficient with fists and swords.'

We both glanced at Osric. We all knew he couldn't fight: Ava's abysmal lesson on the road to Kaya had been evidence enough.

'So I'll go to protect him,' she said.

I shook my head impatiently. 'People take one look at you and know exactly who you are. I'm completely unrecognisable, and I have a natural shield. I will enter as Isadora did, on a work permit. They'll read only what surface thoughts I give them.'

'Say you're right and they *happen* not to probe any deeper. Then what? You ask the Mad Ones nicely to let her go?' she snapped.

I shrugged. 'I'll improvise.'

'Gods almighty.' Ava rubbed her eyes wearily. 'Are we going to talk about the fact that your own argument excludes you from the task? You asked Osric if he could fight, which he can't. But Falco – neither can you.'

I folded my arms, resting my throbbing skull against the wall. My headache was getting worse. 'I have a few tricks up my sleeve, cousin.'

Her eyebrows furrowed. She was at her wits end.

'And if she's dead?' Osric asked.

'She's not dead.'

'You won't feel it if she –'

'She's not dead.'

'How do you *know*?' Ava demanded.

I nearly said it. *Because Isadora is the Sparrow, and when they learn that there's no way in this world that Dren and Galia will kill such a powerful tool.* But my tongue stayed. Why? I didn't owe her anything. I had certainly never agreed to keep this secret for her. It was a matter of national security – Isadora was an enemy to Kaya. Still, I didn't tell them. 'You'll have to trust me.'

My cousin stared at me and then shook her head. 'Fine. Do as you will. But remember one thing for me, and remember it with every decision you make.'

I waited.

Ava leaned forward and held my eyes. 'Your life is more important than hers, every time. Understood?'

I let out a breath. And nodded.

ISADORA

The royal hall was unusually full. Dozens of servants and guards lined the walls, while warders and nobles who had once belonged to Falco's court mingled and drank. It was not one of the grotesque parties enjoyed in the pool rooms, rather it seemed I was interrupting a more formal celebration. Dren and Galia sat on their thrones covered neck-to-toe in richly woven gold. Hundreds of birdcages had been brought in from the smaller entertaining chambers and hung from the high ceiling and marble pillars. Coloured feathers glittered unnaturally and I struggled to look away from the captive creatures, their chirps and flutters and squawks echoing in my ears. The enormous room was filled with noise, colour and expectation.

How disappointed the courtiers would be when they discovered it was just little old me who'd been captured.

I did not come before Dren and Galia as I had many times before, cowering and carrying drinks, hair and skin tanned to make me acceptable. No, today I was brought forward by six well-trained palace guards – who, unlike the warders, knew very well how to fight – and by Gwendolyn the Viper. Today I was brought forward in all my freakish splendour, skin and hair white for my hatred, eyes the red of my fury, which lived in me always.

Our arrival caused a stir. Everyone in the room turned to see me being paraded through the parting crowd. I heard gasps and whispers at my appearance: *how dare I even* exist *here among the perfect people*? It made me smile. Because with the bond gone from me, I was at last able to determine what remained.

Perfect clarity: I was the gods-cursed Sparrow of Kaya, leader of the southern rebels and ruler of three hard-earned southern realms, and I would destroy this palace and all in it – whether they be warder or soldier, servant or noble – just as I had always planned. The bond had made me soft; its absence made me brutal.

The world created its monsters, so here I stood.

We stopped directly before the thrones. 'Did you contain whoever used such power?' Galia asked. 'Where are they?'

'I'm afraid they had already fled by the time we followed the trail to their residence, Majesty.'

A storm of fury crossed Galia's face and she lashed out at the nearest servant, snapping the poor man's neck with a burst of pressure. A flicker of fear passed through the nobles in the crowd. I felt no pity for them. Not for those whose loyalty could be bought and traded.

'And did you *follow* them?'

'No, Majesty. They were cloaked.'

'Who could possibly have enough power to cloak against *you*?'

'Osric.'

Dren and Galia both froze. I might have missed it. But I was different now, intimately acquainted with pain and terror. So see it I did. Their fear.

'*Osric* is here?' Dren demanded.

'He is.'

'And you let him get away.'

Gwendolyn was the picture of detached calm; in her there was no fear whatsoever. 'We were detained, Majesty.'

'Detained. What exactly was it that *detained* you from tracking down the only disloyal first-tier warder in the world?' Galia asked. 'And you'd better pray you have a good enough answer, Gwendolyn.'

'The girl before you.'

Dren and Galia's eyes swivelled to me. A long silence filled the crowded hall.

'She's hideous,' Dren muttered, his silver gaze fixed on me as though he couldn't believe what he was seeing.

'What is she?' Galia asked.

'I don't know.'

'She must have done something quite terrible to have crossed paths with you, Viper,' Galia said.

'Not only did we discover her entering the residence where the resistance had been hiding, but she attacked my team and harmed several of my warders. She is most certainly an insurgent.'

Dren was frowning. 'Harmed several warders? Why did you let her do that?'

I heard Gwendolyn hesitate for the first time. 'She is impervious to our magic.'

The Mad Ones' eyes whipped back to me. I smiled. And for the first time in my life it was an easy expression.

A rustle of unease moved through the hall. The birds flapped nervously in their cages, the echoing sound lifted by the dream to wrap me in protection. I could feel their feathers against my face.

Galia crossed to stand very close to me; in the dream she smelled rank and true. 'How?' she wondered aloud. I knew she was trying and failing to enter my mind. I could feel her poisonous *tap tap tap* to get in. 'What is your name?'

'You know my name.'

'Not blocked from your mind as we are,' Dren snapped.

I kept my eyes on Galia and saw anger spark. She didn't like my lack of fear, didn't like how much power I seemed to hold over her. She slapped me across the face and I was grateful for the pain as I used it to hone the edges of the dream realm.

'There's more, Majesty,' Gwendolyn said. I might have marvelled – she was as calm as I'd ever been. 'She was not the only one we found at the rebel house.' The Mad Ones shifted their attention back to the Viper. 'Hiding in a cupboard was Penn of Limontae. Your son.'

Dead silence. Into it Galia asked, '*Excuse me?*'

To her credit, Gwendolyn held her ground. 'He's clearly in league with the insurgent. She risked her life to free him.'

Any anger I had seen Dren and Galia display previously was as nothing to what came over them now. Both sets of eyes shifted white and Gwendolyn hit the floor, writhing in pain. The birds screeched; some of them dropped dead. Fear pressed the guests back as they urgently tried to escape the violence.

On the ground before me the Viper was screaming and clawing at her head. I watched without an ounce of sympathy. *Try having your bond severed, you bitch.*

The grips of the guards holding my arms tightened. Gwendolyn's scream finally cut off and she sagged in relief as the pain stopped.

Slowly she climbed to her feet and straightened her shoulders. I could see a trickle of blood in her ear.

Galia was trembling with rage. 'What is the first law of our rule?'

The Viper replied and still, *still* she was without fear. 'That your son is to be found at all costs.'

Interesting.

'You will be punished. Make your way to the dungeon until I have decided by which means.'

Gwendolyn bowed her head and strode from the hall, shoulders and spine straight. I didn't have time to admire her strength – something wasn't sitting right. If Penn's capture was the most important rule of the warders, then why had Gwendolyn let him get away? I was impervious to her magic, yes, but Penn wasn't. She could have wrapped him in a ward so I couldn't touch him and then dealt with me separately. I had trouble believing she was foolish enough for it not to have occurred to her – she was the Viper for a reason.

'You are acquainted with our son,' Dren said, interrupting my thoughts.

Silence.

'Answer me!'

'You didn't ask a question.'

He visibly restrained himself from flying into another rage. I restrained myself from grinning. Some part of me had snapped. I'd gone so far beyond pain that nothing was registering anymore, and frankly, I just wanted to hurt people. Watching Dren and Galia squirm was a steady thrill to my pulse. It was the point of it all.

'How do you know Penn?' Galia asked. 'Is he working with your insurgent group?'

I tilted my head slightly. Did they really think I'd just tell them?

'Are you manipulating or controlling him to help you?'

When I didn't answer, Dren turned to his partner. 'She must know of his power. Why else risk her life for him?'

Both sets of eyes returned to me, but now the Mad Ones watched me with a different kind of wariness. As if I were a creature who possessed the key to their undoing. It didn't once occur to them that I might have saved their son out of love.

A commotion sounded at the back of the hall, murmured voices and shuffling footsteps.

'What's wrong?' Dren called.

One of the guards answered. 'A guest. He's . . . unconscious, Majesties.'

'Did he drink too much?' Galia rolled her eyes.

'I don't think so –'

A second commotion started on the other side of the room and I craned my neck to see that another body had dropped. A third went down amid gasps of fear, then a fourth, all unconscious for no apparent reason.

'Warders will immediately extinguish all use of magic,' Galia ordered.

A fifth body hit the floor.

'It's no ward,' Dren told Galia softly.

'Then someone is here,' she muttered, eyes darting around.

I peered through the crowds. The guards were patrolling with weapons at the ready, looking for any sign of disruption.

'Warders to the edges of the room,' Galia called.

The warders moved back so that Dren and Galia could study those who remained – the guests. But no one was studying the servants. The pretty, dumb servants, overlooked every time. Among them I saw a flash of golden hair – not unusual in a land of golden-haired beauties. But I had not been bonded to any of the other golden-haired beauties.

It was the shock of seeing him that made it happen.

I woke.

Galia's gaze snapped directly to me and a terrible smile curled her lips. We both knew that I was no longer the hunter.

'Hello, pet.'

FALCO

It was easier than I'd thought to get in. I didn't have a work pass but the guards took one look at me and waved me through. I understood now why Isadora made herself look the way she had – all the people around me were golden-haired, tan-skinned copies of each other. It repulsed me that I looked like them. But I was no stranger to it:

these were the kinds of people with whom I had taken my pleasure as Emperor Feckless, ever weary of their endless *sameness*. Beauty lived in imperfection, in difference, and if I knew nothing else at least I had always known this. For a moment I saw Quill's incredible black hair, so unusual for a Kayan, and felt the loss of it in my chest. I wouldn't see her glorious raven hair again, thanks to the ruthlessness of the woman I was now forced to rescue.

I swallowed the nauseating bitterness – now wasn't the time. I was dressed in loose white pants and no shirt, and then ushered to the kitchen area for serving duty.

It will look like a brown leaf in a bunch, Sara had told me before I left, for I'd noticed she knew a little of such things. *Combined with valerian root, it will drop them like flies.*

Becoming a servant reminded me – ironically – of becoming an Emperor. Both were acts. Both required attention to detail. To be Emperor was to manifest arrogance and elegance. For a servant my body would need to shift. Turned-in shoulders, shuffling feet, head lowered. Erased was all trace of privilege or arrogance. And as different as the two men were, I now felt the same kind of invisibility I'd felt as Feckless. As an Emperor, I was forbidden to be looked upon. As a servant, nobody bothered. Lucky, too, for although no one had ever seen them, rumours of my strange eyes had been circulating for years. I could will them and will them to shift until the world burnt out, but I had no control and never had. So it suited me just fine to be utterly ignored.

The trouble was getting access to the food, but I knew the palace like the back of my hand. I tracked around to the back entrance and picked through rushing cooks and their assistants, passed roaring fires and industrial stoves. Servants ran trays in and out. One of them shoved me roughly out of the way, but the poor boy looked petrified with fear. A couple of guards were watching over the staff so I moved with purpose straight for the food stores. It took too long to find the herbs, but I managed to spot the brown leaves and stuff a few into my pocket.

'I haven't seen you before.' I turned to the guard watching me. 'Where's your kitchen pass?'

My eyes moved to his weapon – a baton at his belt. I could take it from him so easily, use it against him before he'd drawn breath.

A young man dressed as a servant appeared behind him. He looked at me irritably. 'Not in here, idiot,' he chided. To the guard he muttered, 'He's new. I sent him for drinks.'

'I didn't know where . . .' I blustered.

'Deal with him,' the guard snapped.

The man who'd chided me ushered me out into a hallway. His annoyance dropped the moment we were alone. 'What are you doing?' he asked softly, glancing left and right. He looked like the others – tall, well-muscled, blond and tan. He also had whip scars all over his shoulders.

I didn't have time to be suspicious of him. 'Thank you for your assistance.' I was about to push past him when he laid a hand on my arm.

'You're good. You look right. I wouldn't have picked it if I hadn't noticed you watching. I watch, but I'm not meant to. So when I see someone doing the same I get curious.' His fingers tightened and I looked into his wide azure eyes as they shifted lilac. 'Whatever you're doing, let me help.'

I studied his face, turning the idea over in my head. 'Why?'

'I *hate* them.'

'Don't they know if you hate them?'

'They know it well,' he bit out. 'Everyone in here hates them. They don't care.'

This was reckless, but so was the whole bloody thing, and I was pressed for time. 'I need valerian root. And a needle. Two, if you really want to help.'

He nodded and turned back to the kitchen, pausing only to say, 'I'm Ryan.'

'Pleasure, Ryan. If we survive this I'll tell you my name.'

I waited for him beneath a set of stairs where I'd hidden as a child. It was just as dusty as it had been then. My brothers and I had coughed and giggled and waited to see how long we could stand it before bursting out for a gasp of clean air. Later, I had come here alone to hide from the servants, nobles, informants, assistants, chancellors and warders who all wanted more and more and *more* from their new emperor, forgetting he was but a ten-year-old boy.

Ryan returned and I whistled to get his attention. When he was safely squashed under the stairs he showed me his loot. 'Why'd you get four needles?'

'There are a couple of others who'll help, if you want.'

I nearly smiled. This was looking more and more like a suicide mission by the minute. 'Why not?'

As I mushed the root and leaves together I explained to Ryan what I needed. We dipped the tips of the needle into the paste and he took the extras to pass onto his friends. 'Whatever you do, don't accidentally prick yourself.'

We emerged from the stairs and ran headlong into two guards. I slammed my elbow into a temple and swung a fist into a jaw. Both guards dropped unconscious to the ground. The simple physical movements exhausted me and I blinked woozily against the spots in my eyes. I started dragging one of them to the alcove beneath the stairs.

Ryan stared at me.

'*Help*, kid,' I urged, and he jumped into action, dragging the second body.

'I had this ridiculous notion that you were the Emperor,' he said with a laugh. 'What an idiot.'

I almost laughed too.

We split up and made our way separately to the main hall. I managed to convince a server that she was required back at the kitchen so I could pinch her tray of delicacies. Holding it high to cover my face, I moved into the hall and was met with the sight of hundreds of people, and at their center, Isadora.

Six guards held her prostrate before Dren and Galia. They were on *my* thrones. Thrones that had once belonged to my ma and da, and to my own Empress Quillane.

The rage in my heart was unquenchable.

I remembered their faces from long ago, from the day I had them captured and sent to the prison, the day they screamed their threats and vowed to return. I had laughed, arrogant and humiliating. Quill hadn't, though. She'd taken it as seriously as she took everything.

'You are acquainted with our son,' Dren said to Isadora.

I moved swiftly through the crowd of onlookers, keeping my face turned away from the thrones.

'Answer me!'

'You didn't ask a question.'

My lips twitched. The Mad Ones continued to question her but she remained silent. She had to be asleep, if they couldn't force her to answer. Which was good – if I freed her from the guards she'd be able to get herself out.

Keeping the needle hidden within my sleeve, I pricked it into the back of a man's hand and kept moving past him. It only took a minute for him to drop to the floor, asleep. Across the room Ryan and his friends were doing the same and more bodies dropped. Fear rippled through the hall. People weren't sure what to do. Dren and Galia ordered all magic to cease, which was exactly what I wanted. I pricked a few more nobles, trying to drive the crowd to panic, but their fear of Dren and Galia outweighed even the threat of being rendered unconscious. I would have to spill some blood.

That was when Isadora flew straight into the air.

A communal gasp tore through the crowd, a woman screamed and the birds went nuts in their cages, flapping and screeching desperately. Galia had her hand extended to hold Isadora frozen. The little Sparrow had woken.

I cursed. I couldn't prick her back to sleep while she was in the air. Ryan arrived at my elbow with a questioning look. I motioned for him to wait.

'Silence!' Dren yelled and the room fell to a terrified hush.

'Not impervious after all,' Galia said. 'But her mind is still closed to me.' The woman was studying Isadora with a wicked smile. 'Just like *pet's*.'

'No,' Dren breathed.

'It is,' Galia laughed. 'You fooled us, poor pet.'

'Gods above,' Ryan whispered beside me.

'You know her?' I asked.

'Yes. She . . . didn't look like that.'

I started weaving closer to the thrones. Ryan followed.

'It was you, then.' Galia was still addressing Isadora. 'You killed twelve warders in this palace.'

A rustle of outrage from the warders in the room.

'It's not possible,' Dren argued. 'She's defective.'

'Don't be obtuse,' Galia snapped.

I caught sight of Isadora's face. She was impossibly cold. If I were to cut open her chest I would find a heart made of chiseled ice sitting in the cavity. Softly, very softly, she said, 'It was so easy to kill them. Warders are such cowards.'

The hall went still.

Dren and Galia stared at her and she looked right back, eyes a deeper red than ever. Red like vein's blood. My heart pounded in an unfamiliar way.

'We can't let them kill her,' Ryan whispered urgently.

Leaning close, I said, 'When this all turns sour, get your friends and family out of the palace and take them to the wharfs under cover of dark. There you'll find a tunnel – a way out of the city. Say I sent you.'

'You haven't told me your name.'

'I have a feeling you'll soon learn it.'

'You're going to regret that,' Galia told Isadora. 'You're going to regret everything: your entire life, your very existence in this world.'

I watched as my bondmate writhed in the air with sudden pain.

No. Not my mate.

Blood trickled from her ears and nose and eyes. *What the fuck were they doing to her?* I didn't stop to think – I smashed my tray into a nearby guard's face and blood splattered onto the marble. The sudden violence pushed everyone past their stress limits and they started scrabbling for the exits. I melted into the chaotic melee, forcing my way towards the Mad Ones. I had to stop them somehow from breaking into Izzy's mind –

A single, ear-splitting scream tore from her lips. Lips I had kissed as I sheathed a knife in her heart. She dropped to the ground and crumpled like a tiny, broken doll.

And Dren and Galia turned as one to me.

They knew.

They had broken through whatever natural shield Isadora had over her mind, and they'd learned all that she was and everything she knew of me. My body locked. I couldn't move a muscle. I was too late, unable now to prick Izzy back to sleep. We were both at the mercy of the Mad Ones.

The whole room froze and I realised I was not the only one who'd been locked. Everyone – all the guests, all the guards, all the servants – were bound by warder magic so heavy that I could feel its prickle in the air. The birds dropped dead in their cages, and in the absence of their screeching it felt like someone had sucked the sound from the world.

An invisible hand dragged me forwards until I stood next to Isadora. She'd regained consciousness but looked drowsy with pain as she struggled to sit. I tried to reach for her but my body was no longer mine.

'This might be the best day of my life,' Dren crowed.

Galia was just as delighted. 'Ladies and gentlemen. I'd like to introduce two very famous people.'

No. *No no no.*

She turned all the bodies in the room to face Isadora and me; their feet moved with a collective, military step that echoed. Then Galia spun the two of us to face them and it was hideous, it was a puppet show, not a single set of eyes able to blink of their own accord. We just stared and stared and waited.

'Before you stands Falco of Sancia, dethroned Emperor of Kaya, and the rebel Sparrow of the South herself.'

Shock hit, and disbelief. They didn't need to move for me to feel it, it was so potent.

'Both are enemies of Kaya,' Galia went on, her anger rising. 'And they will be punished for their crimes against our proud, exultant nation.'

That was rich.

'Death is too good for such destructive terrorists,' she said, appealing to the crowd, though for what I had no idea, since not one of them could show her any agreement. 'Death is freedom. No, instead we must seek a more apt punishment.'

No doubt something humiliating, torturous and traumatic, just for fun.

'Emperor Feckless,' Galia mused. 'The man of a thousand faces. What an embarrassment you've been to us.' She glanced at her mate. 'What kind of man doesn't recognise his own reflection?'

'The master of disguise inevitably forgets his true face,' Dren agreed.

They were rifling through my soul and speaking the truths they found. I'd never felt more naked, more revealed, more like an empty husk.

'Their punishment is too precious to waste,' I heard Galia murmur. 'Let's think on it.'

'The dungeons then, for now.'

The Mad Ones gestured and the world went dark.

ISADORA

I woke slowly to the sound of soft voices floating around me. My head pounded, trying to crack through its own skull.

'So what did you do?'

'Failed to bring you in.'

'Oh, well, then I'm rather glad you're in here.'

Blinking carefully, I managed to slide my aching body upright against a wall. When my vision returned I saw a dungeon cell, and in cells on either side of me sat Falco and Gwendolyn, chatting with no apparent concern for their whereabouts.

'She wakes,' Falco said.

I rubbed my temples, trying to ease the ache. I'd need my wits about me for this, whatever this was. Being held captive between two of my greatest enemies. Who were apparently completely at ease in each other's company.

'What are you doing here?' I managed to ask Falco without looking at him.

He smiled flippantly. 'Saving you. Obviously.'

'Why?'

'Because you know what I know. Which is now also what the Mad Ones know.'

Of course. I glanced at him surreptitiously, trying to weigh how I felt. There was no longer a tide pulling me to him. My skin didn't itch to touch his. My lips didn't tingle with his absence. But my soul still screamed and my heart held an endless weariness I now understood was the lack of his heart alongside it.

I turned my thoughts to more important things, taking in the prison cell and its trappings. 'They don't know everything,' I muttered.

'What do you mean?'

I couldn't mention anything to do with our friends or the tunnel with the Viper right there, so I met his eyes. 'They don't know what's important.'

He understood, the fear that had clouded his expression easing. 'How?'

I swallowed and shrugged. I didn't know how to describe the battle that had taken place in my mind. When Dren and Galia had waged an assault on my thoughts I had cloaked myself in the thickest, calmest lake I was able to conjure. I made every surface reflective and gave them back their own thoughts. When they went down one path I flooded it. They turned down another and I flooded it too. And yet I hadn't been able to block everything. They were too strong. They found Falco, despite how I fought. They found him because he was right there at the surface, impossibly raw. But I wouldn't let them have anything else. Never would I let them have what mattered. So to distract them from the people currently fleeing through the tunnel and the army hidden in the forest, I had given them me. My childhood, my life, my fury. All the secrets I'd kept for so many years, the ones I had shared with no one. I gave them my cage, even though it was giving them my very soul.

And I *would* give them my soul, if it bought Finn, Jonah and Penn's freedom. I would give it freely. Only I wasn't sure who would take that deal. There wasn't much of my soul left.

I turned to Gwendolyn. 'You let Penn go. Why?'

She studied me, then glanced at Falco. 'You wouldn't believe me.'

'Try us,' Falco said.

'I couldn't allow myself to know I would do it before I did.'

I stared at her, confused. Then it sank in, the only thing such a statement could mean.

'You've surprised me,' Gwendolyn said. 'And few are able to.'

'Why?' I demanded, so sick of physical appearance being all anyone saw or judged. 'Because I look small and weak I should also behave so? That thinking will be the downfall of even the strongest.'

The Viper inclined her head. 'You must prepare yourselves,' she warned. 'They will be planning something very bad for you.'

Falco met my eyes for only an instant before turning away. 'We have already known something very bad,' he said. 'I dare them to try.'

And though he hadn't meant to, he bolstered me. Fortified my edges, my shields, the surface of my lake. His courage inspired my own. *I dare them to try.*

'When the time comes, remember – it's not as far as it looks,' Gwendolyn said.

We had no time to question what she meant. The Mad Ones had come. They blacked out the world once more, and this time when I woke it was to find . . .

A cage, hanging over a chasm.

And the end of courage.

The end of calm.

CHAPTER 14

AVA

In the dark we crawled. It was a bad place, this tunnel. A bad night. People wept as we led them through the narrow space, the blackness a heavy veil upon us. Some panicked, tried to get out but there was no going back, only forward, and slowly.

Finn, Jonah and Penn had already led a group of a hundred people through and Osric and I were bringing up the rear of the second group we'd managed to wrangle: another two hundred.

Only three hundred citizens of Sancia. Pitifully few. We would keep going back for more but not until tomorrow night, and we would only have time to do so many trips before the warders discovered us.

As dawn broke we emerged, Osric and I the last two out. The crumbling cliffs broke away beneath us but we were close enough to sea level that scrabbling our way down was easy enough. From here we would head north along the rocky coastline.

An hour or so later Osric made his way back along the line of weary people. I was at the rear, making sure no one was left behind. 'We're far enough now,' he informed me. 'It's safe to connect you to your husband. Tell him to hurry.'

I nodded and a thrill quickened my weary heart. Osric closed his eyes and placed his hands on my temples. A tingling sensation ran down my spine, and then it hit me.

A tidal wave of pain. Excitement fled; there was only bone-deep terror. *The girls?* I screamed through our throbbing bond. *Where are our children?*

But he couldn't answer; he was a maelstrom.

Osric let me go and I staggered to the ground, a guttural moan pulled from my lungs. I was almost blinded by the pain but I squinted up at the warder and gasped, 'He's dying. My husband is dying and I have no idea where my daughters are.'

THORNE

For days and nights I ran, Howl by my side. Up through ice, through a cold deeper than any, flanked by wild, howling wolves.

I had traced the scent of my family through the city, slowed by soldiers who either attacked or offered help. Not all the soldiers of Vjort followed Sigurd – some still remained loyal to Ambrose and me. I followed the trail to the temple where Finn and I were married, my heart swelling in relief. Of course this was where they'd come.

But the temple was empty, the old couple dead. The scent had gone cold, and though I hunted every inch for a sign that they'd been here I found nothing, only the broken bodies of the people who'd married my wife and me. Which meant one thing: to find my family and avenge my King I needed my berserker army.

So through ice I ran until I reached the creatures under the mountain and bid them follow me south to war.

*

We stopped on a hill overlooking the city wall, taking a knee to catch our breath. Goran, once King of the berserkers and now my second, crouched beside me to survey Vjort. He was twice my size, a hulking boulder in the dark. He bore that rough, earthy scent of strength and threat, of animal, but never again would I be bothered by it; I took pride in knowing his strength belonged to me.

'Entrances?'

'The main gate is to the south. There are several further points of entry both east and west. All are guarded by no more than a few men but have warning bells to alert the barracks inside.'

'The number of men?'

'Ten thousand. But not all with Sigurd.'

'How many with him?'

I shrugged.

'Ten thousand, then.' Goran grunted.

Against one hundred berserkers.

'We take Sigurd and the six who work his trade and I guarantee the rest will fall to us.' Civil war in Pirenti was almost nonexistent. Despite Ambrose's noble beliefs about violence, our means of ascension to the throne caused the country to respect and fear its leader, forestalling any uprisings or dissent. We were, at heart, a loyal nation. It took a large disruption for someone like Sigurd to mount an open rebellion.

'They will fall,' came Goran's reply. Sigurd might feel safe rebelling now, but by dawn he most definitely would not. A lesson was coming for him.

There was a gaping wound in my chest that I would fill with blood; the treachery of disloyal men had now taken two fathers from me.

*

The plan was so simple it was hardly a plan at all. We walked straight up to the north gate in full view of the sentries on the wall and waited for them to ring the bells before we smashed our way through the locks. Let them know we were coming, let them all know.

My dozen wolves lifted their heads and howled our approach, long and chilling into the night. They flanked Goran and me at the forefront of our army with Howl at their head. I heard men shouting, saw them running. The bells had reached the barracks in the distance so it wouldn't be long before the troops organised. I had little fear that they would try to fight us. Pirenti men didn't fight berserkers. Pirenti men hoped and prayed that berserkers would fight with them and for them, but never against them.

We walked straight for Iceheart's.

The Jarl was nowhere to be found tonight. I signaled and Goran took his men inside to kill every soldier. This was where the business was done, where the women were sold, where Sigurd built his new empire. So it would be the first place to fall. They fought back, but not for long. Once the tavern was empty of the living, I burned it to the ground.

We surged through the streets; it had begun to snow. Past the square in which I'd committed my first executions. That night was clearer in my memory than any other. I remembered swinging my axe into the necks of those four men. I remembered their expressions, their mouths and eyes, the way their blood had fallen on the snow, the scent of their fear and then their deaths. I remembered how I'd felt that night, how heavy with despair, and with a cool kind of detachment I realised I felt no such thing now, on this eve of many, many more executions. I felt nothing, only hunger.

Da spoke up then, but not in the way I'd come to expect from him. He stalked through the snow at my side, and said, 'Easy, son. We kill the guilty – the traitors, the threats, those who have harmed or seek to harm us. We don't kill for pride, and we don't kill the innocent.'

He stopped in front of me, staying my feet. Then my father said, 'Strength is not bloodlust.'

My mouth twisted into a bitter grimace. I felt betrayed. *After all these months of you poking and prodding and pushing me to be like you – to be ruthless and brutal – now you pull away scared?*

I shook my head and strode forward, leaving him behind. My real father was Ambrose and he was dead. I needed no other and never had. Thorne was soft after all, just like Sigurd and the rest of them, like all but my berserkers and me.

We reached the castle and I waited at the bottom of the steps. By now there was a wide crowd of onlookers. Contingents of military lined the street, waiting for commands. Men and women had come from their houses, drawn by the promise of violence.

'Fetch the traitor,' I said. Goran smiled and took the wide stone steps three at a time.

He was not long in the castle. Soon Sigurd emerged and, after only a slight hesitation, descended to meet me. He was flanked by a dozen of his own men, but he smelled like he was about to piss his breeches in terror. He managed to maintain the mocking act, pausing several steps above me. 'Princeling.'

I clasped my hands behind my back. 'Where are the royal princesses and the Lady Roselyn?'

Sigurd frowned. 'Lost your women, princeling? Don't look at me – we couldn't find them either.'

'And the King?'

The Jarl leant forward, holding my eyes. 'I killed him. Nice and slow, while he begged for mercy.'

My lips curled, baring my teeth. The wolves sensed my intent and let out low growls. 'My berserkers want blood,' I told Sigurd. 'Shall I set them free to destroy this cursed city once and for all?'

'I have ten thousand men at my back.'

I turned and surveyed the street. 'Actually,' I murmured, 'they look as though they're at my back.'

Sigurd made a gesture to the soldiers who'd been with him in the castle. 'Sound the order to attack.'

I looked up at these soldiers. They were watching the berserkers spread out behind me, and glancing at each other uncertainly. I met the eyes of the one in front, Sigurd's right hand. 'Feel free,' I told him. He hesitated, weighing us up, weighing it all, and then he bowed low to me. The rest of Sigurd's soldiers were quick to do the same.

Goran gave a shout and lifted his fist high in the air. Within moments a hundred berserkers were giving the guttural shouts of battle – *awhoo, awhoo, awhoo* – and within the din I walked forward, placed my hand around Sigurd's neck and lifted him off the ground.

'You fashion yourself a king. But usurpers have small souls and small hearts, and are the smallest men of all.'

His fear spiked, and his shame. I breathed them in.

And that was when somewhere in this world Finn broke the bond between two lovers, using the power that had been born into my soul, and it caused my head to explode. I dropped Sigurd and sank to my knees, clutching at my skull.

And the bastard slid his knife between my ribs.

AMBROSE

As I lay in a tomb beneath the city, waiting to die, I looked at my hands and no longer recognised them. They did not belong to my body, to my heart or my mind; they were foreign, corrupt things. How did I once bear them with confidence and pride? How did I not see them for the weapons, the monstrous blights that they were?

I saw the blood they spilt, the flesh they tore, the death they wrought. Untold pain, from these hands. Havoc, from each and every finger. They were strong – *too* strong, absurdly strong. Their violence . . . and always seeking to commit more. To fight and fight and fight and *fight*. This endless, unendurable scrabbling tooth and nail for life, but what was that life worth?

Who was the man greater than the acts of violence he committed? That man did not exist.

Cut them off. Look where they've brought you. Look how deep the violent hands of men have buried this nation –

The semi-lucid thoughts ended there. My body had been brutalised and was not long for this world.

THORNE

'You coward,' I grunted.

Sigurd crouched over me. 'They say it of you both, you know,' he murmured. 'Not just your uncle, but you too. That you're immortals. Giants. Impossible to kill, impossible to vanquish. But what do you know? You have both proven human after all.'

My head was throbbing. Whatever Finn had done had drained me to within an inch of consciousness. I couldn't yet feel the wound from his knife, but I knew it must be deep – the blade had disappeared to the hilt. The Jarl whispered, just for me, 'When I find her, I'll have your mother against her will, and then I'll do the same to that delicious little wife of yours.'

There was blood seeping from my side and long, sharp steel embedded in my abdomen. It didn't matter. Did he truly know *nothing* of what it meant to be King of the Ice? Even he, a man who called himself a son of Vjort?

I rose. The battle chant rang out around me. *Awhoo, awhoo, awhoo.* I took Sigurd's neck once more and this time I didn't waste my breath on him. I sliced my axe down the center of his chest and then dropped the blade carelessly. I reached into his chest and wrenched out his heart. Then I devoured it while his body fell like a ragdoll to the cobblestones. I devoured it while all the souls of Vjort watched and my wolves howled.

Never again would someone threaten my family.

Chapter 15

Falco

I sat up with a lurch and felt the ground beneath me sway. *What?* Eyes darting, I took in my surrounds with a dizzying sense of disorientation. I was inside a small iron cage, hanging over a disastrous drop. Hanging in her own cage beside me was an unconscious Isadora. I lurched towards her and the cage swung dangerously, planting me on my ass. She was too far to reach, even had I not been swaying woozily. The cages hung on chains attached to long metal poles that protruded out over the rocky chasm. I couldn't see what was above the lip of the chasm, nor could I see what was at the bottom of it – the sun's angle made the shadows below deep.

Unease crept in and before I knew what was happening I had begun to breathe too fast. My hands were trembling and the swaying seemed to worsen. *Stop it*, I bid myself. *You were born and raised at the top of a rocky aerie. You do not fear heights.*

I wrestled for control of myself by concentrating on my cage. I could find no door and no lock. If I stood . . . no, not even close. There was only enough room to kneel, and my head brushed the metal above. I could hold both sides at once, it was so narrow, and as I gripped the hard steel edges bit into the skin of my palms. I gave a sudden roar of fury, wrenching at the metal, shaking the cage as violently as I could. I would break it apart, rattle it so hard it fell to pieces.

The metal held; my palms bled.

What the fuck was going on?

The racket I was making finally reached Isadora. She stirred, and I felt a wild stab of relief at the mere thought of not being alone here any longer.

But as her eyes opened and she saw it, her cage and this chasm, a terrible scream erupted from her lungs.

And in that sound I realised why we were here, why this was the punishment the Mad Ones had chosen over all others. Whoever Isadora had become was because of this cage. This was what had scarred the inside of her sick, twisted heart. Here lived her madness.

She didn't stop screaming. I reached through my bars for her, but I was so far away and she couldn't hear me saying her name over and over, begging her with it, all she could hear was the swell of her own screaming, as though something had snapped in her mind. It went on and on until her throat was hoarse and nothing more would come out, just a rasping scrape and a gasp of pain, and then she curled into a ball and sobbed and sobbed and sobbed and sobbed.

I was sick with the horror of it; I couldn't stand it, couldn't make it stop. Night fell and she continued to weep. Morning rose and she continued to weep. She rocked back and forwards, covering her eyes with trembling hands. I tried to soothe her but I could think of nothing to say except her name, over and over as a mantra, as though I was Penn. She needed to be touched but I couldn't reach her. Even when we had been bonded, I realised, I hadn't been able to reach her.

My fury faded: it was impossible to hate someone who suffered so badly. Instead I closed my eyes and listened to the result of the world's cruelty.

As the sun sank on our second day in the cages, Isadora abruptly stopped crying – I could have started with relief. She looked utterly exhausted. But instead of falling asleep as I'd expected her to, she sat up and blinked swollen eyes.

'Forgive me.'

'*Are you alright?*' An immeasurably stupid question. 'I . . .' Fuck, what could I say? 'That was . . . that was really scary, Iz.'

'I'm alright,' she rasped.

'Do you . . . Where are we? What is this?'

She rubbed her eyes. 'Not yet.' And then she curled up and slept. I forced myself to do the same, even though my nerves were shattered and I couldn't shed the sound of her weeping from inside my pulse.

★

A cage was not a good place to sleep. My muscles twisted and cramped and as I woke all I wanted to do was stretch but there was no damn room. Grooves were gouged all over me from the sharp-edged metal, and my wounded hands throbbed. With a groan, I wriggled around to see that Isadora was already awake, the morning sun shining on her white hair.

'Massage your muscles,' she told me, sitting cross-legged.

I rolled my neck painfully. My stomach was rumbling with hunger pains and my head was pounding from dehydration. I wasn't sure how long we could survive here without food or water. But now that the wailing had stopped I was determined to find a way out. I set about inspecting every inch of the cage, as well as the chain above. It was solid, no sign of the forging joins. Which meant the damn thing had been sealed by warder magic.

'Don't bother,' Isadora said.

She'd never seemed so listless. So . . . adrift. It was easier to be angry with her now she was composed, but those hours of agony were etched on me. 'When were you here?'

She didn't reply. I followed her gaze and saw a flock of tiny birds in the distant sky. Isadora covered her mouth with her hands and gave a soft whistle. She did it twice more, and then we waited.

Two small birds circled closer and then landed on her cage, peering inside inquisitively. My mouth fell open in astonishment. It closed when Isadora's hand darted out to snatch one of the birds and snap its neck. She brought the dead creature to her face and whispered something to it, and then started to pluck its little feathers. I didn't say anything, but she felt my gaze. All she offered was, 'Sparrows.'

Sadness struck my heart. I felt ill-equipped for it, and wondered how long she'd had to survive on the meat of her namesake. When she finished plucking the bird she poked it through the bars and made as if to throw it to me.

'Wait!' I scrabbled to stick my hands through. 'Don't – you should eat it.'

'I'll catch another.'

'Well – wait, don't *throw* it.'

'Don't move,' she said. I kept my hands still as she tossed the dead bird straight into my palms, her aim as perfect as always.

Pulling it into my cage, I couldn't help feeling repulsed. 'How do I cook it?'

She didn't reply but she laughed. It was a striking sound, trickling water and falling ash. I abruptly saw myself through her eyes: a spoilt, entitled palace brat. I steeled myself and bit into the raw flesh of the small bird. It tasted awful and I struggled to keep it down.

'It will make you sick the first time,' Izzy warned me, 'but your stomach will get used to it.' She was busy seducing another sparrow to land on her cage, and let out a few more trills.

Indeed it did make me sick. The only blessing was that I managed to get most of my head out of the cage to vomit.

'Water?'

'Rain.' She shrugged. 'And urine.' I made a face and she smiled. 'It's wet around here. It rains every few days. But if you have to drink your piss, catch it in your boot.'

'How did you learn all of this?' I asked her, but she didn't reply. 'How did you get out the first time?'

She caught a second sparrow and killed it effortlessly. As she plucked it she said, 'I was meant to survive the first time. They needed me alive. When I fell ill they came to treat me and I escaped. But you and I are meant to die out here. There's no one coming to check our health.'

'So – what? That's it? Settle in and wait to die?' Just like that my anger rekindled.

We sat in silence for a long time. I pissed and caught it and drank it, and it was gods-awful. I tried to work my muscles as much as possible, doing sit-ups in the small space, hindered by the sway of the cage. Isadora sat utterly still as if in some kind of trance. Another night passed and we both slept a few uncomfortable hours. We didn't speak. I couldn't bring myself to address her or look at her, and she was silent by nature. If I didn't break the quiet no one would.

I used the time to think of Quillane and strengthen my anger. I told myself stories of her, as I did of my family – that was what you had to do to ensure the dead didn't fade with time. But they did fade. They did. And the stories became all that was left, drops of water in a desert. I would never let go of these stories of Quill and our time together. I tortured myself again and again with the possibilities, the *what ifs*. What if I hadn't been feckless? What if I had ruled alongside her as she deserved? What if I'd been all that I could be? Would she have loved me?

It was nice to fantasise that she would have, but the truth was plain. I had asked her outright on our last night together. She could never have loved me because she'd always been in love with someone else.

It came to me that I hadn't thought of Quillane in this way since before I was bonded to Isadora. A kind of uncurling took place inside me, an *easing*. I was free to think and feel what came naturally to me. Free to mourn the woman I loved by *choice*.

But that was when Isadora began to speak. And as her words reached me, and settled upon me, I hated her. *I hated her.* Because she was making it impossible for me to hate her at all.

ISADORA

I didn't remember the hours between waking and sleeping. I knew I had behaved poorly and embarrassed myself, but it was all a blur. Once the shock was purged from my system I felt sane, and miraculously calm. This was, after all, the world I knew best. No matter the fear, no matter the despair.

And so.

We sat in our cages, him and me, and I came to understand that this was not quite the world I knew. It had one extraordinary difference – his presence. This was why I spoke. Into the quiet of our third night in the cages. Or maybe it was because there was no lake anymore. And that meant the end of everything.

'I don't remember a time before this cage,' I said, my voice still rasping painfully. We were both watching, not each other, but the starlit sky. 'I must have been brought here as an infant. At first they delivered me food and water. Gave me blankets to keep me warm. Later they made me find my own sustenance. They called me Demon. A demon child to guard the precipice against monsters. In a cage where I belonged.'

219

I closed my mouth, regretting it, regretting every word. Fear made a mockery of the momentary courage speaking had taken.

Minutes passed and then he asked, 'How long?'

This was it, wasn't it? The moment that would change the way he thought of me forever. I'd never wanted another soul to know this truth about me, to understand in which conditions I had been forged, to pity me or think me weak for it. But this was a man my whole existence had been bound to until only very recently. This was a man I could no longer hate.

'Twelve years.'

There was an infinite silence. I stretched and shifted within it. And then I looked over to see that he had rested his face in his hands.

'Would you have been saved if I'd reclaimed Sanra?' he asked, and I could hear the tears in his throat.

I'd imagined this all my life. A chance to hold someone accountable. I could tell him the truth, I could punish him with it. But I found, quite simply, that I no longer wanted to. I knew – I *knew* – that even despite his hatred of me, the truth would cause him terrible heartache. He was not a selfish ruler but a cunning one, a ruler disempowered by the brutality of his family's death.

A world opened in the sky above me and I gazed up at it, at the thousands of stars and through them. To punish someone for the cruelty done to me would be selfish and very small.

'No,' I said.

'*Iz*,' he demanded, moonlit tears in his crystal eyes. 'Don't. If we had come here to Sanra to take it back from Pirenti, this never would have happened to you.'

'Pirenti didn't do this,' I said. 'It was warders who offered me as tribute in hope that the gods or their magic would banish the Pirenti. They were mad, Falco. Corrupted.'

'I could have stopped them.'

'You didn't know.'

'I should have!' he gasped, and then he was weeping. This was a very old sorrow, a deep shame, the kind of grief that builds from the loss of self, of identity, of the life you were *meant* to live. Who was ever strong enough to shoulder the weight of such unfulfilled possibilities? The weight of *what if?* There was nothing as destructive as waste.

At least I had never been born to be anything. I had never risked anything in this cage, had never needed to become anything. But Falco had been born huge and had been forced into something small small small. He had spent his entire life on the knife-edge of risk, in constant danger and under perpetual threat. Those things were their own cages.

'You were my other half,' Falco said into the darkness. 'I should have known somehow. I should have felt it, and come for you.'

FALCO

Days passed and we ate more raw bird meat. I stopped getting sick. I'd pointed out that I was losing a lot more energy and fluid vomiting up the rancid food I ate than by just sitting quietly and not eating, but Isadora pointed out that it was worth the initial danger because I would acclimatise to it before I died of starvation. It was wet season so it rained most afternoons; we drank as much as we could, catching water in our shoes, drinking it before it seeped away.

But I was going stir-crazy. I needed out. My body was fading, weakening. My mind was full of nothing but *twelve years.* It made no sense to me, how someone could endure that. And a *child.* Someone who was meant to be developing into a human being, learning about the world and life and her place in it. There had been no one to show her love or kindness. What *did* make sense now was her inability to connect with people, and her violence. Frankly, after what she'd been through I was surprised she wasn't a raving lunatic.

I noticed she was keeping the bones of her sparrows, piling them in the corner of her cage. 'What are they for?'

Isadora shrugged, looking bored. 'I killed my captors with these. Not much good now. Must be habit.'

She was far smaller than me so she had room to do pull-ups on the top bars of the cage. I watched her athletic form as she reached fifty, watched her muscles tighten and release. She was strong, despite her size.

'When did you learn the knives?'

221

Isadora's eyes moved immediately to the bottom of the chasm and the darkness down there. She let go of the bars and tucked her knees under her chin. 'I learned aim because of the monsters.'

I frowned, peering into the depths. I couldn't see anything, and wondered if the 'monsters' might exist as nothing more than a facet of a little girl's frightened mind.

'They've been quiet,' she murmured, 'but they're down there.' Shaking her head, she added, 'The knives came when I got out. I practised when I lived in the forest.'

'And your army?'

'Started small. A handful found me. Sheltered me. When I was . . . not good. I hadn't yet learnt to speak, so they helped me.'

More silence fell. I had never experienced such long bouts of quiet. I'd spent my life surrounded by people and questions and requests. With Isadora there was none of that. She asked nothing of me. There was only contemplation and it was confronting. Within it there came a kind of stillness. The quiet I'd never understood in her. I used it to think about what she'd been through, about my part in her life, about what she had done to Quillane and Radha. And I used it to examine myself, though I had no idea what I would find.

'What did you plan on doing with the world when you had killed me?' I asked her abruptly.

She took her time replying. 'Disempower the warders.'

'All of them?'

She nodded.

'How?'

'By teaching people to lucid dream.'

'What about the warders who aren't corrupt?'

I was afforded a sceptical glance.

'So you'd punish them all for the actions of a few. Eradicate magic entirely.'

'I don't have a problem with the people. I take issue with the magic. With anything that can be manipulated by some humans and not others.'

'Then why do you carry weapons?'

She shot me an impatient look.

'What you're saying is no one should have a skill that others don't,' I pressed. 'No one should have superior strength or speed, or carry a sharper weapon. No one should excel at anything. If I'm stronger than you it must mean I'll hurt you.'

'Human strength doesn't corrupt souls. Soul magic destroys those it inhabits. It's not a matter of if, but when.'

'What of Jonah? Finn? Osric? You would condemn them before they've committed a crime? Wipe them all out to avoid danger? That's negligent. A ruler who thinks of all as one can too easily commit democide.'

'And allowing a problem to fester and grow will be the ruin of all. I would have thought you'd learned that by now.'

I closed my mouth, surprised she'd engaged in a political conversation.

Time passed. I was trapped in it, wanting it to speed up or slow down, anything but to move at its normal pace. Something was missing, some piece I couldn't remember, couldn't fit into place. It niggled at the edge of my mind, just out of reach. It was the answer to this mess, I knew it.

I questioned Isadora constantly, starting to lose my handle on things. She stopped answering, stopped communicating except with looks. She'd obviously fulfilled her quota of words and I was left to my own company.

★

'So what do we do?' I demanded days later. 'I don't accept this end.'

Isadora didn't say anything.

'*Speak*, Izzy. You have to speak. I tried to do this on my own but I can't. The silence is sending me spare.'

She met my eyes as she rarely had. I let my desperation rise to the surface – I was literally begging at this point. Swallowing, she clearly made an effort. 'I don't know what to do. I was never able to get free on my own.'

'The sleepwalking?'

'Can't move me through metal bars.'

'Does anyone pass by here? Your people?'

'We're in the wilderness,' she replied. 'It's dangerous rocky terrain and there are no roads nearby. My people live south-east in the forest.'

'*Fuck.*' I peered into the dark below. 'What's really down there?'

She shook her head, incensed. 'I told you.'

'They haven't attacked us.'

'Yet.'

But the niggling thing, the missing piece. I had the edge of it now, and turned it over in my hands. '*It's not as far as it looks* . . . Gwendolyn said that. Right before.'

We frowned, peering down. I could hear Izzy's scepticism in her silence.

'She intentionally let Penn go,' I said. I got to my knees and studied the loop connecting the chain to the cage. 'I think I can get this free.'

She shook her head quickly.

'It's the only way to break the cage,' I insisted. 'It might crack if it falls from a great enough height.'

'As will we!'

'Maybe not.' I started calculating, mapping it out in my head, working out angles and timing. 'How far is it really?'

Izzy bit her lip, considering. 'Fifty meters, maybe. More?'

'That's how far it looked. Which means it's less.'

'Says the *Viper*.'

'What do we have to lose?' I studied the cage while I worked it through aloud. 'It will hurt. The damage will be proportional to the force at which we hit the ground. Which is great for breaking the cage, but not so great for us. Force depends on momentum, momentum is mass times velocity. If we can change our velocity even a little it will lesson the force. So we jump within our cage. But we have to do it right before we land, otherwise we could increase how far we fall.' I looked over to see that she was staring at me. 'What?'

'How do you know all that?'

I shrugged. 'I'll go first and call up if I survive.'

'*Stop*. Think a moment.'

'I just did.'

She shook her head helplessly. 'Falco.'

I turned to her.

Her mouth opened but nothing came out.

'Don't worry.' I smiled. 'If I die, you'll still be alive to think of another way out.'

Stop him. Don't let him do this. But too old were my wounds, and too deeply scarred upon me. I nodded and said, 'Then it's lucky we broke the bond.'

Falco's smile turned gentle and knowing. 'Aye.'

Something passed between us, a little piece of truth. He reached up through the bars and took hold of the chain, removing his weight from the cage. Then he unhooked it and he was falling.

My chest lurched as he disappeared into the darkness. I heard the crash of his landing, quicker than I expected. 'Falco!'

A groan reached up to my ears, and then pained words. 'Still alive! But *gods* that hurt.' I listened to him shuffle, wishing he'd waited for the sun to be higher. 'It worked!' he shouted. 'The cage broke! When you go, keep hold of the bars above so the bottom of your cage will break most of your fall!'

He'd actually worked it out.

I took the sparrow bones I'd meticulously sharpened and slid them into the waistband of my breeches. Then I reached up and hung onto the bars of the cage.

Something made me pause.

An inexplicable, irrational fear threaded my pulse. Not of falling or dying, but of leaving the cage. Of returning to the overwhelming, crowded, intimate, *violent* beyond. In the cage I was nothing. I was safe. In the beyond I was a monster drenched in blood, and worse — there were people out there who wanted something of me, wanted to be always talking or touching or questioning, giving me things and asking for things and expecting and wishing and requiring and taking. In the cage, I needed no words. In the beyond, I never had enough.

In the cage, I didn't have anyone. In the beyond, I didn't have Falco.

I closed my eyes and tried to reach for the lake of calm, but it was gone.

'Isadora,' Falco shouted up to me, 'you can do it!'

But he didn't understand. I was panicking.

'Don't let Dren and Galia choose your fate,' he called. And it was enough, it was where my hate lived.

It took me a few goes to unhook the cage and then I felt the world drop out from under me. A hollow whoosh swept through my stomach and crushed me against the top of the cage. I held onto the bars as tightly as I could and –

I hit with a huge crash. My hands were ripped free and I slammed into the ground, dislocating both my shoulder and hip. A gasp of pain stole my breath and for a too-long moment my entire world was eclipsed by the fire in my left side.

Then Falco was there, dragging me out of the bent and broken metal and lying me on the earth. 'Where?'

'Hip and shoulder,' I panted, squeezing my eyes shut.

'Hip first.' He took my leg and I tried to prepare myself, tried to count or breathe or something, but I didn't have a chance before he wrenched it up and to the side. I screamed as the joint twisted back into its socket.

Falco didn't give me a single second to recover – he moved straight to take my wrist.

'Wait, wait –'

He pulled it up so the muscle could rotate back into place, and I blacked out.

As I came back around the pain was dizzying, but less. I breathed in, feeling queasy. I could see, even wreathed in shadows, that both my palms were bleeding profusely.

'Good advice,' I snapped, noting that he was in much better shape than I was.

Falco turned and showed me the back of his skull, which had a bleeding gash. 'You're better off without the head injury.'

I tore strips from the ankles of my trews and wrapped them tightly around my palms. Then I made him carefully remove his shirt so I could wrap it around his head with as much padding as possible. He could be badly concussed or have a brain injury, which meant he'd deteriorate quickly. We shared a look, both aware there was nothing to be done about it but hope.

'You managed to do what I couldn't in twelve years,' I said.

'I spent my adolescence studying physics and mathematics. You spent yours sitting in a cage. You could hardly be expected to know how to get out.'

'Even without all the gibberish you went on with,' I muttered, 'it was still common sense to drop the cage.'

'And when did you have a chance to learn common sense?'

I flushed with embarrassment. Moving awkwardly to the wall of the chasm, I began the climb despite the pain in my body.

'There are tunnels,' he protested. 'Look. We don't have to climb.'

'You don't wish to face what lurks in those tunnels,' I replied softly. 'Not for anything in the world. Climb, Falco, and do it quickly. They will have smelled the blood.'

They did come, and they followed us up the wall in that swift sinister way of theirs, never emerging entirely from the shadows, though their eyes glowed red just like mine. Their teeth were sharp but they were no match for the sparrow bones I darted into their mouths and eyes and soon, soon, Falco and I made it into the sunlight and up over the lip of the chasm.

Together we sagged to the ground and stared up at the sky. My wounds hurt, but Falco was worse. His eyes kept losing focus and drifting shut.

'Don't go to sleep.'

He smiled. 'Strange. You're usually telling me not to wake up.'

Something in my chest tightened in fear at the fading quality of his voice. I forced him to his feet.

★

We walked. On and on for days. We ate what we could and drank from streams. We didn't speak. Falco went in and out of feeling well or drifting into a barely conscious haze. I silently pleaded with him to make it to civilisation where we could find a physician.

My body hurt too. But it didn't hurt like the very heart of me was beginning to, the greatest of all the wounds, where he had been cut from me. He was the other half of my soul, after all, and we'd never been born to be parted.

★

'Which way?' Falco asked.

I shielded my eyes against the glare of the white salt lake. It stretched as far as I could see into the distance. To travel around would slow our path considerably and I wasn't sure Falco could make the extra leagues – so we would have to hope for rain or we'd die of thirst trying to cross the enormous expanse.

I led him onto the surface, feeling the crunch of salt beneath my boots. It had formed winding circular patterns a long time ago, made by the movement of the earth and the wind, I supposed.

'I wonder what the world looked like before the ocean here dried out,' he said.

'There was no ocean here.'

'The salt remains to tell us of another time, another world. We're standing in a spot that must have once been hundreds of leagues underwater.'

It was a strange notion, and I found myself comforted by it. It made me feel powerless in the face of time and the earth beneath my feet, and the feeling wasn't unwelcome. 'So much is lost,' I said.

'But look at what beauty remains.'

I frowned. It was just . . . white. And painful to look upon. The salt glistened in the sun like ice or snow and yet the land here was incredibly hot. I had difficulty sometimes determining what was beautiful and what was ordinary. I'd always thought I knew what was ugly, but maybe I didn't really know that either. I swallowed, unsure how to voice my question. 'Do you not . . . does it not make you feel insignificant?'

Falco peered around, letting his eyes travel over the horizon. He was more lucid than he'd been in days. 'Strange, I suppose, but I find myself not all that bothered by insignificance.'

'Is a ruler meant to think that way?'

He shrugged, smiling crookedly. 'I have no idea what a ruler's meant to do.'

I dropped my eyes and as we walked I thought hard about what that meant.

We'd covered about half of the salt lake by the time the sun went down. Exhausted, we stopped to rest a few hours on the hard ground, neither of us inclined to keep talking. I took watch, searching the dark for signs of movement.

I woke later to a painful thirst. Rolling over, I was met with Falco's staring eyes. I sat up quickly, embarrassed to have fallen asleep. The moon was huge above us and lit the salt with an eerie, lovely glow.

'Wait,' he said, 'don't move.'

I paused, unsure if he was warning me of danger.

'I dreamt of you like this once,' he murmured, frowning. His gaze traced over my skin and hair. 'Covered in salt.'

I looked down to realise I was indeed covered. My fingers drifted up to feel that my hair was filled with coarse grains – it, too, was coated. There wasn't a great deal of difference in the colour. I was surprised he'd noticed.

'It shimmers a little,' he offered, like he'd read my thoughts. But he could no longer do that. The notion was a trick, a seduction of my heart. This moment felt like a dream.

I rose to my feet and carried on, prompting him to follow.

The rain started that night and was at first a relief, soon a burden. The cold crept into our bones and made it hard to walk. But we continued on through morning and reached the edge of the salt lake. With a last look back at the roiling grey sky and luminous earth, I turned my sights and thoughts away from whatever beauty it held and towards what I had to do.

I would reach my army and march them east to Sancia. I would destroy everyone in the palace. And for that I would need to be the Sparrow once more, not a salt-covered girl sparkling in the moonlight.

★

We were two days' walk from the village when he collapsed. We were so close, had made it so far already. The rain continued to pour, turning everything soggy. It was how he slipped, and why he couldn't get back up again.

'Falco!'

He stirred groggily and muttered, 'Quill?'

We'd reached a muddy road, but I could see nothing through the curtain of rain. We were a long way west and none wandered these parts for fear of getting lost too near the border of Pirenti.

'Stand up,' I ordered him, water persistently running into my eyes. 'You must stand and walk.'

He moaned but his eyes remained closed. The shirt around his skull was soaked through not only with rain but with blood. I slapped him on the face and shook his shoulders but it didn't rouse him.

'*Please* get up,' I urged. 'Falco, *I need you to get up.* I'm not strong enough to carry you.'

I wasn't. I wasn't strong enough. I was so small and he so much bigger.

And why should I care? Truly, why? Was this not what I'd wanted? This man's death was meant to be the purpose of my life. I wasn't blind to what I'd felt for him when bonded. I'd honestly believed I was in love with him. But the remnant of a thing I had never chosen and had fought to end should not be enough to nullify *the very purpose of my life.* How had I become so weak?

Leave him. Leave him here for the crows to pick at and take what you are strong enough to take from a broken world. Eradicate what monstrosity you are strong enough to eradicate.

Here was what I believed.

That you were either the hunter or the hunted. The butcher or the meat. The caged or the free. I believed that I would use my daggers to cut out the hearts of the Mad Ones.

But no longer was that *all* I believed.

The terrible truth made itself clear as I watched a man die. He may not believe in himself, but I did. I believed in Falco of Sancia, and knew he would be the one to free us from the warders.

So even though I wasn't strong enough, I rolled him onto my shoulders and I rose trembling to my feet. My hip and shoulder hurt so badly that tears were in my eyes, lost in the rain as they streamed endlessly down my cheeks, but I took step after slippery step towards the village ahead, for hours and hours. Sometimes I thought I wouldn't take another step, but step I did, because I was forged in a cage by cruelty and madness, and I would not let the distance between my feet and that village be the thing that defeated me. I would carry him forever if I had to.

★

I couldn't make it to the nearest village in Sanra. So I did something I'd vowed never to: I veered north-west and crossed into Pirenti. We were just as likely to be killed as helped so close to the border. Those on the edge of the two countries had never been able to put old enmities to bed – fights and skirmishes still broke out to this day. But it was Falco's only hope.

When I saw the village in the distance I sank to my knees and felt his body tumble from my shoulders. With the only strength I had left I stretched out to catch his poor head, protecting it from the hard, wet ground. Then I lifted my other hand and held it high in the air. Sentries would be posted at all times and lightning struck often; I prayed for them to see me.

It was two boys who at last came running. Small figures at first, slipping and sliding through the storm to reach us. When they arrived I saw they were very young. I licked my lips and rasped, 'Run for help.'

One of the boys sprinted away, but the other stayed and sank to his knees beside me. I looked up to see that he was dark-haired and dark-eyed, his hair shaved short in the fashion of adult Pirenti warriors. Water ran in rivulets from his long eyelashes to his lips.

Falco had been shivering with fever for hours. My vision grew spotty and I fought a wave of nausea, of fear.

And that was when the boy reached to lay his cool hand gently on my cheek. 'Don't be frightened,' he said. 'I won't leave you.'

It broke something inside me and I began to weep.

He waited with me until help arrived, speaking soft words I was too tired to comprehend. Four Pirenti men and two Pirenti women came, all wearing oil cloaks against the rain. The women were beside themselves with worry, trying to rouse us while the men lifted us onto stretchers and carried us at a run into their village.

'His head,' I told them. 'He's hurt his head.'

'Shh,' one of the women soothed me. 'You're safe now.'

So I allowed myself to drift to sleep in the arms of the brutal northern pigs, the first people who'd ever offered to take care of me.

Chapter 16

Ava

Migliori was tiring badly by the time we reached Vjort. He and I had spent many long days flying to my fortress in Pirenti, only to be told upon arrival that Ambrose, Rose and Thorne had taken my daughters north for the solstice. They were expected to be in Norvjisk already, so I set off without resting a moment. By the time we reached the city my family were nowhere to be found. Fear turned me cold as I angled north-west. I sent energy to Migliori and begged him to last a little longer, praying with everything I had that we would find them at our next stop, though if Ambrose, Ella and Sadie were in Vjort it boded badly for their safety.

I couldn't banish my husband's pain from my body. It lingered still, even though I was too far from him to truly feel much through the bond. I only knew that he had not yet died. I would certainly feel that, I would feel it every day for the rest of my life.

Night fell. The cold deepened. I would never grow used to it, no matter how many times I travelled north. Exhausted to my bones, I circled low over Vjort and kept my eyes peeled for archers happy to forget our peace with Kayans long enough to shoot one out of the sky. But there were no guards on the wall. Instead I saw movement through the streets, in and out of buildings, a whole lot of hurried bodies and distant shouts. What was going on?

I aimed for the castle and angled Migliori into the grounds. No guards here either – something was wrong. 'Wait here,' I told him, then strode up the steps of the front entrance.

The door was wide open.

I moved warily inside, feeling the weight of my sword sheathed over my back. I had a dagger at my left hip and a whip at my right. All three weapons had been forged for me, designed and commissioned by Ambrose as a gift for our wedding anniversary a decade ago. I did not think, given his recent change in attitude, that he would give me the same gifts now. Regardless, I loved all three, loved the feel of them in my hands and loved too that they were engraved with our initials entwined together.

I could hear the noise of people and the moment I entered the hall I saw dozens of servants in a frenzy of activity. Not one of them glanced in my direction as they rushed sacks and trays towards the kitchens. I cleared my throat. Loudly.

One or two looked my way and a young girl dropped her armful of firewood with a gasp. She tripped to her knees and lowered her head to the stone floor. 'Your Majesty.'

The other servants in view noticed her, spotted me and then hurriedly did the same.

'Rise,' I bid, moving to impatiently gather the fallen wood for her. 'Are my family here?'

The girl rose, a look of fear in her face. And pity. There was pity there.

My stomach bottomed out.

'Whose orders are you following?' I demanded. Dread made me short and rude; the frost had worked its way up through my throat and into my tongue and now coated each one of my words.

'His Majesty the King's,' the girl replied.

I let out a breath of relief; my hands trembled with it. I placed the firewood in another servant's grasp and told the girl to fetch him.

'He's —'

'*Now.*'

She dashed off to do so. I waited, sheathing my sword and folding my arms. 'What's all this about?' I asked the remaining servants, gesturing to the flurry of people in and out of the kitchens.

'Supplies, Majesty,' a man replied. 'For the searchers.'

I frowned, not liking the sound of that and sensing that whatever needed to be explained would be best coming from my husband. 'You may resume.'

They launched back into their duties. It was taking all of my restraint not to tear through this castle and find my husband and daughters myself. Jarl Sigurd was regent here though, and storming through his home before he'd greeted me could be seen as an affront. *Respect those who serve you*, my husband often counselled, *and they will respect you in return.*

It was not Ambrose or Jarl Sigurd who flew down the steps, but Thorne. We were across the space in less than a second, clutching tightly at each other. In his enormous arms I was lifted off my feet.

'Ava.'

'Thank gods you're alright.'

He released me and I stepped back to get a look at my nephew. He was ghostly, with bruised hollows under his eyes and a sickly pallor to his skin. I wondered when he'd last slept. He smelled like he hadn't washed in weeks.

'Where are they?' I asked. 'Where's Ambrose?'

Something left him. A sound that liquefied my insides, it was so stricken. 'You felt it,' Thorne said roughly. 'That's why you're here.'

'Felt what?'

'It's all gone to shit, Ava.' He laughed, and it sounded like a sob. 'It's all gone.'

'*What*, Thorne?'

'He's been killed. Ambrose has been killed.'

My whole body went numb. I shook my head. No. 'Where are my daughters?'

'I don't know,' he whispered. 'I can't find them. I've had everyone in this whole damned city searching for days and nights without rest, tearing the place apart, but . . .' There were unshed tears in his eyes as he spread his hands. His voice broke. 'I can't find any of them.'

AMBROSE

I couldn't be certain, but I had come to believe there was someone else in my tomb with me. Buried alive, as I was.

I could hear breathing. It had taken me a long while to distinguish it from my own. It now took me a long while to work up the strength to use my swollen, dry mouth.

'Hello?' I rasped. It was more a scrape than a word.

'Good gods,' burst a woman's voice. 'I'm here – I'm here! Don't go back to sleep!'

'Who are you?' I couldn't see anything, couldn't open my eyes.

'I thought you were dead. *I thought you were dead.*' She was weeping.

'It's alright,' I grunted, wanting to comfort her. 'Who?'

'I . . . you captured me. I'm the warder. Maisy.'

I didn't understand. Didn't know anyone called Maisy. Had no memory of capturing anyone. Was too confused. I swallowed and tasted blood. Pain was a sixth sense, a fifth element. I'd lost track of the things done to me – I was only nerve endings searching around for mercy.

'You've been unconscious a very long time.' The girl's voice found me in the darkness. 'I thought I was alone.'

'No,' I said. Because that was a thing I knew. I was here. I was.

'They tortured you,' she said. 'It was . . . they were so brutal.'

'Where?' I rasped.

'We're in the tombs under the city. Under the castle, I think. But it's been sealed. We can't get out.' She was panicking. True terror filled the tomb – I could almost smell it like my brother used to be able. My brother. I wanted my brother so desperately, so urgently, that for a moment the longing eclipsed the pain. He would fix this. He would fix everything as he always, always did. *Where are you, Thorne? You're supposed to be here.*

'There's no way out,' the girl kept saying.

'Your magic?'

'I've been trying,' she wept. 'I can't . . . My mind is too . . . and my hands are bound, and I can't . . .'

'Shh,' I murmured. 'It's alright.' My voice was coming back a little. My clarity. 'Rest. You're safe. I won't let any harm come to you.'

A gasp left her. 'You were dead! I have no idea how you're still – *you were dead*, Majesty.'

'I'm still here,' I whispered. 'I'm still here.' Like a mantra, or a prayer, or a vow.

But threads were unravelling again, too quick to catch in my clumsy, loathsome hands, all the pieces of me being wrenched upon and unspooled into a mighty, infinite tangle.

'Majesty? Wait, no, *please* don't leave me . . .'

Maisy's voice faded.

My body faded.

Even the darkness somehow faded.

I was lost and there was screaming all around.

And a man, standing in the middle of nothing and everything. It wasn't my father or my brother. It wasn't any of the people I expected. He was a small thing, slight and skinny. He had long, straight black hair. Dimples in his cheeks when he smiled at me and crooked front teeth, and warmth in his pretty brown eyes, my gods so much *warmth*.

I took a trembling breath. It felt like I had been walking towards him all my life.

'Who are you?' I asked, even though I knew.

His smile widened. 'My name's Avery.'

I sank to my knees in the void. 'Is this real?'

'I don't know. Maybe. Does it feel real?'

'It feels like everything.'

He moved to my side and knelt with me, reaching for my head as the tears fell from my eyes. 'You can't stay here,' he told me gently.

'Why not?' I wanted to, very badly. The blaze of his smile was warming me all the way through.

'You have so much more yet to do, King of Pirenti.'

'I'd burn the name if I could,' I whispered. 'Scour it from me.'

Avery shook his head, leaning so his lips were near my ear. 'Don't burn it. Remake it.'

'I'm not strong enough. Not for the magnitude of what it will take. Have I not proven that already?'

'If you are not strong enough, then make of yourself something stronger,' he replied. 'To help you, you have the soul of a woman strong enough to bond twice. Who else in this world can say that?'

I smiled.

'Can you feel her now?' Avery whispered, his lips against the skin of my cheek. It was incomparable sweetness to experience his touch. 'And those girls of yours. My gods, what girls they are, what women they will be.'

I could feel them, my daughters, and I could feel the echoes of her, of his other half, of my other half.

'Go back,' Avery bid me. 'Go back, Ambrose.'

The threads were reweaving themselves. I could feel pressure and a great pain I couldn't bear to return to.

'Avery –' I cried desperately, scrabbling to hold onto him, but it was no use. I was gone from him.

AVA

Fury was a second skin. My teeth chattered with it. My hands were iron steady with it. He wasn't dead. He wasn't.

I could feel him, but I didn't know *where*. Somewhere close, somewhere maddeningly close but *where where where*. The streets were chaos; nearly every citizen of Vjort was out, either searching through houses or fighting the searchers. Fires had broken out and buildings burned, their owners working desperately to douse the flames. A riot was in the air, I could feel the danger approaching. Brawls were already taking up entire streets.

I didn't care about any of it. If that's what it took to find my husband and my children, then let them kill each other, let it all burn. Let them tear down this vile city and be done with it.

I came to a press of people fighting wildly, all men who towered over me.

Instead of drawing my blades I uncurled my whip: I had no patience for anything in my way. With a swing and a snap of my wrist, the leather snaked out and made a mighty crack, slashing at those before me, carving a path through which I strode, ignoring all but the feel of him, the whisper of him, that tingling, pulling, tugging ache of the heart.

Blades swung at me; I cracked my whip through the hands that wielded them.

Hands came at me; I cracked my whip through the spines that controlled them.

At the end of the street I heard a distant whinny. Peering into the night, I spotted Migliori sweeping the city, searching as I was. I whistled to him and he angled down, spreading his wings wide that he might glide to a thunderous landing.

'Where?'

He tossed his head, stamped his foot. I swung up onto him and he flattened his wings, instead plunging into a gallop along the cobblestones. He was carrying me back towards the castle and as he did so I realised that he was right. My feet and my panic had carried me too far. It was here, back here where I began, that I could feel the tug grow stronger.

'Gods curse it,' I snarled as my mount careened up the steps and I dismounted in the damned entrance hall once more.

Ambrose was here. I could feel him like a limb that had lost sensation, a prickling tingle, not exactly pleasurable and not exactly painful. He was near, but *where*? As I ran up stairs and through halls and searched through each of the four towers, I felt the bond between us flicker on the edge of being doused. The pinpricks grew severe. I was about to be too late.

So I stopped. I closed my eyes, and I concentrated. Allowed the tug to guide my feet.

Down it led me.

Down further than I even knew was possible. A tunnel at the base of a set of steps I hadn't known existed. I followed this tunnel at a sprint, at the end of which was a small antechamber, inside of which was a stone table, around which sat three men.

I halted abruptly and took them in, just as they whirled to do the same. They wore military garb and were heavily armed. On their table were strewn the remnants of several meals, bottles of wine, playing dice and a pile of coins. From the smell they'd been down here a long time.

'What are you doing here?' I asked.

'Waiting for you,' one replied.

All three rose to their feet, hands moving to axes. There was a door behind them. Slow, flickering heat filled my limbs, my guts, my mouth. My teeth chattered with it. 'Move.'

'We're not to move,' a second man said, 'until the sounds stop coming from within. So you'd best take your sweet little ass back up those steps. *Majesty*.'

I drew a slow breath, trying and failing to calm myself. The heat was an inferno.

I took two huge booted steps, one onto the empty chair, the second up onto the stone table. As I moved I uncurled my whip and with a flick of my wrist I cracked the end of it straight through the soldier's throat.

Flesh tore and blood spilled; he clawed at his neck, trying to keep it together. The others moved to attack, but I did the same to the second guard, curling my whip once around my head and then straight through his jaw.

Now I paused, gazing down at the third and last, who'd halted in shock. 'Do you think you can keep me from my husband?' Unbridled fury made my voice tremble. Only a foolish man would mistake that tremble for weakness.

The guard glanced at his comrades, both bleeding out on the ground.

'Open it,' I ordered. A beast like Thorne's had taken control of my body – it *would* get inside that room, there was no question of that.

The soldier decided to take his chances against my whip. And died.

I jumped heavily to the ground. After searching through the belts of the three dead men, I found the keys to the padlock and unlocked it. It wasn't the only deterrent – the door was made of heavy stone and took all my strength to drag open. By the time I'd hauled it far enough to squeeze through, my hands were blistered and bleeding, my head dizzy with exertion.

I stumbled inside to find myself in the pitch-black of a windowless room. It was very cold, the air stale. I heard the sound of a girl weeping as my eyes adjusted slowly to the darkness. I made out a shape. Rectangular, like a tomb. Something lumpier atop it.

I drew closer, reaching out to touch it. Someone yelped, moved, the weeping cut off. 'Help! Help, please –'

'Shh, I'm here,' I said quickly. 'It's alright.'

The girl was tied to a slab but I couldn't see well enough to work out how to free her. She was struggling wildly, bucking against the restraints.

'Hold,' I tried, 'Let me –'

'He stopped talking,' she sobbed hysterically. 'He went quiet and left me alone . . .'

I whirled, searching in the dark for another slab, another body. Reaching out, I felt until my hands connected with . . . Something cold. Too cold to be a living thing.

Nausea struck but I swallowed it and felt around until I found his face. 'Ambrose. *Ambrose.*' I shook him but he wasn't moving and I couldn't hear him breathing, couldn't feel it against my skin.

Footsteps echoed in the tunnel beyond the door and I heard the stone slab being dragged wider. And as it moved the light from the antechamber moved across the floor, closer and closer, casting light first over the poor girl tied to the rock, and then over me, over my face, and when I turned my back on it so that I might look at my husband I saw, at last, what had been done to him.

He was beaten black and blue. No inch of skin remained its colour. Parts of him were swollen and disfigured. Bones were pointing the wrong way.

But worse, so much worse, were the two severed hands lying inches from where they should have been attached to his wrists.

My eyelids slammed shut and the world spun around me.

No.

This couldn't be. It would see him dead. If by some impossibility Ambrose survived this tomb, those lost hands would be the end of him. They would make him the weakest man in a country he could only survive in as the strongest.

I couldn't breathe, I couldn't breathe, I was going to scream scream scream *scream* –

'Ava!' Thorne's voice brought me back to the room, this cold stinking torture chamber. I breathed through my mouth until I knew that the next thing from it would not be a scream.

I leant to hold my husband's face. 'Ambrose. Wake. Please, *wake.*'

'Give him breath,' Thorne prompted, feeling for a pulse.

I pressed my mouth to Ambrose's and breathed air into his lungs, just as he had done for me once upon a time in a watery cave on an island far away. His lungs inflated and I did it again and again until he coughed and started breathing on his own. I sagged in relief, stroking his cheeks. 'Ambrose. Wake.'

He swallowed but didn't open his eyes – they were swollen shut. A dry, rasping noise came from his throat. Not quite a word. And then a weary sentence: 'There you are, pretty boy.'

AMBROSE

Better I cut them off, before they strangle the life from my body.

Had I not wished for this? Fate was cruel indeed. And sported a very dark sense of humour.

AVA

I sank over him, kissing his swollen eyes gently. 'I'm here.'

Ambrose grunted, smiling. When did he ever stop smiling?

Thorne was seeing to the girl, who'd calmed considerably now that she could see and her bonds were untied. Most of her fear was undoubtedly from being left down here with only a dying man for company. She was very weak and frightened to her core, but she sat up and watched Ambrose with a fierce protectiveness, for which I loved her.

'I can heal him,' she said. 'If I can see him and my hands are free. I have a little power in such things.'

My eyes went to his hands, the fingers gently curled as though resting and well and not separate from his body. His breathing changed.

'Ambrose!' I glanced at the warder girl. 'Quickly – he's going again.'

She stood unsteadily and Thorne supported her to Ambrose's side.

I shook him. 'Stay. *Stay.*'

What kind of monsters brutalised people and then left them to die so badly? I could hardly bear it.

The girl started to cry again. 'They hurt him so much,' she wept.

'Don't,' I begged her. 'Don't cry. Please.'

But she was overwrought. It was too much, this was too much to ask. She was just a child and she'd been tortured with this imprisonment, held down here for gods only knew how long. I wished I could do it but I'd never been able to heal anyone but myself – not even my bondmate.

Thorne forced the girl to meet his eyes. 'I can smell how much courage is in you, Maisy. *Find it now.*'

She swallowed and her eyes shifted to a beautiful orange, the exact shade of her hair. She went to Ambrose and her eyes changed again, this time fading to white. She sagged and Thorne caught her, supporting her as she worked. I watched Ambrose's horrendous wounds start to close over and the dark bruises gradually lose their colour. The swelling around his eyes shrunk back down until they looked almost normal again.

But his hands didn't reattach. I didn't know if any magic had the power to make them.

Once her eyes returned to normal, Thorne lifted her into his arms and held her tenderly. 'Don't take me from him,' Maisy mumbled deliriously.

'You're both safe now, you can sleep,' Thorne told her, and with a last look at me he carried her away.

I turned back to my husband.

He was conscious and looking at me. I tried to swallow my tears but they were thick and prickly. Because he knew. I could see it in that blue gaze of his.

I helped Ambrose slowly sit, and then he looked down at the stumps on the ends of his wrists where they rested in his lap. Next he took in the gruesome severed hands on the slab beside him. His hands. His very own. His lips were bleached bone white.

Desperate grief struck me and I wanted to find the heinous brutes who'd done this and torture them just as badly. Worse, I wanted to kill them and I wanted to smash my fist into this wall and break the bones in my own hands and I just wanted to fucking *scream*.

It wasn't fair. It was so desperately unfair.

Then he spoke. Gently, honestly. 'It's alright.'

I closed my eyes. Went to him and threaded my arms around him. Kissed his cheeks and his eyelids and his lips. 'I'll protect you,' I whispered fervently. 'I won't let anyone hurt you ever again. I don't care how many come. I'll face them all.'

'I don't doubt it, my darling, but you won't need to,' Ambrose told me. 'Not in the world I'm going to build.'

He didn't move his arms to embrace me, not yet, but he kissed my lips and he whispered, 'I saw him. I saw Avery.'

242

My heart seized. I looked into Ambrose's eyes as they shifted to a blazing gold.

'He was perfect,' my husband said, and he was smiling, this man who had just been tortured almost to death, who had just lost both his hands. He was smiling.

CHAPTER 17

ISADORA

I woke to find myself dry and clean in a room made of heavy stone and draped in tapestries of wolves. My shoulder was bandaged, as were both my palms. The bed beside mine held a sleeping Falco, his head also heavily bandaged. And in the corner was the boy with dark eyes. He watched me unblinkingly as I awkwardly pulled myself upright in the crisp bed.

'I'm Davin.'

'Isadora.'

We watched each other. He brought me a cup of water and I drank greedily. He didn't seem interested in speaking, which was a relief. After Davin and I had sat in silence for some time, a woman entered. She was tall and broad as a man, with the gentlest brown eyes I'd ever seen.

'How are you feeling, little lady?' she asked me.

I nodded my thanks.

'My name is Elsa. We forced fluids into you, but you won't be right again until you've eaten your weight.' She pressed a compress to my forehead. I forced myself not to flinch away from the touch.

'My friend?'

'He has a crack in his skull. It will mend itself with time. If he wakes, he will be alright.'

'Why . . .' I cleared my throat. 'Why are you helping us?'

Elsa peered at me as though she didn't understand the question. 'Because you were injured and poorly, child. What kind of people would refuse to help?'

I swallowed. 'But even . . . even with my appearance?'

Elsa's wide smile made her quite pretty. 'I think perhaps you were born in the wrong country.' Then she checked Falco and walked for the door. 'Come, my love,' she said to Davin.

'No,' I said quickly. 'I mean . . . he can stay.'

Elsa nodded and left the child. He peered at me just as he had been. 'Here we worship a snow and ice goddess. She looks just like you,' he said, round eyes unblinking.

I didn't know what to say.

'But the goddess Skaði is not only a goddess of ice,' the boy went on. 'Before that, always, she is a goddess of the hunt. She drapes herself in salt and ice and hunts with the wolves of the mountains. She married, but the huntress in her was too cold, too ravenous, and overcame any love she had. She returned to the ice to live the lonely life of the hunt.'

I stared at him, feeling a prickle on the skin of my arms. At his age I hadn't yet learned to speak, let alone speak like this.

Davin broke the spell cast by his words with a grin. 'If you believe that stuff, anyway.' He shrugged to dismiss the story, then brought in a board and pieces so we could play chess. The pieces were a little different to the ones used in Kaya but I got the hang of it and didn't let him win, to his frustration.

'Move your hersir forward three squares and you have her, kid.'

We both turned to see that Falco was awake and watching our fifth game.

Davin followed his instructions.

'Cheating,' I pointed out.

The boy grinned as he knocked down my king.

The three of us played as the light faded. Falco spent the whole time helping Davin. It embarrassed me how much better at chess strategy Falco was than me. Elsa eventually returned and was pleased to see Falco awake. She sent Davin to fetch us food and then hovered, checking us both. She didn't ask any questions about where we were from, even though Falco was blatantly Kayan. I wondered if the Pirenti men would be so accommodating, then remembered how carefully they had carried us, how gentle their deep voices were as I drifted out of consciousness.

What blindness, what assumption. The kindness I had found here was unlike any I had experienced in Kaya, except from Penn, Jonah and Finn. Thorne, I realised, was the only other truly kind person I had encountered; the discrepancy between how we saw these northern folk and how they really were astonished me. Kindness, offered freely, was the rarest of treasures. This I only learnt after escaping the cage.

Falco asked Elsa the same questions that I had, and more. When she was gone we ate our food quietly.

'They don't know who we are?' Falco asked softly as we sank onto our pillows.

I shook my head.

'How did we get here?'

'You collapsed but their scouts found us,' I lied. 'They had a carriage.'

'Fortuitous,' he said. 'Are you well?'

Another nod. It seemed to satisfy him for he shut his weary eyes. 'In the morning we'll part,' he said with a yawn. 'And the world will be righted once more, you and I on different paths going in different directions.'

I felt my pulse quicken.

'Before we do, we should discuss strategy,' he added. 'Your people and mine will need to work together until we have our end. So perhaps for a while it will be a similar path after all.'

'Where will you go?'

'I'll ride north and then east. I need to find Ava and those from the city. I hope the Pirenti managed to reach them in time.'

'Do you think they know we're out of the cages?' I asked softly. *Dren and Galia.*

'No idea. Let's hope not.'

I rolled to lie on my back and peered at the tapestry on the opposite wall – an ice-swept mountain glistening with blue fissures. It reminded me of my skin. I let my mind reach out to that northern wilderness, so unforgiving that no one dared go near it. I ought to have been born there, where no one could see me.

I contemplated my lie and couldn't endure the thought of Falco knowing the truth of how I had carried him. Just as I couldn't endure his pity, the thought of him feeling indebted to me was equally repulsive. Cutting all ties, except in a political capacity, was a wise idea.

Silence ticked on, as did the night. Falco fell asleep but I remained awake. Sleeping this close to him, in a bed not a cage . . . something happened. His hands found me, in the dark. His mouth on my body. His tongue against mine. Pieces of him inside pieces of me. My breathing quickened and I was back there, in that glass room overlooking the ocean as he made love to me with the strength of his beautiful body and I felt it again, that thrill of knowing a secret of his, one nobody else knew, the secret of what his heart felt like –

'Do you think about it?' Falco asked suddenly, shocking me half to death. 'The *why* of it?'

I gathered in my treacherous thoughts and stuffed them inside my overheated body. I knew what he meant and it caused a frightened thump of my heart.

'The reason we bonded,' he clarified. 'Do you think about why? I can't help worrying at the meaning of it. Thinking about *why* we were fated to each other.'

I licked my lips, clenched my trembling hands. 'I don't believe in fate.'

'I know that well,' he murmured. 'Maybe you're right. Maybe you've been right all along, and it's just a big joke. A chaotic mistake.'

I closed my eyes.

'Either way,' Falco went on softly, 'it's . . . I feel . . . very lonely. Without you.'

Tears slipped beneath my lashes and down into my hair. And I didn't say anything, but it wasn't because he didn't deserve my words. It was never honestly because people didn't deserve my words. It was this curse of mine that meant I never had the words to speak. I was caged within my own body, with none of Falco's physics or mathematics to get me out, with only an endless, lonely lake of calm for company.

*

I woke with dawn and listened to the birds singing the return of the sun. I went to the window to look out at the garden and breathe that fresh rain smell. Flowers of every colour bloomed. I spotted Davin through one of the rose bushes and without hesitating I swung over the windowsill and dropped onto the wet grass. It felt nice under my bare feet as I crossed to the boy's side.

He was standing by a fish pond, skipping stones.

I picked up a few and joined him. When he grew bored, he knelt and put his hands in the water. I watched curiously as he sat very still and waited. Fish returned from hiding to resume their exploration of the leafy depths. Several swam through Davin's hands, but he didn't move until the arrival of a particular fish. Closing his fingers gently, he caught the white creature and held it there in the water.

'Go on, touch it.' He grinned at me.

'Why?'

'He feels nice. Go on.'

I reached into the water and traced a finger along the smooth scales of the fish. It had fins tipped in orange.

'Nice, isn't it?' Davin asked. I looked at the sheer pleasure on his face and couldn't help smiling. Was this what it meant to enjoy a life? Finding joy in such simple things? My heart yearned for this, to be able to have this always, but I straightened. It was never mine to wish for.

He released the fish and we watched it swim a while longer.

'Davin!' His ma's voice reached us from the house and we turned back. Davin sprinted across the grass to meet Elsa, but as I approached I could see all was not well.

'There you are!' she said to me. 'Come inside, little lady.'

I didn't particularly enjoy being called 'little lady', but Elsa said it with such endearment that I found I wasn't bothered.

'There's been a change in your friend's condition.'

I froze. Elsa prodded me towards a kitchen table, where a man who must have been her husband sat. He was huge, but I couldn't tell if his girth was fat or muscle. Probably both. 'My husband Jarl Garth, son of Gus.'

I nodded to him, too distracted for a proper greeting.

'He's the ranking Drenge here,' she added. Which meant he was in charge of the village and surrounding lands because he was both the strongest warrior and had the oldest bloodline.

'My friend?' I asked.

'I have women in there with him now.'

I turned to go to him.

'Hold, child. Sit down.'

Though it was the last thing I felt like doing, I sat stiffly.

'The bleed in his head has started again,' Elsa said gently. 'He did not wake this morning when I tried to rouse him.' She paused and then reached to touch my hand. 'He will not wake again, dear.'

I stared at her blankly. 'For how long?'

'He will not wake *ever*.'

That didn't make any sense. I was just speaking to him last night and he'd been fine. A terrible panic was taking hold of my chest. Very calmly I said, 'He must wake. Do whatever it takes, please.'

'There's nothing more to be done,' she said. 'I'm not a surgeon, but even if I were I wouldn't cut into a man's head. It would only kill him quicker.'

'Where is the nearest surgeon?'

'Three villages north,' Garth rumbled in the deepest voice I'd ever heard.

I stood.

'He won't make it that far,' Elsa protested. 'And a surgeon will make no difference. Truly. Spend this time holding his hand and bidding your goodbyes – it is a rare chance at the end of a life.'

I looked helplessly at this woman. She didn't understand.

'The magic,' Garth said. 'Your Kayan black magic. It would save him.'

I stared at him. 'There are no warders in these parts. Not for hundreds of miles.' *I killed them all.*

And then it occurred to me. 'The prison,' I whispered. There were no warders so far south, except in the prison that sat deep within the dead forest, where even my people dared not trespass. 'I will take him there. Do you have a horse I can use?'

'I have none to spare, I'm afraid,' Garth replied.

'Please,' I tried.

'It isn't a matter of pleading for them. I truly have none to give you.'

I could force them. There were knives in the kitchen that I could reach before either of them knew what I was doing. I could steal their horses. Those were things that I could do with ease.

Or I could try for words.

Drawing a breath to calm my heart, I met Garth's eyes. 'Do you know of the unrest in Kaya?'

'Of course.'

'Then you know of the massacres taking place.' I floundered, not knowing how to continue. With a breath, I drew myself up. To do this, I would demand more of myself. I would channel Falco's cunning tongue. 'You have shown me such kindness already, I don't wish to ask you for anything further. But for what it's worth, know this. That man is no ordinary man. He is the fallen Emperor of Kaya and he *must* live to regain his throne or the Mad Ones in the east will finish with Kaya and turn their power to Pirenti. They will take control of the entire world and the massacres will never stop.'

Elsa had gone white with shock. Garth didn't blink. Slowly he passed a hand over his face. With a look at his wife he said, 'I can't ask my men to give up their horses – they depend on them. But I can give you mine. Hallr isn't fast, but he is strong enough to carry you both and his fortitude will not fail.'

I felt a great rush of disbelief. 'Thank you,' I whispered, unable to express my gratitude.

'I wish I had more.'

'The debt will be repaid, I give you my word.'

Elsa rushed off to prepare Falco, and then Garth carried him out to the stable. I paused only long enough to pull on my boots and ask Elsa if she might have a blade of some kind. She gave me a blunt and unbalanced hulk of a carving knife.

'Will that do?'

'It's perfect,' I lied, stowing the weapon in my waistband. I would have been better off with sewing needles. She also gave me a hooded cloak to travel in, which would come in handy.

Spotting Davin carrying a saddlebag, I surprised myself by pulling him into a hug. 'Thank you,' I whispered, kissing him on the forehead. I didn't know how to express that he had shown me something I'd never known: true generosity of spirit, given without agenda. The touch was incredibly strange to me, as was the sudden wash of affection. Had I ever shared a hug like this? Made of nothing but a sweet, true fondness?

Davin returned the embrace tightly. 'The goddess gave in to the hunt and the ice because she wasn't strong.'

I pulled away and searched his face, unsure what he meant. His dark eyes gazed back at me and then he grew abruptly shy, smiling and pulling away.

Garth helped me swing onto the mighty black horse. Its white fetlocks were shaggy and almost bigger than my head. Garth stroked the animal's muzzle – this was a truly beloved creature.

'Talk to him,' Garth said. 'He will understand you. He'll need water and food each day, but not much rest.'

Falco was bound tightly in a sheet and propped against me, his padded head lolling back onto my shoulder. Without warning Garth slapped Hallr and the horse plodded forward. I almost lost hold of Falco, and clutched him against me.

'Good fortune!' Garth boomed. 'The Sword be with you!'

I twisted my neck to look back at the three of them, lifting my hand. All three raised theirs in return and I kept my eyes trained on them, refusing to turn back around until they had completely vanished from sight.

★

Falco was so big I felt I would suffocate any second now, or collapse under his weight. Poor Hallr was doing exceptionally well, unrelenting at a rapid trot, which seemed to be his quickest pace. But this was not going to get us to the prison in time to save Falco. His breathing was slowing and rivulets of sweat drenched me.

I ran my hands through Hallr's mane, trying to think of something to say to him. Speak to him, Garth had said, as though it was that easy.

'I . . . could you . . .' I cleared my throat, feeling infinitely stupid. 'He's fading, Hallr. Please hurry.'

The horse broke into a big, heavy canter. Brilliant creature.

We rode without stopping for eighteen hours and came to the first village on our path. Hallr brought us into the stables and I called for the horse master. A small man emerged and peered up at us.

'I need to trade this horse for something faster. He has unrivalled stamina and strength.'

'I've no need of a carthorse in these parts. Sparrow wants us on warhorses.'

I removed my hood and let him see me. 'I am Sparrow-sent. Get me the fastest horse you have.'

He jumped to do my bidding. Not because he knew I was the Sparrow – few knew that beyond the man lying across the front of this horse – but because the Sparrow's people were notoriously ugly, and because no one dared use my name in these parts unless they had truly been sent by me. I'd made sure of it.

The stable master brought out a huge white stallion, and he was glorious. 'He's called Elof.' A true warhorse, a creature of impeccable breeding and speed. He stamped his hoof and tossed his head, barely contained by his master. I smiled at the wild spirit in him. He'd be keen to run.

'Are you able to ride him, lady?' the man asked worriedly. I wasn't surprised – the creature was barely broken.

I nodded and swung up onto the enormous stallion and got my knees in tight around his flanks. He tossed and stamped and almost bucked me free, but I held my seat with tight knees and soft nonsensical murmurs. I took a few moments to settle him, leaning low over his neck and stroking his mane. He trembled with adrenalin and I held him firmly, not giving him any room to step out of line. When I was sure I had him under control I called for Falco to be mounted. It was not a good idea to load a horse like this with so much dead weight – he would chafe under it – but I had no choice, and soon I would be riding him hard enough that he wouldn't care what was atop him.

As the stable boys secured Falco I gave a few quick orders. 'Treat Hallr with care. Deliver him to Jarl Garth just across the border.'

I didn't give them time to be shocked by such an order, but kicked Elof forward, thrilled at the power that surged through his body. It was difficult to get low over his neck with Falco in the way, and it took

Elof a few moments to find his stride, but soon he was blazing across the earth with breathtaking speed.

We rode like this for a long time before he began to slow. I could feel him labouring and it killed me to press at him, to urge him faster. The unbearable truth dawned: I would have to ride this horse to death. I'd been opened, somehow, to things like fish in the hands of children. The death of this magnificent creature beneath me would hurt. It was not a good omen for the kind of strength I needed.

'Keep going,' I whispered desperately. I could feel Falco fading in my arms; his breaths were so few now. The horse flagged beneath me, trying with all his might to continue. I kicked him harder, felt his need to keep running even as his heart floundered. There were no more villages. We were drawing near the dead forest – we were *so* close.

Without warning something moved in the corner of my eye – the flap of a snowy wing – there and then gone. A bloom of sudden, belated clarity.

I pulled Elof to a halt and felt him tremble beneath me. Carefully, I dismounted and the great warhorse lowered both his front legs so I could gently pull Falco from his back. I soothed the stallion to the ground and cut off the top half of my canteen to let him drink from it. I laid my hand on his sweaty neck and felt him slowly start to calm. He would be alright, if he could let himself rest.

Falco would not. So I turned to the sky and prayed that my idea might work, that I had not entirely severed the connection when I severed the bond. With two fingers I whistled as loudly as I could, sent all of my need with that note of sound.

I waited. Would she forgive me for sending her away? Would she even feel me? I surely didn't deserve for her to, but Falco did. I sank to my knees beside him, keeping my fingers pressed to his neck to be certain he was alive. I let my eyes travel over the lines of his face as I hadn't done since before we'd broken the bond. Let myself remember those final moments when he'd looked inside me and known me, his eyes so gold. Gone were all the facades, the pretenses. I wasn't sure what he'd seen, but I knew it had been true. Just as I had seen the truth of him. The real truth, at last. When first we bonded I'd known he was more than he seemed, I had known of his masks and his faces and his names. I had known of the versions of himself that he drew about him as cloaks of protection, as means of survival. But I had not known the depth or extent of these until the night I died. I'd looked into his eyes and felt myself uncurl like a bloom, and felt him do the same. As though our souls were trying desperately to stop what was about to occur by giving us a glimpse of the infinity of each other. And in those moments I heard his mind, just as he'd heard mine – with an incomparable sweetness.

Farewell, little Sparrow. In dreams we will find each other once more.

And then he'd kissed me and pressed a blade into my heart.

I watched him now, allowing my fingers to trace the shape of his face. The angled jaw and cheeks. His eyelids and brows, his lips. I searched my heart for what remained, trying to understand the urgency in me. My terror at his death.

I feared the guilt of having brought it about. That was certainly part of it. My own fear of the cages had seen us imprisoned, resulting in his head wound. Was fear of adding to my shame all this was? I didn't have the same blind madness for him. I wasn't sick with love, or mad with it. Wasn't on fire with the thought of his touch.

But I . . . there was something subtler snaking itself through my veins. And perhaps it was simply the seduction of a life other than the one I lived. Perhaps in my mind he represented the idea of a life in which I was not a monster.

'That's weak,' said a voice, and I looked up to see Quillane. She was on her own today, her black hair swaying silkily. 'You are free of your cage.'

Something gave way inside me. 'Am I?'

'Yes.'

I swallowed. 'The monster doesn't need to be caged to be a monster.'

'Just as the monster may cease to be a monster if she so chooses.'

My heart hurt.

'Are you not compelled by the very idea that *choice* matters above all else?' the dead Empress of Kaya asked me softly, gently. And for the first time I felt frightened of her ghost.

A rush in the trees above us caused me to jerk in shock, and then I felt the great *whoosh* of power in my chest and I knew, I *knew* it was

Radha. She flew through the sky and circled down to the grass, the feathers of her wings glinting in the sunlight. She had the deepest brown eyes and *these* I knew to be beautiful.

I pressed my forehead to hers and gave her every scrap of myself, every tiny piece I had left. I didn't know if she could forgive me, or if I would ever look at her without remembering the lives I had taken, but she was here when I needed her and that meant everything.

She lowered herself flat so I could drag Falco onto her back. I sent Elof back to civilisation with a light whack to his rump, then quickly mounted Radha. Her powerful body leapt forward and the muscles in her enormous wings stretched and contracted. She trembled with the adrenalin and the effort of getting into the air, but once we were up with a lurching struggle, the pockets of wind helped us rise. The ground fell away beneath me as she worked to gain height, angling us up over the trees.

'Hold on,' I whispered to Falco. '*Please* hold on.'

CHAPTER 18

ISADORA

The sap of the magic in the dead forest was no less grievous in the air than on the ground. I had walked this forest once before, though Thorne and I had hung back and waited for Penn and the twins to reach the prison. I had been ill from the effects then, and I was doubly so now as we flew deeper into the heart of it. A brutal nausea overtook me and my limbs trembled with fatigue. I worried about Radha, though her wingbeats remained steady, and worried about Falco, though he continued to breathe.

I spotted the building in the distance and saw that it had no guards and no roof. Radha angled down and into the guts of the prison. The moment we moved within the sphere of the walls, the magic in the air ceased to drain me and I felt bizarrely energised.

We landed in a large central space, around which seemed to be levels of cells. People flocked from these cells to circle the pegasis and I looked down at them warily, leaving my hand on her neck to calm her. Equally composed of men and women, many looked normal, but there were several pale-eyed warders. With a wave of repulsion I angled Radha away from them, though none seemed to want to hurt us – not yet, at least.

'Move aside!' a voice hollered and a figure pressed through the crowd to Radha's side. He was bald and scarred and staring at Falco with dawning horror.

I drew my poor carving knife and held it where he could see. My eyes didn't stop moving; I didn't like being surrounded by potential threats. All these people crowding in so close, wanting to touch my horse –

'Get back!' I snarled, and Radha stamped her hoof.

'Give them some room,' the bald man shouted. The press of bodies eased a little.

'Your name?' I asked, getting a better look at the scars in his skull – they gouged brutally deep.

'Brathe. Once general of Kaya's army. Imprisoned by the Mad Ones, as we all are.'

I let out a breath. 'Then you can help. With me is Falco, Emperor of Kaya. He needs medical treatment.'

There was a variety of responses to that. Some gasped in delight, others in worry. Some swore in anger. I locked eyes with Brathe, allowing the question in my gaze to be clear.

'I would die for this man,' came his response, and he lifted Falco from the pegasis.

I dismounted and looked around. None of the cells were locked – the whole place had an atmosphere of unruliness. There didn't seem to be anyone guarding it, so I had no idea why anyone would remain here.

I followed Brathe and his entourage, leading Radha inside. They took Falco into a cell and laid him on the bed. There were people hovering – three warders – so I kept my hand protectively on Radha's flank, and on my single knife.

'What's wrong with him?' Brathe asked me.

'Cracked skull.'

The general turned to the warders. Two women and a man. They moved to stand over Falco, their eyes rolling back in their heads. I fought a wave of panic at the sight of them near him.

'He's too far gone,' one of the women said through tightly gritted teeth. She had dozens of elaborate braids in her hair and a ring through her nose. 'We cannot . . .' She groaned. Brathe was there to catch her limp body.

'Find more,' he urged her. 'Please, love. Take mine.'

My blood was rushing in my ears as I heard myself speak. The voice was barely recognisable to me. 'And mine. Have all of it.'

What are you doing?

The warders reached for me and I felt the repulsive drain of my soul. It was all I hated of the world, all the power I condemned. I had gone from being a monster who at least had principles to a creature who threw them away for a man who'd been her next kill. None of it made sense – *I* didn't make sense, but I didn't tell them to stop. They stole from me, took the guts of me, and that was strange, too, for how could they want the use of such a desolate soul?

There was a mighty wrench on my insides and I heard a gasp from the bed. I managed to stay conscious long enough to see him wake, to see his eyes open, and then I let the world disappear.

FALCO

In dreams we will find each other once more.

She has salt skin. Her eyes drip blood, as do her knives. Her corpses litter the ground beneath her feet. The bars of her cage blot out the sun and the moon; they make it very dark, very cold.

She is tiny, no more than two years old, shivering in the cage.

She is older, maybe ten, sharpening the bones of birds into weapons.

She is being jeered at, ridiculed, beaten and abused. She is a sea of bones. Wolves howl in agony from their mountains. Her heart is made of ice and I reach into her chest and crush it with my hand.

But now there are more hearts, and these are not made of ice. They are made of flesh and blood and they beat even when I take them in my hands. One of them belongs to Thorne, my Thorne. One of them to Finn. One belongs to Ava, another to Ambrose. There are more hearts in my hands, these belong to my family, all five of them. They are precious, and I destroy them. Another for Penn. One for Quillane. And two that are made of moth's wings and spiderwebs. Two that belong to Ella and Sadie. These I clench hard enough to make sure they cannot flutter any longer.

Watching me all the while are red eyes, my own and Isadora's. Her fingers are made of blades and I take one of them to sheathe in her heart, but before I can do this she looks into my eyes, into my soul, and she says, *Don't wake up, Emperor Feckless.*

★

My chest was wrenched upwards and I felt a great gush of air fill my lungs. The nightmares fled and I was pulled bodily into reality.

I lurched awake to a very strange sight. General Brathe stared down at me, flanked by three unknown warders. Behind them Isadora collapsed at Radha's hooves.

I scrambled to my feet.

'Majesty! Please –'

But I crawled to where she had slumped and scooped her into my arms. As gently as I could I carried her to the bed and laid her out.

'You are unwell –'

'I'm fine!' It was true. I felt as healthy as I ever had in my life. 'What's wrong with her?'

'She's only drained.'

'You took her energy?'

'She gave it freely.'

I breathed out. 'Where are we?'

'In the warder prison, Majesty.'

My head swivelled to look at Brathe, properly taking in his presence. 'Why did she bring me here?'

'Your head wound.'

The last thing I remembered was the Pirenti house, a bed beside Isadora's. This would have cost her a great deal, bringing me here. To the people she hated most.

I sat on the bed. 'We'll talk when she wakes. Have my pegasis taken care of until then.'

'Falco,' Brathe said as the others left the cell, 'it is dangerous here.'

I nodded, meeting his eyes. 'Have you access to a weapon I might use?'

I saw concern and pity. 'What will you do with a weapon, Majesty?'

'I will use it.'

He nodded and retreated, sliding the bars closed behind him. To his credit, he hid at least some of his doubt.

★

I sat with Isadora for an hour before she woke. She slept soundly, but her eyelids flickered with dreams and I wondered if she was conscious in that head of hers, lucid within the walls of those dreams. I wondered if I would ever walk the dream world again, or if that had been a single miraculous night of beauty. How strange, to walk such a place each night. How glorious. Did she know the fortune she had in stepping through the fold and seeing a world no others had access to? Or was it as normal to her as breathing after twenty-five years of it? It didn't seem right that someone who was capable of seeing the bizarre loveliness of the world was also capable of such hatred and violence. Then again, that was hardly her fault.

Eventually, her red eyes opened.

'I know nothing more than you. Are you ready to face them?'

She nodded. Then, 'Radha?'

'I have Brathe seeing to her. You . . . called her? To carry me?'

Isadora nodded. She got to her feet and we emerged from the cell. A couple of young warders flanked the entrance. Before us was an expanse of people, above us was open sky. The warders were grouped together, the ordinary humans a distance away, separate but larger in number. They weren't happy to see us, and I could sense a bristling tension in the air.

'Where's Brathe?' I asked.

The warders led us down several snaking hallways. I got the sense they weren't only showing us the way, but guarding us against the cold gazes of the other prisoners. I heard fights raging, and shouts of anger. Isadora subtly twisted so she could keep an eye on our rear as we made our way through the prison. A wise idea, it turned out, as our passage was riling everyone up. Several young men shouted obscenities and threw things at me. Isadora managed to cut most of the items out of the air, but she missed a heavy metal cup. I fought the urge to duck, and instead let it clip me hard in the ear. She took one look at the trickle of blood on my face and turned back with a frown.

'Keep moving!' one of our warders barked.

Isadora visibly hesitated, then acquiesced and followed us swiftly.

We found my general in a large kitchen, sitting at a wooden table opposite a female warder I didn't know. More warders kept watch at the entrance, but it was quiet within.

Without warning or permission, Emperor Feckless arrived.

My posture and mannerisms shifted slightly, turned more flamboyant, a little more effeminate. My expression took on an arrogant disinterest, a touch of distaste, as though the prison had offended my sensibilities. I offered a flourishing, theatrical bow, because Feckless was always, always mocking. 'General Brathe,' I greeted, and even my voice was tweaked, more of a purr. 'How the tables have turned, what with me dethroned and you king of the criminally insane. Shall I bow and kiss your hand? Perhaps I should avert my eyes! What a kingdom you have built here.'

There was silence in the kitchen.

I could almost hear my heart pounding. *What are you doing, you maniac?*

But Brathe was unsurprised by my behaviour. I'd never been anything else with him. 'You will be Emperor until the day you die, Majesty,' he disagreed, always generous despite his impatience with my antics. He was impeccably loyal, stemming not from belief in me, but from a wayward perception of royal blood and its divinity.

'Emperors have palaces and servants,' I said with a sniff. 'And *wine.*'

I could feel Isadora's gaze, but was careful not to look at her.

I seemed to have lost control of my masks. For Brathe I had always gone to extremes, had pushed Feckless as far as he could be pushed. For Brathe I was careless, disinterested and given to vices. I joked a lot, asked stupid questions, turned up to meetings drunk or hungover. His reach had been wide - he'd passed more intelligence through Kaya than any other, which made him the perfect tool. Without meaning to he spread knowledge of my idiocy and incapacity into even the least touched corners, where enemies were more likely to be hiding.

Which was all very well, but did not explain why I was still carrying on with it, while he was captive in a prison and could share information with no one.

'You'd best explain, then.' I sighed with an impatient wave. 'What right mess are we in now? Please tell me it can be solved without too much involvement from me.'

Isadora and I perched ourselves opposite the general. The female warder beside him eyed me with such scorn that I could have burst into flame. I liked her facial piercings though.

'I was imprisoned here six months ago in the initial attack,' Brathe answered. 'The warders and soldiers here are those who would not bow to Dren and Galia.'

'Why weren't they killed?'

Brathe shrugged. 'Don't know, Majesty. But there are factions here. Warders on one side, soldiers on the other.'

'Why do you stay?' Isadora asked.

'We can't use our magic within the prison,' the female warder replied. 'And –'

'A lie,' Isadora said flatly.

The warder studied her a moment, then glanced at me. 'We can use *some*, but at great cost. The warders who helped heal His Majesty remain unconscious from the effort. There are incredibly strong wards draped over this place like a veil, weakening us and making it impossible to escape.'

'It makes the warders targets for the soldiers, who hate their kind,' Brathe added.

'My condolences,' I said, 'but if the Mad Ones were able to escape then I haven't much sympathy for warders unable to do the same.'

In the irritated silence that followed, Isadora leant close to my ear and muttered, 'It's not necessary here, Falco.'

I didn't respond, keeping my eyes trained on Brathe and the warder. She was wrong, and I knew it suddenly. With people of my court it would always be necessary. I couldn't loosen my grip on the way things had been. Not when everything had gone to shit and Feckless was the last vestige of normalcy. I had to protect even the possibility that things could go back to the way they were, that I would return to the throne of Sancia and Brathe would be my general, and he'd spread knowledge of the nation's foolish Emperor, an easy target.

An underestimated man was a dangerous man.

And I was surrounded by enemies. I would *always* be surrounded.

I saw them then. Five bleeding hearts, removed from their bodies and placed tenderly on the edge of a fountain for a little boy to find –

I swallowed the wave of panic and pulled my mask more firmly into place, armour against the memory.

'What's there to do in here?' I asked. 'I imagine you must get up to all kinds of mischief.'

'Mostly we try not to die,' the pierced woman said bluntly.

I let my lips twitch a little. 'Forgive me – greeting beautiful ladies is usually my first priority. Emperor Falco of Sancia at your service.'

She looked unimpressed. 'I am Inga.'

I leveled Inga with a look, one I happened to be very good at. She could have been almost anyone in the world – married, in love, interested in women, another man – it didn't matter. This look caused people to blush, drop their eyes and imagine very dirty things.

Inga blushed, dropped her eyes and was no doubt imagining very dirty things.

I allowed Brathe to spot my smile before donning an innocent expression. He ignored my behaviour as he always did, explaining that Inga was a second-tier warder who'd lived in Limontae. He touched her hand, an idle finger to the beat of her pulse, and I recognised in it the familiarity of lovers. He went on to say that the leaders of the human soldiers in the prison were none other than the royal assistants Sharn and Valerie, who had been the stewards of Limontae. They now opposed all warders, even the ones in the very same captivity.

'It's bloody,' Brathe told me grimly. 'We fight constantly for territory and power. We hold the kitchens, which is no small thing. They hold the library and weaponry. We'll need to keep you sequestered safely out of the way, Falco. It's . . . starting to get out of control.'

'Do you have any weapons at all?' Isadora asked.

'Very few,' Brathe answered.

I turned to Izzy. She was expressionless, her huge red eyes searching. 'What do you think?' I asked her.

'Secure you. Fortify the space. Keep it well guarded until I can find a way out.'

I frowned. 'You want me to hide?'

Isadora turned back to Brathe and I saw it so clearly: her dismissal. 'Where is secure?' she asked, and they started discussing spaces in which I could be hidden and protected, but I heard none of it. There was a ringing sound in my ears.

That dismissal, so blatant. I'd seen it in so many, but never in her. It made something shift. A complete, enormous refusal reared up inside me, absolute and undeniable. Nothing had ever been so acute, so *propelling*.

I'd thought, somehow, that she knew. That she saw me. But even Isadora was convinced by Emperor Feckless.

And I was abruptly unable to abide that.

My heart, I realised, may as well have been removed and placed alongside the hearts of my dead family; I too may as well have died that day twenty-five years ago. But I'd made a plan, I'd been strategic and clever.

I was tired of being clever. The world Emperor Feckless had ruled over was destroyed.

So let me be brave instead, just once.

'A meeting,' I demanded clumsily, interrupting them and swivelling their gazes to me. 'Set up a meeting with Sharn and Valerie.'

'Majesty, I must tell you . . .' Brathe hedged. 'They hate you. They all hate you. They blame you for their imprisonment.'

'Because I was weak enough to let Kaya be overruled?'

Brathe opened his mouth, closed it again and simply nodded.

Fluttering wings brushed against my face as I stood. 'I need cloth.'

'A meeting is far too dangerous,' Brathe tried, but Inga found me some cloth. I wrapped it around each of my fists. 'Falco,' Brathe was saying again, 'Wait -'

But I'd had enough of waiting. I strode through the hallways to the arena. The dark heart of me circled. Thirty-five years of fury took root in my chest, the course of adrenalin whispered to me. It said *fight fuck kill, use fists guts balls spine, use it all, use everything, all of it, and finally, finally let it out, let it be seen, let the truth unveil you.*

Brathe and Inga were trying to reason with me, question me. I shut them out, allowed the fluttering wings to take control instead.

The prisoners were all in the arena. They'd been waiting for me, and the shouting began. Gods, how they hated me. I could taste it in the air as I pressed through them to face Sharn and Valerie. He had always been serious, she had always been flippant. Now they were both furious. I needed the library and the armoury. I needed the fighting here to end. I needed every person in this prison aligned at my back, so that when we broke free I could lead them to face the Mad Ones. And I could think of only one way to make that happen. I had to give them someone to align behind.

Isadora had followed me and was hovering at my side. 'No matter what happens,' I said, 'don't let anyone step in for me.'

She looked confused, even concerned. 'An inability to do something does not make someone weak,' she said. 'You have nothing to prove by putting yourself in danger. You may make things worse.'

I smiled a little. 'Maybe,' I agreed. Then I turned, even as she reached to stay me, and walked into the middle of the circle. It was strange, where fate led you. Excitement uncurled at the base of my gut. How thrilling the notion of showing her something other than inability or laziness. To show her, after all this time, that I didn't need protecting. To be seen as someone who could not only survive without her help, but could also help protect *her*. Not that she would ever need it.

I didn't want to feel useless anymore, I didn't want to be pitied. I didn't want to be fucking Emperor Feckless.

'Stand forward,' I ordered crisply amid the chatter of curiosity and scorn.

Sharn and Valerie glanced at each other and stepped forward. 'You look ready for a fight. But we would bid you not to embarrass yourself further. You no longer hold power over us.'

'Because you are traitors to your country.'

'Because *you* are!' Sharn exclaimed.

'How am I a traitor?'

'You let them win. You let them take. And you're too weak to take back.'

'So you mean to kill me?'

They nodded in sync. 'Kaya needs strength, not the cowardice you have shown.'

I straightened my shoulders and looked around at what had to be hundreds of people. They filled the arena and lined the balconies of the cells. 'I am Emperor Falco of Sancia, son of Emperor Falonius. I have ruled Kaya for twenty-five years, since the day I turned ten.'

An unimpressed silence filled the prison: my name held no respect.

'Twenty of those years were peaceful. Now there are corrupt warders in my city, in my country, and I will do whatever it takes to scour them from this earth. I want every one of you to join me in facing them.'

'We're imprisoned, fool!' someone shouted angrily.

'Why would we follow Emperor Feckless?' Sharn asked. 'How could you ever stop anyone?'

'I have the support of both the Sparrow and the King and Queen of Pirenti.'

'The Sparrow is your enemy!' someone shouted.

'You're a coward!' another yelled.

'He's a fucking joke.'

'Miserable whelp.'

'Fool.'

'Incompetent.'

'Pathetic.'

'Useless.'

'Good-for-nothing.'

I heard it all, all the insults they'd been longing to throw at me for months, maybe years.

I stretched my neck, my shoulders, felt the pull and release of my muscles, my healthy, strong body. Let their hate wash over me. None of it touched me. Not now, not in this place. Because not a single person in this hall knew what I was. Not a single person in this world.

Valerie shouted and six men ran forward.

My eyes shifted scarlet.

CHAPTER 19

ISADORA

I was confused, at first. I thought he intended to get himself killed. Then when he told me not to send anyone in to help him I thought he must have some kind of plan. I kept expecting it to show itself; for some elaborate, genius scheme to unfold. Because he was smart. That was what I knew of him. He'd spent his life covering it up but he was cunning - this I had learned. Indeed, he had just morphed as I watched into a creature of such simpering, vain idiocy that I had barely been able to believe my eyes. The way he'd shifted himself, his mannerisms, his expressions, his words, and all so effortlessly until he seemed like an entirely different person . . . the way he had looked at Inga, with a deep, barely controlled heat. Once upon a time he'd had reasons for it, I knew, but now I wasn't so sure. Now I thought maybe it was pattern, habit, familiarity. Either way, it was amazing, this chameleon-talent of his.

As the six soldiers ran at him, I realised his intelligence was not the only thing he had been hiding.

They attacked and my thoughts shifted to how I would step in, how I would kill them. If he planned to martyr himself I would not allow it. I took several steps forward, then stopped.

In the warder prison of Kaya I saw a thing unlike any I had witnessed. I saw an impossibility. Something not a soul in the world would believe were they not to see it with their own eyes. He had done such a thorough job of convincing the world of his uselessness, the very idea of anything else was laughable. The Emperor – a man so feckless he had been gifted a new title, a man renowned for his clumsiness, his inability to fight, his complete lack of courage – ducked gracefully beneath the first soldier's fist, swinging an incredible right cross straight into the man's jaw. It was flawless, and it dropped the soldier instantly.

My first thought was that I had slipped into the dream realm, where things were beautiful and false.

But I was very much awake, and the attacks were continuing. Falco dodged a blow, twisting to use the man's momentum to hammer him in the back of the skull. Without pausing Falco continued his turn, lifting to smash his boot into the ribs of the third man. He kicked again, smashing the ribs to pieces. Two men came at him from behind, but he spun low beneath their blows and smashed them both in the solar plexus, one and then the other. The first fell to his knees, unable to breathe, but the other came at him again. Falco advanced, swiftly ducking the blows flying at his head and then throwing his own. His fist landed hard on the man's face: one, two to the cheek, breaking the bone, one to break the nose, a third to the jaw to knock him out.

The final soldier was big – Pirenti-big. He took Falco by the shoulders and sent him flying through the air. Falco twisted into a roll and was on his feet again, running at the Pirenti attacker. He slid low, bending backwards beneath the man's arms and taking out his legs. Falco rose fluidly alongside the stumbling brute and reached – almost casually – for the man's thick neck, slamming it to the ground. The soldier was out like a light, his skull hitting the floor with a boom.

Falco rose to his feet and looked around at the six injured men. He turned his eyes – red as blood – to Sharn and Valerie. And he waited.

I realised my mouth was open and closed it with a snap. My skin prickled and my pulse was quick, wonderfully quick. The prisoners were just as overawed. *How did we not know?* they were thinking. The sheer magnitude of his deceit hit me, and the loneliness of that life. It wasn't just that he could fight. It was *how* he was fighting – the *discipline* of it, the infinite hours he must have trained in secret and all the hours he must have spent training to hide that ability. He'd made every gesture blunt and clumsy, had dropped things, stumbled over nothing and made it look perfectly real. The mask was so heavy and so tightly attached that it was a cage in itself.

Now he was free of it.

And, oh, how I had fallen for it, sneaking into his palace and believing he would be the easiest man in the world to kill. How arrogantly I'd crept through those hallways, towards the waiting blade fish with his shimmering scales and unseen deadliness.

How he would have destroyed me, had he not bonded with me instead.

*

Sharn looked deflated, but Valerie was angrier than ever. It wasn't over, I realised. Valerie now yelled at the armed men at his back and four of them rushed forward, swords at the ready. Which changed things. Fists could break bones and debilitate easily. Blades meant blood, and real danger.

'Don't do this,' Falco warned. They ignored him – one or two sniggered, too stupid to have properly understood what they'd witnessed.

I still had my heavy butcher's knife, whatever good it would do him. 'Falco!'

He spun as I lobbed it through the air; his hand plucked the hilt and spun the blade into the hand of a sword-wielder, and that was all Falco needed it for – the knife was promptly discarded in the same moment he caught his attacker's dropped sword. The unarmed man bolted away, but there were still three swordsmen coming at him, another two circling behind.

He spun to inflict dozens of quick shallow wounds. His movements were elegant and fast; the long curved sword moved with a dazzling flicker of light.

I watched and came to understand that I *did* know how to recognise beauty. This was beautiful – *he* was beautiful. Not his skin or hair or his pretty face, but his skill, his resolve. I let my worry for him fade with the spectacle unfolding before me, as special as a white fish to a little boy.

FALCO

I disarmed them without inflicting too many wounds. Most were shallow, but two had deeper gashes in their abdomens and thighs that would need to be dealt with quickly.

The control was a familiar drug to me, a powerful stimulant in my veins. Manipulating my body and feeling its precision, the way it did my bidding – this was what I lived for, how I got through the days. It was strange being watched. My awareness of their eyes returned as I lowered my sword, the fight over. The blade in my hand wasn't my father's, but it had done the job.

Silence reigned, but for the soft whimpers of an injured man. As my pulse cooled I looked around. Sharn and Valerie didn't send any more soldiers to attack. Instead, they stared at me.

I cleared my throat, ran a hand through my hair and said, 'An under-estimated man is a dangerous one. That was the why of it. I plan to use the power of my false name to destroy the Mad Ones and rebuild Kaya. But I can't do it without you. My people. I need your courage. Will you help me?'

Sharn and Valerie smiled in sync. 'Aye,' she said.

And a huge cheer went up. A wall of sound and movement washed over me.

What a strange, heady thing, to feel admired, even respected.

I turned to find Isadora in the crowd. She was watching me, and her eyes were black.

★

I had to endure an hour of Brathe barraging me with questions: who taught you to fight, when did you learn, why didn't you tell anyone, why weren't you leading my forces and so on. When I escaped I found Isadora sitting on a bed in an empty cell. Radha was standing just outside the open bars, keeping watch over her.

I stopped by the pegasis and pressed my forehead to hers. 'I've missed you.' She nuzzled against me and I stroked her, feeling her hair and her feathers beneath my fingers. Then I sat on the bed opposite Izzy's and folded my hands over my knees. Her eyebrows arched, but that was all. The only acknowledgment she made. My own lips twitched.

She nodded at the door and I craned my neck to see that two young soldiers had arrived to stand by Radha. 'What are you two doing?'

'Guarding you, Majesty.'

Isadora hid a smile.

'That's alright, mate,' I told him. 'We can guard ourselves.'

They left reluctantly.

'You're adored,' Izzy said, a little mockingly.

'It's stupid. That all you have to do is fight a couple of novices and they forget about twenty-five years' worth of embarrassment.'

'It's not that you fought, it's *how* you fought, and what it means.'

I scratched my chin, avoiding her eyes. 'Now we just have to get out of here.'

'How did it feel? For them to see you?'

I shrugged, unsure of the answer. There was something scratching at me, at the edge of me. I didn't know what, but it scared me.

We lapsed into silence. I considered her covertly, pondering our situation and how we'd come to find ourselves here. In the cages I'd wanted to be away from her – had planned to leave her the moment we escaped. At Elsa's house I had been ready for the two of us to part. And yet here we were again – stuck. If fate did exist, then it was certainly having a good laugh.

I couldn't hate Isadora, not with the same burning fury I'd felt when I found out about Quill. But there was still a kernel of bitterness in my heart every time I looked at her. She'd stolen something precious from me, and from the world. I didn't know how to forgive that, or even if I should.

'I want you to know something,' she said softly, uncomfortably. She wasn't looking at me, so it was safe for me to study her face, the fine, delicate angles of it. 'You and I have agreed to align for the course of this war. But even after . . . as the Sparrow, I have decided I will not contest your rule.'

I felt myself go still. Was this some kind of ploy? She was certainly clever enough to make a long play that would get her closer to the throne – her tactics in the past had been to deceive and assassinate.

Mistrust overtook. She couldn't possibly mean it. Not after all these years, not just because I could use a sword.

'Not because of the fighting,' she said. The hairs on my arms stood on end at her ability to read me.

'Then why?' I demanded. Confusion made me angry. I wasn't ready for her to be kind. I certainly wasn't ready for her to expect anything of me – there was way too much pressure in that, way too much panic.

271

I watched her struggle for words. Nothing came from her open mouth and her expression turned helpless.

It was a lie. It had to be a lie, so I rose to my feet. 'Generous of you,' I muttered coldly, and left.

I walked through the prison. Most prisoners were in bed by now but those who weren't bowed as I passed – a far cry from throwing cups at my head. I explored the armoury first, noting the weapons stock and choosing two long swords with scabbards that would strap to my back nicely. Then I made my way to the library. This was where the warder records were kept, which had always bewildered me: why keep them with the prisoners instead of safe in the warder temple? It seemed now that the secrecy of the warders was so extreme that even their information needed to be imprisoned. What were they hiding in here? All the warders who'd been stationed to guard the prison and maintain these records were now dead, so there was no one to ask. I strolled through the stacks, opening scrolls and flicking through books. Lists of those with soul magic, training techniques, types of magic, history of magic – it was all here.

If there was a way to defeat the warders then it would stand to reason they would lock that secret inside an inescapable prison. All I had to do was find it.

★

Hours passed without me noticing. I was surrounded by a pile of half-read scrolls when I looked up to see that I was no longer alone. Inga was perched on a table, watching me silently. 'What a funny, tricksy one you are,' she commented. 'What a lonely pursuit.'

'Couldn't sleep?'

She shook her head. 'Her dreams are too loud.'

'Whose?'

'Your strange travel companion's.'

I closed the book I'd been flipping through. 'You can hear her dreams?'

'It's the part of my magic I can't control. Not even in here.' Her eyes were a pale orange. 'She has terrible nightmares.'

I looked away, muttering, 'Not my problem.'

Inga frowned. 'But are the two of you not . . .?'

'We're nothing.'

She shook her head. 'Why so angry?'

I blinked. 'I'm not. I just don't trust her. You wouldn't either if you knew who she was.'

'But I do.'

My hands paused in opening another book.

'She offered her energy to help heal you. I saw inside her.'

'Then you know what she did.'

Inga nodded. 'I know all that she has done, and I know what you both did. But I don't understand why, or *how*. How could you do something so destructive?'

I shook my head, frustrated. 'We didn't *love* each other, but were bound unto death. It was unnatural.'

Inga gave me this look then, like I was supremely foolish. Like I was Emperor Feckless, even though I hadn't donned his mask.

I took a breath and tried to explain. 'Isadora believes in choice above all else. She didn't choose the bond, so no matter how right or wrong or fated or mistaken it was, having it forced upon her turned it to ash. That could never be undone, no matter what grew between us.'

Inga considered this, then nodded. 'I understand.'

That surprised me. 'You don't think we ignored what fate had planned for us?'

She smiled. 'If we believe in fate, then by its very nature it means that breaking the bond must have been part of its plan, too.'

I couldn't help returning her smile. The small silver pieces threaded through her long dreadlocks flickered in the candlelight, as did the ring in her nose. Her orange eyes shifted to a pale sky blue as she pinned them on me.

'But let me tell you a secret, Emperor Falco. The bond is a force and can be forced, that is true. And perhaps it was right for the two of you to break free of it. What cannot be forced is love.'

I stared at the warder, feeling the words sink like stones to the bottom of my guts. I had to clear my throat before I could speak. 'Isadora was never forced to love me.' *The bond hadn't even been able to do that much.*

'You're right, she wasn't.' Inga rose, her long legs untangling. She had the look of a gangly foal, unsure on her feet, or a child who had grown suddenly tall and was still unused to it. I wondered how old she was. It was often hard to tell with warders. She grinned, seeming suddenly much younger. 'I'm going to do something that neither of you want. But I'm a meddler. It's my fatal flaw, according to Brathe.'

Without waiting for my permission Inga placed her hands on either side of my head and I felt a rush of sight. Memories flooded my mind, not my own. Isadora looking down at me as I collapsed in the rain. *Please stand up. I need you to stand up. I can't carry you. I'm not strong enough.* But she did carry me, doggedly, slipping and falling, on and on. I saw memories of her sinking to the mud, of being found by children, of weeping, of being carried on a stretcher, of watching me sleep, of a fish inside a child's hands, of cradling me on a horse and pushing it further and further. I felt the fear she harboured of this horse dying and knew that she would ride it to death if she had to. I saw her dismounting and calling for Radha, felt the overwhelming nausea of carrying me into the dead forest, saw her landing in the prison, her fear and repulsion, the soul-deep betrayal she felt at giving her energy to the warders . . .

I returned to the library in a rush, blinking to see that Inga had removed her touch. I swallowed and ran a trembling hand over my eyes. For a good few minutes I let the memories settle in my mind, trying to make sense of them. 'I didn't know. She told me . . .'

'She doesn't want you to feel indebted to her. But I thought you ought to know.'

'Why? So I might feel guilty?'

'Of course not.'

Angry, I stood and strode into the hallway. Unsure, I stopped, turned, swivelled back again. I walked towards the arena, towards her cell. Stopped again.

Don't. It doesn't mean anything. Nor does it change anything.

Except that it did. It changed something inside me. Being stuck with me was one thing, but endangering her own life to save mine was something else entirely. Was it guilt? A lingering connection? I didn't know what the fuck was going on. *She* was the one who had always hated *me*.

I had loved her.

There it was. The reason I was so angry. Because I had loved her and she had hurt me in the most brutal way possible. I'd told myself that my fury was about Quill. I was sure now that I also hated Isadora because she had never surrendered to me like I had to her. She had been stronger than me, and I the fool for it.

I continued angrily to the cell, but stopped and turned *again*. I was lost, too full, too empty. I was a mess inside, a chaotic mess of uncertainty.

Curse it.

I strode into the cell. She woke instantly, jerking from whatever nightmare plagued her. 'Why did you do that?' I demanded. 'Why did you save me?'

Isadora sat up slowly. It was dark, though a window above shed a little starlight. Not enough for me to see the colour of her eyes. Mine felt very black and I couldn't control them, couldn't calm them.

'Why?'

But she didn't answer. She never answered. I crossed to the bed and knelt, reaching to take her arms. I shook her a little, my grip too tight. I could see her eyes now – they were deep scarlet. 'You shouldn't have done it,' I snarled. 'You can't hate me and want me dead and then turn around and save my life. You can't.'

She swallowed and I was distracted by the way it made her throat move. My eyes went to her parted lips. I could see the rise and fall of her breathing. I leant closer, holding her eyes. 'If it was some trick of yours . . .'

'What?' she murmured. 'What would you do?' Her breath was on my lips. I could feel the heat of her against my body.

'I'd kill you,' I whispered.

Her lips curled and her irises slipped black to match mine. 'You could try.'

My heart was hammering against my ribcage. Unable to help myself, I dipped my mouth to hover over her jaw, her throat, not quite touching, but breathing in her skin. She was frozen still, as though I would attack her at any moment. Slowly, I brushed my lips against the corner of her mouth. It was the slightest of touches, the ghost of a touch.

We stayed there, in that moment and all moments, perched on the edge of a precipice. Time stretched, thinned, stopped. She took up the whole world, she *was* the whole world, and my desire for her even greater.

Isadora turned her lips to meet mine and it all dissolved around us and we were clutching at each other and kissing kissing kissing. I was so hungry for her, ravenous, impossibly so, I couldn't get enough, I had to have more –

Without warning I was shoved from her and found myself sprawled on the floor.

Dazed, I looked up. Her cheeks were flushed, lips swollen.

'What madness is this?' she whispered.

Slowly I shook my head. Because it felt like the tide again, the great ocean tide pulling me towards her, and what mortal man was strong enough to resist that? It felt like fate and inevitability; it felt like magic.

Which was impossible. We were free of the magic. We had survived it. This wasn't fair – it wasn't *right*.

I climbed onto the bed opposite hers and stared at the ceiling. I willed my heart to slow. My lips and hands felt like traitors to the rest of my body. I thought of Quillane, or I tried to make myself think of her, but my thoughts kept returning to the woman in the bed beside mine. I thanked the gods she had stopped me before I got any further. She was not mine and could never be mine. And not only because she had murdered my Empress, but because she still didn't know the truth.

How did it feel? For them to see you?

I'd wanted it to be so different, but it wasn't. It felt the same as wearing any other mask. It felt hollow.

ISADORA

I listened to his breathing slow and couldn't understand how he was able to fall asleep. I lay awake, tense and anxious, for hours. His nearness was a flame of mortification. This gods-cursed temptation again. This ripping of my heart from my chest, when I was supposed to have endured enough already. Was this my punishment for surrendering to him once? To be forever bound to the longing for him? He fell so easily to sleep, unconcerned by how mad this was sending me.

It wasn't his fault, I supposed. He was used to this sort of thing. Had spent his whole life in the arms of women and men, if rumours were true. He was amorous and desirous and desired. He could have no idea how momentous even a kiss was for me, a kiss chosen freely.

A thousand years ago, a million, we made love. But that had been a dream, as fleeting and unreal as all the illusions I saw when I walked the dream realm. Our bond was as bright and brief as the shooting stars that fell through the dream sky. The pleasure was a tease, a taunt, a way to remind me of what was missing from my real life, the life I had earned.

In this real life I had never felt desire or been desired. There had never been space for it. Against all odds desire had found me tonight, at last. Whole body, whole mind desire, with no coercion or magic to fuel it. But desire, I understood too well, was a fleeting thing. It was not connection or affection and when it fled it left an even greater absence in its place. My wound, the scar where his soul had been connected to mine, hurt unbearably. I missed him. He was two meters from me and I missed him terribly. I felt small and invisible and pathetic.

The answer was clear: I needed to stay as far from Falco as possible. I would reforge myself into steel and iron and be done with everything.

I was deciding this when the morning sun crept through the prison window and wreathed him in golden light. I turned my head and looked at him - a mistake, as it turned out. For he was lovely, lying so peacefully sunlit, and my thoughts turned away from steel and iron.

If only I had known what it would feel like to lose the sweet tenderness of your touch or the love in your eyes when you looked at me . . . If only I had understood how much those small pieces of you were worth, how big an absence they would leave in their wake . . . If only I had understood what it would feel like for you to fall out of love with me . . . I'm not sure I would have been strong enough to tread this path.

Chapter 20

Finn

The dead were a noisy bunch. *Scream, scream, scream* they went, all day long. It was my ma's legacy, that I could hear them. She'd been born to raise the dead, but she hadn't been very good at it. One try and that was it, lights out for her. Being thrice-born also helped me to hear them – made it so I couldn't *stop* hearing.

As I lay halfway between sleep and waking I listened to the screams of the dead souls shift to become the mindless chatter I knew would soon turn into the melodies of the otherworld. If you listened closely enough the screams weren't screams at all, but beautiful, mournful songs.

Someone moved beside me and I was drawn further into the waking world. The sound of the waves crashing against the mouth of the ocean cave mingled with the hum of dead voices in my ears. Hundreds of bodies slept pressed in around me. Living, breathing warm bodies. Penn was to one side, his hand curled inside mine. Jonah was to the other. And there were *eyes* above, milky eyes gazing down at me.

I jerked in fright. 'Ugh. Are you *trying* to be creepy, Os?'

The warder nodded his head towards the mouth of the cave and made his way over to it. I grumbled sleepily and picked my way through the bodies, stumbling clumsily over several and receiving curses for my efforts.

'You have a particular talent for being annoying,' I told Osric as I joined him on the moonlit shore.

'I often think the same of you,' he muttered.

'We must make a good pair then. What's wrong?'

The sea lapped against the rocks at our feet. Its black reaches smudged into the black of the sky in the distance, distinguishable by its smattered silver stars. The smuggled people of Sancia were scattered throughout caves along this coastline, sleeping as well as they could after having left loved ones and homes behind. It felt vulnerable out here, despite the shroud of stone and night we hid beneath.

'We can't stay here.'

'I thought Falco told us to wait for a Pirenti entourage.'

'And will we wait ourselves into the grave? They have a long way to travel to reach us and we don't even know if they're coming – we should move to meet them.'

I shivered, though the night was warm. I didn't know how it had happened, but suddenly without either the Emperor of Kaya or the Queen of Pirenti in our retinue, the leadership and protection of three hundred hunted souls had fallen to Osric and me. It was rather horrid.

'The road follows the coast and will be riddled with warders.'

'We won't take the road. We'll go around the marshes.'

'And if we're spotted?'

'We won't be. You and I are going to erect a cloak,' Os said.

A flicker of fear found me. 'Cloak three hundred people over a distance of hundreds of miles, for a length of time spanning weeks?' I gave panicked laugh. 'I'm flattered by your assumption, Os, but you're a first-tier warder. I'm a no-tier warder. I can tell you right now, you won't be getting much help from me.'

Osric turned his head. His eyes were very pale in the moonlight, his hair glowing a little. In this light he reminded me of Izzy, and I wondered yet again where she was. Falco hadn't returned with her, which meant he'd failed in his rescue mission. And which of us had believed he *wouldn't*, anyway? It was a steady gut-sickness, thinking about the two of them and what I had done to them, thinking how even now they might be dead and separated for all eternity because of the power in my bondmate's blood.

'Who is the corrupted warder?' Osric asked.

I sighed – this was the way he finished every one of our lessons. 'The powerless warder.'

'Don't just say it, Finn. Understand it.'

'How? I ask you and ask you what you can possibly mean by such a backwards statement, but you never tell me, Os! Power is what corrupts, not the other way around.'

'You're clever, kid,' he said. 'At least you're meant to be.'

I rolled my eyes, irritated. He never bloody well *explained* himself.

'Do you know how many warders are born with power over the dead?' he asked.

'No.'

'Almost none. You are a very rare creature, Finn of Limontae. So let me tell you a secret, but don't mistake it for a compliment.'

'From you? Don't worry, I won't,' I muttered.

'Whatever that deep, rare thing inside you is, it's exponentially stronger than anything that exists in me.'

I frowned. His words disturbed me more than I wanted him to know. 'That's ridiculous.'

He shrugged.

'So if I'm apparently so powerful then doesn't that mean, according to your logic, that I'm incorruptible?'

Osric gave a sigh of long suffering. 'What is power?'

'Magic, but —'

'Gods almighty, Finn! That's exactly what Dren and Galia believe! Magic is *not* power.' He grabbed my shoulders and shook me a little, and I was shocked — I'd never before seen him anywhere close to this animated. Osric's perpetual state of being was boredom and mild annoyance. But now I could see ferocity in his gaze, in the twist of his mouth.

'Power,' he said, 'is strength of spirit. It is kindness. Generosity. Loyalty. Love. The second you start thinking that power is magic is the second you surrender to it, the second you give it control, the second it begins its corruption. Instead, *you* must control the magic.'

I swallowed, holding his unblinking eyes. 'I understand,' I told him. But it was easier to conceive of than make real. Easier to want strength of spirit, harder to have it.

Osric returned to the cave but I sat on the rocks to listen to the waves a little longer. *Crash, crash, sway,* they went. *Whisper, whisper, hiss* went the voices in my ears. And *Thorne, Thorne, Thorne* went my heart, not knowing what else to do.

THORNE

I sat on the edge of my bed in Vjort's castle, dizzy with exhaustion and refusing to sleep . . . *not yet, not until they are found.* I tried to reach out to Finn, willing it to work, desperate desperate *desperate* for her voice. But there was nothing. I couldn't feel her, could barely feel myself.

A sound left me, some breathless noise of pain. I looked for Da, but couldn't find him either. He hadn't appeared to me since the moment I cast him off, and I was terrified I'd lost him forever. Lost him to my own shadow, this shadow I had stepped into and cloaked myself beneath.

I struggled to my feet and paused before the mirror. Carefully I lifted my tunic and then the soggy bandage to see the swollen, puss-infected wound between my ribs. It looked bad, felt worse.

Grimacing, I pressed the bandage back down and straightened my tunic. No time to show weakness. The deep night needed its Berserker King. For a moment I caught my reflection in the mirror. Beads of sweat rolled down my forehead and over the clammy skin. My eyes were hollow and bruised, but worse than that, they looked empty.

I hardly recognised myself.

AVA

The search of the city produced one conclusion: Roselyn, Ella and Sadie were no longer in Vjort. We had parties sent south, east and west, though we sent no one north. To send someone north would be to kill them.

Thorne went into the streets and forcibly contained the violence. He sent people to their homes, reined in his berserkers and set tasks for the soldiers. It would not hold Vjort for long – something within its walls had snapped, some piece of sanity, some sense of calm. The city was bent on destroying itself with a determination not even the King of the Ice could halt. When he'd finally returned home he was exhausted to the point of illness and could no longer argue about needing sleep. I saw him to bed and ordered guards to keep watch over him.

I circled back to one of the castle's central living rooms. The space was large and had unusually high ceilings. Maps hung on each of the walls, and ornamental weaponry was mounted in every conceivable spot. It felt at once busy and cold: I hated this room. My husband was sitting in a low velvet chair, looking relaxed with both his arms in slings. The stubs had been seen by multiple physicians who had cleaned and tended the wounds, and now his arms were heavily wrapped. I was far from used to seeing him this way – the absences at the ends of his wrists were like a trick of the light, or a dream you were supposed to be able to blink away. He masked it well, but I knew he was in a great deal of pain.

Goran, once King of the berserkers, stood before a roaring fireplace and stared into the flames. Danger lingered in the air; there was no easy relationship between berserkers and the Kings of Pirenti. I had no patience for male rivalry.

Maisy was perched at the end of a side table, watching over Ambrose as she had been since the second she woke. I suspected she was easing his pain.

'So,' I announced as I strode in, 'where will our search begin?'

'The search,' Goran growled, 'is a waste of time. Two girls and a woman? The concern now is war.'

'Say that again, you dumb brute,' I snarled, ready to draw my whip against him.

'Settle,' Ambrose said. I paced the room to get a hold on my temper. 'We'll all move south. We can't leave Falco and the Kayan people without help – they're waiting for us even now.' To me he said, 'We can search on the way. It's the most likely path they will have taken, in any case.'

I nodded.

'And you?' Goran asked, turning to face Ambrose. 'You can't think it will be *you* who leads us south to war?'

'Watch your mouth,' I ordered him coldly.

'I said south,' Ambrose replied. 'I said nothing of war.'

Goran and I both stilled.

'You don't mean for us to fight the warders?' Goran demanded.

'I've yet to decide, and won't until I know more.'

Goran took several lumbering strides — it was like a hurricane forcing its way through the room, or a maddened bear attacking. I wasn't quick enough to get between him and my husband before Goran leaned in with bristling threat. He was seconds from losing it, and then we'd have a wild berserker in the room with us. 'No man comes between my kind and war with the warder filth,' he breathed. 'We'll have their blood, regardless of what the handless king says.'

Maisy stood, and I could see she meant to use her power. I motioned sharply for her to stop and the girl lowered her hands slowly. Her boldness impressed me.

We all looked at Ambrose.

He hadn't moved, hadn't replied to the threat. His face was calm as he slowly rose to his feet. No easy task without arms to balance or push him out of his deep seat. But his strong legs lifted him until he stood face to face with the berserker. Goran was far larger, and he had one of his meaty fists clenched around the hilt of his enormous axe.

'Stand down,' Ambrose said softly.

Goran chafed with anger and disbelief. I couldn't imagine a berserker had ever been given an order by someone so extraordinarily disabled before.

'Your King is *my* loyal prince and second,' Ambrose said. 'It is by his grace that you live to kneel before him. And just as he kneels before me, so too will you.'

The silence in the room was palpable. The eyes of the two men were locked together. Goran was a rabid mess of fury and bloodlust. But in Ambrose there was no animosity, no ferocity — no violence whatsoever. There was only certainty, and that turned out to be worth more, in the end.

'Kneel,' he said.

And Goran did.

★

After the berserker had gone, Maisy pulled me to the side, her voice dropping low. 'I offered to try, but he refused me.'

'Did you tell him you could do it?'

'I won't lie to him,' she said. 'I don't know if I can. But for him I would have tried.'

My gaze traced the girl's face. She was tired – I could see the hollows under her eyes and the drawn pinch of her mouth. But she was fierce, and no doubt a little in love with the man she'd shared a tomb with. She would try, and he was willing to throw that generosity away.

'Thank you, Maisy. Get some rest.'

'I'll stay with him, Majesty.'

'Am I permitted to be alone with my husband?'

She flushed pink and dropped her eyes. 'Of course. Goodnight.'

When she'd gone I warmed myself before the fire and Ambrose reclined once more in his chair. There was silence between us. I thought of our daughters and I'd never known such deep, resounding worry; it ate at my insides, gnawing and chewing me hollow.

'Get some sleep, darling,' Ambrose said. 'You've been awake for days.'

'Why won't you do it?' I asked, no longer able to hold the anger at bay.

'It isn't possible.'

'At least try,' I begged. 'It might work!'

'I no longer need hands to wield weapons.'

I gave an aching gasp of betrayal. 'And what else have you no need of? Holding your daughters? Protecting them? Holding *me*? Do you not wish to touch my body again?' I shook my head, turning away from him. 'I don't know how you could do this. How you could *choose* it.'

I heard him climb out of the chair again and this time he struggled a little more, wearier and in more pain. 'Ava.'

I didn't turn, didn't offer to help. 'You would lie down and die. You would give in and leave us to face the danger alone. Like a coward. If you do this, I'll never forgive you.'

'*Ava*,' he repeated, and there was so much fire in his voice that I spun to look at him.

'*What*?'

'Women are being raped!' he exclaimed, his words flung out into the gaping dark, furious and sure. 'Violated and abused because in this place violence is normal.' Ambrose shook his head. 'I will not have it. Not in a land I rule.'

I swallowed. Clenched my trembling fists. 'Of course. *Of course*. But your hands. How will you stop it without your hands, my darling?'

'You're the only one,' he said. 'The only one who might understand: you were the first to live when you shouldn't have. You forged a new path, an entirely new existence, through sheer force of will. And look how the world has changed for you. *Someone must always be first.* For this, in this, I will be the first. No matter what it costs me. I will forge a new path for this nation, a path that will stop us from destroying ourselves. I will do it without weapons, without bloodshed, without *hands*, because the time for those is past now. I will show our people that strength has nothing to do with fists.'

My skin was on fire and my pulse was racing, swooning, intoxicated. After twenty years together he could still do this to me.

'I killed both my parents for the dishonour of my throne,' he said, voice dropping low and dark to match the expression in his eyes. 'Even if nobody else ever understands this, I need you to be the one person who does: to give that same throne honour, I will kill no more.'

Every part of me was rushing towards every part of him, in love, in awe. But I stalled, just for a moment, a moment enough to whisper, 'They'll come for you. Like they did the last time they thought you weak.'

Ambrose drew himself to his full height, tilting his chin with unyielding certainty. He removed his arms from the slings and let them drop to his sides, determination thrumming through every inch of his remaining muscles. His eyes blazed a blue fire.

He asked, 'Do I look weak to you?'

I shook my head, a heady breath leaving me. 'No,' I told him. 'No, my love. You look very far from it.'

ROSELYN

Three hundred and ninety-eight, three hundred and ninety-nine, four hundred.

I stopped with an ache, unable to go on.

My arms tightened around Ella and Sadie. They were sleeping restlessly on either side of me, just as we slept each night. I didn't let my grip on them falter. I would never let it falter.

'What is it that you count?' a resonant voice asked me over the gentle lapping water.

I peered out from under my furs to look at Erik sitting at the prow of the tiny boat. He was armed heavily and held himself with complete alertness. This was the punishment he would bestow upon himself for the rest of his days – never resting, never sleeping, never lowering his guard. The unendurable guilt he felt for having been trapped behind a locked door.

It made me as sad as anything did.

'Many things,' I replied softly, not wanting to wake the girls.

The night was very cold. But we four had become used to cold. Cold, Ella said this morning, was a joke.

One night when we sheltered from a storm so frigid it made our bones tremble, Erik told us the story of the gargoyles – monstrous creatures who'd been fashioned out of stone as decoration for the wealthy, hideously designed and sculpted to scare away attackers. Much to the consternation of the wealthy, the monsters had come to life and spread their terrible, glorious wings, as desirous of the cold air of the north as any berserker. The wealthy men and women had gathered their armies and hunted the monsters, seeking to destroy them, though the creatures had harmed or frightened no one on their journey north. In their haste, the people followed them into the ice and froze solid. Now it was said that the gargoyles perched on the frozen corpses of their hunters, the better to admire the beautiful world around them.

Both girls were rapt by this story, and finding a tale they'd never heard was quite a feat. But that was what Erik did – he told stories. Like Finn, he wove them with skill and emotion, sweeping us away from reality. In reality things were simple. We were just four bodies, searching day to day for shelter and sustenance. My own body was a little different, of course: it was a thing waiting to be removed and discarded. It was an old cloak that didn't fit me any longer, a thing that had been sullied. I would keep it until I didn't need it, and then I would shed it, hang it up and leave it forever.

Except . . .

Except that Erik kept asking. 'What do you count now, my lady? What do you count tonight?'

I swallowed, tightening my arms around Ella's shoulders. 'Stars.'

'Why?' I could hear in his voice the burden of what had happened, the self-loathing he bore.

'Because my husband bid me to, moments before he died,' I admitted. It was the first time I'd mentioned any part of those final moments to anyone.

'Even though it's impossible?'

'I think probably because it is.'

'So then why?'

'He knew the counting would ease me.'

Erik was silent and I watched the side of his face, trying not to live in that moment, that most brutal moment of Thorne's death. His smile, when I told him I was pregnant. A smile to end all smiles.

I rolled onto my back, struggling to draw breath.

'Would you . . .' Erik cleared his throat. 'Would you like help?'

Air filled my lungs. 'Yes, thank you.'

So he helped me to count the stars, for no other reason than that it calmed the painful edges and nudged us quietly into sleep.

Life had become about tiny generosities, as many as the four of us could find to give each other. Life had become simple enough to make three wishes in the dark, even though wishes weren't allowed anymore. Wishes were fool's hope and fate's curse.

One wish for my son's safety.

One wish for the girls on either side of me.

And one wish for my husband's soul, pricked through with stars as it was.

CHAPTER 21

FALCO

I rounded the corner of my palace hallway, reaching the entrance of my bedchamber. There were no guards here, and my footsteps echoed off the marble floors. The door was wide open and something wasn't right. Something was coming. Something was waiting.

I moved into the chamber and saw a delicate hand lying on the rug, attached to a body that seemed to be hiding behind my bed. Slowly, heart pounding, I edged around until I could see.

There before me lay Quillane. Her gold eyes stared sightlessly at the ceiling and her stomach had been torn open. Crouching over her was a small, pale creature, a colourless wraith. It had its head inside Quill's body and it was tearing and chewing at her guts, eating her remains. The creature heard me and looked up, startled. It was Isadora, blood smearing her mouth, eyes dripping with it as she bared her teeth –

I woke with a gasp. My head pounded and I reached to clutch it. Not in the palace, in my chamber. I was in the warder prison. The bed on the other side of the cell was empty.

The dream lingered on my skin as I rose and dressed, lingered even as I made my way to the kitchens and was served a morning meal. It lingered as I called for everyone to meet in the arena, and as I spent the next hours dividing the warders and soldiers into groups and organising their training.

Figuring out who were the best fighters was a slow process, but I eventually had half a dozen strong warriors – including Brathe – to lead the groups. I wanted those who hadn't been trained – such as the warders – to learn, and I wanted those who could fight, to fight better.

At one point Isadora appeared and my head and my heart were over-lapping cloaks that did not match in colour or texture. There she was in my dream, blood-smeared, and there she was in the bed beneath me, and there she was standing in the prison. I asked her to lead a group, but she shook her head, instead watching the proceedings hawk-eyed with a knife twirling between her fingertips.

I'd never trained anyone before, but I did my best with one of the warder groups, recalling the lessons Da had given me as a child. I took them through basic self-defense, how to correctly hold weapons and find the weak spots on an enemy. 'You want to inflict maximum damage in minimum time and effort.'

As they awkwardly ran through grappling drills I sat beside Isadora. She was leaning lazily against the wall, legs propped up before her. The dagger spun fluidly as though it had a mind of its own.

'Alright?'

She nodded, attention squarely on the trainees.

'How would you do it?' I asked her.

She gave a half shrug that could have meant anything.

'Don't you train your soldiers?'

'I have people to do that for me.'

Right. Obviously. I had to stop imagining her army as a ragtag bunch of misfits running around in the forest. They had proven time and again that they were a ruthless, deadly force. She had forcibly taken three realms of my country, bringing them under her control using an army smaller and better trained than mine.

'When we escape here I will rally them and move north-east.'

I nodded. 'I'll do the same with this lot.'

That got her attention, at least. She flashed me an arched eyebrow. 'This lot will get themselves slaughtered in minutes. They are no force worthy of you.'

'They were the only ones loyal and brave enough to stand against Dren and Galia. For that they were imprisoned. They're the worthiest of all.'

Izzy met my eyes. 'I apologise.'

'Iz, you don't need to apologise to me. I think we're a bit beyond that, don't you?'

She returned to watching the training.

'I wanted to talk to you about last night,' I said. She didn't react. 'There's obviously a lot . . . that remains. It took me by surprise and I wanted to make sure you're alright.'

'It was nothing,' Isadora said. 'Nothing but a passing moment of weakness.'

I blinked. Turned back to the arena. If last night was weakness then I was a very weak man indeed, because I still felt it now and could hardly refrain from touching her.

'Who taught you?' she asked, eyes still on the fighting.

'My da.'

'And after he died?'

'No one. I taught myself.'

The knife stopped twirling briefly, then started again.

'Younger sons,' I murmured, thinking back. 'Not born to rule, but to fight. I was never going to be Emperor. Not with two older brothers. I was to be the soldier in the family.'

'Then they died and you spent the rest of your life playing dead.'

I looked at her. She was as cold as the knife in her hands. Pushing myself off the wall, I strode back into the middle of the arena and called for a halt.

'I'm seeing a lot of hesitation,' I said. 'You hesitate and you die.'

'It's only sparring,' Brathe interjected.

'I don't care.' I looked around at their faces. 'You walk into a fight – any fight – and you have to be willing to get hurt. You have to be willing to die. I know you are. So show your opponent the same respect. Fight hard. We don't have much time so make every blow count.'

Their energy picked up after that, warders and soldiers throwing themselves wildly into the sparring bouts, doing each other a fair bit of damage. But that was good. I wanted them to feel the pain a blow could inflict. They couldn't be frightened of it.

Sharn was by far the smallest in her group. It was obviously the first time she'd tried her hand at combat and she was struggling. I watched as she was slammed to the ground and pinned. I could see her frustration growing, her focus waning. She wanted it though, which I appreciated, remembering how precious she had once been.

'Hold,' I said, walking to her side. The man she'd been paired with – Clyde – was a head taller and far stronger through the body than she was. I knew how *I'd* beat him, but Sharn didn't have my strength. I had no clue what to tell her.

Spinning, I motioned for Isadora to join me. She peered at me for a moment, expressionless. Then she wandered reluctantly over. 'Isadora. This is Sharn. If you'd be so kind as to show her what to do with a larger opponent, we'd appreciate your expertise.'

She rolled her eyes at my saccharine manner and I grinned. That was all I managed before she pivoted off Clyde's thigh, flipped her body over his shoulders so that her legs were around his neck and then used the momentum of her fall to slam him so hard against the ground I wasn't sure he'd ever get up again.

I blinked as Isadora straightened gracefully.

Clyde groaned and started struggling to his feet while Sharn cheered and I remembered how to breathe. Having Izzy kill someone wouldn't leave a great impression on day one of training.

'Thank you,' I told her. 'How about this time we try the beginner's version, without the showing off.'

Izzy's lips twitched as she hid a smile. She turned and motioned for a new opponent to come forward. Henrik was the largest in our group and hesitant as he stepped up to be her next training dummy. I might have chuckled at his expression had I not been so preoccupied with Isadora and her smile and –

'Groin, throat, eyes.' She addressed Sharn shortly.

Henrik immediately covered his groin, but Izzy went for his eyes. The moment he reached up in response to her first hit, she sent a knee to his groin, and as he doubled over she hacked his throat. Luckily, she'd only given him love-taps.

'Obviously not in the order you announce,' she added witheringly.

Henrik blushed, but looked quite relieved to be left unscathed, and the rest of the group laughed. A few other groups had circled around to watch by this point, the women pushing their way to the front.

I gestured for her to keep going.

'Groin causes extreme pain. But if you're being attacked by someone stronger your only chance of survival may be the eyes. This is a vicious point of attack.'

As she looked at the women surrounding her she was the Sparrow, in complete control.

'Secondary vulnerable spots,' Isadora went on bluntly, pointing each out. 'Ankle, knee, wrist, elbow, solar plexus, collarbone, nose. Each will incapacitate. If it's a joint, you must compromise the range of movement; broken bones or dislocated joints are optimal. The knee, from the correct angle, requires the least amount of weight to dislocate. A clean hit to the jaw could knock him out, but isn't likely to kill. To strike a death blow, aim for the temple.'

She glanced at me. 'As we saw last night, a bandaged hand will generate more power in your punch. Wrap your hands before a battle. But it is *always* preferable to fight with a weapon.'

A slightly curved, serrated dagger appeared in her hand, a wicked and beautiful weapon she had obviously found in the armoury and concealed within her shirtsleeve. I wondered how many more she had on that body. She approached Henrik once more, but this time he jerked away.

'Relax,' she ordered impatiently. There were a few titters from the audience.

Isadora placed the tip of the blade at his thigh. 'A thick artery runs here. Sever it.' She moved it to his kidneys. 'A blow to the kidneys causes sickening pain.' She moved the knife to his stomach. 'Forget the stomach – a wound here kills too slowly.' The blade slid up to his neck. 'Cutting a throat will make them bleed, but it won't instantly kill unless you also sever the spinal cord, so use a swift, deep incision starting from this point.' Next she moved the blade to rest over Henrik's heart. 'To reach the heart, don't go through the breastbone.' The blade traced up to his armpit. 'Slide in under the arm, or –' here it moved down to his ribs, '– up through the ribs.'

At this she glanced at me and the knife pierced my heart again. The pain was in my chest; Isadora's pain, my hand pushing the blade through her ribs and into her heart, her death and my own. A lifetime ago, and also seconds. Another person who'd inflicted that fatal wound, or perhaps the real version of me, whoever he was.

I dragged my mind back to the prison. Each group was watching Isadora sum up her lesson. 'Momentum will help you use his weight against him. But don't let him pin you. Look for weaknesses or injuries. Use anything you can find as a weapon. In battle use the attack points to kill swiftly and move on – it's a numbers game.'

She turned to push her way through the crowd, done with it. Applause broke out and Izzy froze as though she'd been attacked. I crossed to her side. 'Why are they clapping?' she muttered.

'Because that was brilliant,' I said with a grin.

'Show us!' a woman shouted. They started yelling for Izzy to demonstrate. She shook her head, trying to push away again, but they wouldn't let her through, good-naturedly pushing her back into the middle.

'It's not a game,' she said.

'So show us,' Sharn replied. 'Inspire me, because I have no damned idea how I'm meant to walk into a battle being what I am.'

Isadora stared at her. 'What you are,' she said clearly, 'is anything you choose to be.'

Then she moved towards Henrik. He nearly peed his pants. 'Not with *me*!'

Izzy waited for an opponent to step forward. There were, unsurprisingly, no takers.

'I'll fight you,' I heard myself say. As she turned to meet my eyes my heart quickened. I didn't imagine she would agree, but then she smiled a dangerous smile. If she did not destroy me in this fight my own desire for her surely would.

A cheer broke out as our audience pressed back out of the way.

'Weapons or no weapons?' I asked.

She looked at me like I was an idiot.

Weapons it was, then. 'First blood,' I told her and she nodded.

We walked to opposite sides of the floor. I drew the twin swords and felt their weight. I breathed deeply. The palace was not my home, Sancia was not my home, not even Kaya was my true home: my swords were.

I locked eyes with Isadora across the space. She hadn't drawn any weapons, but I knew where they hid. I'd been wondering lately if I'd be able to survive an attack from the Sparrow's daggers. Now I would find out.

The danger would lie in the first few moments. The distance between us was to her advantage, not mine.

We readied ourselves.

Sharn shouted, 'Begin!'

And I was running, pressing myself forward into the hail of knives. One flew straight at my head and I managed to duck to the side, straight into the path of the second knife, which I avoided by lengthening my trajectory – it was so close I felt it brush through my hair. The next blade was too quick to dodge, aimed straight at my sternum, but I managed to get my sword into place and cut it out of the air, doing the same for the next two daggers that knifed towards me, slicing left and then right and sprinting into the gap.

I reached her and she leapt at me in the same moment, sliding beneath me and jabbing up with her remaining knife as I sailed over, twisting mid-air to avoid being cut. I landed low and slashed backwards with both swords, watching her arch out of the way to press off her hands, launching her weight up and over in a graceful backflip. I followed swiftly, slashing at her with twin blades winking in the light. She danced backwards and to either side, watching my swords, moving so quickly it felt like she was pre-empting my movements. *Damn* she was fast.

I had her on the back foot, but noticed too late that this was what she wanted. She reached where one of her daggers had landed and with a fluid motion she kicked it up off the ground and into her empty hand. Without a moment's hesitation she lunged forward beneath both my swords, slashing the knife up at my hand.

But I was quicker than she thought, and I'd been expecting her to do this at some point – my hands were the furthest extended parts of me and the only unguarded spots on my body. Instead of jerking them up or to the side as she anticipated, I threw my whole body forward and slammed her backwards. She was thrown off her feet and rolled to the ground. I was upon her, slashing the dagger from her clasp and disarming her. I pressed forward to get the tip of my blade at the exposed flesh of her collarbone and I saw the exact hit I would make, the shallow slice of her perfect white skin –

– and just as he was about to make contact I threw my head all the way back so his sword tip grazed my skin too lightly to spill blood, and in the same moment I slammed my boot heel up into his groin.

I heard his grunt of pain as I shot my fist up and into his wrist, sending his left sword flying. I dove to where it landed and rose to my feet.

We circled each other, both now armed with a sword.

Falco didn't seem too bothered by my kick. He grinned. 'I was hoping you'd do that.'

'Too scared of my knives?'

He gave a breath of laughter and lunged forwards with a huge strike. I got my sword up in time to block it, but the impact jarred through both my arms and up into my jaw. He was *way* too strong to face this way. I had to either disarm him or get to one of my daggers.

We spun and slashed, blocked and jabbed and parried and hacked, dancing backwards and forwards. His footwork was beautiful – far better than mine. He angled me where he wanted, keeping me away from my fallen knives. My only chance at fighting him this way lay in my speed, and in maintaining a smaller target. But I couldn't fool myself for long – in swordplay he was unrivalled. He blocked every one of my manoeuvres with ease, seemed to foresee every attack. I got the feeling he was playing with me, and my heart quickened not only with outrage, but with secret pleasure.

I had to get inside his arms, to where his sword couldn't touch me.

Falco went in for a long strike to my stomach. If unblocked, it would skewer me like a pig. So I did something absurd and possibly suicidal. I dropped my sword.

He saw it at the last second and wrenched his arm up, dragging his own blade from its path with an urgent grunt. I curled backwards, kicking his sword from his hand. It only left his grip because he was in the throes of a completely unplanned movement, but whatever the reason, it flew up into the air and bought me time.

I used it to scramble backwards and dive headlong for one of my daggers. He used the time to dash after his fallen sword and reclaim it, and when we came at each other again I didn't make the mistake of throwing my blade – this time I held it close as I ducked *into* his sword attack, curling up within the space of his arms to press my blade to his throat –

Only to realise that he had done the same thing.

We froze, our blades at each other's necks, pressing ever so gently to spill a single drop of blood from each.

I was unable to hide my smile.

'You've ruined me,' he muttered, his eyes black, black, black.

I swallowed. *And you me*, was what I didn't say.

FALCO

It was her will. This *will*, my gods: a will to redefine the world, a will to deny even the ocean tide. A will that endured iron cages for years on end, that ate the raw meat of birds and sharpened their bones into weapons. A will that killed, but more than that – a will that fought, and practised, and learnt, when all of those things should have been impossible. That will had *carried* me, across so many miles of land, even when she wasn't strong enough.

It was her defiance. A defiance that stood against the one thing no one in the world had ever dared to deny before. Defiance of a magic so old it defined our people.

It was her fury, her deadliness, the weapon she had made herself into when she could have cowered in her cage.

It was the fact that she went back for Penn, even though it would mean her capture and maybe her death.

It was her smile, rare as it was. It was the daggers. Her red eyes. Her words when she gave them, like hiding jewels, and even more so it was her silence.

More than anything it was the fact that she dropped the sword, and trusted me to be quick enough not to kill her.

These were the reasons I fell in love with Isadora for the second time, and why it was a much harder fall. Because I *knew* her, knew all of these things about her. Standing here, in the middle of a roaring crowd, I was limerent, sick with love, *mad* with it.

And I knew that *this* love – a love chosen freely – would actually be the death of me.

I tore from the arena amid the chaos, losing him in the crowd. I ran through the corridors as fast as I could, ducking through doors and finding myself in the armoury. Falco was right on my heels and as he slammed the door shut behind him I gave a breathless laugh. His eyes flashed as he followed me around a bench. He moved left, so I moved left; it made him laugh and then launch himself over the table to push me against the wall. His mouth ducked to mine and hovered just over my lips, almost touching but not. I could feel the heat of his breath and it made me tingle.

'Why did you drop the sword?' he asked.

'I knew you wouldn't kill me.'

'How did you know?' His body was hot along the length of mine, only a hair's breadth or two between us. I couldn't think straight, was scrambling to find some distance.

'Because you've never killed anybody. Have you?'

He let his hand travel down and link with mine, our fingers threading together. It startled me; felt more intimate somehow than any other touch.

I swallowed. 'I envy you that.'

His eyes were red, I saw, and for a moment I thought he must be angry. But then I recognised it as *my* shade.

'What colour are my eyes?' I asked urgently.

Falco swallowed. 'They're no colour. Like mine.'

I breathed out. Our eyes had shifted for each other. And they were not no colour, but every colour.

The door banged open. 'Are you in here killing each other?' Brathe boomed.

Falco stepped away from me. I reached for clarity, putting distance between us. Our eyes returned to our own colours, the moment between us popping like a bubble or a dream, another dream, endless endless dreams I was no longer able to control.

CHAPTER 22

FALCO

'We've found a weak spot,' Inga announced as Izzy and I arrived in the kitchen. 'In the corner of the library. We couldn't feel it before because Sharn and Valerie weren't allowing us access to the area.'

Sharn had the grace to look sheepish, but Valerie simply folded his arms.

'Great,' I said. 'How can we use it?'

'Don't get too excited,' Inga sighed. 'It's still warded powerfully, it's just . . . comparatively weaker.'

We looked at her, waiting. Isadora perched on the edge of a bench, while Sharn, Valerie, Brathe and Inga sat at the long central table. I hovered at the end of it, too much energy in my limbs.

'With more warders we might be able to break through, but with only a score, all of which are third, fourth and fifth tier . . .' She shook her head helplessly.

'There must be a way to use it,' I said, pacing back and forth.

Isadora leaned forwards to grab my attention so I went to her, ducking my face close. 'Warders use soul energy, right?' she murmured. 'There are plenty of people with souls in this place.'

I straightened, considering it. 'Could you use our energy?' I asked.

The warder frowned, shaking her head. 'It's too dangerous. We'd need everyone and I'm not sure what it would do to them.'

I glanced at Isadora, who shrugged. I agreed. 'We risk death and get out of here,' I announced, 'or we sit and rot while the country goes to shit. Not much of a choice. But I'll explain it to them and you'll

298

use only volunteers. Get your warders together and start preparing. Isadora – can you keep training the women? They respond to you.'

I didn't expect her to, but she nodded.

'Brathe, keep pushing the men. We use every second we have left in here to harden up.'

There were a few moments spent coming to terms with my new ability to give serious orders, and then they dispersed to their tasks while I went straight to the library to continue my search of the warder records. I knew there was something here, something important, and I was running out of time to find it.

It was late when I came across some of the writings of Agathon, first warder of Kaya. He was the one who forged the first bond between lovers thousands of years ago, the one who'd then foretold of Thorne and Finn's power to break that same bond. The furthest foretelling in history – a foresight so immense I couldn't imagine his power.

His story was sad, though. His bondmate was beloved throughout the land, so when she leapt to her death from the top of one of the shining towers in Limontae the nation was distraught. Agathon had waded in and drowned alongside her, and these deaths had started the tradition of Kayan bodies being sent to sea.

It was older, though, the human connection to the sea. Far more ancient than Agathon and his tragedy. It stretched all the way back to those first days of life, when we had washed up on the shore as a piece of driftwood. This was why we went back, because it was where we had come from in the very beginning. I found myself imagining, once again, the horizon beyond the ocean. My mind was fixated on it. I imagined taking a boat out into the waves and sailing it until I came to a new shore, to explore a new world. But unlike before, in this fantasy I was no longer alone in my boat.

Rubbing my sore, tired eyes, I closed the book of Agathon and made my way back through the corridors, passing the other cells – no one was awake. Even Radha was asleep outside Izzy's cell, her soft horse snores endearing as I crept past.

Isadora was curled towards the wall. I watched her for a while, ordering myself not to do what I wanted to. I knew she didn't feel the same as me, and no matter how much I wished for it, she could not be forced to love me.

Be reasonable, I begged myself. *Be wise. Find some measure of self-preservation.*

And yet. Powerless once more, I moved against all better judgment to slide into her bed and wrap my arms around her. If I had a choice at all, then I would choose to plunge beneath the surface of her lake and hold onto her as tightly as possible, no matter what either one of us had done to the other.

She stirred, but didn't push me away. Instead she threaded her fingers through mine. I pressed my lips to the crook of her neck and breathed in her scent, and we stayed like that until morning.

★

When I woke it was to find that she'd turned in the bed and was watching my face. Her eyes looked huge and bloody up this close. I blinked sleepily. 'Have you come from somewhere wondrous?'

She shook her head.

'No lucid dreaming?'

'Not since the night we broke the bond.'

I searched her pensive face, unsure what to say about such a loss. 'You'll get it back.'

Her hands were clenched so tightly the knuckles were white. I reached down and gently eased their stranglehold on the sheet.

'What are you . . . Why are you in my bed?'

My heart sank.

She sat up against the wall. I remained where I was, reclined and comfortable. I stopped being comfortable the moment she said, 'Quillane. What about Quillane?'

I closed my eyes, turning my face into the pillow.

'I don't know what you're doing, Falco.'

'I don't either,' I admitted wearily. I shook my head and rose to dress. She wanted me to punish her – probably indefinitely – just as she would punish herself, but I didn't have the energy for it. I didn't know if I had forgiven her, or if I ever would. I didn't know if I was *allowed* to. But there was no space in my heart for fury or hatred.

'We should get started on the day.' Without waiting for a reply I headed for a quick meal and then got back to work in the library. I was trying to scan through hundreds of years' worth of records of warder activities, plus all their training techniques in case there was anything about covering weaknesses.

I needed to find Ambrose. He'd been trying to teach me how to kill warders, but one or both of us had been failing miserably. Apparently his brother, the late King Thorne, had been the one who excelled at it – the slaughterman found a way to make himself completely impervious to warder magic and had been in the north torturing them for information. As far as we knew he hadn't done it by sleeping; he'd found another way. And it certainly wasn't as simple as Ambrose seemed to think it was – his only method of teaching had been to repeatedly tell me to 'clear my mind'. Shame I wasn't able to ask the slaughterman himself.

Groaning, I let my forehead fall onto the page of a book.

I felt a hand trace lightly over my hair and looked up to see Isadora. The touch was gone as quickly as it had appeared, and as she slowly rounded the table and took in the chaos she seemed far away again, the touch like something I'd imagined. I could see her circling with wary suspicion, unsure if she was the predator or the prey after this morning. Trying to feel me out, trying to see through my facades. She didn't trust me one bit, I realised, but I'd never given her much reason to.

'Taking a break?'

She nodded.

'How are they going?'

A shrug.

'I can't find anything. I need more eyes. Want to go through that pile for me?'

'I'm a poor reader. It would take me hours to get through a page.' She made it back around the table to my side, tracing her hand idly along the books.

I snatched her fingers and placed a kiss to her palm. 'I'll keep you anyway.'

She removed the hand to flick me in the temple, hard.

'Ow. Careful – you told everyone that's the death blow.'

Isadora smiled. 'If I could flick people to death I'd save myself a lot of time.'

'Oh. You're not very good at jokes, are you?'

I watched her walk through the stacks of books and wondered if she could understand their titles. How strange to be almost blind to the language of text.

'Radha's entertaining everyone by stretching her wings,' Isadora murmured.

I smiled. We'd hopefully be out of here by tonight so I had to get a move on. My current scroll brought me up to the start of my reign twenty-five years ago. There had been less than a hundred warders in Kaya at that time, only one of them a first-tier – Osric. Which meant he was obviously a lot older than he looked. Lutius had been training as a novice at that time, but he'd been flagged already as a possible head warder when he graduated. From what I could gather it was something about the type of energy coupled with the type of mind. But obviously not even their careful choices yielded any security, since the man least likely to be corrupted by his magic had been the worst traitor of all. I scanned accounts of magic use throughout the first few years of my reign, looking for more on Lutius, but something else caught my eye.

The warders I dispatched when I was ten to find the murderers of my family, Callius and Raziel, had both nurtured future-telling gifts, which was why I'd chosen them – foresight was the hardest thing to evade. They had searched for two years and reported regularly that they'd found nothing, and then they'd relocated to continue a more permanent watch on the border in case the killers had gone north into Pirenti.

But this scroll identified Callius and Raziel as having lived in Sanra – or *Yurtt*, as it became – for a full twelve years after I dispatched them, until the day they both died. I'd been informed that their magic had worn through their bodies – they were both very old at this point – and they'd perished on the hunt. Only it now seemed like an awfully big coincidence for them to have died on the same day unless they were secretly bonded. And why hadn't I been told that they were living in Sanra?

Then there was the fact that twelve years was the same exact amount of time that Isadora had hung in her cage – in Sanra. Which might not mean anything, and yet . . . I frowned, thinking it through, reading for more information. Izzy had come to sit on the edge of the table to watch me. I felt on the cusp of something and it was making my heart pound.

'Look for these names,' I told her, showing her Callius and Raziel on a scroll.

She peered at them and I saw her lips move as she sounded out the letters. Her face suddenly cleared as the letters became words. She was stone and iron. She was calm fury. 'These are the names of the first two warders I ever killed.'

I went still, a terrible dread blooming in my heart. 'Why?'

'Because they were the men who put me in the cage.'

I stared at her.

'What, Falco?' she asked quickly, seeing my expression.

'Do you know why they did it?'

'I told you. Superstition.'

I shook my head, tearing through scrolls to find the stack of reports from Sanra in those years. I read through Callius and Raziel's accounts of their time in the region. They had been reporting back to the warders with an entirely different set of information to what they'd been sending me. And what I read made my blood go cold.

'What?' Isadora demanded, and for the first time since I'd met her she sounded scared. I got to my feet, pushing the chair out so quickly that it nearly toppled over. I didn't have any words, had no idea how I could explain this, or what it meant, or how she would . . . Shaking my head, I gathered up the scrolls and headed quickly for the door.

'Falco!'

'It's nothing,' I said. 'Nothing you need to worry about.'

ISADORA

I didn't allow myself to think about whatever had happened in the library. Falco had read something that deeply unsettled him, some-thing about Callius and Raziel, whom I had killed, but he wouldn't tell me what it was. So I wouldn't waste time on it.

Every prisoner had offered their soul energy in the service of breaking out, even those who loathed the magic. The warders took hands, while the rest of us waited around them. Falco was atop Radha, who flew up to the barrier above so he could press free once the weakness in the ward had been ruptured. He thought his energy was going to be drained along with everyone else's, but I had spoken privately with Inga and Brathe and they'd agreed that he would not be used – even if the rest of us perished, Falco must live.

A wall of energy smashed against me, taking my soul with it. A collective groan sounded as we all sank to our knees. Blood trickled from my nose and ears. I hadn't expected it to be this bad. Through the pounding in my head I watched Inga and her warders. Just as the pain threatened to overcome me she gave a terrible scream and the pressure ended as abruptly as it had started.

My body felt boneless. As my head hit the ground I saw wings beating across my vision, and then his pale eyes as he lifted me onto our pegasis. 'It worked,' he told me, and then his gaze erupted into flames. I gasped, reaching for him.

'Falco – your eyes!'

He stared at me, unaware. I twisted my neck to glance behind. Something was coming, I could feel it. The walls of the prison burst into flame but Radha wasn't moving, and when I pulled at Falco he wouldn't come. The sound of mighty wings beat behind us, drawing ever closer.

'Run!' I told him.

He shook his head. 'This is real. Don't you get that?'

The prison finished burning and there was a blizzard of white-grey ash, dancing and falling upon his skin and hair and in his eyelashes. It leeched the colour from him until he looked just like me, nothing but a white, colourless creature.

Had I turned him into this? Had I made him what I was?

'Run,' I whispered. 'Run.' And this time I meant for him to run not with me, but from me.

FALCO

With the severing of that first ward the magic of the entire prison crumbled. It unravelled like spools of string and as I landed Radha in the dead forest outside the prison walls, I watched an impossible thing.

The forest came back to life.

304

Blackened bark fell away from skeletal trees leaving them brown and green with budding new life. Withered grass found green, wild-flowers bloomed and a huge breath of air was taken into the uncurling leaves of the canopy above. It was so beautiful my eyes prickled, and I wished Isadora had been awake to witness it.

Those who were able emerged from the prison. Most were deeply fatigued from the magic, while others remained unconscious. We spent the night under the newly awakened trees, waiting to recover. I made sure Izzy was wrapped tightly in her cloak and I had Radha lie beside her, though it was warm so far south. It was more for comfort than temperature. I didn't want her to wake alone.

I checked on my people and discovered that two had died in the escape, and though Brathe told me I ought to be relieved it was not more, I felt the deaths keenly. Inga had not yet woken. She looked pale and clammy, more so than anyone else. I sat quietly with Brathe for a while as he held her hand. Next I checked on Sharn and Valerie, who had both woken and were seeing to others with admirable aplomb. It was like walking through a battlefield. The unconscious bodies laid out on the grass made it seem like a great fight had taken place. But I knew we had yet to see the real beginning of bloodshed.

I circled back to Izzy and found her tossing restlessly in her sleep. As I sank to the grass beside her I heard her teeth grinding, and then words forced through them. 'Run, run . . . *run*.'

'Isadora,' I said, touching her shoulder. She lurched awake, breathing wildly. 'Easy, it's alright.'

Blinking, she struggled to sit and lean against Radha's warm belly. Her hands moved of their own accord to thread through the horse's wing feathers.

'What were you dreaming of?'

She shook her head a little, her eyes fixed on something distant, careful not to stray towards me. We were several hundred meters from the rest of the prisoners, behind a large fir tree for privacy. But even here, so alone with her, she felt terribly far from me.

Radha snorted softly.

I changed the subject, hoping to pull her mind from whatever nightmare she'd endured. 'Which way are your people?'

'West.'

I got her a canteen of water from the prison. I could feel things inside me reaching out, pieces of me trying to grab hold of pieces of her. I wanted to tell her things, but I couldn't think of any – I had nothing to tell and I could feel nothing from her, just as I always felt nothing from her. She was a cold piece of granite before me, untouchable. She was the snow goddess of the north, and I the sea's fool.

There was one thing I could tell her. One thing discovered in the library. What would she become when I shared it? What would *we* become? Enemies, no doubt. There wasn't really any other fate, once my terrible culpability was revealed.

'Where will we regroup? Your people and mine?' I asked.

'I will take my army around the marshlands and wait on the far side. If you don't come in time, I will attack the city myself.'

'You can't face the warders in open warfare. They'll decimate you. Nor can you lay siege to the city – they'd outlast you with ease.'

'I know that,' she replied.

'Then what's your plan?'

Isadora said nothing.

Frustrated, I stood. 'How are we to be allies if you won't tell me your strategy?'

'I will tell you when I know it,' she answered me, and I saw an abrupt anger kindling behind her eyes.

I let out a breath. 'Very well. We regroup beyond the marshlands. We plan our attack *together*.'

She said nothing. Didn't agree or disagree, and I had no idea what she was thinking. I left her, at my wits' end. Went to gather up the prisoners and get them ready to move.

*

Isadora pressed her forehead to the space between Radha's eyes, nuzzling her and whispering something I couldn't hear. From my seat on the back of the pegasis I looked down at Izzy's snow-hair, pulled into a thick, messy braid, and at the long lines of her pale neck. With a final kiss to Radha, she turned and walked for the trees. She carried a small pack with water and some rations, along with several knives stashed on her person. Her boots were worn, her clothes ratty. She was small like a child heading alone into the forest, graceful as one of the fey creatures of old.

Brathe and the rest of the group were waiting for me in the other direction, but seeing her like that, without a single word of farewell . . .

'Isadora!' I called, panicked.

She stopped and looked back. The sun was behind me so she had to shield her eyes. Could probably see nothing but my silhouette. She waited, but I could think of no words.

'We will meet again,' I blurted out. *In our dreams.* It didn't sound like a question, but it was.

Isadora nodded, then vanished into the trees.

I felt as though I'd had a sword taken to my ribcage, splaying it open for all to see the gruesome mess within. Dazed, I manoeuvred Radha after the rest of the group, already on its way north-east to find Ava and the Sancian citizens. Brathe had waited for me, choosing to walk alongside my pegasis.

'Parting is the wreckage of us all,' he said gently.

I blinked. 'Pardon?'

He nodded to where we'd left Izzy.

'We're not . . .' I shook my head, giving up. 'She bears no real fondness for me.'

'And I thought the fool act was done with.'

That was just it, wasn't it? The fool act no longer felt an act. And there was thick, thick dread in my guts. I pulled Radha to a halt.

'Sire?'

She'd given me nothing, not even a farewell. She'd given me no words or looks or touches, had never shown me but a glimpse into her thoughts or feelings.

But she had carried me on her back across miles of land, saving my life even when she shouldn't have been strong enough. She had told me the truth about Quill, even when she didn't have to, when in fact it would have protected her to stay silent. She did give me things. She gave me acts of courage, and those meant the most. When put like that, what had I ever given her in return?

I swung down from Radha's back, my boots landing lightly on the grass. To Brathe I said, 'Carry on. I will find you.'

'Sire – we need you,' he argued.

'You're still my General, Brathe. Act like it.' With a clap to his shoulder, I left him with my pegasis and I turned back for the forest, pushing myself into a run. Trees whipped past me in a blur.

'Izzy!' I shouted, unable to spot her. 'Isadora!'

Slowing to a halt, I peered around, now thoroughly lost. *Shit*.

Something caught my ears, a sudden *ziiiip* of sound and then a loud *thunk* right by my head. I looked at the knife quivering in the tree trunk; it had passed so close it took a few strands of my hair with it. Searching the forest around me, I still couldn't see her.

'Not a wise time to let your guard down, Majesty,' came her soft voice from above.

Tilting my head, I spotted her sitting on a high tree branch, red hawk-eyes watching me. 'What are you doing up there, little Sparrow?'

'Heard you coming from a mile away. Great lumbering idiot.'

'Like to join the lumbering idiot on the ground?'

She shook her head.

I breathed out. 'Very well.' Here I was again, with words all dried up and a cold wind rushing through my chest cavity.

'What are you doing, Falco?' she asked more quietly. 'Turn around and go with your people.'

I swallowed and said, as calmly as I could, 'I'm not yet capable of being parted from you. If you'll have me, I would come with you to find yours.'

A long, silent moment stretched out. It was madness. My own men and women needed me to guide them. I knew it and she knew it. But finally, almost imperceptibly, the Sparrow nodded, her eyes shifting green to match the veil of leaves about her head.

Chapter 23

ISADORA

I could no longer tell where the dead forest ended and my lands began. All was green and lush with new life.

'Are we near?' Falco asked.

'Scouts will spot us. You had best not look like that.'

He frowned, peering down at himself. He was dressed in worn, dirty garb – the same we'd been sent to the cages in. It had been dragged through salt and mud and dust, and ripped to within an inch of its life. 'Granted, I'm not looking my best, but where am I meant to get a change of clothing from?'

I couldn't help it. I smiled. 'Your clothing isn't the problem. It's the rest of you.'

His frown deepened.

'You look wealthy and noble, Falco. No matter what you wear.' I gestured to his beautiful face and glorious locks of golden hair. He still moved with the refined, pompous entitlement he was having trouble casting off. 'They'd kill you on sight.'

'Cut it off then.' He flicked his lovely hair.

My eyebrows arched sceptically.

'You think I could care less about hair?'

Grinning, I drew one of my daggers and set about hacking at the locks. I worked as quickly as I could, cutting close to his scalp, making sure to leave parts uneven and to nick his skull a few times to make him look rougher. When I was done I stepped back.

'What?'

I shrugged, not sure what to say. The bloody haircut had made his cheekbones and jaw more severe, and the colour of his eyes now shone with an undeniable glow. They looked haunted in the afternoon light, set under brows that seemed heavier without the halo of silky hair. If anything he was *more* beautiful, stripped back like this.

'Break my nose,' he told me.

I hesitated, then sent a hard palm into the bridge of his nose, making sure to break the bone. Falco yelped, raising a hand to catch the streaming blood. 'Ow! *Iz.*'

'You told me to.'

'I thought you'd at least argue first.'

My lips twitched. 'It'll be crooked forever.'

'Do I look ugly?'

The smile disappeared. 'I never said you needed to be ugly.'

'Sorry,' he said quickly. 'I didn't mean –'

'Not all are so fortunately born to physical beauty. It's an illusion and it teaches you to care about the wrong things.'

Falco looked at me helplessly. 'It's not what I meant. Forgive me. My nose really hurts.'

'Is that the first time you've been hit?' I couldn't remember him taking a single blow in the prison fights.

He nodded.

'A rite of passage then.'

'How violent,' he said.

I shrugged. Waved at his face. 'I prefer it. You're not so pretty.'

'Then feel free to break some more bones!' he announced wildly. 'How about my jaw? My eye socket? You could give me a disfiguring scar!'

I strode ahead to pick up the path. He joked and laughed so easily about disfigurement, about *choosing* it as though it meant nothing and made no difference, but he had no idea what it truly meant to be born different.

★

310

By nightfall we were surrounded. There was a faint rustle in the trees that meant they wanted me to hear them. I stopped and gestured for Falco to lift the torch higher, casting my hair and skin into the light.

Out of the darkness emerged six cloaked soldiers. They sank low to the ground before me. The figure at their head rose first and withdrew her hood, revealing a misshapen mouth and nose.

'Greer.'

She smiled a little, but kept her tone formal. 'You've returned to us.' Her words, as always, were slurred.

I nodded and gestured for them to lead us home. Greer fell into step beside me as we walked, while Falco fell a little behind, keeping the torch aloft. 'Your companion?' she asked me.

'A servant. He knows who I am.'

Greer's eyes widened slightly as she darted a wary glance back at him. Most of my soldiers didn't even know who I was – they thought the albino girl was the Sparrow's second.

The camp wasn't far, a place we had come to refer to as Cloth City. It moved constantly, its structures easily erected and disassembled. My people were at least two thousand strong and the sea of canvas huts stretched before us, lit by scattered campfires. Soldiers sat around the fires enjoying a meal before sleep. In the morning they would be roused early to train or to take up the necessary duties that kept our mobile community running. Food and water had to be constantly dealt with on a large scale, along with the washing of clothes and maintenance of weaponry. Scouts were constantly prowling the area and battle parties went out each day to protect the people of the three realms I reigned over. If need be they enforced my law, which consisted mostly of the punishment of theft, violence, mistreatment or cruelty. My soldiers also offered free labour to struggling farms or sustenance to those who couldn't feed their families.

The system worked, but only because I didn't have to pay my soldiers. They offered their lives freely to the cause, which was a huge difference between my rule and Falco's government. In his three realms, citizen taxes paid for the maintenance of peace, security, law and order.

My tent had been kept for me, awaiting my return. It was simple and small, with a bedroll on the ground just like the rest of my soldiers had. The only difference was a small wooden table, necessary for meetings.

I bade Greer send for Lade, who quickly joined us. I then sat with my two commanders around the table, while Falco lit the lamps and poured us wine. It was remarkable to watch him don the servant's cloak; it fitted him astonishingly well. Every detail of the deception was attended to – I seemed to have a stranger in my tent, evident in the respectfully downcast eyes, the abruptly blunt and solid movements of his body, the bowed shoulders, the disappearance of his effeminate delicacy and quick flashing smile. I didn't have time to continue admiring the disguise though, because Greer and Lade were both waiting for my explanation.

'Thank you for your service in my absence,' I said, clearing my throat. I hated these moments, in which I was expected to speak. I hadn't *chosen* to lead these people, they'd simply begun to follow.

Lade inclined his head. He had suffered terrible burns as a child in a house fire that took his parents. Half his skull, face, neck and most of his body was puckered and shiny with the scars that even now caused him pain. But no one had strength quite like Lade – no one had the same spirit with which to laugh at misfortune in loud, obnoxious defiance.

Greer, in turn, had a sharp intelligence I was grateful for, and a mistrust of every person in this world. She was now watching Falco with that same suspicion, eyes cold. I could not truthfully call either a friend, though they were the people I knew best. We shared little more than politics and strategy and the running of this army. But they respected me, and I them.

I listened as they outlined the movements of my soldiers over the last eight months, and the workings of the realms. We'd held firm, but had still lost ground to warder intrusion. Their magic was impossible to fight, even with courage and skill. All of Ora and some of Querida had been conceded, which was a substantial blow and left us with half the land we'd had six months ago.

It occurred to me that if we helped Falco win this war there would be nothing to stop him turning around and taking back the whole of

Kaya. And if I had learnt anything about him in the last weeks, it was how single-minded he could be in the pursuit of what he wanted. I had all but offered him my lands back when I'd pledged to support him, but it wasn't as easy as just handing over control. There was a great number of people whose welfare needed to be considered. They were better off under my rule, but was a unified Kaya more important?

'I've been trapped within the walls of Sancia,' I informed Greer and Lade. 'I had the opportunity to kill the Mad Ones, but failed.'

Lade cursed under his breath. 'They'll die very badly, Sparrow — we'll make sure of it.'

'And to do that our forces will join with those of the northmen, and with the Emperor of Kaya.'

There was silence at that.

'I have his man,' I said, gesturing to Falco, who stood near the entry. 'He's issued a formal offer of alliance and I mean to accept it.'

Greer was up in a moment, lifting her bow and aiming an arrow directly at Falco's heart. 'You brought one of Feckless' soldiers into our home?'

'He isn't to be harmed,' I said flatly, and the tone of my voice was more than enough to force her weapon down. Greer made a hissing sound out of her mangled mouth and paced before Falco, keeping her eyes on him. Saliva slid from the corner of her lips, but she didn't wipe it away as she normally would, too intent on her enemy.

Falco lifted his eyes to her. I saw nothing in his expression to indicate he was uncomfortable in her presence. With his short warrior scalp and his crooked nose he looked dangerous and unruly. He also looked underfed and poor, which was probably the only reason Greer had not shot him already.

I stood and all eyes returned to me. 'We align, or we die. How long will it take to ready my forces to march east to war?'

'Two days,' Lade replied, ever eager to fight.

I nodded to dismiss them. I would not explain my decision further, though I knew it had deeply offended them both. I refused to allow my people to suffer under my hatred any longer. Against the threat of the warders, the rest of Kaya couldn't afford to be divided.

Falco relaxed, breathing out. 'You're scary when you're the Sparrow.'

I thought it an odd thing to say. No matter which disguise he wore, he was still blind to the truth of me: 'I'm always the Sparrow.'

FALCO

She slept on her bedroll and I on the floor near the flap of her tent, like a good little servant. I couldn't calm my mind for long enough to drift off, but I heard the sound of Isadora's breathing deepen more quickly than usual. She was very tired.

It was thrilling to see her wield her power. Thrilling to see the inside of the Sparrow's world after so many years imagining it. I hadn't realised the extent of her army – Cloth City boasted far more soldiers than I had imagined and I felt grateful, lying here, that she was now on my side in this war.

Izzy sat up so suddenly I got a fright. 'You alright?'

She didn't reply, but rose from bed, stepped over me and walked straight out of the tent. Confused, I scrambled to follow.

She wound her way through the dark shapes of sleeping soldiers and the dying embers of campfires. She was wickedly quick, and I had to jog to keep up with her as she reached the edge of Cloth City and melted into the forest.

'Izzy?'

I caught up to her and glimpsed her vacant eyes – she was sleep-walking. I kept pace with her, unsure if she was controlling it or not, but certain I wanted to see where she was going.

We walked for at least two hours, plunging deeper and deeper into the forest. There were no paths here and I was amazed at her sure-footedness in the dark. My feet tripped over vines and tree roots and slipped into ditches, caught by sharp thorns of wild blackberry bushes and the gnarled, low-hanging branches of oak trees.

Not long after I'd begun to consider waking her up and ceasing this mad venture, we emerged from the thick trees into a huge clearing.

In the center of which was her lake.

I had seen it before, in dreams. I'd felt the cool liquid calm of it in her mind.

The reality was so strange it felt like I'd stepped into her dream realm. The lake was completely, impossibly still. It was glass. The night held two identical moons, one in the sky and one reflected in the surface of the black water.

Isadora walked straight into it, so fluid that the water barely moved at her disturbance, seemed instead to swallow her and return to glass. I had watched the reverse in our dream, when she emerged just like that, like she was floating, removing the water like a second skin. Now she had donned it once more, returned to its depths.

My sense of reality unbalanced; this was too surreal, too strange.

I waited for her to break the surface, but she didn't.

Horror dawned. I ran into the water, destroying its clarity with huge splashes. I took a breath and plunged under, swimming through the pitch-black, so dark it was tar. I searched but I couldn't find her and panic made my lungs burn. I kicked for the surface and took another breath, then ducked under again. Where was she? It didn't make sense – I had just seen her but now she was gone, there was only endless black . . .

I twisted around and around, swimming forwards and doubling back, sure I was going mad in the darkness.

Until – a wisp of white in the depths, like a plume of smoke. Or a long tendril of hair. Relief shocked me and I kicked for her, taking her tiny body in my hands and surging for the surface.

We broke free and I swam her to the bank, hauling her out onto the twigs and bark of the forest floor. She coughed and spluttered, spitting up water with a shudder.

I could hardly breathe as I paced before her, too filled with adrenalin to stop moving. I was so frightened, deathly frightened. Isadora's unsteady eyes found me. She was awake now, pale and small and scared. There were wet leaves all over her body, brown smudges in her hair and on her skin.

'I can't tell what's real,' she whispered. 'Falco. I can't. I can't tell the difference.'

'This is real,' I promised her, sinking to my knees. 'You're awake.'

She shook her head. 'You said that before. In the dream. You say it in every dream.'

I reached to smooth her wet hair off her face, trying to make her believe me, to see me. 'That really scared me,' I admitted, shaken to my core. I couldn't calm down, couldn't come back from the fear. My hands on her face were trembling. 'I couldn't find you, Iz. *I couldn't find you.*'

'Shh,' she whispered. 'I'm here.' And then she pressed her lips to mine.

She was sweet and we were feverish as we kissed beside the lake of calm that had tried to drown her.

Chapter 24

ISADORA

Neither of us was able to face the trip back through the brambles and wild heath to the camp, so instead we slept in each other's arms, tangled together on the bank of the lake. The calm, calm lake.

I woke, unsure of the time of day. Heavy clouds hung overhead, hiding the sun, though it had to be daybreak. 'Don't,' he muttered, his lips in my hair. 'Don't wake. It's too nice here.'

'A storm is coming.'

'Let it.'

I uncurled from him and sat. He gave an annoyed grunt. I was cold to my bones from having slept in my wet tunic on the wet ground. Too strange. Last night had been too strange. I truly couldn't work out what had been dream and what hadn't.

But he was here with me, so that was one true thing I could hold onto.

Had I dreamt his kiss? Was the taste of his lips a phantom pleasure, gone now with day?

His hand rested against my spine. I felt it acutely. Just as I'd felt it after we made love in Sancia. It had rested just there, in that exact spot, and then he had taken it away for hatred of me and I'd been left with only cold absence. That had been a dream, had it not? Was I dreaming still?

'Is this real?' I whispered, confused.

'Yes,' he said, sitting to rest his chin on my shoulder, his lips to my ear. 'Yes.'

'How can I be sure?'

It felt too sweet to be real.

'Trust me.'

I tilted my face to his. 'You're like this in both realms. Which version of you am I to trust?'

The question hit him like a blow. He pulled away from me. Drew his knees up to rest his arms upon. 'Neither, I suppose,' he murmured. 'None. No version.' Falco swallowed and met my eyes. 'Maybe all my versions are just dreams.'

'Leaving what?'

'Nothing.' He looked away, eyes resting on the lake.

'Do you want to know a secret?'

He nodded but I could see that he was a long way away, hardly listening. Trapped inside some kind of self-torment he had created.

'Maybe,' I said, 'all your versions, all your masks, all your disguises – every single one of them – is real.'

Falco's eyes returned to study me. Up this close there were a thousand colours in his irises, and inside each colour was another thousand colours, and inside each of those another thousand.

'I don't understand,' he said, blunt as a challenge.

'What kind of person,' I asked, 'is one thing only?'

Falco shook his head, climbing to his feet with an abrupt burst of energy. 'You don't get it.'

I watched the surface of the lake, no longer calm and undisturbed but shivering with the wind of the approaching storm. Ripples moved out and out and out. *Whoosh* went the trees, scattering leaves through the air. I rested my head on my knees and looked up at him in the grey light, standing there above me.

'Maybe it's alright to be feckless,' I dared to murmur.

Falco looked at me as though I'd mortally wounded him. His mouth opened and closed, filled with wordless betrayal, and then he strode into the forest.

I turned back to the lake.

Calm, calm, calm it had whispered. Right up until the moment it drowned me.

FALCO

Irresponsible. Lazy. Indifferent. Useless. Incompetent.

Those were the qualities of being feckless. She must not understand the word, had not yet learnt its meaning. It was not alright to be any of those things. Not for an Emperor, not for anyone.

My pulse was racing as I sprinted back through the forest. Because there was also the possibility that she did know the meaning of the word, and had wanted to wound me with it. Did she truly think me feckless?

Was I?

ISADORA

I was still beside the lake when I heard it. The soft shuffle of footfall, the snapping of a nearby twig. Assuming it must be Falco returned, I remained where I was.

And was rewarded with the blade of an axe appearing gently and precisely to sit against the soft flesh of my throat. I didn't make the mistake of reaching for any of my knives, but rose to my feet as the axe bid me.

'Easy now, demon,' said a rich voice behind me. A man's voice, heavily accented with the northern Pirenti form of speech. 'Turn slowly and I will look upon your face.'

Very well. If he wished to look upon my face before he died, I would let him.

I edged around, while he kept the blade always at my neck. I could feel in the pressure of it that he was skilled with the weapon. He knew how *not* to nick the skin.

The man was leaner than I'd come to expect from Pirenti men. He had long limbs and long hair, with outlandish markings on his face and skull. And black, bottomless eyes, brimming with expression. I regretted that they would shortly be empty.

How, I wondered, *was one meant to live without killing, when killing sought one out at every turn?* The world made its monsters indeed.

'How do you fare so far south, snow demon? Your place is north under the ice mountain, where no babes might stray into your path.'

I titled my head at the peculiar words, studying his face. I didn't think he feared me, despite naming me demon, despite holding an axe to my throat.

'I'll say a prayer for you, and hope your soul finds its way back to wherever it's from.' He paused and added, almost sadly, 'That's if you have a soul. Certainly the gods will forgive me for sending it back.'

His grip changed – he meant to kill me. Before he could move, the dagger at my right forearm came up, slashed through the unprotected wrist of his blade hand and then flipped to rest against his carotid artery. His axe fell to the ground as he lost the ability to grip it – I had severed the tendons in his arm.

The man's eyes widened, but I saw acceptance in them, and understanding. A man used to walking at the edge of death.

'I'm no demon,' I told him softly. 'But I've also got no wish to die today. On your knees.'

He went calmly to his knees and gazed up at me. The wind picked up, rushing through the trees around us. The lake was no longer anything resembling calm.

I hesitated, looking down at the dark-eyed man. *Don't, you fool,* I screamed inwardly. *Never hesitate.* But hesitate I did. And in those brief moments, someone else moved.

A small child was running along the bank towards us. Her dark hair whipped about her and she struggled against a particularly strong gust of wind. 'Wait!' she cried. 'Don't!'

'Get back, love!' the man roared. And I realised that he hadn't been trying to murder me for the sport of it – he'd been protecting his daughter from a creature he thought dangerous.

My dagger remained at his neck as the girl arrived, panting hard, hair and eyes wild. I saw with astonishment that those eyes were an incredible shade of violet. 'Please don't kill him,' she begged me. 'He's a good, kind man.'

'*Step back,*' he ordered her. 'Do not be fooled by the small and weak look of the creature – it is disguise for its bloodlust.'

But the girl ignored her father, reaching to place her hand on top of mine, holding the dagger along with me. I blinked, astonished by her courage.

'She's no demon,' the girl said, looking into my eyes with an unblinking stare. She calmly removed the blade from the man's neck; my hand obeyed hers for no fathomable reason. 'She's the snow goddess,' the child said, and then she flung herself on me, clutching at my neck.

I stumbled back, the dagger dropping from my hand. I was so shocked that I could hardly remember to breathe. What prepared you for the unburdened generosity of children? For the affection they so easily afforded?

Absurdly, my arms lifted of their own accord to return the embrace, and as I held onto her tiny body I was embarrassingly close to tears.

'Put her down,' the man ordered me, ever fierce.

I met his eyes over the girl's shoulder. 'Whose blade was drawn first? Your daughter's in no danger from me.'

The girl gave a trickle of laughter as she pulled away. 'Erik's not my da. He's our hirðmenn.'

I had no idea what that was but I frowned, wondering why a man would be traveling with a child not his own.

'Sade! Rose! Come out!' she shouted, but her voice was lost in the wind.

The man – Erik – reclaimed his axe and held it at the ready, pushing the girl behind him once more. His wounded right arm was used to keep her back. She rolled her eyes, flashing me a conspiratorial look. I couldn't help it – my lips twitched.

'We'll pass, and there'll be no need for bloodshed,' he shouted over the gale force.

Two bodies emerged from the copse of trees, following the water's edge. A woman and a second child, treading the smooth pebbles of the shore.

'Don't come any further!' Erik ordered them although I wasn't sure they heard. He started backing away from me, tugging the girl with him. 'We're leaving peacefully,' he said.

But I was looking at the second child, noting her similarity. Noting, in fact, the identical features. My eyes went to the woman, incredibly beautiful with her red hair and fine features. I had heard those names before, had I not? Or some very alike?

'What's your name?' I called to the girl.

I saw Erik's mouth move to warn her.

But she shouted, 'Ella!'

A breath left me as my eyes moved between the four of them. An unlikely group. I smiled, and it was a real smile, an unguarded one. 'I know someone who will be very pleased to see you,' I said.

FALCO

Cloth City was in chaos. The storm had arrived and there was no doubt in my mind that its source was not nature, but magic. Which meant Dren and Galia knew exactly where we were, had probably been tracking our movements since the moment we broke free of the cages.

The sky had turned black. Tents flew from their pegs, whipped into the air and slammed into people. A man flew past me, dragged by a tent caught in a gust of wind. It smashed him straight into the trunk of a tree with a sickening sound – I didn't need to check to know he was dead. Campfires reignited and gales sent the flames into the surrounding cloth. I saw with perfect clarity what was about to happen. The whole camp was seconds from igniting.

A huge creak rent the air and I barely had time to dive out of the path of a falling tree. It crashed to the ground, flattening at least three people who'd not been quick enough.

How did you fight a storm? Where could you take shelter if you had but *cloth*? Everywhere was a danger – the only cover was the trees, but they were falling left and right, aflame with the ever growing fire. This forest was a deathtrap and I felt impotent in the face of it. Screams were rising above the sounds of the burning campsite. I hoped Izzy would stay where she was, near the relative safety of the water, and in the same heartbeat I desperately needed her here – she would know what to do.

A faint noise reached me, a wild whinny. I spun to see a glorious pegasis rear onto its back legs to avoid another falling tree, its wings stretching in alarm. *Radha*. She manoeuvred herself bravely around burning logs and debris to reach my side with another whinny. My strength bolstered, I swung up onto her back and leant low to her ear. 'You wonderful, brave, foolish creature.'

With my knees I moved her forwards and she navigated the chaos as though born to it, fluid, graceful and sure-footed. 'North!' I shouted at everyone I could see. The plane was north, and safe from the fire. 'Run north and don't stop until you're free of the forest!'

Radha jumped over a burning log and pivoted her legs as she landed, twisting us around an iron tent pole and then flattening herself under a sheet of flying canvas. She was glorious, pounding through the campsite so I could direct the Sparrow's army to run north. Most seemed to be listening, despite not knowing who I was.

I spotted a woman pinned beneath a tree branch and swung off Radha. 'I've got you,' I grunted as I took the woman's arms and dragged her free. Smoke was in my lungs, ash in my eyes as I mounted once more.

We spotted a group of soldiers trapped within a circle of burning tents, the flames biting higher with each second. Radha turned and flapped her enormous wings, working to douse at least a portion of the wall so people could leap through it.

'Now!' I shouted as the wind she had created briefly flattened the flames. The soldiers dashed through, sprinting north. But the length and breadth of Radha's wings were designed to find any pocket of air the sky might hold, and as they were now spread wide they caught a mighty gust of wind. It launched her off her hooves, flipping her over into a wild tumble. I tried to tuck myself into a ball but was thrown to the earth and caught by the horse's flailing legs. The right side of my body scraped along the ground and I felt skin split. Miraculously I wasn't pinned or knocked unconscious. Struggling dizzily to my feet, I stumbled to Radha's side. She was splayed over the ground and my heart stopped, thinking her legs or her wings must have broken, but she lurched abruptly to her hooves, tossing her head and shaking herself off.

'Good girl,' I breathed, stroking her trembling neck. She snorted and stamped her hoof, bidding me remount.

We cantered through the remaining area of the camp in search of trapped or injured people and dragged them out of immediate harm. The flames were growing, everything was alight including the grass and bark of the forest floor. It would be a miracle if the fire did not take out the entire forest at this rate.

'Falco!' I heard, and I jerked towards the voice.

I couldn't see anything at first – there was heavy smoke now – so we leapt over burning tents and galloped to where the camp ended. There, pounded by wind, stood Isadora and my nieces.

My heart exploded with terror. *What in gods' names are they doing here?*

Roselyn was here too, and a Pirenti man I didn't know.

'Take them!' Izzy shouted. I reached down and lifted first Sadie and then Ella onto Radha's back, tightening my arms and knees around them.

'Where are you taking them?' Roselyn demanded.

'Out of this madness,' I replied over the howl of wind. 'They're my blood, Lady Roselyn – on my life I *will* keep them safe.'

She hesitated, clearly torn, then nodded.

'Hold onto each other and lie flat,' I ordered the girls and they flattened themselves against the horse's neck. To Izzy I called, 'Get north, clear of the forest.'

She nodded and I turned Radha and kicked her into a wild gallop. We streamed through the burning forest, flat and fast, ducking our way under and around flying debris. I pressed myself over the tiny bodies before me, sheltering them as best I could in the hail of bark and twigs that lashed at me. Many times the storm tried to force us back into the flames, but Radha was strong as she denied the gale, running straight into it, never allowing it to dictate our course.

It was too dangerous to try flying – uncurling her wings once had nearly gotten us both killed. Instead she held them flat and we tried to make ourselves small that we might slice through the chaos like an arrow finding its mark.

We should have been clear by now. But the storm held the dark madness of the warders. Just as we spotted the beginning of the grassy plains, a huge wall of flame erupted directly ahead. Radha reared back in fright and I gripped tightly to hold my seat and ensure the girls weren't flung free.

She landed and turned swiftly, running along the flames' edge, but it wasn't long before the fire cut us off again, and soon we were surrounded. Radha slowed, jerking her head to find a way out, but there wasn't one. The heat was magnificent; the air itself burned.

My eyes scanned the ground for anything at all that might be used to shelter us. Radha had already seen something, and carried us to a ditch in the earth. I slid off her back and reached for the girls, tugging them to the small trench. 'Stay down, curl up tight,' I ordered. Then I took Radha's mane and steered her to where they were huddled.

I didn't know what to do. She wouldn't fit. I might not even fit. Could I press myself over them and protect them from the worst? Radha snorted, nudging me towards the ditch. I turned to look at her, realising. As the flames leapt closer my heart broke. It was in her deep eyes, her knowing eyes. I took one too-short moment to press my forehead to hers, thinking I would die before I let her do this for me, but for the children – anything.

'Forgive me, love.'

She tossed her head and lowered herself onto her front knees. I curled myself over Ella and Sadie, and then Radha lay close to spread her wings over us. The glorious feathers cocooned us tenderly in a tiny inferno.

I heard her give a whinny as the flames rushed closer, and I *prayed* to the old gods, the gods with enough power to give life to a piece of driftwood, I prayed that they find enough power now to make this cursed fire pass.

ISADORA

Was I dreaming?

Around me everything burned. *Run*, people screamed. Had I dreamt this before? It felt like I had. There was a woman with hair of fire shaking me and screaming at me to run, run, but she was not real, surely. Too lovely to be real. All of this too nightmarish to be real. Someone was carrying me because I hadn't thought to run and I couldn't see Falco anywhere –

The heat. The heat was real enough to burn, and I found clarity like a blister upon my skin. 'Put me down!' I ordered. It was Erik, the man who'd tried to kill me beside the lake. He set me on the curling crackling bark and we took off once more, faster now. The woman, though – Roselyn – she was so slow. As the fire chased us, ever gaining, she stumbled awkwardly again and again, until Erik gathered her over his shoulder and ran with her as he'd done me.

We made it free, gasping for breath. My lungs were on fire, scorched by the heat of the air. I still couldn't see Falco.

Spinning around, I ran through the expanse of people who'd made it to the plain. Flames spread through the long grass but were beaten back, more manageable here. I couldn't find him anywhere and couldn't spot Radha either, who should have been plain to see.

I turned back to the forest. The fire was eating its way through, moving west.

'Wait,' Erik said, appearing beside me. 'Wait for it to pass.'

I shook my head. If he was in there with the children I would find them. But Erik said, 'You're very much awake, girl. You kept asking and asking, so I'm telling you. You go in there, you won't wake up – you'll die.'

It stalled me. I couldn't remember asking if I was awake. All my memories were slipping together, my realities blending. I didn't know what I had dreamt and what I hadn't. *This is real*, I told myself. *All too real.*

FALCO

I prayed for it to pass and it did, quickly due to the force of the wind. But so extreme was its heat that when we emerged from the cocoon it was to see the ravaged remains of the forest, a burnt out husk of blackened skeletal waste in every direction.

And Radha.

I sank to my knees beside her. She had covered herself as best she could, curling beneath the feathery shield, and so her body was relatively undamaged, a little singed. But her wings . . . her wings were burnt to ruin, the feathers disintegrated, tissue and muscle scoured away leaving only the fine bones and tendons. She bore the skeletons of wings, the ghosts, and she was in so much pain. She tried to stand but her legs wouldn't hold her and she sank back down.

My throat was thick as I tried to soothe her, stroking her and pressing my face to her neck. She was trembling and hot to the touch.

'Falco?' Sadie asked, in tears. She had been crying since we climbed into the ditch, but Ella was solemn-faced and silent.

'It's alright,' I managed to tell them, though it wasn't, it wasn't.

Abstractly, I remembered Ella's words to me from months ago. *You're a chrysalis*. It seemed she'd been right, but the world I had emerged into was a macabre kind of underworld indeed, and I less of a man than ever.

'Shh,' I whispered to Radha. 'I'll find you a healer, my darling, and you'll be well, I promise.'

Distant shouts rang out. People searching for us, for any survivors.

It was Isadora who found us first, perhaps pulled by the feel of her pegasis. She sprinted through the coals of the forest and stopped dead. Her eyes landed on Radha and even over the distance I could see her red gaze disappear, shifting instead to something grey and faded, something halfway between black and white. *Pain*, I thought, *her colour for deepest pain*.

'She saved us,' I rasped. 'Get help.'

Sadie draped herself over Radha's neck, holding her tightly and whispering to her. Ella reached to place her hands on the horse's hind, stroking her gently. But Isadora didn't touch her pegasis. She seemed frozen, locked.

'Izzy – we have to get her to a healer!' I said. 'Find someone!'

But she didn't move.

More people were arriving, the Sparrow's soldiers crowding around. Roselyn appeared at a run, scooping her nieces into her arms and kissing them repeatedly. There were tears in her eyes. Her companion was nearby and seemed almost as relieved to see them safe.

But I didn't have space for relief in my chest. It was pounding pounding *pounding* because I could see the look on Izzy's face and I thought I knew what it was for, but I couldn't believe it, I wouldn't.

She drew a dagger.

'Don't you dare!' I snarled.

Her eyes were that awful grey as she looked at me. Ashen, I realised, like the forest around her. 'Step aside.'

I shook my head. She couldn't be serious. She couldn't think I'd ever step aside.

Her eyes flicked to whoever was behind me and I was too slow, unforgivably slow, shock and grief making me stupid. Hands took me, several sets, all strong and rough enough to pull me from my pegasis. I grunted and struggled, but there were at least four of her soldiers.

'Bind his hands,' Isadora said. 'He's more dangerous than he looks.'

I struggled, screamed. 'Get away from her! It's only her wings – the rest of her is fine!'

Isadora walked a few paces closer to where I had been dragged. 'How could you be so cruel?' she asked me softly. 'She's in agony. Half of her has been destroyed.'

'I know the feeling,' I exclaimed. 'Would you slaughter me too?'

Her eyes flickered scarlet, black, back to grey.

'I'll do what I must,' Isadora said. 'It seems you are, as always, too weak.'

A scream left me as she turned back to Radha. 'Don't. Isadora.'

'Take the children away,' she ordered Roselyn, who hurriedly did so. I heard Sadie's crying grow softer and softer.

'Don't,' I begged again, over and over. 'Don't, *don't –*'

ISADORA

I sank to the ground beside her. Her agonised eyes pleaded with me. 'Yes,' I whispered. 'I will. I'm coming.'

Running my hands over her nose and forehead, pressing my cheek to hers – these were the little things I had not done enough. These were the small acts of affection I had never allowed myself, too frightened of what they might open within me.

But now I let all the fear leak out of my cracked edges, all the brittle and sharp thorns grow dull and then smooth. 'I love you,' I said. 'I love you, I love you.' True love, chosen freely and given completely. Stronger than any magic.

I looked into Radha's brown eyes, with Falco in my ears – *don't, don't, don't* – and I said 'thank you' and I sliced my knife straight into her carotid artery and I killed her. Her blood poured free, all over my hands and arms. She slumped against me and I sat still for long minutes, feeling the weight and warmth of her pressed to my body. I didn't think I could move, didn't think I was capable.

But I was and I did. I climbed out from under her and without looking towards Falco, I walked through the burnt forest all the way to the river. Alone now, I waded in and lost my footing, sinking awkwardly to sit in the water.

Wind still blew through the charcoal trees. Ash floated in the air, landing on my face, my eyes and my lips, on the surface of the river. I watched it floating, making patterns in the ripples. The world was grey.

Someone stepped into the water beside me.

I looked up to see the red-haired woman. Roselyn. She sank to her knees and with the ends of her skirt she began to gently scrub the blood from my arms and hands.

I dropped my head and wept, great heaving sobs that had been building all my life. She cleaned my skin and then smoothed her hand over my head, tenderly stroking my hair as I sobbed.

When finally my tears came to an end I wiped my eyes and nose with the back of my hand and rested my head on my raised knees. 'I always have to do the ugly things,' I said.

'They take the most courage,' Roselyn replied.

I would never have imagined the afternoon could turn cold in the wake of such a blaze, but it did. The clouds hung heavy over the sun and though the wind had lessened, it grew frigid. My teeth chattered and all the submerged parts of me went numb and wrinkly as a prune.

'Where did you come from?' I asked.

'Vjort. It was violent there. We stole a boat and sailed it downriver.' She sighed a little, as though the whole thing was wearying. 'We grew lost, swept up in the current. We came too far, I imagine, because now it seems we are in Kaya.'

I shrugged bleakly. 'Who knows where we are. Yurtt, Sanra, Kaya, Pirenti — it's all the same when it burns.' I glanced at her face and was struck by how pretty she was, how prominent her cheekbones. 'I thought it was always violent in Vjort.'

Roselyn nodded. She seemed lost in thought, before realising I was waiting for further explanation. 'The men of Pirenti fight always for power. I'm not sure who rules there now.'

I straightened, studying her. 'Your brother-in-law. Your son.'

'Perhaps not.' There was an ocean of fear in her brown eyes. And something else. Something darker. 'They didn't come for us. But the Jarl's men did.'

'Did they harm you?' My skin prickled at the thought of anyone raising a hand to such a fragile creature.

She took her time answering. Tendrils of burnt-ochre hair blew across her face, catching in her eyelashes and against her lips. Roselyn brushed them away and met my gaze. 'There are worse things than being harmed.'

At first I didn't understand, thinking of my cage and imagining that she mustn't know a great deal about harm. But as we sat hip deep in the river I considered her words and realised she was right: watching someone you loved be harmed was worse. Committing the harm yourself worst of all.

I looked at Roselyn and saw her for what she was. Not fragile after all, but quite the opposite.

'And you?' she asked. 'Where have you come from?'

The answer was so clear, suddenly. Not the cage. That was not where I had been born or raised or forged. I had been forged in this forest, and on the road with her son, and in the city with Falco. Pressed flat to Radha's back, her heartbeat thumping against my ribcage. Not by cruelty, but with kindness. I didn't know how to explain that, so I said nothing.

We rose to our feet and waded onto the bank, both of us soaked through. As we began the walk back, dread filled my stomach.

'What is your name?' Roselyn asked.

The time for secrets was over. The time for truth had come. I needed to bear my name with pride and use it to win this war. 'My soldiers name me Sparrow.'

But she shook her head. 'What is your true name?'

My heart thumped. I garnered my courage and told her. 'Isadora.'

★

I found Falco digging a grave, alone in the graveyard forest. Her body had been wrapped in a singed tent cloth. I hoisted a second shovel salvaged from the camp wreckage and I dug alongside him, and neither of us spoke a word. This time the silence was not chosen by me, but by him.

★

Sometime in the night the ash beneath my feet started creeping up over my boots and wrapping itself around my ankles, my legs, my hips. It snaked upwards, covering me in a fine, stinging layer, covering my hands and arms and throat and mouth and eyes. My entire body became a burnt-out husk and I called for help, shouted it as loudly as I could, but Falco couldn't hear me or didn't care, and without looking at me he finished burying Radha and walked away, leaving me to suffocate in ash.

Chapter 25

Finn

There was a film between life and death; I could feel it so easily now that I often took to slipping my fingers beneath it as we walked. A veil, something entirely insubstantial, a sensation more than anything else. The delicacy of a moth wing or the gossamer of a dragonfly. It had the same texture as sticky, trickling sap, the finest sheen of it. How little the living knew of the truth: they moved so close to death that the only thing between was as thin and ethereal as a shadow. It was probably a good thing they knew so little – the truth was terrifying. So I didn't tell them how I was manipulating it: we survived the journey to the marshes only because I was able to feel that film and stretch it a little, molding it over all three hundred of us, coating us in the invisibility of death that we might not be spotted by warders.

After all, warders were unable to glimpse the dead.

Well, unless they were me.

Falco

I was attempting to get as drunk as humanly possible. It made for an interesting walk through the long grassy plains of Querida. I had walked here before, but with Ava, Finn and Osric, whom I loved, instead of with an army of enemy soldiers I'd spent the last ten years trying to kill. The Sparrow was at their head, composed and unreadable. She was the ice queen, the snow goddess, a statue made of granite. I finished my bottle of rum, stumbling as I smashed it on the ground. People looked at me, but what did that matter? What did any of it matter?

Emperor Feckless had returned with a vengeance.

Roselyn and Erik were keeping the twins away, even though anyone could see how desperate they were to be near him. Greer told me to pull him into line, but I ignored her. Falco was none of my concern. The final thread tying us together had been severed by my blade.

A scout appeared in the distance, sprinting back to us. As I waited for her I glanced at my army – we were fifteen-hundred strong after the casualties of the fire. Plus two children, a Pirenti hirðmenn, a Pirenti woman, and one drunken fool.

The scout arrived and took a moment to catch her breath. 'A group of people, lady. Very large people – they look Pirenti. Some on foot, some on horseback. Heading towards the marshes as we are.'

'How many?'

'Maybe two hundred.'

I cursed inwardly. Two hundred was too few.

I called for my army to make camp and then I waited for nightfall. The darker it grew the louder Falco's drunken singing became. When I could stand it no longer I donned a black, hooded cloak and drew it over my hair, then I crept silently through the dark hills. Every shadow seemed a dream; I kept thinking I must have slipped into sleep at some point.

Hold it together, I urged myself. *Keep control of your senses, at least for tonight.*

It took me several hours to reach the group and I tracked their movements for some time longer as they seemed disinclined to stop for the night. Eventually they paused, most of the enormous men taking a knee, some water, a little rest, but no sleep. It wouldn't be long before they took off again and at this pace they'd reach Ava and Osric's group of Sancians within days. It occurred to me to let them continue on their mission to protect the fleeing citizens, but no – I would need even these two hundred on my side of the battle. The best way to protect the people was to destroy the warders.

Flattening myself over the crest of a hill, I peered down on the group, searching for its leader. I'd never met King Ambrose and it was hard to distinguish any of the men in the dark – they all looked similar. Huge bodies, shaved heads, heavily armed.

Something snapped behind me and I whirled too late. How had I not heard him? This was turning into a habit: dropping my guard and letting men sneak up on me.

He was a giant. I had never witnessed a human so large. He plucked me by the back of the neck and lifted me from the ground. It hurt the base of my skull and my first instinct was to slash him to ribbons, but I held my temper and remained still, hanging like a ragdoll in his grip.

'Well, well,' he growled. 'Forgetting the simplest rule: you can't sneak up on someone who can smell you from a hundred miles away.'

I felt a chill run through me. All my animal instincts were screaming at me to get away from this thing, whatever it was. Hardly a man as I knew them. He carried me down the hill and I schooled myself to be calm. I wanted to talk to them. I just hadn't counted on being apprehended and carried in like both an enemy spy and a helpless child.

As we drew near I realised that the larger soldiers were berserkers, and my skin crawled. I was carried through and they crowded around, sniffing at me. I was thrown roughly to the hard earth, where I sprawled and quickly righted myself.

'He reeks of blood and emptiness,' my captor reported.

Sitting on a log on the other side of a fire was a handsome man with no hands. I blinked, confused by the bandaged stumps. This helpless man was no berserker, so why was he here?

'Who are you?' the handless man asked.

The berserker snarled, 'He's a warder. Only ones who have that empty, cold scent. Let me kill him.'

'Are you a warder, kid?'

I lifted my hands to my hood and lowered it. There was a collective growl from the men around me. Some called me names – monster, witch, demon. I straightened my shoulders, streaked through with rage. For being caught, for being called a man, a child, a warder, and all those other fucking names, for this cursed prejudice, these fools, and the endless, endless assumption that I was exactly what I looked like. I'd had enough.

Twisting low and fast, I took hold of the berserker's wrist and used it to swing up behind his mighty shoulders, snaking my legs around them and pressing the blade of my dagger against his throat. He froze.

'Yes, I'm a demon,' I snarled, lips near his ear. 'A witch, a monster. Anything at all that you can think of to call me, I will be. But if you ever name me warder again, I will drain you of every last drop of blood.'

There was an astonished silence.

The berserker didn't move. I watched the handless man. Who laughed. 'How about instead of calling you any of those things, I just call you by your name? Greetings, Isadora.'

'Have I leave to kill her?' the man between my legs asked.

The handless one laughed all the more. 'If you think you can, be my guest.'

My knife bit into his neck.

'Easy. I was kidding,' the handless man assured me with a smile. His eyes were impossibly blue. 'Climb down from poor Goran and let's talk.'

I could feel Goran bristling beneath me as I swung down and landed in a puff of dust. I sheathed my blade, keeping my unguarded back to him in what I hoped he would take as an insult. Then I stepped forwards to face the King of Pirenti.

'Ambrose,' he confirmed. 'I would shake your hand, but alas . . .' The smile he gave then astonished me, and I couldn't help glancing at the stumps. He would not remain King of Pirenti long, in this state. 'Thorne and Finn have told me much about you, Isadora. Where have you come from? Last I heard you were trapped in Sancia.'

I shook my head, no idea where to start. Now that I was here, and had them all staring at me with varying degrees of fury and curiosity, my words dried up. This mutilated king was watching me with such kindness that it unnerved me, scattered my thoughts.

Just then a small group of people arrived at the edge of the fireside, carrying huge buckets of water over their shoulders. One of them was Ava, another Thorne.

The prince stopped dead, staring at me. He looked sick – much thinner than I remembered him, much older, much wearier. But he smiled, slow

335

and wide, and the boy I knew shone from his pale eyes. Lowering the buckets to the ground, Thorne said, 'Come here, snowflake.'

And I felt myself moving to him, was wrapped up in his tight embrace, lifted from my feet and hugged for a long time. 'I've really missed you, my dear friend,' he said. The best I could do was a nod, struck by how much I'd missed him too. His quiet, steady gentility made me calm. And not the forced false calm of the lake, but a true peace.

★

I explained – awkwardly stumbling over my words – all I could about the nearby army of the Sparrow, Falco's presence, the prisoners from the warder prison, the fire, our journey to the marshes and our plan to attack the warders. Then I looked at Ava, feeling guilty for not having led with: 'Your children are safe.'

She gave a gasp, a sound sucked from her lungs, and then she was up and sprinting – *sprinting* – to a pegasis, leaping onto its back and galloping into the darkness. The whole thing had taken about five seconds, and I blinked.

A few soldiers stood to follow her, but Ambrose told them to let her go – they'd all follow first thing in the morning. He too was grinning ear to ear and had to wipe his moist eyes with his shoulder. Thorne placed a meaty hand on his uncle's back and they shared a quiet moment of relief.

'My mother?' Thorne asked me, and I nodded.

He clapped Ambrose even harder.

'I knew they were fine,' Ambrose said. 'I could feel it.'

'What of the people from the city? Did Ava get them out?' I asked.

'She did. Osric and Finn are with them.'

'They'd better not have been found by the warders since then,' Thorne muttered.

'I don't know what kind of power could vanquish the indomitable Finn of Limontae,' Ambrose said wryly. 'Now, to this Sparrow. You said Falco has allied with him? And he's willing to accept our alliance?'

I nodded.

'Is he trustworthy?'

I opened my mouth, closed it and then nodded again. I wasn't sure how to explain, how to reveal it without sounding idiotic.

Once we'd exchanged information I looked again at Thorne. 'Would you walk with me a moment?'

He nodded and we made our way through the grassy hills, both watching the moon above. He was very unwell, with a constant stream of sweat running down his temples.

I cleared my throat. 'Are you alright, Thorne?'

He smiled sideways at me, reaching to squeeze my hand once and then letting it go.

I heard new footsteps and with a sinking heart I turned my head to see Quillane and Radha walking nearby. They did not look at or speak to me, but they were there, an eternal reminder.

'You've killed people, haven't you?' I asked Thorne abruptly.

He nodded.

'Do they haunt you?'

'No,' Thorne said, 'but my father does.'

Startled, I looked at him in the dark. His eyes flashed in the light of the almost full moon.

'Or,' he amended, 'he *did*. Until I banished him.'

I swallowed, searching for the words. 'You regret that?'

'Every second of every day.'

'Why?'

'I miss him,' Thorne replied.

I breathed out, considering that. 'Then you are not . . . haunted. Not by your own monstrosities.'

'I used to carry a lot of shame, Iz,' he said. 'Then I accepted the part of me I'd been frightened of. I welcomed my beast and now we're one.' Thorne cleared his throat. 'There's . . . a bigger darkness than that, one that lies beneath our feet, an easy thing to slip into. It's not something we can escape if we have been born walking atop it, as all kings of Pirenti are, and as I think you have been.'

The words made me cold inside.

It was no wonder Falco hated me – who wanted to be bound to a woman who walked over a gaping, sucking darkness? One that made her kill the things he loved?

Swallowing, I said, 'Falco isn't well. He will need you.'

'He has me.'

We walked in silence a while, cresting a hill and pausing at its apex. Quillane and Radha started humming a soft song and it moved its way into my blood, into my heart, reconciling me to the bleak truth that I would never be rid of them, not for all the days I lived.

Some part of me started making plans.

'I didn't even meet my da,' Thorne said abruptly. 'I have no idea who he is and yet I imagine him talking to me as though I know him. How ridiculous is that?' He gave a choked kind of laugh, and then looked straight into my eyes. 'I think I've gone mad, Iz.'

I glanced up to see stars fall from the sky, every one of them a glittering arc through the infinite abyss. I knew the feeling.

FALCO

I had sobered up a tad by the time dawn approached. I didn't sleep – I hadn't been able to since Radha, not for more than a few minutes here and there. Lurching to my feet, I tripped my way through the chilly predawn grey, fog draped heavily over the sleeping campers and dousing the last embers of the fires. I was in search of more drink.

I came across a canteen, but found it filled with water, and begrudgingly swallowed some before throwing it down and continuing my mission. My feet led me near to where Roselyn was curled between Ella and Sadie. I couldn't help but pause, looking at them and feeling a woozy pang in my chest where my heart used to be.

Memories of some version of me reached for them, but the mask I now wore had eclipsed any other Falco – this one had no more love. This one was a useless waste of a person who wanted nothing but to numb the world. So I moved on, refusing to look back at the sleeping girls, once two of my favourite people in the world.

I had not gone far when I heard hoofbeats. Someone was approaching through the fog. I stopped, still too drunk to fully comprehend the potential danger. I was sure the Sparrow would make quick work of whoever dared to draw near, the blades on her body already covered in thick layers of blood. In a move my mother would have been mortified by, I spat on the ground, but the bitter taste remained in my mouth.

And then I recognised the figure dismounting to dash through the sleepers, peering down at them, searching. 'Ava!' I called before I could stop myself.

I pointed to her daughters and watched her scared, twisted face crumple into tears, and I watched her walk the last paces to her children, and I watched them wake to fold into her arms and hold her as she wept.

But there was a pegasis standing nearby and when I caught sight of it I decided I didn't want to watch any more reunions. I picked up a bottle and walked with it into the mist.

AVA

Getting an account of recent events from two eight year olds was not the wisest idea. I sat on the grass with a daughter hanging off either arm, chattering away as though they might lose the ability to speak at any moment. I couldn't stop smiling, my heart too big to fit in my chest.

They were working backwards for some reason, and as they got to the account of what had happened to them in Vjort, I realised why they hadn't been so excited to describe that part of the story. A slow horror uncurled in my stomach as they explained how they had escaped through the night, underdressed and carrying the unconscious Erik, how Roselyn had gotten them to safety and hidden with them for two days straight. Their words slowed as they went back further, to the attack in the castle, to hiding in the closet while Rose tried to convince the soldier she was alone.

They stopped, both of them, something bleak in their eyes and I knew something very bad had happened, and I changed the subject entirely. There was a trembling in my fingers that I couldn't seem to clench away. My eyes went to where Roselyn and Erik the hirðmenn sat in companionable silence by the morning embers of the fire.

★

It was a couple of hours before Ambrose arrived with the rest of our soldiers.

339

I had warned the girls that Da had been hurt but was well now, and just as strong as he'd ever been. When they saw him they both burst into tears and hugged him, and he did his best to hug them back, kissing the tears from their faces. It was both sweet and painful, a bit much to manage, so I used the moment to go to Rose. She was ensconced in a reunion with her son so I turned instead to Erik, who had heavy bandaging around one of his wrists.

He bowed low.

'You, Erik,' I told him, 'must never bow to me again.'

He blushed as he straightened, the markings on his face taking on a beautiful look over such a sweet expression.

'For what you've done for my children, I can never repay you. I can't even come close.'

He shook his head quickly, eyes darting to the red-haired woman nearby. 'Majesty, it was not me who saved them.'

'What happened?' I asked.

Erik met my eyes. His were a very dark brown. 'My lady . . . do not ask her. I beg you. Just know that she has courage unlike any I have witnessed, and if you and His Majesty will allow it I mean to pledge my life to protecting her.'

I swallowed, managed only to nod. Then I turned to her, leading her away from where we might be overheard. Roselyn's eyes were bright from having seen her son, but something in her expression stilled as she saw mine.

'Rose,' I whispered. Because I knew what the men of Vjort were like. The vileness of the place bred a deep cruelty in its people. I didn't understand how one person could be so endlessly strong. 'How can I possibly . . .?' I shook my head. 'I love you. I thank gods every day you're in my life. And now I owe you an impossible debt, the greatest anyone can owe another soul. *My children*. Rose . . .'

'You owe me nothing,' she said. 'Nothing.'

'I love you,' I said again, taking her in an embrace.

'And I you,' Roselyn murmured, holding me so tight.

I thought I saw a flicker then, in the corner of my vision. A flicker of dark, silky hair. But I closed my eyes against this trick of the light, tears blurring my vision.

THORNE

After making sure Ma was alright, I went looking for Falco. He was nowhere to be found within the camp, but I followed his scent into the hills. Everything looked the same out here – there was no difference between these particular grassy slopes and the ones Isadora and I had walked last night, except that these were shrouded not in moonlight, but heavy fog.

I found him balancing on a wobbling rock, half-empty bottle in one hand, a sword in the other. 'What are you doing, brother?'

His head whipped up, his ankle rolled on the rock and he lost his balance, crashing onto the bottle and nearly skewering himself with the blade.

I winced. 'For pity's sake, Falco.'

'So you pity me now too?' he asked, words slurred. He rolled off the miraculously unbroken bottle and took a swig.

'It's first thing in the morning and you're already drinking,' I said. 'So yes, I do.'

He brandished the sword wildly. 'But I can use this blade!' he announced, then cracked up laughing. 'That means I'm not pitiable, right? It means I'm not the man everyone thought I was! Emperor Feckless knows how to fight with a sword, so he must not be feckless anymore!' He seemed to find this hysterical, doubled over and clutching his stomach with mirth.

I placed a hand on his shoulder and forced him to sit on the rock, then I perched next to him, grateful to be seated. The pain of my wound was getting worse by the day.

'What happened, mate?' I asked. 'Isadora said you weren't well.'

'You've spoken to the ice sculpture, have you?' He gave a bitter laugh, swigging more. I snatched the bottle from him and held it out of his grasp. 'Curse you, you big lug.' Falco rested his head in his hands. 'Nothing happened. I'm just coming to terms with what I've known all along.'

'Which is what?'

'The masks only mask the fact that there's nothing beneath them.'

I shook my head, stood. 'You're drunk. Sleep it off and when you're sober we'll have a real conversation.'

'Sleep, he says. But in sleep dreams wait, and in dreams she waits.'

I peered at him. But that was when we heard a shout and a scream, and I ran back to the camp with the smell of blood in my nose.

CHAPTER 26

FALCO

I was actually less drunk than I'd let Thorne believe. And I was even less drunk when I arrived on his tail to see a berserker holding Greer over the fire, dangling her face-down, close to the flames.

'Stand down!' Thorne boomed.

The berserker reluctantly put Greer on her feet – thankfully not in the fire – and she spat at him in rage.

'We are allies,' Thorne barked. 'This is unacceptable.'

The berserker bowed his head to Thorne and I was awed by the young man's power, though not surprised. Ambrose and Ava arrived, and I could see the Sparrow making her way around behind the altercation. 'Will you not punish him?' she asked Thorne.

He frowned. 'Tensions run high, Izzy. It's over now – there's no need.'

Isadora eyed him calmly, her huge red eyes turning very cold. 'Seems I must punish him for you.'

There were a few laughs of disbelief, a few angry mutters.

'And who the fuck are you to punish *me*, little girl?' the berserker asked her derisively.

Isadora's gaze moved to him, then travelled over the crowd of onlookers and finally rested on me. She said, clearly, 'I'm the Sparrow of the South, and these are my lands you stand upon, my army you have asked to join.' Without further ado, she sliced off one of the berserker's fingers.

ISADORA

There was chaos. Fights broke out between and within groups. Ambrose was shouting for a cessation of violence. But people were

343

shocked at the revelation of my identity and the sudden brutality in the morning, and it didn't help that the two sides hated each other.

I saw Falco coming for me but I couldn't face him, so instead I disappeared into the fog.

'What, you're running from me now?' he called, following. 'You're a butcher!'

I whirled to face him, wrenching my arm from his clutch. 'Do you want berserkers thinking they can attack those smaller and weaker and not endure any consequences? *They're dangerous, Falco, and now they're among my people.*'

That seemed to stop him. He was breathing quickly. 'You exacerbated the problem.'

'Do I look like someone to be respected? Obeyed? Followed?' I shook my head. 'I have to make them or I get a sword in the back.'

'There are better ways to lead than with fear.'

'Shall I amuse them, then? Disappoint them? Because we know how well that has worked for you.' As soon as the words were out I regretted them, imagined snatching them out of the air before they reached his ears. I didn't want to fight with him, didn't want to throw barbs back and forth, especially when I didn't believe the cruel words I spouted.

His expression hardened. 'This has got to stop,' he said, and I almost breathed a sigh of relief until I realised he didn't mean our fighting, he meant something else entirely. 'I need to tell you something, and when I'm done, *we're* done.'

I froze. Could feel my muscles seizing up, turning to bone.

'Your ma's name was Iona, your da's name Steven,' Falco told me, and my heart thundered. I shook my head. Whatever this was, I didn't want him to tell me, but he kept speaking and he couldn't even meet my eyes as he did so. 'Steven had six brothers, all of whom had natural shields against warder intrusion. The seven of them stole into the Sancian palace and slaughtered the royal family. When I was crowned, my first act was to send the warders Callius and Raziel to find the murderers. What I didn't know, until the library, was that they were found, almost immediately. Steven and his brothers, along with Iona, were tortured to death for crimes against the throne, treason and the murder of five royals. The warders kept it to themselves as some part of a power play I can only imagine. And then they placed Iona and Steven's white-haired baby in a cage for the remainder of her life.'

It fell into place suddenly, the last nails in a coffin.

The fog around us was clearing, falling back. My mind was whirling too hard to notice. The cage was not because of how I looked, not because I was a demon baby, but because my parents were rebels. They were the ones who had chosen the path of my life when they butchered Falco's family. I bore the punishment of that. And now I had become just as bloodthirsty. Blood begat blood, death begat death.

'Isadora . . .' Falco said, almost desperately. 'All this pain we've caused each other – it dates even further back than our lifetimes. It's my fault – *directly* – that you were born into such horrific brutality. I finally think you were right. Whatever brought us together and bound our lives was nothing more than a cruel joke. Let it go now. Let it be over, that we might not punish ourselves for it any longer.'

I opened my mouth but nothing came out.

'Wasted lives,' he whispered. 'Two utterly wasted lives.'

At that moment the fog cleared enough to reveal that we were not the only two people left in the world, nor had we moved as far as I thought. We were right beside the recently warring camp, now filled with at least fifty staring faces, all of whom had overheard our argument. Including Ava, Ambrose and Thorne. They gazed at us and I had a vague thought that at least our embarrassing conversation had stopped the fighting.

But I didn't feel any embarrassment for the weaknesses I had just revealed. I felt only a terrible heartache as I watched Falco walk away from me. I wished there was some way to tell him that I didn't care about our parents, I didn't care what his warders had done to me or to my family. I didn't care about the cage or the brutality – I was so far beyond it because of him. I cared only for him, I *loved* only him, desperately and endlessly, no magic and no bond needed to make it true.

*

We marched west for several days until we arrived at the edge of the marshlands. The question now was which way to skirt them, and as we stopped for a quick lunch break I joined Thorne, Ambrose and Ava to figure it out.

'Well hello, stranger,' Thorne greeted me pointedly. I lowered my eyes, not wanting to discuss why I'd avoided the lot of them for the past few days, travelling ensconced in groups of my own people.

None of the Sparrow's soldiers were particularly surprised to learn my true name. I had always been known as the Sparrow's right hand, and I got the feeling many of them had suspected the truth. Ava had been watching me with cold suspicion ever since, whereas Thorne had yet to make his opinion clear.

'A little white sparrow,' Thorne mused now.

'It's wonderful,' Ambrose said.

'How do you figure that?' Ava said.

'The Sparrow was an unknown before. We didn't know if he could be trusted. Now that "he" is a "she", and one we happen to know and love, we have a powerful new ally we can count on.'

I tried not to blush at his use of the word love, astonished that he would throw it around so lightly. He had met me mere days ago and since witnessed me slice off the finger of one of his men.

'The Sparrow is an enemy rebel who started civil war in my country, rose up against my cousin, the rightful ruler of Kaya, and incited untold bloodshed,' Ava said coldly.

I lifted my chin, letting her see no regret. I would not reveal myself as the ruler of three realms only to cower before a foreign woman, no matter who she was or how respected. 'The subjugation of my people by yours,' I said, 'the unforgivable misconduct shown by Kaya's rulers, and the constant, insidious hand of the warders in any and every decision of state merited intervention.' I paused, holding her violet eyes, watching them slip to a bright fuchsia. 'I did ask first. I asked for Sanra's freedom, I asked for new laws to be placed on warder use of power, then I warned what would happen if I continued to be ignored. And *then* I acted. Emperor Feckless has only himself to blame.' I sat back, uneasy about how much I had spoken.

'You mean your bondmate?' Ava asked pointedly.

And I replied, 'No, Majesty, I don't.'

She sighed, and I could hear her sadness.

'I *never* would have guessed, but I should have,' Thorne offered with a shake of his head. 'Why didn't you tell us, Iz?'

'I never told anyone. That was the point.'

'But Falco knew?' Ambrose asked.

I nodded.

'For how long?'

'Since we bonded,' I replied.

'That little cheek,' Thorne muttered. 'Lying through his teeth this whole time. Finn will *die* when she finds out.' I couldn't help smiling as he laughed at the thought.

'Ambrose, could I have a word with you?'

We turned to see Falco a few paces away. His crystal eyes glittered in the sunlight.

'Of course you can, my short-haired, broken-nosed cousin,' Ambrose said cheerfully. 'Take a seat.'

Falco hesitated with a glance at me, but sat beside Thorne.

'We were just talking about you,' Ambrose said. 'Who's on wine duty this afternoon?'

'I've got it,' Thorne offered, lifting a bottle to the King's lips and wiping away a trickle down his chin. I watched, thinking Ambrose might be embarrassed, but he didn't look it. He just swallowed and thanked his nephew, finally turning back to Falco. 'I've been hearing some fairly wild rumours about you.'

Falco flapped his hand flamboyantly and with a droll sigh said, 'Lies, all.'

'Drop it, Fal,' Thorne growled.

Falco looked at him and I watched the colour leech from his cheeks, along with any pretense. He suddenly seemed tired and dead-eyed. 'Do you know anything about your brother's ability to torture and kill warders?' he asked Ambrose.

The air was sucked from the space.

Ava glanced at her husband protectively. Thorne clenched and unclenched his fists. But Ambrose smiled a lovely smile as he thought about his brother for a few long seconds. With a shake of his head he said, 'No. His actions under the ice mountain were always a mystery to me.'

'Might his wife know?'

'You're not to ask her,' Ava said. 'She's been through enough lately without remembering her husband's violence.'

Thorne's jaw clenched. Falco looked like he might argue with Ava, but let it go. I could see the two halves of him battling for power, could see his own certainties and opinions vying for space, but all of it was cowed by his need to be ignorable.

We did the same thing, him and me, always seeking to make ourselves smaller – to make ourselves *invisible*. He had a showy, beautiful way of being invisible, but it made him invisible in the ways that mattered. How in the world we had found ourselves leading half a country each was utterly beyond me.

You're a butcher! The words walked with me, ran and breathed and slept with me. They hadn't stopped racing around in my mind since he'd said them.

It was what I'd believed, was it not? For as long as I could remember? The butcher or the meat. But the way he said it – with such repulsion – made the very idea vile. The truth became something else entirely: I still believed in being the butcher or the meat, but now I thought I would far rather be the meat.

'How then?' Falco asked. 'How do we face them when they can render us immobile with a look, and we have no access to the one man who understood how to beat them?'

Ava looked at me. 'I've been waiting months to ask the Sparrow how she's been leaving warder corpses all over the city.'

I swallowed, unsure how to explain. My eyes darted to Falco. He said, 'Isadora has a peculiar talent for lucid dreaming. She can control her body while her mind sleeps, and the warders have no power over her in that state.'

'Of course.' Ava sighed. 'Sleepwalking to get Penn free.'

'Since the night we broke our bond,' Falco said, 'she's been unable to.'

'Did you learn the skill?' Ambrose asked him.

Falco shook his head.

348

I remembered acutely the beauty of that night and its strangeness, remembered how infinitely lovely it was to share the dream instead of always walking it alone. I cleared my throat a little.

'Who taught you, Iz?' Thorne asked.

'No one.'

'How did you teach yourself?'

I didn't know what to say. It wasn't that I minded them knowing, it was simply that if I explained they would pity me, and I couldn't stand the thought of that. Rupturing my heart, Falco reached to take my hand. His eyes shifted but I couldn't tell what colour they were in the glare of the sun. He said, 'With courage, boredom and practice.'

My lips quirked. I considered removing my hand, but decided pity was marginally better than hatred.

Falco reached for the bottle of wine, exchanged a very pointed look with Thorne, and then took a small sip. 'Happy?'

Thorne nodded.

'Has anyone told you that you look like shit?' Falco asked him bluntly.

'We have more tact,' Ava said.

'Honestly, why do you look like shit?' Falco pressed.

Thorne shrugged.

'Ambrose looks like shit too, but we all know why that is.'

'Cheers to that,' Ambrose announced, jutting his chin pointedly until he was fed more wine. 'So which way do we go?' He looked at Falco and me, whose country we found ourselves in.

We glanced at each other and he seemed to remember that he was still holding my hand, quickly removing it. 'South.'

'And when we get there?' Thorne asked.

Falco used a stick to draw a map of the city in the dirt. 'The wall is impenetrable and covers all but the ocean side. This western gate here is the largest, and will be most heavily guarded. Just inside this southern wall are the palace buildings and the warder compound – the magic here will be thick.'

'Can we use the cliffs?'

'They're too steep to climb without significant casualties.'

'What about the tunnel you built?' I asked Falco.

He marked it on the drawing. 'We could potentially feed soldiers into the city slowly, if they don't catch us in the act.'

'Meaning we need to occupy the warders with a sustained diversion to give the infiltration time to work,' Ambrose said.

We all peered at the drawing.

'The berserkers and I could attack this western gate with enough force to draw the bulk of the warder defenses,' Thorne said.

'You want to take all the heat on one hundred men?' Falco demanded. 'You'll be annihilated.'

The prince shook his head. 'Warders don't have the same kind of power over berserkers. Can't get into their heads as easily.'

'Why?' Falco asked. This was really getting under his skin. But Thorne only shrugged.

'We can distract them long enough to give you a shot. We're probably the only ones who could.'

I was the first to nod, but I was silently making my own plans.

★

I peered into the marshlands. Hundreds of rivers snaked through the swamp and it was impossible to follow their banks through the expanse, as more often than not they became thick, sticky mud. The air was humid, mosquitoes and other insects appearing to feast upon our flesh. There was a sweet, rotten fruit scent; Thorne and the berserkers had to tie cloth over their noses, and looked ready to vomit from the pungency of it.

Just as the call to move was about to be announced, I heard, all too clearly, a few sniggers. Lade and a group of my soldiers had lined up behind a berserker and were wafting horse dung through the air to irritate his sense of smell. The enormous man was almost double their size, and whirled around with an angry growl, clearly about to lose his temper. *Not again.*

I kicked my horse into their path and levelled them with a look. The Kayan men were instantly contrite, while the berserker struggled to contain his temper with deep, long breaths. 'Your immaturity would tear us apart before the warders get a chance,' I said softly, directing the words to Lade.

'Forgive me, Sparrow,' Lade said quickly.

'I beg your pardon?' a voice said from behind me. A voice I had come to know well.

I rounded my horse, but found myself staring at nothing. Literally, the space before me was empty of anything except the long grass of the plain.

'What did that man just call you?' the voice asked.

Gods, I'd lost it. Or I was dreaming.

'The veil, Inney,' a second voice said, a boy's voice.

Several things happened very fast.

First the air before me flickered, shimmered, and instead of nothing I was abruptly staring at a bedraggled group of several hundred people. My eyes widened. *What*? Standing at their head were Finn, Jonah and Penn, gazing at me in shock, and –

And then I was lifted right into the air, an invisible hand around my throat.

Voices shouted below me, chaos breaking out at both the appearance of the invisible people and the fact that I was dangling by my neck at least ten feet in the air, choking.

'Let her down, Osric!' I heard Falco roar.

But I was not let down. There was magic in the air, a thick crackle of it sizzling against my skin and hair, singing just as the fire had done. I couldn't breathe, couldn't get anything into my lungs and my vision was starting to cloud –

With a great *whoomph* I fell through the air to land heavily on my ankles, crashing sideways onto the hip I had recently dislocated. I blacked out for a second or two and it couldn't have been any longer than that, because when my eyes opened, it was to see Finn of Limontae standing before Osric, first-tier warder of Kaya, her hand outstretched towards him.

She clenched her hand as if squeezing and he fell heavily to one knee, trying to gasp air, but unable to. 'That doesn't feel too nice, does it, Os?' she demanded, squeezing tighter.

'She's the Sparrow!' Osric managed to cough, and with a burst of power he rose to his feet and shook off Finn's ward. 'I vowed to kill the bloodthirsty Sparrow and so I shall.'

I rose to my feet despite the pain. 'Let him try,' I growled, flicking free two of my daggers and spinning them between my fingers.

'Are you out of your minds?' Finn snapped, and then she did what should have been impossible: she contained the first-tier warder, froze his body and his power with a burst of her own.

'Finn!' he roared. 'Let me go! *She must die!*'

'Stand down, Osric!' Falco ordered again.

'Majesty,' the warder gasped. 'She has sought your death for years! You cannot trust her, no matter who she is to you!'

Falco glanced at Finn, whose eyes were completely white, hair floating around her with the force of her power. It was sending the berserkers mad – I could hear them growling in fury, chafing to get at her, to destroy the magic they could scent. Things had become very dangerous.

'Knock him out, if you can,' Falco ordered Finn.

Finn sent a burst of power so intense that Osric slumped unconscious to the ground. She lowered her hand, breathing slowly. Her yellow hair fell back into place and her white eyes regained some of their colour. Disturbingly, they didn't return to their normal brightness. They were faded – a fainter shade of yellow that made her look sapped.

'Finn,' a voice said.

I watched as she turned, her eyes moving over me as though I barely existed – in that moment no one in this world existed, only Thorne. She spotted him and twin expressions lit their faces. I felt the love that breached the distance between them more intensely than I had felt the heat of the fire or the wind of the storm. Their eyes were gold as we watched them cross and melt into each other. A warder and a berserker.

CHAPTER 27

FINN

While everyone else was dealing with serious things, Thorne and I crept away to the edge of the marshes. We hid ourselves behind the gnarled roots of a mangrove tree, kissing kissing kissing until we couldn't breathe. There was a lot to deal with – Isadora was the Sparrow and Ambrose had no hands – but it could all wait. I needed my husband.

I didn't realise at first that he was trembling. 'What?' I whispered. 'What is it?' I searched him, running my hands over his face and arms and chest. He looked gods-awful. 'Are you sick?'

Thorne shook his head. I'd never seen him so exhausted. His face was gaunt, eyes hollow. 'I've missed you,' was all he said, but the way he said it made me frightened of how much. I kissed him again, tasting his lips and remembering the feel of him with a pleasure so intense it was almost painful.

'Your eyes, Finn,' Thorne said. 'How much power have you been using?'

'Magic,' I corrected.

'What's the difference?'

I shook my head, almost overcome with weariness. 'I had to get them here and there were warders everywhere. The north-west is crawling with them, Thorne.'

'How did you do it?'

'I cloaked them.'

He frowned, studying the colour of my eyes. 'Well, don't do it anymore, alright? Don't use any more magic for a while.'

'On the eve of war?'

'You go with Ambrose and the twins – get to safety and don't look back. You've done enough.'

I pulled away from him, my boots squelching in the thick earth. 'I've no wish to fight, but in what world do you think I'd leave you to face them alone?'

'I won't be alone -'

'It's done, Thorne. You're going to need my help.' Because one thing had become clear this morning: if I could contain Osric, then I might be the only one with a chance against Dren and Galia. It did not sit well with me – my control over magic was rudimentary at best; the only real skill I had was in manipulating the fabric between life and death – but I had spent most of my life being frightened of my magic and I was tired of it. I would use it for good, one way or another, or there was no point in it at all.

I swallowed, running my fingers over his clammy skin. 'Are you wounded?' He shook his head, so I asked, 'Is it your da? Are you still seeing him?'

Thorne looked pained, his eyes dropping. 'No.'

An idea had been forming throughout my long walk, with the film sitting between my fingers and the singing of the dead in my ears. I wasn't ready to share it with him because I didn't know if it was possible, but this idea continued to fixate me.

'Things got very bad in Vjort,' Thorne admitted, looking haunted. 'I had to —' He cut himself off abruptly.

'What?' I asked, but his jaw remained clenched. 'Where are you?'

'With you,' he said bluntly, lifting his eyes to mine. 'I've been with you this whole time.' Then he amended, almost angrily, 'I've needed to be.'

'Why? What's going on?'

'I'm . . . *balanced* with you. Alone I'm just . . .' He shuddered. I waited for him to explain, could see how much he was struggling with the words. 'I can barely recognise my —'

'Thorne!' someone's voice sliced through his sentence, and I sighed.

'This conversation isn't finished,' I warned him. 'You look awful, and I'll get to the bottom of it.'

I turned, but he snatched my hand and pressed his lips to the inside of my palm. Eyes closed, he breathed in the scent of my skin. 'I'm lost without you.'

I ran my free hand through his short hair. 'No, you aren't, my darling.' After pressing a kiss to his temple, we reluctantly rejoined the rest of the world.

'Meeting,' Falco said after giving me a kiss on the cheek.

'You look rough, Fal!' I exclaimed, touching his short hair and prodding at his crooked nose hard enough to make him wince and knock my hand away. It was too much fun antagonising him.

The others had grouped together at the head of the massive expanse of people spread out over the plain. I took the Emperor's hand, stalling him. 'Are you alright?'

Falco's unchanging eyes shone clear in the sunlight. He nodded.

'But was it . . . the right thing to do?' *Breaking the bond.*

He hesitated, then shook his head. 'I honestly don't know, Finn. But either way, it's over. It's all over, and we're both still alive, so there's that to be thankful for.' The words sounded distinctly hollow.

I had yet to greet Rose or Ella and Sadie, and I didn't know where Jonah and Penn had got to, but it seemed we were launching right into a discussion about things I was now abruptly involved in, because of what they'd seen me do to poor Os.

'Finn and Osric will go through the tunnel with Isadora and her contingent of soldiers,' Ambrose said. 'It's a great gift that we now have your powers on our side.'

Noooooooo. Not the bloody tunnel again. I did my best to contain my complete irritation.

'Try not to look too happy about it, Finn,' Ambrose said.

'Trust me, if you'd been in that tunnel, you'd know,' I muttered.

'Thorne and Ava,' the king said, 'along with the berserkers and the second half of Isadora's soldiers, will lead the attack on the west gate, distracting them from your infiltration.' He was speaking mostly to me, I realised, as I was the only one here who didn't yet know the plan. My eyes, flooded with a pale azure made entirely of horror, shifted to Thorne. He was the distraction, meaning he was the bait, meaning he was the most likely to die. Awash with nausea, I felt him take my hand.

'Because the civilians have been delivered to us,' Ambrose said, 'I will escort them to Pirenti, with my soldiers as guards. Falco, you can come with me. You need to be protected to take up your throne when this is over.'

It was obvious what Ambrose *didn't* say: Falco also needed to be out of harm's way since he couldn't protect himself.

Falco shook his head once. 'I will fight with Thorne, and the men and women from the warder prison will stand at my back.'

There was an uncomfortable silence.

'Falco —' Thorne started.

'He will do more than fight,' a voice said. 'He will lead the attack.'

We all turned to where Isadora stood, a little apart from the rest of us, idly spinning a blade in her fingertips. The conversation seemed almost to bore her. She was painful to look upon in the sunlight, and the glinting blade sent a beam of light into my eyes every time it flicked my way.

'Iz,' I said, shielding my vision. 'Come on.'

'The bulk of the force will be made of my soldiers,' she said calmly. 'I leave them under Falco's leadership, as this is his land we stand upon, his city we are about to attack. He will also lead Thorne and his berserkers, whom he outranks.'

My eyebrows arched. When had Izzy become so audacious? There were a few uncomfortable movements and mutterings. The huge berserker man beside Thorne looked ready to attack.

'They're here to help us,' Ava pointed out.

'And we thank them for that,' she replied, unruffled. 'But there are many voices in this circle, many leaders with their own right to authority. This happens one way, with one leader, or we fall to chaos and conflict, and die.'

'You're right,' Ambrose said. 'You're exactly right. We do need one leader. But . . .' His eyes moved to Falco. To Emperor Feckless.

'But it shouldn't be me,' Falco finished for him.

There was an awkward silence.

I watched Falco look at Isadora, watched their eyes meet and I heard her say, softly, 'Find the version who was born to lead us, and don his cloak until this is over.'

Falco's eyes shifted red. He looked at the rest of us. 'We'll attack in the dark, three nights from now when the moon is at its thinnest.'

'We won't make it there in three nights,' Ava pointed out.

'We will if we go straight through the marshes.'

'How are we meant to do that? There's no path through.'

'We don't need a path. We're going to swim.'

★

It was clever, as it turned out. Those guarding the city walls would have no visual warning of our approach, the marshes opening out right on the edge of Sancia. We'd get there quickly, which gave us the element of surprise. Dren and Galia knew of our approach, but couldn't assume we'd reach them so fast. And we would be coated in mud, making us difficult to spot at night. Falco explained all of this and then went on to describe how best to use the warders in his team of prisoners, having spent the last weeks learning how to break through wards and walls made of stone. By his reckoning, he would have an entire western portion of the wall destroyed by dawn of that first night of attack. It was a bold statement, but something had come over him, a certainty that made a mockery of what we'd known about him. I wasn't sure about the others, but I couldn't help believing him. He seemed an entirely different man.

He finished by saying, 'Without Thorne's advantage we will take heavy casualties, but that was always to be expected. Essentially, the more power we force the Mad Ones to send at us, the better, because every piece they use takes a piece of their own soul and draws them nearer to death. We just have to be able to withstand that power, like your brother could.'

I was confused. But, as *my* Thorne turned and strode away from the group, so raw at even the mention of his father, I understood.

'What is it that you don't know?' I asked.

'My brother had a way to withstand a warder's powers,' Ambrose said, then turned to Falco: 'Only we don't know what it is so we should stop bringing it up.'

Falco shook his head, obviously frustrated. 'It's got to be within our grasp. They haven't always had this much power over us – the warders weren't originally undeniable.'

'They've grown stronger.' Ava shrugged.

Falco didn't buy it. 'It *must* have to do with what we know about them. They've been building their power base for decades now, in preparation for when they might take over. But once upon a time they were less of a threat to normal folk. Thorne taught you to withstand their mental powers, Ambrose, but if he was torturing them he must have also understood how to withstand their physical powers, and that is no small feat.'

My eyebrows arched. Since when did Falco spend time thinking so strategically? A slow curl of excitement snaked around my heart. I'd *known* he wasn't what he seemed. I'd felt it in his touch, in the weight of his beautiful heart. Some part of me had been waiting since that day, waiting for the reveal, and now I savoured the moment, watching him in the sunlight.

'With Thorne's knowledge we could have won this war,' Falco muttered.

Alright. A thrill ran through me and I grinned. With a quick check to make sure my husband was out of earshot, I said, 'Well, then. Why don't we ask him?'

Chapter 28

Finn

Nobody understood how difficult it was to bring someone back from the dead. The effort had killed my mother and could very well kill me, but that wasn't the issue. It was about *finding* him. Stepping between the veil was easy enough, listening to the screams become songs was a pleasure with which I grew more fascinated by the day. But recognising one soul over millions of others was no simple feat, given I couldn't actually *see* anyone behind the veil. I could only hear them, and sense a shadow of them.

'What did he sound like?' I asked.

Ambrose was almost giddy with excitement, but I could see Ava was wary. I'd asked them not to tell Thorne what I was attempting because it was far more likely it wouldn't work.

'His voice was rough like gravel,' the king said. 'You'll know it – you won't have heard a voice like it.'

'Alright. I'll *try*. Keep Thorne and Rose away from me for a few hours.' I walked far enough to not be distracted by the sounds of the massive camp. Then I lay on the grass and stared up at the cloudless blue sky.

The veil was shrouding me, pulling me in, and this was never the hard part because it *wanted* me to walk within it. Death wanted more and more and always more. It was leaving that grew harder each time. Voices reached me, screaming and shrieking, hissing and whispering. I concentrated on individual sounds, allowing them to disentangle. Moving through, it was hard to distinguish them, but souls pulled to each other, even through the veil. Love pulled souls together, which meant that the dead who loved, and were loved, by the people here on the plain should be closest to the divide.

'Thorne,' I whispered, and listened, listened. They were humming and the sound of the endless collective swelled to be addressed by me, by the living.

And then I heard it. The rough edge, scratchier than the sounds around it. I reached for that shadow, feeling it between my fingers like I could feel the film of life coating the space.

'I'm here,' the shadow said in a voice unlike any other.

I tugged at him, drawing him with me through the veil, but as I did the surge of voices returned to screams and I felt a wave of pressure. More were following, trying to get through with us. This had never happened before and I didn't know how to stop them. They flooded me, suffocated me, shoved at me, more substantial than I'd realised. Their wails grew so loud I thought they would burst my eardrums. A scream left my mouth, one of shock and pain. I lost hold of the veil.

'Follow me,' said the deep, rough voice in my ear. I latched onto the sound of it, reaching for his body as it grew fleshier with each second. He hummed through the screaming, hummed and hummed so I could follow his voice and know it from the rest, so I could use it to anchor me and reach to find the film of life and draw it over us.

I gasped, utterly drained, staring at a dizzy, spinning sky. Someone else was breathing as I rolled over, onto my elbows and knees, struggling to rise. A sense of victory assailed me – I'd done it. I'd brought him back.

A thud of pain struck my spine and I came down flat on my stomach, unsure what had happened. Someone rolled me over and I was looking up at a man. I blinked in confusion. This wasn't how I had pictured the famous and feared Slaughterman of Pirenti. This was a small man with pitch black eyes and a cruel twist to his lips. This *wasn't* Thorne – I had seen paintings of Thorne. So who in gods names had I brought back? I had been so sure . . .

He placed his hand around my throat and started to squeeze, dousing my confusion. It didn't matter who he was, only that he was about to kill me. Without thinking I sent an outraged burst of power from my hand into his body. He flew off me and landed in a crumpled heap. I tried to rise to check on him, but couldn't seem to move my body, and then –

The sky had turned to night. There were stars glittering and I was being lifted into a pair of large, strong arms and I sighed in relief. 'It didn't work,' I tried to say.

'Shh,' my husband said. 'It's alright, sweetheart. Sleep now.'

I could hear other voices and a name being spoken, a name I recognised but I couldn't work out how. *Vincent*. Sleep was pulling my exhausted mind and body away, but I had a last moment of lucidity, and with it dread. Because I had distinctly felt others come through the veil with me, and I had no idea who or where they were.

ISADORA

The dead man we found in the grass beside Finn's unconscious body was called Vincent. Once upon a time, Ambrose had killed him in a dungeon cell for poisoning King Thorne. Prince Thorne didn't even look at this snake of a man as he lifted his wife into his arms and carried her away.

'Throw him in the swamp to rot,' Ambrose said coldly, kicking the corpse with a heavy boot. An old fury had appeared in his demeanor for the first time since I'd met him. It said much about how formidable he had once been, and how disappointed he must be at Finn's failed mission.

We'd been waiting for Finn all afternoon, but as night fell Thorne wanted to know where his wife was.

'How dare you?' he demanded. 'How dare you let her do this for you, knowing full well that it could kill her?'

I'd never seen him so angry.

'Thorne –' Ambrose tried.

'Neither her life, nor her magic, is to be used for our gain, and she certainly isn't to be lost in favour of the long-dead,' he snarled, then stormed off. We followed, discovering not a risen king of Pirenti but a dead creature in the night.

I made my way back to one of the campfires, seeking a break from all their unwieldy desires and sorrows, from the memories they shared and were eternally connected by.

I found Greer beside a fire, boiling water for tea. I was grateful when she didn't talk, but allowed me to quietly watch the flames.

I thought of what one ought to do had she the skill. Was it arrogance to have a skill and not use it? And what if that skill was in killing? What was *right*?

I stopped thinking of questions I couldn't answer and thought instead of the plan I had been forming. Its pieces were yet to reveal themselves entirely, but the pieces mattered less than the result. Of that I was certain. There were people sitting around me with families. Husbands, wives and children, brothers, sisters and parents with whole lives of their own: people with an abundance of love, with true wealth. I hadn't known that in my life, but perhaps that made me the best person to protect it.

'Can I have a word alone with the Sparrow?'

I looked up to see Ava.

Greer waited for me to nod my permission, then left us alone. I looked at the wolf scar gouged into the Queen's face.

'Your faith in him is not surprising,' Ava said, 'but it's also unfounded.'

'Who needs enemies with family like you?' I muttered, not in the mood to explain myself to a woman who still suspected me of treachery.

That thought caused a shot of adrenalin to run through me – it crystallised another piece of the plan. If half these people didn't trust me, perhaps I could use that.

'I don't say it to be disloyal or unkind to Falco. I love him. I only say it to be realistic at a time when fantasy will get us killed.'

'Do I seem like a woman who lives in fantasy?'

'No. You're a woman who hated her mate enough to sever the unbreakable bond between you. And now you're a woman who has turned around and shown both political and personal support for that same man. What's your game, Isadora? Or should I be talking to the Sparrow?'

I didn't reply, but I studied her. She was shrewd, far more suspicious of me than anyone else.

'Listen carefully, Sparrow. If you imagine yourself sweeping in during the chaos, unhindered and free to take what does not belong to you, you should expect a fight on your hands.'

I allowed the very edges of my lips to twist. She left.

Most had settled down to sleep.

Food was becoming a problem – my stores weren't going to support so many extra mouths for long. I would make my move tomorrow, when the army took to the marshes. The sooner this was over the better. And if there was a thorn in my heart at the thought of leaving, of proving Ava's fears about me true – well, I knew how to put things in boxes.

Two figures trickled their way through sleeping bodies and tents. I recognised his shape, of course, and the monkey-like way he moved. Penn flung himself on me, holding me so tightly. 'You were taken,' he said.

'I'm here,' I promised, clutching him in relief. With his touch, as always, I felt peaceful.

'And a liar, as it turns out,' Jonah said coldly.

My eyes flicked to him, but I was uninterested in whatever he wanted to start.

'It doesn't matter,' Penn said, sitting beside me. I took his hand, not willing to lose his touch yet. He let me.

'How can you say that, Penn?'

'Has Izzy ever hurt us?' he asked his best friend. 'Or has she saved us, time and again?'

'For what?' Jonah demanded, eyes shifting lime. 'What was it all for, if not to use us for her own ends?'

'And so what if she does?' Penn replied. 'Has she not earned everything from us that we can give her?' Though I couldn't see them in the dark I imagined the freckles on his cheeks and the constellations they made across his skin. In Sancia I had made pictures of his freckles as I fell asleep.

'The Sparrow hates warders,' Jonah said softly. 'Everyone knows that. So what of me? And Finn? Do you hate us?'

I swallowed. What I felt for the twins was very far from hate. I didn't know how to say that, so I just shook my head. Jonah peered at me, maybe making up his mind.

There was a thudding sound to my left and looked down to see –

A small, naked body curled and shivering on the ground, where an instant before there had been nothing.

A breath left me: I was dreaming again. At least this time I was aware of it. But was Penn's hand in mine a dream, or was he really here with me? The girl on the ground was stretching herself, trying to climb to her feet. 'Leave me alone!' I begged her, because in dreams words didn't reveal you, they were swept out and lost in the void. 'I get it – killing you was a tremendous mistake, and I am paying for it with the destruction of my own life.' Is that what this ghost wanted to hear? Was this how I would have to prostrate myself before my dead would let me be?

I frowned to see Jonah crouch beside the woman. Definitely a dream, then – not a ghost or a hallucination if he could see her too.

And then Falco appeared a few feet away, skin and lips turning bone white as he stared at the dream woman.

With a swift flick of his wrist he removed his cloak and swept it around her naked body, helping her to her feet. 'What . . .?' He was lost for words.

'Who is this?' Jonah asked. 'She . . . *appeared.*'

'Is Quill here?' Falco asked urgently, his hands shaking on her cloaked shoulders.

The dream woman didn't seem to know what was going on. She was slender and short, though nowhere near as slender or short as me, and she had strawberry blond hair and a pointy, pixie nose. These I knew well. I saw them every day.

'I don't know if she got through,' was what the woman finally replied. As we stared at her she stretched her arms, wriggling all ten of her fingers with an astonished laugh. '*My body,*' she whispered.

'What's going on?' Jonah asked. 'Who are you?'

'My name is Radha,' she told him. And then she looked at me, straight at me, and it didn't feel like a dream at all as she said, 'I was murdered.'

★

I'd never imagined how I might react to being faced with one of my victims reawakened. I'd never imagined I would turn and bolt into the marshlands, my chest constricting until I could no longer breathe. She was not a ghost or a dream, but a flesh and blood woman who could speak and touch and remember and *exist*.

My lungs shuddered as I gasped for breath, pressing into the sodden, smelling stretch of marsh. When I couldn't run any further, trapped on every side by mud, I swung up into the branches of a mangrove tree and climbed to the very top. Emerging out of the heavy canopy, I was met by a sky filled with thousands upon thousands of stars, and a slice of moon so bright it didn't look real. The air finally moved inside me and I felt my pulse slow.

Exhausted, I lay in the crook of a branch and watched the world above, wondering if there were other places out there like this one, or if it was just endless emptiness. Maybe I was altogether wrong and the sky was the roof of the world, as most believed, placed there by the gods to stop us from escaping. I had always felt as though I could stare into and beyond it – the sky didn't feel like a cage, but the opposite.

*

I must have fallen asleep, dreamless, for the moon had moved when I next opened my eyes. The branches were shaking with the weight of someone climbing them and abruptly I was anxious again. I didn't want anyone to find me, held myself very still. But find me he did.

Falco poked his head out of the canopy a few meters away and sighed in relief. 'There you are.'

FALCO

I sat Radha down beside the fire and made sure my cloak was firmly covering her. I kept peering around for Quillane, hoping she might melt out of the air like her mate. Jonah and Penn had run off to find Finn and ask her what in gods names was going on, so I waited alone with the dead woman.

She seemed dazed, content to watch the flames and feel their heat on her skin. I had a million questions for her, but held my tongue. One of her eyes looked glassy, maybe blind. I honestly had no idea who this person was, and yet she'd been mated to the woman I'd spent my life with, living within my palace for years.

I couldn't hold it in any longer. 'When did you and Quill bond? Was it before she became Empress? How long were you living in the secret tunnel? What did you do before that? Where did you come from?'

She smiled. 'Oh, Falco, you tactless oaf.'

I couldn't help returning the smile, surprised. 'You say that like you know me.'

'I do. Quill spoke of little else.'

'Let me guess. The idiotic Emperor Feckless and his laughable antics.'

'Of course. Was that not what you wanted? Did you not design the world to be a place that spoke of the Emperor of Kaya's foolishness? Was there not some masterful plan in place in which acting weak made you strong?'

I didn't know how to respond.

'Why do you recoil from it now?' she asked. 'You were dedicated for so many years, Falco. Loyal to the plan, no matter what.'

'It didn't work.' I shrugged. 'It's over.'

'It would have worked,' Radha replied. 'Don't we all know it? Isn't it obvious now how you would have killed the Sparrow that night she came to find you, had fate not chosen a different path for you both?'

I looked at her, waiting for the point.

'Your enemies are not dead, Majesty,' Radha said. 'You are a master of disguise and deception. *Use* the weapon you put in place so long ago. Use him.'

There was a prickle along my spine at the very idea, but she wasn't yet finished.

'I don't know why I'm here – perhaps it was luck that I happened to be so close to the fold – but I do know that it won't be indefinite. The veil won't release me for long. So listen.' She leant closer, holding my eyes. Hers, I saw, were sea-green, one of them definitely blind. 'It is cowardice to direct your anger where it does not belong. And you are no coward.'

I looked away from her and in the following silence listened to the crackle of the fire.

'Now that's done,' she added, 'please, *please* will you go and fetch me some clothes. Your Majesty.'

I rose and left her sitting by the fire. Jonah and Penn were already hurrying back with clothes, so I let my feet take me to the tent that had been erected for Finn's recovery.

Thorne and Ambrose were standing outside when I arrived. 'How is she?'

'Not well,' Thorne answered bluntly.

'Why am *I* to blame?'

'Because you wouldn't leave it be,' my best friend said. 'Worrying at it and worrying at it, desperate for my father's secrets. Maybe those secrets are best left dead with him, Falco. Did you think of that?'

I looked into Thorne's face and reached for his shoulder. 'I'm sorry. She'll be alright, brother. We all will.'

He softened, some of the tension easing. I knew he was shaken by the whole thing.

'Has she explained?' I asked.

'She says she felt more dead come through,' Ambrose said. 'Says she couldn't stop them, and can feel them now.'

'Where?'

'She's delirious,' Thorne said. 'It isn't the time to be questioning her.'

I squeezed his arm. 'Did you see Isadora?'

'She ran into the marshes.'

I spun to gaze at the tangle of darkness looming before us. It was incredibly uninviting and I pondered the possible stupidity of dragging an entire army through it. What was Izzy doing in there?

With some quick thinking, I made my mind up. After telling Thorne of my plan, I grabbed a pack filled with rations, armed myself with the prison swords and stopped off to farewell my cousins. The little things were sleeping between Ava and Roselyn, and didn't stir as I ducked to kiss them both. I silently apologised to them for being such an ass, so easily given to vices, so poor at handling grief.

'Where do you think you're going?' Ava asked, one eye open.

'Your husband will explain.'

'Falco . . .'

'If I mess it up, Ava, at least you'll be there to take over.' I flashed her a grin and then hurried into the dark.

Tracking Isadora was easy enough. She'd broken branches and left footprints in the mud. When the prints ended I assumed she must have started climbing, and after glimpsing a few out of place boughs I followed her up. She was lying in the branches with a perfect view of the sky, looking at me as I emerged. A dagger was in her hand, but when she recognised me it took to spinning in that lazy way.

Settling in, I braced myself for what I prayed would not be another argument. A box had been opened, never again to be closed. I wouldn't let it be closed.

I said softly, 'I've behaved very badly, and I can blame it on no act or pretense. I wasn't angry with you about Radha – I was furious with myself for not being strong enough to do it, and for always allowing you to do what was most difficult. I wanted to be braver for you, but when the time came I was a coward. So I took it out on you and on everyone, and I became the worst version of myself. For that I'm ashamed.'

She listened silently. I couldn't see her eyes in the dark.

I drew a breath and forged on. 'Finn said there will be more of the dead yet to rise. So it's going to get very complicated in that campsite for a while, and it's going to slow everything down. I intend to move ahead and make a proper surveillance of the wall. I don't want to rush into this blind. Thorne will bring the others when he can.'

'What if Quillane rises and you've left?'

This was where the courage came into it, I supposed. Though it physically pained me to miss my one chance at seeing the Empress again, I said, 'I can't be focused on the dead when I have so many living yet to protect.'

Isadora considered this, tilting her head. Around and around went the blade, an extension of her thoughts and mood. The moon shone on her pale hair and eyelashes. She was glorious, a creature meant to be looked at under moonlight.

Swallowing, I tried to quiet my nervous fluttering heart as it beat its wings to escape my chest. 'I packed rations enough for my bondmate and me.'

The knife froze. Her fingers stilled. 'We're no longer bondmates, Falco.'

And I replied, 'Of course we are, Isadora.'

Chapter 29

Ambrose

I woke with the sun, having fallen asleep while keeping watch outside Finn's tent and listening to the soft murmurings of a young husband soothing the delirium of his young wife. I woke to find that the fog had settled again, draping us in white. The early morning sounds of rising people reached in from the distance and the smell of stoked campfires wafted pungently.

And my brother. I woke to find my brother.

He was sitting beside where I lay, watching me, and he was exactly as I remembered him. Larger than life, draped in fur, the paleness of his eyes an ever-intrusive cold.

I took one breath, and then began to weep. Because there in him was the understanding I had never once glimpsed in anyone else. There in him was the knowledge of why I had to do all of this without hands.

I had missed him more acutely than I had ever thought possible. I was never meant to do any of this without him. Thorne nodded, pulling me to him, and held me as I cried. 'Soft as always, little brother,' he said, and I gave a sob of laughter. In my ear I heard him ask, 'Where's my boy, Am?'

Thorne

I was returning to Finn's tent when it happened. I'd left her early, stepping over a sleeping Ambrose to make my way to where Jonah slept. She would need her twin brother.

We were in the middle of a huge expanse of sleeping or rising people. The fog had cleared a little so I could see a fair distance beneath the heavy white of the sky, and a fair distance worth of people could see me – were watching me – as I made my way through them. Warily or with awe, they stared. I was King of the berserkers. I supposed I was quite a sight to the Kayan soldiers. My mind wasn't on any of it, but with Finn and how tormented she was by what she'd done. They sapped her, these dead who had crossed. The breach was not weighing easily on her. My thoughts shifted to the move we would need to make as soon as we could get several hundred people up and ready; they shifted to the battle that loomed, to the growing pain in my side, to the almost certainly suicidal mission of attacking a host of warders who fought from behind the safety of a wall . . .

My mind was a jumble, and so I wasn't paying attention to the ruckus that had begun working its way closer.

What wrenched my focus from the jumble was the stench. The unmistakable, thick sweetness of *fear* that permeated the air. Hundreds of people's fear, their terror. My beast roared with sudden hunger, with the awareness of danger. I stopped, pressing Jonah behind the safety of my body. I breathed deeply, overwhelmed but searching for the cause. I heard a few shouts, a few alarmed voices, and then I saw it.

A giant of a man running directly towards me.

My instinct was to draw my axe, but what followed was a wave of relief. It was Da. He'd returned to me at last, thank gods. But what the Sword was he doing? And . . . wait. Wait. People were looking at him. They were scared of him – I could smell it.

All other thoughts vanished because he was bearing down on me and I had a second to think, incredulously, that he must be *attacking* me, but then he was –

Holding me.

Shock unlike any I had ever known hit. He was flesh and blood. He was warm, and breathing, and I could feel his heartbeat against mine and my mind caught up to the sheer force of his physicality for long enough to think, *It worked*. Finn's magic had worked and he was really, truly here with me, holding me, a creature no longer dead but *alive*, impossibly alive.

'Da?' I whispered, barely daring to believe.

And he was saying over and over again, 'My boy. *My boy.*'

The Slaughterman of Pirenti. Most feared and loathed man of a nation. My father. Here. Saying, 'My boy,' over and over like a prayer, like it was the only thing that mattered or would ever matter.

I felt my arms come up and around his mighty frame, so tentatively. And like the thawing of a great glacier I felt my heart – this heart that had grown up hating him for all that he'd been and all that he'd failed to be, hating him for leaving me to be feared just as he was, for his legacy that meant I could never be forgiven, and hating him most of all for being absent – I felt *this* heart fracture like a fine sheen of ice over a winter river, cracks snaking out and out and out until the whole broken surface sank. I was submerged in his scent, my father's scent, in the magnificent physical presence of him, his size and strength, and more than that. Ambrose spoke often of giants and never once described a giant as being large in size, but in spirit. Even this most fallible of men, this person who had fallen prey to his most monstrous side, even a boy who'd been so easily manipulated by his mother . . . even such a man, Ambrose called a giant. I had never understood it. Not for a second. Violence, in my mind, had never meant spirit. And yet here he was, holding me like I had always in my most secret heart of hearts wished my father could. Once upon a time I'd asked my uncle, who raised me, how he could love such a monster. How he could forgive such a monster. And he said that his brother had one quality more than any other, and that I would realise one day how much that quality meant. He had been right – it was my wife, in the end, who taught me how much it meant. Taught me so that now, in the grip of his trembling fingers, I knew how to recognise it, could feel and understand it, could be awed by its power. Here in the grip of a giant I had never met, in the unexpected love of a slaughterman, I felt it: loyalty.

ROSELYN

I woke with my children by my side and a hirðmenn watching over us. I disentangled myself from Ella and Sadie's arms and Erik moved so I could sit beside him on the log. His poor wrist needed to be sutured, but I didn't have my kit, so instead I'd had to bind it very tightly and hope we could find him proper treatment soon.

'Do you ever sleep?' I asked.

'Would that I didn't have to.'

He didn't look at me, never looked at me. In his averted gaze I felt the shame of what had been done to me. I knew he didn't mean for me to feel it, but I did.

'Erik,' I said.

'Yes, my lady?'

'Look at me.'

He did so with extreme difficulty. A clenched jaw, a clenched fist. 'Yes, my lady?'

'You're free.'

He frowned. 'How so?'

'You've done so much. You've saved us. And for anything that came before, you are not responsible. I'm freeing you from this burden, the honourable, *kind* man that you are.'

His face twisted in pain. 'My lady, the three of you are no *burden*. You are the point. The entire point.'

I didn't understand. Searched his black, black eyes.

And then.

'Roselyn,' a voice said, and

I

dissolved

into

dust.

In that one word a thousand wishes were fulfilled, a million impossibilities. I counted them, tried to count them, could not slow my heart or my tears, could barely manage to stand. But he was there to help me. His hands touching mine, his rough voice in my ears, his smell in my nose.

I turned and looked up and saw him. My husband.

'Step back,' a voice was saying. Erik's voice. He was holding an axe.

I tried to tell him to stop, but no sound came from my mouth and I was trapped in the pale, pale eyes.

'All's well,' Thorne told Erik without looking away from me. 'I'm no threat to her.'

'I don't know you, sir. Step back.'

'My wife knows me,' Thorne said, and I faintly heard Erik stammer in confusion. 'Might you walk with me?' my husband asked, and in his voice I heard a tremor of nerves.

It was all I could do to nod.

People were here, watching us, but I could barely comprehend who they were. Ava, I thought. Ambrose maybe. And our son. But Thorne was already leading me away, my hand in his, and I barely felt the ground beneath us. My weary, grief-stricken heart said *no. This isn't real. Don't let it carry you away.*

But my soul was his, as it had been from the day we met, despite all that had passed.

Love was inexplicable. This I knew to be true.

We reached a mangrove tree and stood between its gnarled roots. We watched the water, side by side, hand in hand. He said, 'There is a place in which I live, and that place is you.'

I closed my eyes. In the mangroves his lips found mine.

*

When my mind had found its way back from the sky, or the earth, or somewhere I had no chance of following, we looked at each other. He frowned, as though trying to understand something.

'That boy,' he said in slow wonder. 'I think it was a gift that I was not here to ruin him.'

My chest ached.

'A far greater man than me, and solely because of you.'

'Have you . . . Where have you come from?' I managed to ask. My first words.

Thorne shook his head, unsure.

'Did you see . . .?'

His gaze was shadowed. 'I saw it all.'

I dropped my eyes and turned for the plains, but he took my wrist and gently stayed me.

'Rose. I saw it all.' He took my chin and tilted it so that I was forced to look at him. 'I can wish until the end of time that I had been there to stop it. I can wish an eternity of regrets away –'

For the first time in my life I was a she-wolf, furious and defiant. 'It didn't even touch me,' I told him. 'He was small and weak and it was *nothing* to me.'

Thorne nodded and pressed his lips to the tears on my face. 'You didn't need me,' he said. 'You have never needed me. You are unquenchable, my love, stronger than any king of the ice or berserker warrior. Stronger than any warder of the south, your spirit an impossible, humbling thing. Had I recognised this sooner our lives might have been very different, and that is a shame I will carry always.'

I had no desire to be named strong. It was arbitrary. But this: *You have never needed me.* Twenty years without him and he could say such a thing to me. Though, really, he was still a young man, frozen in time and space, with no way to learn or grow. He was as he died, just beginning to find his way. I was much older now, had lived many more years. And as this occurred to me I found the space between us that had always been reserved for my certainties, for my needs and demands, and yet which I had never filled. Stepping into it, twenty years too late, I said, 'I've never needed you to protect my body from harm. My father taught me long ago when he tried to drown me that harm was a thing I could endure; harm did not quench the spirit. All I needed you to do was love me.'

'I did.'

'And punished me for it.'

He winced.

'Love is not possession,' I told him clearly at long last, as I should have done the day we married. 'It is kindness. Generosity.'

Thorne grew pale and sank to rest against the tree roots. I'd never seen him look so ill, so lost. I sank to the muddy earth before him, heedless of how it dirtied my skirts. My hands reached for his face, holding it gently. 'You were a child when we married, as was I. Neither of us knew how things should be. You were brutalised by a cruel and twisted woman into believing gentility a weakness. For that, and for the way you treated me, you carry an ocean's worth of guilt. I can see it. I can *feel* it, Thorne.'

There were tears in his eyes, slipping down his cheeks. *Tears*, from the slaughterman. How strange, how impossible.

'But know this, my love,' I finished, holding his pale gaze. 'Were I given the chance now, today, knowing all that I do and having endured all that I have, *I would still choose you*. A hundred times, a thousand. Each time I look at our son I can *feel* the way you would have loved him. For that I will cherish the heart you left inside me, just as my heart will find its place within you.'

He closed his eyes. '*Rose*.'

I kissed him, because I wanted to, because he was mine, because it was all that I wished for, and I felt a mighty rush of truth from my heart to his, and more than that: a rush of power, of self, of certainty. This was what I'd been petrified of when he lived: his indifference, his rejection, his scorn. I feared it no longer, safe within this certainty of the woman I was.

Things would be different this time. We had a second chance, an impossible second chance. We would ask for more and give more. We would do it right. It was the only thing I felt sure of.

Chapter 30

ISADORA

It was not swimming so much as wading. The murky water reached our hips and we trudged through it as quickly as we could, stopping only to take a few water breaks. I had been bitten in every conceivable place by buzzing insects and had become so sick of slapping them dead that I now just let them feast upon me. Falco was swearing and cursing and swatting wildly every single time. I couldn't help laughing as he made another outraged noise, as though still surprised he was being bitten.

'What?' he demanded.

I rolled my eyes, and he splashed muddy water at me.

'This is the worst idea I've ever had,' he muttered. I wasn't about to argue with him, although I could certainly think of a few worse. 'I have mud in every crevice of my body. And bites. And it smells weird. Also it feels like we're being watched. Every time I turn my head . . . that tree just moved. Seriously, Iz – it moved.'

I hid a smile, motioning for him to hurry up.

It took us the good part of a day and a night to make it through the swamp. We emerged into a grassy ravine, and after climbing the ridge to lie flat at the lip of it, we had the perfect view of the valley below. About half a kilometer away loomed the western wall of Sancia.

As we started our surveillance it reminded me of the night we watched the warder temple from the bell tower. I thought about how much had changed since that night, when we'd silently marked the movements of warders in the compound. Now we marked the movements of soldiers and warders on the wall, but it was not silent.

The air was heavy with unsaid words, thoughts and feelings – we shared them without sharing them. When he reached over to smear mud through my hair and over my skin I didn't flinch away, but watched his face as bravely as I could. I allowed him to touch me. In fact, I craved his touch and leaned into it. When I did the same to him he held himself very still and I could feel his desire burning the surface of his skin.

We are no longer bondmates.

Of course we are.

Night fell, the sun sinking behind the city and casting a halo. 'I should have faced her,' I murmured without meaning to. We were flat on our stomachs, eyes glued to the wall.

Falco looked sideways at me but didn't reply.

'She deserved that at least.'

'You have time yet.'

I marked down the patrol of a third guard in as many minutes. The security on the wall was tight.

'Am I meant to make amends to every person I have killed?' I asked him, honestly wanting to know the answer.

'To what end?'

I didn't know.

'Making amends is for you, not them. Do you need that?'

I didn't know the answer to that either.

'I suppose it depends why you killed them,' he said.

I shrugged. 'I don't even know. I feel drenched in blood.'

'When this is over, when the Mad Ones are dead, you won't ever have to kill again.'

I thought of the hirðmenn finding me by the lake, thinking me a demon. Of all the times violence had found me because of how I looked. I thought of soldiers who'd attacked me in battle, I thought of warders who'd tried to torture me for being something they didn't understand. Glancing at Falco, I asked, 'Do you really think that's possible, being what I am?'

He considered this, reaching to smooth a piece of mud-caked hair from my eyes. 'Why did you want to break our bond?'

'Fal –'

'Don't worry, I'm not dredging it up.'

I frowned, knowing the answer well. 'I wanted to be the author of my own fate.'

He nodded and replied, 'Then do not make of yourself a monster.'

I looked away. 'It's not so simple. Things aren't as clear as they once were. Everything is . . .' I struggled to find the word, then caught sight of my mud-smeared hands. 'Muddied.'

'How so?' he asked.

I thought of Radha, of both Radhas. I thought of the bond Falco and I had severed, and of whatever still lay between us, impossible to quell no matter how we tried. I thought of the plan I had been formulating, the one in which I would need to be violent to save others from having to be. 'I can't . . .' My tongue felt clumsy in my mouth. 'I don't know how to . . .' My fists clenched in frustration. Why did I have such difficulty with words?

'It's alright,' Falco said. 'Slow down.'

Drawing a breath, I let it move through my body before I tried to speak again. 'I always thought I could be stronger than fate, or the tide. I thought I could make my own path. But I have never felt so small or so insignificant. A mote of pollen battered in the wind of a hurricane. I've never felt so caged. I fight it and fight it, but still I walk blindly forward, doing everything I was meant to, and I can't help feeling like fate is laughing at me. If I am a monster, it is because I was meant to be one, and there's no changing that.'

Falco cupped my cheeks and his eyes slipped red. 'No. You're wrong. I thought you were foolish in the beginning, always trying to fight something undeniable. But I've come to know something, and of this I am absolutely certain. Your will, Isadora, is greater than anything in this world.' He drew a breath, and then added, 'It's why I am completely in love with you. Why I would fall in love with you over and over again, even if magic stripped it from my heart a thousand times, a million.'

I slammed my eyes shut.

'Don't,' he said. 'Look at me, Iz.'

I forced my gaze to his, my heart thundering in my chest.

Falco smiled a little. 'I'm just versions of a person, and I don't really know what's underneath those versions. But for what it's worth, every one of them loves you.'

I exhaled and laughter left me. 'Fate's fools once more.'

'No.' He grinned. 'You're my choice. My very own, little Sparrow. If fate wants to take credit for you, then let her, but you and I will know the truth.'

My smile and his found each other, lips touching softly. 'And you're mine,' I said. Though the words might have been swallowed by our breaths.

★

Each time I tried to leave him, he woke and held me closer. Every time I planned to sneak away, he started some conversation that required my input, or he kissed me until I wanted nothing but to make love to him on the sunny grass. He was watching me like a hawk, and I was almost certain he knew my intention.

He asked me things, so many things, and he waited patiently for me to struggle with the answers. Things like, why do you like solitude so much? To which I answered, being alone is safe. Like the cage was safe? Yes. Do you miss it? Sometimes. Do you ever imagine leaving here? Where would I go? Don't you find it disconcerting not to believe in the gods? No. Then how do you think we came to be here, if not by their power? By our own power, the power of our bodies, the power of all living things. Do you still hate all warders? No. So after this, how do we determine what magic is safe and what isn't? I don't know. Do you think about your parents? No, not much. Why not? I don't know how to think of them. They aren't real. Do you think about children? No. Why not? What kind of mother could I be? Do you think about life with me, after this? No. Why not? I can't afford to.

On and on it went. He never asked twice, but he probed and prodded and plumbed things I hadn't even determined for myself. It was strange, trying to be as honest as I could with him. A strange vulnerability that came only with speaking truths.

But there was one question he asked that I would never answer. *Who humiliated you so badly that I felt it halfway across the country? How could they possibly make you feel that?* That had been the first day in the palace, when the Mad Ones had made me enter the pool with Ryan. I told Falco never to ask me about that again, and he promised he wouldn't. That was one thing I would not give voice. It was one thing I would not burden either of us with.

'What are the things that you like?' Falco asked me, finally.

I looked at him blankly, not knowing what he meant.

'The little things. The things that give you pleasure. The things that make you glad to be free of the cage.'

I frowned and couldn't think of anything. But he waited, and slowly I began to recall. 'Rain,' I said, and he smiled. 'The smell of it. The sound of it. Chilli. The taste of it, the burn of it on my tongue. Steel. I like the weight and feel of steel in my hands, I like knowing my blades are in their spots on my body.' I paused, hesitating. 'I liked Radha's wings. The colour of them. And her eyes. They were very brown and very deep, and they always seemed wise.' Falco nodded, his smile growing sad. 'I like the scars on Lade's skin. I think they're pretty, like the shimmering scales of a fish. I liked the storm over the salt lake, when we were there. The feel, or . . .' I shook my head. It was like coming alive, this sensation of taking pleasure from things. It was like realising that I was not dead, after having believed myself a ghost.

'What are the things that you love?' Falco asked.

My heart thumped and I shook my head. Nothing. I didn't. I couldn't. It wasn't part of my life.

'Tell me, Izzy,' he pressed gently.

Closing my eyes, I felt his hand in my hair. 'Penn,' I said. 'I love Penn. His counting, and . . . everything about him. Finn. Her stories. How sure she is, how brave. The way she looks at me sometimes, as though I'm hers. Jonah's thoughtfulness, how generous he is in caring for me, even when . . . Thorne, his kindness. I loved Radha. I love her still.' My heart was unfurling, blooming. It was opening so wide I didn't know how it could ever fit inside my body again. 'I think I even love Roselyn.' For what she said to me, for washing the blood from my hands, for that one moment. 'And Ella.' For seeing me and smiling, for saving me from killing a good man, another one.

I opened my eyes and looked at Falco. *And you,* I whispered without opening my mouth. *You, you, you. For your cleverness and sweetness. For that grin of yours. For your questions, difficult as they may be. For your loneliness.*

'That's a lot of love for one little Sparrow,' he murmured. 'You must have a very generous heart.'

Tears filled my eyes and as I closed them they slipped down my cheeks. Because he was right – it was a lot of love. I did have people in my life, whether or not they loved me in return. And it was enough, finally, to ease the uncertainty inside me, the questioning and the worrying and the *what am I, what should I be, what should I do?* I knew now what I should do, and so I would do it, without any hesitation. With only love.

The rest of the army arrived in the ravine below us. I had meant to be gone by now, but this was better. It gave me a chance to face my ghosts, because when I left I wouldn't be coming back.

★

After the unpleasant journey through the marshes Ambrose wanted to give his people a night to rest. Ambrose, who hadn't gone with the civilians to safety, but had come this final leg of the journey with his wife and daughters. It was obvious why: his brother was alive, and they were clinging to each other, all of them.

Dead King Thorne was a very frightening person. He waded from the mud, his hands and legs coated in it while his scarred face and scalp remained clean. His slender, beautiful wife was beside him, dwarfed at his side, and his handsome son, almost as large as him. They didn't speak to each other, but the three of them stood close as Ambrose regrouped the troops. There was a pull of gravity between them. From my spot atop the ridge I watched them curiously, noting the way father and son glanced repeatedly at each other as if to covertly learn the other.

'Gods almighty,' Falco breathed, following my gaze. 'The slaughterman stands in Kaya and no one is trying to kill him. Never thought I'd see the day.'

'Many will be trying soon enough,' I muttered.

The slaughterman in question had an enormous axe over his back – it was about the size of me. Ambrose was explaining something to him, and his pale gaze swung up to us.

'Uh oh,' Falco said. 'Here comes the beast.'

King Thorne strode up to where Falco and I sat and sank into a crouch. I was surprised at his agility beneath such heavy furs and weapons, but then I supposed he'd had an entire life to get used to carrying such weight. There was something cold about him, something cruel in the lines of his face as he took in the city below. This was the frightening thing. Not the size or strength or tattoos or scars, but the violence in his eyes and in the twist of his lips.

'I've never met a dead man before,' Falco said brightly.

Thorne glanced sideways at him – just a glance – and his disdain was clear before his gaze flicked back to the city.

'Emperor Falco of Sancia,' Falco said, holding out a hand.

Without looking at him, Thorne said, 'The boy who plays at being a man and has his city snatched out from under him. The boy who lets men reclaim his throne for him.'

My anger erupted. 'I've never cut out the tongue of a ghost before. I wonder if they bleed like the living.'

King Thorne turned to behold me and his expression changed. He took a deep breath through his nose and smiled wolfishly. His eyes were alight with a strange fascination as they moved over my body and face. 'And what kind of creature are you?' he asked softly. The only way to describe his voice was to call it a growl.

'Just a woman,' I replied, holding his eyes.

'A blood and snow woman. An ice woman.' His smile widened, and when his gaze darted back to Falco he gave a low rumble of laughter. 'This one has more spirit than you, boy. Endeavour to fight in her shadow and you might just last the night.'

With that he strode back down the ridge to talk with his brother. It felt a little like a hurricane had passed through.

Falco and I shared a look, and he started laughing. After a few seconds even I cracked a grin. Things weren't often better than the stories described them.

FALCO

We could have moved. We should have – the moon was barely there, the night dark. But Ambrose seemed to want one last night with his family, and for that I could hardly blame him. After all, it was me who'd asked him to endanger each of their lives for a cause not his own. So I sat with them, looking around at their faces and realising that this was my family too. Ava and Ambrose had a daughter in each of their laps. Sadie was giggling as she fed her father bread, purposely missing his mouth and shrieking as he snapped his teeth at her fingers. King Thorne was next to his brother, gently holding Roselyn's hand and talking softly with his son. Finn was upright, sipping at whisky to calm her nerves and leaning her head wearily on Jonah's shoulder. I couldn't see Penn anywhere, nor Izzy.

After a quick search I found them sitting on a branch of a mangrove at the edge of the marshes, silently swinging their legs in time with each other. 'Come on, you two,' I bid. 'Join the party.'

Penn jumped down happily, but Izzy shook her head.

I walked closer. 'I want you beside me.'

She hesitated a long moment, then allowed herself to be tugged back to the group. All eyes went immediately to our linked hands as she sat beside me.

'You two are the biggest idiots I have ever met,' Finn snapped. 'I'm really glad we all went through what we did for nothing.'

Izzy removed her hand from mine, dropping her eyes. I sighed, levelling Finn with a look. 'Isadora and I are only here because we broke the bond, that I can assure you. We owe you for that.'

Her expression softened. 'If you say so, Fal.'

I turned to King Thorne. 'Have they explained why you're here?'

'To fight,' came the rumbling reply. Oh, to be such a simple creature.

'We were waiting for you, Fal,' Ambrose said.

I glanced at Ella and Sadie. 'It might be bedtime for the twins.'

'Just five more minutes, Da?' Finn whined, winking at Ella and Sadie so they exploded with laughter.

'They can hear anything you have to say to me, boy,' King Thorne said.

'I'll decide what my children can and cannot hear,' Ava interrupted.

He looked at her, his lip curling. 'And swaddle them like soft little babes?'

'What exactly do you think you know of my children?'

'I know my own blood. My kin.'

Ava rose to her feet. 'You don't get a pardon just because you died, Slaughterman.'

'In what world do you think I'd ever seek pardon from you?'

'*Enough*,' Ambrose snapped. 'There's no place for this. It's twenty years old and well and truly over.'

Ava looked livid – it was clearly with great effort that she shut her mouth and sat back down. Nobody said anything more about Ella and Sadie, so I shrugged, addressing King Thorne. 'We need to know how you were killing warders under the mountain. It's the only chance we have at facing them in battle without magic of our own.'

'You have magic. You have my boy's girl, and the first-tier. And a whole reeking group of them camped north.'

'"My boy's girl",' Finn mused, sharing a look with her husband. 'Better than "the loud magic one".'

'There are about a hundred warders in that city,' I said. 'We don't have anywhere near enough magic.' I was running out of patience – I needed to know the damned answer.

'You don't need magic to face warders,' King Thorne said.

We waited for him to go on.

'Where's the first-tier? Find him, kid.' He seemed to be addressing Penn.

Penn jumped up, unbothered.

'No need, Penn,' Finn stalled him. Then she placed her hands around her mouth and bellowed at the top of her lungs, '*Osric!*'

We all winced, and the girls erupted into laughter again. If they were in the vicinity, Finn would spend all her energy acting like an idiot to amuse them, and it worked every time.

'He's coming.' Finn grinned, and I realised she'd sent for him with some sort of magic, the scream being for King Thorne's benefit. 'What?' she asked innocently. She was out of her mind, antagonising the Slaughterman of Pirenti.

'In my land, young women behave with decorum,' he said coldly.

'Well then, I suppose it's lucky we aren't in your land.'

'It is,' he agreed, glancing between her and his son with scorn. The man was really something. He seemed utterly content to point out every flaw he saw, without giving a damn what anyone thought of him in return.

Osric turned up, preventing any further arguments.

'Don't attack Izzy,' Finn warned him. 'Or you go to sleep again.'

Osric didn't attack, but he did look at Isadora and spit at her feet. His fury was tangible. It was disorienting seeing him like this when normally he couldn't be forced to emote over *anything*. Isadora didn't react.

'You. Can you read my mind?' King Thorne asked Osric.

'No.'

'Why?'

'Because you have a natural shield.'

'Who else does?'

'Falco and Isadora. Ambrose has an even stronger one.'

'The pretty whelp has one?' King Thorne asked, surprised.

'Am I the pretty whelp?' I asked. 'That's sweet of you.'

'Indeed,' Osric answered over Finn's laughter. 'It's even stronger than yours, slaughterman. I could crack through it, but it would be difficult and might kill him.'

'Let's not try that,' I suggested.

'They're not natural shields,' King Thorne said. 'It's lack of fear.'

I frowned, glancing at Izzy. That didn't sound right.

The big man leant forwards, lacing his hands together. He looked at me as he explained. 'Fear is a natural response when meeting with someone who has greater power than you, both physically and mentally. It's an instinctive thing, not a choice or a conscious decision, but part of our humanity. Warders use this, even if they don't know it. This fear creates *avenues* for them to slip inside, allows them much easier access to a mind. Where there is no fear it feels to them like a block or a shield.'

My eyebrows arched.

'So we need to be braver and they won't get inside our heads?' Sadie asked.

King Thorne's expression softened as he looked at his niece. 'It has nothing to do with courage or cowardice, love. Fear, or a lack of fear, is caused by experience.' He turned back to Isadora and I. 'What is it that has scoured away your fear of warders?'

We didn't answer and I didn't think he expected us to. I wasn't sure what my answer was. 'But they can still . . . affect us,' I argued. 'I watched Izzy suspended in mid-air and tortured with pressure in her head.'

'That's because they don't fear *you*,' he answered.

A quiet fell over the circle.

'What do you mean?'

'Lack of fear in you makes you harder to manipulate. The other side of that is in a warder. If *they* fear *you* it makes their powers unwieldy. The greater their fear, the weaker they become. It's an adrenalin thing, an instinct thing.' He looked at Osric. 'You need calm and control to work magic, correct?'

Osric nodded.

'The problem is, they don't fear very much, and they train for years in the exercise of maintaining calm. They certainly don't fear normal humans. But they fear berserkers.'

'Why?' I asked.

King Thorne shrugged. 'A cycle. I don't know how it started – it has always been so. Berserkers don't fear warders, and therefore warders fear their lack of power over us, perpetuating the cycle.'

'How did you make them fear you?' Isadora asked softly, and all eyes went from her to King Thorne.

He smiled at her, a dangerous thing in his eyes. 'My brother says you are called Sparrow. You have been hunting warders longer than any of us, so you know very well how I make them fear me.'

Isadora's eyes glittered, the red in them reflecting starlight.

'Find me later,' he said. 'You and I will speak more of this.'

She nodded. That was going to be one creepy conversation.

I considered what King Thorne had said, which wasn't much of an answer at all. No trick, no tactic. Nothing I could use to strengthen my soldiers. You couldn't order a person not to fear the very thing about to destroy them. You could only hope to instil some courage in them, and courage, it seemed, was nothing against magic. My heart sank.

Isadora rose and left before I could stop her. I watched her vanish into the darkness. I couldn't hope to imagine what made her do the things she did, but I had seen a change in her over the last couple of days. She was no longer the stone queen or the ice goddess. She was flesh and blood, and in a way that was scarier because it made her vulnerable. But she had me now, to protect the unarmed parts of her.

'I would walk with my niece,' King Thorne said, rising.

Sadie jumped to her feet, looking excited.

'Not you, love, your sister.'

Sadie's face fell and I reached for her, pulling her onto my lap. I whispered in her ear, 'He's only worried for her.'

Ella didn't look surprised by her recently awakened uncle's request. She tried to move from her ma's lap, but Ava's hands tightened. 'Alone?' the Queen demanded. 'Why?'

'I've things to tell her that aren't for others.'

'Why?' Ava repeated.

'He can help her,' Roselyn said.

'Why does she need help?'

'It's alright, Ma,' Ella said.

Still Ava hesitated.

'You think I would let harm come to my kin?' King Thorne asked. 'You think I wouldn't die first?'

And that was the thing, wasn't it? No matter how much of a cruel, aggressive brute he seemed, this was a man who gave his life for his family. Didn't just speak of it, or proclaim the intent, but actually did it. That was not something to be taken lightly, a sacrifice of such magnitude. So Ava let her daughter go and we all watched her take King Thorne's hand and walk with him towards the marshes.

Without warning Finn slumped to the ground.

'Inney!' Jonah exclaimed.

Thorne was across the space in an instant, lifting her into his arms. 'What is it, my girl?'

'I just need sleep,' she murmured. 'Sorry.'

'Is it the veil?'

'It isn't meant to be opened.'

'So then close it!' Jonah snapped. 'This isn't fair!'

'I'm fine. Take me to bed, Thorne.' He lifted her into his arms and carried her away.

'This isn't fair,' Jonah repeated, standing with a burst of anger to stride after them.

I stroked Sadie's long hair, rocking her a little to ease her anxiety about Ella. It wasn't working, so I traced my fingers over her back in the shape of moth wings, and felt her pulse slow. Penn was sitting beside me, counting under his breath, strange multiples I couldn't follow. Roselyn was listening to him too and I saw her smile a little. Perhaps everyone was listening, for no one was speaking anymore, but sitting quietly together. The air felt heavy; for some or all it could be our last night alive. I was glad now that Ambrose had made me take this night to spend with them. It mattered, spending last moments together and understanding for what we fought.

ISADORA

I found her with Brathe and Inga, sharing wine and talk. All three looked at me as I arrived, and Radha was the only one who didn't smile. 'We need to have words,' I told her, and she rose to follow me.

'Isadora.' Inga stalled me. 'Is there news on the plan?'

'You'll fight under Falco. He'll give you your orders.'

'And you?' It was Sharn, appearing with Valerie and a host of others from the prison. 'Will you not fight with us?'

'I've another task. But fear not and fight hard, and we will meet on the other side.'

It seemed to bolster them. Sharn bowed her head. 'If you asked, Sparrow, I'd follow you.'

'Follow your Emperor,' I told her. 'That's how you serve Kaya now.'

Radha and I walked along the expanse of soldiers, listening to their voices in the night.

'That's far enough,' she said, turning to me abruptly. 'Far enough for whatever ludicrous apology you seem about to make.'

I let out a breath.

'I don't forgive you,' she snarled. 'I could *never*. You disgust me.'

I nodded, opening my mouth, but she wasn't done.

'You stole the life of the best person in this world, the only one trying to make a difference. And you didn't even steal it from her – you made *me* steal it from her! Like a coward. You – you . . .'

She was trembling as she slapped me across the face.

'I should run you through,' Radha hissed. 'You vile, depraved *monster.*'

Cheek stinging, I forced myself to hold her eyes; she was the first person who'd ever called me names because she knew them to be true.

'I'm sorry,' I said, despite how pathetic it was. Just to have said it once, just to have spoken one true thing to her.

She laughed in my face, a choked sound. 'Of course you are. Of course you're fucking sorry. But you won't pay any kind of price for what you did. No, not having stolen inside Falco's heart. I don't know what he deserves, but it's better than you.'

'I have been paying,' I promised. 'And I will make sure no more die at my hands.' *No more but two.*

'How?' Radha demanded. 'How will you do that? By cutting them off like the handless King has done?'

'I won't need to,' I said. I wasn't long for this world. She saw something in my face, some measure of certainty, perhaps, for she didn't say what she'd been about to. Instead she stared at me for a few agonisingly long moments, and then she walked away.

It hurt inside, all the way through. I dwelled in the pain; it belonged to me and in me, was mine to own and endure. My footsteps took me to the slaughterman. He was with his wife, and Roselyn looked at me worriedly. 'Are you well?'

I couldn't make myself respond.

King Thorne understood, for he rose like a giant and steered me away. We walked and walked, until we got beyond the camp, until we were walking through the empty, grassy floor of the ravine, far enough that no one would overhear us. 'What plagues you?'

'You told me to come.'

'Ask, then.'

'Why did you kill warders?'

His eyes in the darkness were too pale, eerily pale. Paler than either his brother's or his son's. 'Because they are corrupt.'

'How did you learn that? What taught you such a thing?'

I knew the story: a little boy went north into the ice and came back forever changed. There, I later learned, the boy had become a man by torturing warders for the truth of their magic, for a way to end the bond that bound Kayans against their wills. He and I believed in the same things, it seemed.

King Thorne tilted his head to study my face now. It was almost comical, how much taller he was than me. A giant and a child. 'They were travelling north,' he said. 'A ship of them. They wanted to take the mountain, and thought little enough of us to try. The first I caught got inside my head and made me believe the worst kinds of things. I almost killed myself in despair. Truly. I had the knife at my own throat, ready. And in that moment I learnt not to fear what was within me. By torturing me, the warder had taught me to connect with my beast, to embrace him. For that, I returned the favour.'

'Cruelty, then,' I murmured. 'You killed them for their cruelty.'

'I killed them because they threatened my power with their own,' he answered bluntly. 'I do not abide threats.'

It thrilled me, filled me.

'How many have you killed, Sparrow, because their magic threatens all else, because their corruption threatens *life*?'

'I've lost count.'

'Liar,' he breathed.

'Thirty-two.'

His lips curled slowly. I could *feel* the beast in the air, the animal. 'On my chest are five Marks. Five kills. More than anyone I had ever met, until you.'

I realised why I'd come to find him. 'I want you to Mark me.'

King Thorne laughed, long and slow, not in amusement but with pleasure. Then he used his knife to cut thirty-two Marks into the flesh of my inner arm. They bled and hurt, but I enjoyed it, feeling wild at heart. When he was done, he kissed me on the mouth and said, 'People will hate you for being ruthless. But they will be alive because of it. Remember that.'

I licked my lips, tasting him on me long after he'd gone.

With my bleeding arm I found my way back to the top of the ridge. I was still filthy with mud, so I didn't worry that I'd be spotted at such a distance. I stood tall, watching, thinking, readying myself.

'Don't do it,' a voice said.

All of me rushed to him. I was too much in love to bear. So I closed my eyes and I took that gods-cursed lake and I pulled it over me even though I despised it, despised its false calm and its cold cold cold. I let it flood me, coat me, disguise me. It was the lake that made me ruthless. And when I turned to face Falco, I was hardly inside my body any more. I was covered in frost and fading.

'Whatever you're planning or thinking, don't,' he said. I didn't know how he knew, but he did, clearly, which meant lying. 'Come with me. We'll sleep.'

I shook my head.

'Izzy,' he begged, throat raw. 'Don't do this. I need you.'

'I'm not doing anything,' I told him. 'I'm not going anywhere.'

He took my face, smoothing his hands over it, feeling me like a blind man might. Shaking his head, he whispered, 'But you are. You're already gone from me and I miss you terribly.'

Something went very hard inside my chest: the iron closing around my heart and around my spine. 'This,' I told him, 'was always going to happen. Right from the start, from the very beginning, long before either of us was born. We were fated to reap each other's death. I will end your reign as I set out to, and if I can do that whilst saving my three realms and *my* people, so much the better.' I paused, unable to withhold the next words. The easiest I had ever spoken. 'But because you love me, Falco, I'm going to tell you a secret before you die.'

His eyes were black as he stared at me, his lips chalk-white.

I leant close and gave him one truth. I couldn't tell him I loved him, so I would tell him this, and even if the rest was a lie, I could at least hope he remembered this one truth after I was gone. 'You don't have to be masked or unmasked. You can be neither, or both. You don't have to be one true thing and many false. You can be all your masks, each one of them, any time you want, or you can be none. You are fluid, your identity is fluid, your life, your name, your soul. And we are all Emperor Feckless sometimes.'

I pulled out of his arms, out of his reach, and I walked down the ridge towards the wall, leaving pieces of me trailing behind.

He didn't call my name or come after me. He let me go.

★

I had been walking alone in the dark for an hour when I heard it. Footsteps from behind. Whirling, I had a dagger at the throat of my pursuer only to realise it was Penn. 'What are you doing?' I whispered.

'Coming with you.'

'You can't, Penn, I have a plan.'

He smiled; I saw the flash of his teeth. 'Not one as good as mine, I'll bet.'

I hesitated and thought of what I might do were it my parents who'd decided to destroy the world. I nodded and took his hand, and Penn and I walked towards the wall together.

Falco was right. The world did not forge its monsters. It tried to, of course. But if I was a monster it was because I had let myself turn into one. If I was a monster, it was because something inside me had needed to be. And now the world needed it of me. So I would be. I would choose to be monstrous one last time.

It was hate that knew no fear, after all. Love, I had discovered, came with an ocean of it.

Chapter 31

'I knew it!' Ava raged.

'Keep your voice down,' I said.

'I knew it,' she repeated nonetheless, seething with fury.

'She's always been duplicitous,' Jonah muttered.

'No, I can't believe it,' Finn said. 'There's no way!'

'Of course there is!' Osric said. 'Is she or is she not the rebel leader of the south, intent on gaining rule over Kaya? She's obviously made some kind of deal with the warders.'

'But she hates the warders!' Finn replied.

'So she has said,' Ava muttered, 'but she is well versed in deception.'

I said nothing, because I knew the truth. There was no way in any world that Isadora had betrayed us, which meant there was some reason she needed us to think she had, and that meant it was best for me to play along. So I'd made the announcement this morning that the Sparrow had left to join the Mad Ones. And there was yet another argument raging around me.

'She wouldn't do this to us,' Finn said stubbornly, and I could have kissed her for her loyalty.

'What matters is not the hurt feelings of children,' King Thorne said. 'It is the information she takes to our enemies.'

'She knows everything,' I agreed. 'Our entire plan of attack.'

'Then the tunnels are useless,' Ambrose said. 'They'll have them blocked or guarded.'

'So all we have is an impenetrable, heavily-guarded wall.' Ava sighed.

'Not impenetrable,' I said. 'Osric is going to break the wards on the gate, and then we'll smash our way through it. And we're moving the second night falls. No matter what Isadora has done, we here are unified. We are one, with one purpose, one end. That is to destroy the Mad Ones and any who get in our way.'

They nodded, shoulders straightening.

'Disperse and get your forces ready to move.'

While everyone was preparing I went to Ava. 'I need you to lead Isadora's army. They're well trained and they'll respond to you.'

'Because I'm scarred?'

I nodded.

Ava smiled, the wolf scar pulling at her lips. 'Then I will lead them proudly.'

I gave her a quick hug, not bothering to point out what we both knew – if Isadora had betrayed us then her soldiers could turn on us at any moment. Until then, we needed them fighting for us – they made up the bulk of our force.

Next I found Thorne. 'Your berserkers will line the front,' I said. 'Are you happy with that? You'll take the brunt of the attack.'

'I don't think I could keep them from the front if I tried,' he assured me.

'Good. I want to draw as much fire from the wall as possible, and I want the berserkers protecting the warders in my central flank, who will in turn be protecting Osric while he attempts to smash the magic from the gate.'

'Understood.' Thorne stopped me by taking the back of my neck in the affectionate gesture men from Pirenti used with each other. 'Brother,' he said. I met Thorne's blue eyes. 'I'm proud of you and I'm with you until the end, no matter how far it takes us.'

I clapped him on the shoulder. 'I'm honoured to call you my family, King of the Ice, my hot-tempered little brother. The day I met you was when I started living again.'

He smiled, but he looked a very bad colour, and there was sweat dripping from his brow.

'Are you sure you're alright?'

'Of course.'

'What will you do with your father?'

'You say that like I have any control over him.'

I laughed a little, turning to look for my general. Brathe was with Inga and the other warders and I ordered them to line up with the berserkers protecting Osric. They didn't like being anywhere near the huge men, but I made it clear this wasn't up for discussion. To settle them I had the soldiers from the warder prison placed in the same retinue; these people were bonded by their experience of persecution and imprisonment by those inside the wall. They would stand strong together and I'd be there with them when it got bad.

Next I found Ambrose and King Thorne.

Last night's strangeness returned to my mind unbidden. I had been on my way to find Isadora after she'd left the group, thinking she must have gone back to the marshes where she seemed to enjoy the quiet. Instead I chanced upon King Thorne on his walk with Ella. Pausing, I couldn't help eavesdropping on their conversation, hidden behind heavy trees.

'When does it happen?' he'd asked her.

'When I'm indoors. Or when it's hot.'

'Like now?'

'Yes.'

'How does it feel?'

'Like . . . something . . .'

'Speak freely, child.'

'Something clawing to get out.'

I swallowed, disturbed for the poor girl.

'Do you get it?' Ella asked her uncle.

'No, love. But I once knew someone who did.'

'Who?'

'A man from my childhood.'

'But who?' she pressed.

'My father,' King Thorne replied reluctantly.

'I'm not related to your father,' she said. 'I have a different bloodline.'

'It isn't passed through the bloodline, love. It is born in the heart of those wild and strong enough to endure it.'

'But . . . what is it?' Ella asked him, and I could hear her voice trembling. I was on the verge of interrupting them – he didn't have any right to frighten her, no matter who he was to her.

But then I heard King Thorne say, 'You are wolven, my love. It is a rare and precious thing, not to be feared but embraced.'

'What does it mean?'

'It means you are wild. You will struggle with walls and roofs, with any climate but the far north. It means you might change one day into something feared. It means your life will be rich and full and difficult. But here is what we both know to be true: you, Ella, are very brave. You are your mother's daughter in that regard. Nothing will be too much for you, too difficult, too frightening. You are more than all of it, not in spite of, but *because* you are wolven.'

I felt the stirrings of something in my own breast. I didn't understand what he meant, but they were words Ella needed. There was something liberating about King Thorne's particular brand of honesty.

Now I came upon him speaking to his brother, something heated between them.

'You should get clear, Majesty,' I told Ambrose. 'We'll be on the move shortly.'

The brothers were staring at each other as though I hadn't said a word, locked in some silent battle of wills. I shook my head and continued on to find Finn and Jonah looking worried.

'We can't find Penn,' Jonah blurted out when he saw me.

'Doesn't he hide when he feels threatened? He'll turn up.'

Jonah didn't look convinced, but I didn't have time for it. 'Finn. What power can you command?'

She grimaced. Her skin looked grey with fatigue. 'Whatever you need.'

I studied her, then shook my head. 'You only act to open that gate if Osric fails, understood? Save your power for keeping the veil open a little longer.' Now that we had him here, I didn't particularly want to lose the slaughterman from this battle. Already I was seeing what a difference he made to the spirits of the people around him – he stirred some ancient hunger for battle within them.

'And me?' Jonah asked.

I eyed him, having forgotten that he too was a warder. Everyone always seemed to forget. The boy was easily overlooked. 'You're with Osric. Protect him at all costs. Can you do that?'

Jonah nodded, eyes shifting to a pale shade of green. 'Majesty. Did Isadora say anything to you about . . .? Did she say anything before she left?'

Glancing between the twins, I considered quickly. 'She told me she'd been offered a way to protect her people. Any good leader knows when to take such deals.'

Jonah's expression fell, but Finn shook her head again, bluntly refusing it. 'Her people are our people – we are all the same.'

I shrugged, turning. 'If you were given the choice, would you let half live, or all die?' I left before they had a chance to reply. The only way to convince people of Izzy's betrayal would be by making it seem reasonable, smart even.

I was having a very difficult time keeping my mind from her last words to me. From the way she leaned in close and the way her eyes turned crystal. *You can be all your masks.* Some tight, tangled thing uncurled and loosened within me, some terrible pressure finally gave way and I was as light as a feather. I was free to be any damn thing I wanted to be, free even to be all the things I didn't want to be. Free to just *be*.

*

The day wore on as I checked the ranks and checked them again. I finally armed myself and mounted up. King Thorne appeared at my horse's flank, peering up at me. 'Emperor Feckless,' he addressed me.

I grinned, even laughed a little. 'Yes, sire, that is what I tend to be called.'

'Are you dumb as well as useless?'

'I hope not.'

'Then you don't need to be informed of the truth?'

I frowned, searching his face. 'What truth? Out with it.'

'The truth that whatever the little Sparrow is doing isn't what it seems.'

My smile returned. 'She's my mate, King Thorne. What do you think?'

He nodded, satisfied with that. 'Don't fuck this up then, kid.'

'I'll do my best.'

'Do more than your best,' he replied bluntly. 'You smell calm and easy and that's no way to go into a battle. Find your fury. Find your *outrage*.'

I took a breath, trying to do so, but as my eyes scanned the line of soldiers I was distracted by an absence in the rows of berserkers. 'Thorne!' I shouted. 'Where's Thorne?'

His father's voice was grim as he said, 'My son will no longer be joining tonight's battle. I will lead his berserkers.'

THORNE

While Falco spent the afternoon moving through his army and making sure every conceivable thing was ready, I sat with Ambrose, unsure what he was still doing here. Da appeared, having apparently attached axe blades to belt loops. Without asking, he started strapping these to Ambrose's wrists.

'What are you doing? Don't, Thorne.'

'How else will you fight?'

'I won't.'

Da grunted in blatant dismissal of this.

'Brother, listen –' Ambrose started, but Da placed a hand on his little brother's head and pulled his face close.

'No, you listen to me, brother. It's a brave man who tries to change the course of the river, but only a damn fool tries to do that while he's submerged within it. You kick and swim and get the Sword out of there first.'

Ambrose couldn't help grinning. 'Good metaphor.'

'Shut it, kid,' Da growled. 'Point's the same. There'll be time for you to build a new world after this. For now you fight because you're damn good at it, and we need your help not getting killed.'

The smile faded from Ambrose's lips and he stared at the axes being bound to his arms. When he looked finally at his brother, there was something startling in his gaze. Something . . . violent. He'd given in to the tide, or perhaps to his brother, for it was plain to see that between the two of them love ran very deep. 'How many battles have we fought, brother?' he asked softly.

'Many.'

'And how many have we won?'

'All.'

They smiled at each other and I felt the skin on my arms prickle. When Ambrose stood it was to cut through the slings holding his wrists aloft, and to swing those axe blades like he was born to it. 'One last time, then,' he said, and I couldn't help but wonder what this one last time would cost him.

'About bloody time,' was all Ava said when she spotted him.

★

'Walk with me a moment, boy,' Da said to me as the afternoon got older. I followed him into the marshes where we could speak in private. Howl came with us, nuzzling his snout into Da's hand as though they'd been friends for years.

'You've been doing the rounds,' I pointed out. 'Dispersing wisdom to all who'll listen.'

He shrugged, not reacting to the playful barb. 'I've done a lot of watching. And I don't know how much time I have here. Or who'll survive the night.'

My mouth closed with a snap. I waited for him to say what he'd brought me here to say, whatever pearl he needed to impart, but he didn't seem inclined to speak, gazing into the swamp while he petted Howl.

'Was it you I kept seeing?' I asked.

'Aye.'

I breathed out in relief. 'How?'

'Don't know, boy. Maybe that tie to your wife lets you see through the veil.'

'Then I'm not mad?'

Da's eyes moved to rest on me. 'Only the same kind of mad all our kind are. Mad for battle. Mad for blood. Mad enough to fight on and on no matter what harm has befallen us.'

That deep, deep dark that waited below my feet for me to sink into. At least I was not alone above it. At least now I had Da.

'In any other I'd welcome that madness,' he went on in that scraping voice. 'I'd encourage it – to die in battle is a great honour. But you, my boy, my only son, I'll caution. We're violent because it's easy. Because it's been bred into our nature over centuries of war. That doesn't mean it's right. I learnt that the hard way.'

I looked away, folding my arms. The branches of the trees were swaying slightly, everything was swaying slightly, and had been for the last few days. Why was he saying this to me right before we were about to storm the wall of an enemy city? Why take the wind from my sails?

He surprised me by pulling me into an embrace. In my ear he said, 'You reek, my boy. For you the fight is over.'

Before I had a chance to understand what he meant, he was squeezing my head and neck until the world went dark.

When next I opened my eyes the light was fading quickly and my entire body was bound to a tree. Roaring, I struggled against it but found I could hardly move. My mother was here, crouching over me. Da, too, and the twins and Erik. They were peering down at me but I couldn't see them well. My vision was so blurred they were barely more than moving shapes.

'Stab wound,' I thought I heard Ma say.

'It stinks of infection,' Da said. 'I'm away now. Don't let him free, whatever you do. He smells close to death, and that boy will fight himself into a grave.'

I watched them, the two of them. I had never seen them together, had wondered all my life how two such people could love one another, could even inhabit the same space. It was dreamlike and hazy as I watched them now, as I saw him lean down to kiss her on the lips, their shapes entwined for just a moment and then parting again.

I closed my eyes, gave a huge scream of fury. How could he?

'Don't do this, Da, please! I must help! My wife is there, and Ambrose and Falco and *you*! *Let me fight with you!*'

But he was already gone, to battle.

FALCO

Night fell.

Find your fury. Find your outrage.

401

The wings of sparrows beat in my ears as I kicked my horse forwards and galloped down the hill towards the wall. I heard distant shouts atop it. I saw fire-arrows sail through the air at us. I felt the rumble of hundreds of feet following me.

And as I reached the wall, *my* wall, I didn't need to find my fury. It found me.

Chapter 32

Isadora

It took us most of the night to reach the tunnel, and a few hours to climb up through it. Penn and I were both far smaller than the average citizen who'd escaped through this nightmarishly tight hole, so for us it was easier. We talked to distract ourselves from the dark, though. It was a heavy dark that infused the whole world and made it small small small, and for once we each needed words to make it bigger.

'Have you always known you could do it?' I asked him.

'Sort of.'

'But when did it occur to you?'

'Never really thought about it.'

Fair enough. 'Have you ever used it on me? Is that why . . . I feel so good when I'm around you?'

Penn gave a trickle of laughter and I imagined his face behind me. 'I don't use it on people I love, silly.'

It made me flush warm, crawling up and up until we emerged at last into the fish coolroom Falco had discovered. The city was in chaos. Troops of soldiers were running in formation towards the wall, huge lines of them, what had to be hundreds. Citizens were sprinting to the relative safety of their homes. Penn and I wore cloaks with the hoods drawn over our faces as we made our way through the streets. It took a few hours to reach the outskirts of the royal district, and there we hid, biding our time, waiting for the streets to clear. Warders rushed in and out, presumably between here and their temple to the east. Urgency made me jittery – it was an almost physical pain to sit here and wait for the right moment. Every second pulled us closer to Falco's attack on that gate.

I spotted an opening in the rush of people, a rare moment of quiet. 'Ready?' I whispered.

'Hands steady,' he sang.

'You know where you have to get to?'

'Just go, Iz.'

I burst out from behind the merchant building and sprinted straight for the palace. Arrows fired at me as I scaled the gate, but I cut them out of the air with the blade in my left hand. The second I was over eight soldiers were coming at me. And there – there were the warders sweeping down the front steps. Two males and Gwendolyn the Viper.

I was frozen by their wards and beaten to the ground. 'I'm here to offer Dren and Galia a deal,' I gasped, meeting Gwendolyn's faded eyes. 'Tell them the Sparrow has information for them.'

She gazed at me and in her stony face I could read nothing of her thoughts. She nodded, gesturing for the soldiers to bind and escort me inside. My eyes scanned everything they could, noting the hurried footsteps and rushed conversations. The people in this palace certainly knew they were about to be attacked.

I waited in the main hall for the Mad Ones to take their thrones. There were dozens of corpses scattering the floor, left to stew in their own blood and rot. It was horrendous, the stench unbearable, and I forced myself not to look at or think of them.

They strode into the hall quickly this afternoon. No amusement or delight coloured their faces. 'Pet's returned to us,' Dren said.

'How did you escape the cage, little one?' Galia asked as she sat. They didn't seem keen to waste any time.

'Look for yourself,' I said.

'You have a shield,' Dren reminded me. 'Breaking through it wasn't pleasant, if you'll recall.'

'I've learnt how to lower it.'

'Why would you want us to see your mind?' Galia asked, hawk-eyes watching me suspiciously.

'I'm no good with words.'

'How about you try, and we shall see if you can speak the truth.'

My hands clenched impatiently. If I had to seduce them with my tongue this could go very badly. 'I've come from the army that is preparing to attack you. They will move with nightfall.'

'We know of the army. We've been entertained by its progress – sent a few minor obstacles of our own.'

'We do love drama,' Dren agreed.

I curbed my anger at the thought of the fire Radha died in. There was no place for anger right now: it blurred the mind. Coldly, I said, 'But do you also know of the tunnel they will be entering through?'

'The tunnels are destroyed.'

'That's why they built a new one, right under your noses.'

Both their gazes narrowed. 'Where?'

'East cliffs. I'd send troops to guard it, were I you.' They didn't move, so I shrugged and continued. 'That's one piece given freely. The rest you will need to trade for.'

'Very well. Keeping your life seems a sufficient bargain for whatever trifles you think worth a damn to us.'

I shook my head, smiling a little. 'I'm not altogether fond of my life. There are other things I'm more interested in.'

'Such as?' Galia seemed amused now, thought she was toying with me. She couldn't imagine I had anything worth bargaining for, believed she had all the power in the world with which to torment me.

'I want ward-bound contracts that free my realms – Sanra, Ora and Querida – and their citizens from any warder influence or law. I want a contract naming me as rightful ruler of those three realms, and I want a peace treaty with you that spans at least fifty years.'

'Why would we give you more than half of Kaya?' Dren laughed.

'Because my first act as ruler will be to kill Falco of Sancia, and help you take Pirenti.'

There was a silence as they stared at me in surprise. I could see swift calculations going through their minds. Warders lived a long time – fifty years would be nothing to them, and with the rest of the world under their power they could easily take my three realms after the treaty ended.

'Your bondmate,' Galia said slowly. 'You expect us to believe you'd kill him? Betray those friends you've made?'

I met her eyes and asked softly, 'Have you any understanding of how much I hate that man? Loathsome humiliation, to be bound to him, and I will take great pleasure in doing what I was born to do: destroying him. As for the friends, has any one of them looked at me as more than the demon girl? The witch? The ice creature?' I shook my head, letting my lip curl. 'They're no friends of mine. My friends are from the south forests – they're the ones I'll protect with my life.'

'Indeed,' Galia mused. 'For all of that, Sparrow, you must have something very special to offer us.'

'I do. I know how they're going to beat you.'

'Why would you prevent that?'

'I would prevent mass slaughter on both sides. I can stop this battle with a deal, and with the death of one man, simply by revealing the truth.'

'Go on then.'

'Fear,' I said. 'It renders you impotent.'

Dren scoffed, waving his hand in dismissal, but I saw a flicker of concern pass through Galia's eyes. 'Not a problem, child, if you feel no fear.'

'And if you do? If you and every single warder were reduced to a mass of terror? How would you fight the berserkers beyond that wall? How could anyone?'

They studied me, giving no sign that they were nervous. But I knew they were. 'How would that happen?' Galia asked slowly, knowing the answer, fearing it above all else.

'Because your son Penn is outside with Falco, and he is an empath,' I answered simply.

Silence fell.

'Here's what will happen. Penn will cloak your warders with fear, making them powerless. You and I both know he has enough power to do so – it's why you're so frightened of him. That gate will be attacked, and without any magic it will be breached, and then there will be a good old-fashioned battle raging in the streets, during which thousands will die and you will lose. The city will be taken by Falco and his Pirenti family, and my lands will be reclaimed. You're dead, I'm dead, and he wins.' I let that sink in for a moment. '*Or.*'

I went on to describe the plan, and it was the logic of it, in the end, that ensnared them. Not my clumsy words, but the cleverness of the idea, the outcome of which would mean complete victory for them without having to lose a single life.

Well. That wasn't quite right. There would be one life lost.

But thanks to the breaking of our bond, it would remain only one.

★

Dren and Galia picked through my mind to discover if all I'd said was true. I showed them only snippets: the discussion with King Thorne about using a warder's fear, and my last conversation with Falco took the main stage. I also showed them Ava's mistrust of me, Osric's attack when he first discovered who I was. And I showed them how strong both Finn and Osric's magic was. They needed to believe that Falco had an army of formidable opponents, and that I didn't belong with them.

The rest of the truth I kept hidden beneath the lake, where there was no fear, only ruthlessness. I didn't think about it, and they didn't see it. And I certainly did not think about the little boy hiding within the city walls, biding his time.

FALCO

They knew we were coming. That much was obvious. The wards on the gate were incredibly strong, Osric informed me as the night wore on. He had yet to break through, but he was trying. By gods he was trying. All of my warders were working tirelessly to protect him from attack, but the enemy warders on the wall were far more powerful. It was Jonah, it turned out, who was deflecting almost all of the magic raining down on Os.

The rest of us were busy trying to breach the wall. Berserker ladders went up and the mighty men climbed as high as they could before arrows or magic sent them back down and they started again. Some reached the top and fought there, but most were shoved off before they could do enough damage to get us inside. Inga and I had been moving up and down the wall, shields raised against the hail of fire-arrows from above. She was using small bursts of power to crack the stones of the thousand-year-old wall, leaving spots vulnerable to the heavy Pirenti hammers. It wouldn't hold out much longer – I knew we were nearly inside. But it was within the grey light of dawn that things changed.

'Majesty,' a breathless runner gasped, pulling attention from the wall. 'Enemy forces approach from behind!'

I whirled in time to see smudges in the distance. 'Who are they?'

'Don't know, but there are soldiers and warders both, a whole lot of them from either side of the marshes.'

As they drew closer I could see their armour and recognised the colours of Limontae. The two contingents didn't attack; rather, they blocked us in, pinning us with our backs to the wall and then stopping to wait for something.

'Turn!' I called atop my horse. 'Turn and hold!'

Ava swung Isadora's forces around. Ambrose took the other flank, while King Thorne turned the berserkers to take the brunt of the central flank, always hardest to hold.

'Keep at the wall!' I ordered Osric and Jonah.

This was about to become a huge, bloody mess – we couldn't face warders in open warfare. I had never wanted us to engage in that. My heart clenched with shock to see that one of them was Lutius himself. Traitorous head warder of Kaya, the man I had trusted to protect my city but who had instead handed it to Dren and Galia. Fury exploded within me and I drew my twin swords. His blood was mine: I'd vowed it on the night it all fell apart.

That was when a voice called from atop the wall – louder than a voice could without magic. *'Cease fighting. We have a proposition.'*

I peered up and was shocked to see Dren and Galia standing on the wall right there, right above us, vulnerable to attack. My eyes darted to my fighters – King Thorne and King Ambrose to one side, Ava to the other. Osric was still at the gate, but he found me and shook his head, indicating his power had been exhausted.

'No one here wants countless casualties today. So before bloodshed begins, we will offer you a chance at mercy or victory.'

I rode closer and kept firm hold of my swords.

'In ancient times battles were avoided by naming two to meet in single combat. We propose that both armies choose their best fighter. If our champion

wins, you will surrender. All those from Pirenti will leave Kaya, while any Kayan soldiers will be shown mercy under our reign. If your fighter wins . . . well. My husband and I will come down from this wall and face you alone, and you may do your best to destroy us without having to go through an army.'

The Pirenti brothers came to my side. 'It's a good deal,' Ambrose breathed.

'That's what I'm concerned about,' I said. They'd been about to annihilate us. Why intercede and risk their victory?

'I will fight,' King Thorne growled, and I nodded.

'This feels like a trap, Fal,' Ava said.

'Do we have an agreement?'

I hesitated. Ava was surely right, but what choice did we have? I failed to see who could beat King Thorne in single combat. If they tried anything after he won, we would just have to face it then. 'Aye, a deal!' I shouted. 'Send your soldier out.'

'Call your people away from the wall. Any use of magic will immediately void the deal.'

I motioned for Osric and the rest of my soldiers to pull back alongside me.

The gate opened, not all the way, but a little. Enough for a single soldier to ride out onto the grassy plain. A small pale woman, calm and unafraid as she held her head high.

My heart plummeted into my stomach and my pulse rushed. *What the fuck was she doing?* Casting a swift look at my companions, they were all aghast.

King Thorne looked at me, confused. His axe went a little limp in his hand. 'I'll not kill that woman,' he said. 'Not her.'

My mind raced. Why was she . . .? It couldn't be that . . . that she had actually joined them, could it? My soul revolted at the idea, but I could no longer cast it off so easily. If she was willing to fight to the death for Dren and Galia, then how could I think she *hadn't* joined them? And if that was true, if that was the case, there was no one who could do this. No one who could beat the Sparrow.

Except maybe me.

Breathing heavily, I swung to the ground.

'What are you doing?' Ava demanded. 'Get back on your horse.'

'Falco!' Osric snapped.

'Wait, Fal,' Ambrose said. 'It shouldn't be you.'

'You can't fight, Falco!' I heard Ava shout in panic. Then, '*Stop him.*'

'Hold, boy,' King Thorne ordered, placing himself in front of me.

I looked up at him, this giant of a man. Surely he'd be the better pick. Surely he could kill such a tiny girl, if one of us had to. Surely I was a madman, walking to my death and the deaths of thousands. Walking to our defeat. All of that was in his eyes.

'She's my mate,' I told him again. 'This is my land, my country, so it shall be my burden.'

'But you can't do it, kid,' he tried. 'You haven't learned to fight.'

I let my eyes shift scarlet for fury and for blood and for the woman I loved. With these bleeding eyes I said, '*Get out of my way.*'

He did.

I walked and walked to meet her. My boots crunched on the early morning grass. The trill of a bird reached my ears, strangely, and I couldn't imagine in those long moments where it might be coming from. I was desperate to know what kind of bird it was. Desperate, too, for this to be one of her dreams, one of her terrible, terrible dreams.

I reached Isadora. She had dismounted and was waiting for me as the sun rose.

'Tell me this is part of a plan,' I begged her. 'Tell me, little Sparrow, that this isn't what it seems. Because if it is – if you've really betrayed me and all of Kaya – I'm going to have to fight you, and one of us is going to die, and I'll have to do whatever I can to make sure it isn't me.'

Looking into my eyes, Isadora said very clearly, '*Fate's fools no longer, Emperor Feckless.*' And then she attacked.

CHAPTER 33

ISADORA

The idiot wasn't getting it. *Still.* Which was frustrating because he was meant to be the smart one in our pair. I supposed he would know soon enough, and to be fair, my whole plan was designed to make him think he had to fight me to the death.

It came down to this. I couldn't get Penn into the palace without getting him killed, so I had to get Dren and Galia out to him. I also had to stop two armies from slaughtering each other, because no matter who won I couldn't live with that much death, when I alone could fight and die instead. Getting the Mad Ones to agree to this was trickier, but when they heard that the risk was minimised to the possibility that Emperor Feckless – worst fighter in the realm – could beat the Sparrow in single combat, they believed it was a pretty safe bet. I kill him, his army surrenders, my soldiers are loyal to the Mad Ones and they proceed to conquer the world. The only reason they'd believed this, I knew, was because they had so little faith in the human capacity for love.

What was actually going to happen was quite different, if I had any say in it.

And so here we were. Falco with his drawn twin swords, begging me to tell him that this was part of an elaborate plan. As though I could just blurt out that yes, it was, while gods-damned Dren and Galia stood above, listening. *You really are an idiot sometimes, Falco.*

All I could give him was one giant clue. 'Fate's fools no longer, Emperor Feckless.'

AVA

Five seconds ago I was *sure* he was about to die. The Emperor of Kaya was a dead man walking, this whole realm was going to fall under warder reign with no hope of escape, and the rest of us were likely to die here, massacred by magic. Not one of us believed for a second that the offer of mercy handed down by the Mad Ones was anything other than bullshit.

And then he met her beneath the shadow of the wall, and she attacked. I'd seen that girl best everyone she'd ever faced, including berserker kings and hirðmenn. But she didn't best Falco now. He didn't fall to her deadly daggers as everyone else inevitably did. He fought. Like I'd never seen anyone fight. Not even my husband, or this dead slaughterman who'd been awakened for his violence. No one.

His sword cut her dagger from the air and then he was upon her, slashing the second and third blades from her hands before she'd had a chance to use them. He spun and sliced, almost taking her head off, but she managed to duck low and into the swing, coming up inside with a jab of her dagger at his guts. Falco pulled back, slamming her hard with his sword-hilt to avoid the stab and then advancing on top of her as she retreated. He didn't give her an inch or a second, instead using his incredible bladework to attack and attack, pushing her further back. It was brutal and savage in the morning sunlight, a thing none of us had expected to witness.

'Sword,' Ambrose breathed in utter disbelief.

I agreed with a faint nod. 'He's . . . This is . . . How did he . . .?'

'*Quiet,*' King Thorne, the ass, ordered in a growl, his eyes glued to the fight. I refrained from punching him in the side of the head.

Isadora was bleeding in multiple places, but so too was Falco, I now saw. She had used his heavy attack to draw him into an aggressive stance, and when he was halfway through a forward slash she flicked her dagger down into his foot, causing his balance to shift enough that she could step up off his thigh and swing her boot into his face. His head snapped back and he fell, but he was already curling his spine to flip onto his feet. His swords moved at the same time, circling around and slashing through her middle; she leapt above them and sent her knee into his throat. It got a bit unruly then – they both went down and Falco lost hold of his swords, while Isadora punched and scrabbled wildly.

It didn't see what happened as they scuffled, but suddenly she was thrown free, hitting the ground hard. When Fal followed this up he was only brandishing one sword. Isadora slid out of his way, rolling until she was on her feet, and then she was wielding the second sword.

'Gods, damn it,' Thorne cursed. 'He can't let her have the other sword.'

'It's too big for her,' Ambrose argued. 'It'll weigh her down.'

'Isn't that what we want?' I said, but it fell into a hollow space made of horror. Watching this felt instinctively wrong. Because what was becoming clear was how well matched they were – how perfectly in sync their bodies. Whatever had driven her to betray him was brutal, because they weren't meant to kill each other. That was blatantly obvious, witnessing this. They were a match, forged as two halves of a whole.

'I feel sick,' Finn whispered. 'This is *wrong*.'

I hadn't seen her appear, but as I glanced at Finn now I saw how grey her skin was and how deathly unwell she looked. I put my arm around her and gathered her to my side.

'Can't we make them stop?' she whispered. 'I could. I could make them.'

'And then the Mad Ones rain death upon us all,' Thorne grunted.

'If he wins we have to face them anyway,' I said.

'Better than facing that lot at the same time,' Ambrose muttered, waving over his shoulder at the hoard of enemies waiting there for Falco to lose.

He couldn't lose. Wild hope was in my chest at the sight of how he fought. *He couldn't lose.* Not now. Only she wasn't exactly a pushover. They were attacking each other with their single swords, striking and slashing and parrying and dodging. It was so fast I could barely keep up with who did what.

An upwards strike cut straight through Isadora's cheek, and she was only barely quick enough to tilt her head and stop her ear from being sliced off. A thick lock of her hair fell wispily to the grass and was trampled by Falco's boot as he lunged forward, slamming his shoulder into her ribs. We all heard her gasp of pain as several of them cracked. Falco didn't follow through, finishing her as he could have, but paused to give her a moment.

We all moved closer, enthralled by the barbaric scene. 'Stand up,' I heard him snarl.

'Stop holding back!' she replied, and flicked an invisible knife into his right arm. It sank deep to the hilt and I saw the colour leave his face. She was already running at him as he transferred his sword into his left hand and parried the oncoming slash. *Clang* went their steel, again and again. I was sure it could have gone on forever had not one of them faltered, surprising us all.

A gasp left my mouth.

Thorne took two steps forward and forcibly stopped himself.

Finn wailed.

And we watched as one of the fighters sank to cradle the dying one's head.

CHAPTER 34

FALCO

I realised partway through.

Fate's fools no longer. Meaning this was her choice. And I knew her choice – knew it as intimately as I knew my own. To destroy the Mad Ones. It had been this and always this. So, because she couldn't lucid dream anymore, she'd drawn them out and presented them to us. And as she changed the world with one move, I realised what the rest of her plan was. I realised why she'd called me Emperor Feckless: it was how she'd gotten them to agree to the fight. Emperor Feckless had finally done his gods-cursed job. And Isadora's one move was this.

Dropping her wrist instead of raising it.

She was too good not to do that on purpose. Too good not to block my low strike. Too good to allow my sword to impale her body, slicing straight into her stomach and back out again. Her one move was letting me win. It had been her move all along, right from the very beginning.

Shock petrified my body. Everything drained from me, everything.

I sank to my knees. The sword fell from trembling fingers.

I managed to drag her dying body into my lap. Blood from her stomach smeared my hands and then her face as I frantically touched her cheeks and lips. 'Why did you do that?' I whispered. 'Why didn't you block me? You were meant to block me, Iz.' I felt numb. Numb all the way into my soul. 'Why didn't you block me.'

Her eyes opened, clouded with pain. But she smiled. 'Wait for Penn. It should have been long enough now.'

I tried to ask what she meant but what came out was, 'You were meant to block my sword.'

'Falco,' she sighed, blood spilling from her mouth. 'Don't look so worried. All's well. We're not bonded anymore, remember?'

I pressed my trembling lips to hers. 'Of course we are.'

And I felt Isadora smile against my mouth. 'Of course we are,' she agreed.

The last thing I saw before she closed her eyes was the brilliant, blazing gold, not of the bond, but of true love, chosen freely.

CHAPTER 35

FALCO

I had thought I understood pain. I hadn't.

★

There was noise all around. Some were screaming their approval, our victory, others were shouting their rage at her death. Berserkers chanted their battle cry and pounded on their shields. It was hectic and chaotic and no one knew what to do.

I turned my head and looked up at the wall. Dren and Galia were gazing upon me in fury. This was not part of their plan; it was hers. It had been hers all along. To die for us. But I had failed her, because the Mad Ones were honourless and broke our deal by shouting, '*Attack!*'

She must have known they would. So what was the end of her plan? Why go through this? To get them outside? *Wait for Penn*, she'd said, but I couldn't see him anywhere and battle was exploding behind me. Armies met with a rush of steel. Warder magic sent bodies flying and the furious roars of berserkers rung out into the morning air. And within it all I could see Dren and Galia fleeing the wall for the safety of their palace.

'*Stop them!*' I roared.

Osric sent waves of power at them, but they were getting away. I had to get up onto that wall. I *had* to kill them, or Izzy had died for nothing. A sick, tormented grief fuelled me as I surged to my feet.

But then.

'Wait,' someone said. Finn. 'Wait wait wait. She's not . . . Fal, I don't think she's dead.'

My eyes travelled a long way back to her body, dreading what I would see: the evidence not of her monstrousness, but of mine. What kind of creature kills his own mate – *for anything*? She was paler than death, but then she always was. The red on her face and body matched her eyes, closed now. I shook my head. She was dead.

'No, really,' Finn said, fingers pressed at the pulse in her neck. A woozy, urgent hope struck me. 'Osric!' she shouted.

King Thorne and Ambrose had moved to block us from attack, fighting back those who got through our ranks, giving us precious time. Osric arrived, the set of his shoulders exhausted.

'Can you heal her?' Finn asked.

His mouth tightened and he shook his head. Disbelief and something much uglier surged inside me. I backhanded him hard across the face. '*Heal her*,' I snarled.

'Majesty,' he said, spitting out a mouthful of blood. 'I'm drained and she's too far gone. I must focus my last energy on keeping the tracer on the Mad Ones, or they will be lost to us.'

'I can!' a high voice panted. I turned to see an orange-haired girl. 'I can do it!'

'She can,' Ambrose agreed. 'Good girl. Quickly.'

The girl sank beside Izzy and we watched her eyes go white. After a few seconds she was sweating. 'I can't. She's too wounded . . . I can't get her far enough back.'

It occurred to me. An idea. Probably a foolish one. I dropped to my knees and took Isadora's hand. 'Then don't. Leave some of the wound, enough to cause her pain.'

'What in gods names are you on about?' Finn demanded.

'Do it,' I told the warder.

ISADORA

The void was filled with screaming.

But there was a voice within it, his voice, and through the madness it said, '*Don't wake up.*'

Pain exploded through my stomach and my eyes flew open.

The sky was filled with thousands of burning, falling stars. There were enormous black wings flapping above and around, cocooning me, buffeting the heart of the world. And there was Falco. His eyes were crystal, his hair shaved off, his nose crooked. 'Don't wake up,' he told me, and I looked down to realise he'd jammed his fingers inside the wound his sword had made.

Pain tethered me. Slowly I realised what he'd done, what was happening, and I smiled.

I rose, a thrill of dark power rising with me. Over my eyes was a film of blood; through it I gazed at the dream realm. They were all here, staring at me in shock, their edges blurred and flickering. Ambrose and King Thorne and Finn and Jonah and Osric. But not –

'Where's Penn?' I demanded as air rushed my lungs, filled them, buoyed them up off the ground. My hand reached for Falco's, using it to keep my feet on the earth.

'We don't know –'

'Has he done it yet?' Though the answer was obvious. If he'd done it, they would know, which meant something had gone wrong and my plan was in ruins. Battle raged around me. The battle I had meant to stop. But in the dream realm was where my power waited for me, and so stop it I would.

'Finn,' I said. She wasn't as strong as Penn, and she was already holding the veil open. It didn't matter. We all had to find a way to ask more of ourselves before the end found us. 'Manipulate the warders – fill them with fear.' Her eyes widened nervously. I held them. 'It was meant to be Penn, but it's up to you now. It comes down to you. Find your strength.'

Finn drew a long, shaky breath, and then she turned her faded eyes to the battle behind us. 'I've got this.'

'They're getting away,' Falco grunted, nodding up to the wall.

'Deal with this,' I told him, gesturing to the battle. 'I'll get Dren and Galia.'

He hesitated, squeezing my hand tightly. 'Izzy – *they're not the bars of your cage.*'

But they were and I couldn't wait for him to understand that. I had burning Marks cut into the length of my arm and they told the truth of what I was capable of. I took off, gathering my fallen knives from the ground. I heard Falco shout, 'Warders, with her!' and several sets of feet kept pace with me as I sprinted to the huge berserker ladders. Jonah ensured ours remained upright as we climbed and Osric shouted directions, following some kind of trail left by the Mad Ones.

Up the ladder, along the wall. I smashed through the warders guarding it, carving a path for the others to follow. They couldn't touch me, and I would kill them all if I had to. Down the winding staircase, into the city streets. I ordered Jonah to unlock the gates and then he caught up to Osric and me as we stormed the winding path to the palace. If Dren and Galia got back inside the grounds they'd be too hard to follow. Blood pounded through my ears and my guts ached and throbbed.

'Up ahead,' Osric panted.

I could see them running for the gates, nearly there. 'Stop them,' I ordered.

Osric sent a burst of power into the cobblestones directly before them, gouging a hole in the earth and sending the Mad Ones off their feet. They rose and turned to face us.

'No harm done, pet,' Galia said coldly. 'You'll all die.'

I threw four of my blades and watched as they stopped mid-air then clattered to the ground. Galia lifted her hand and squeezed, and I heard Jonah cough. He couldn't breathe. I froze, holding my empty hands out for them to see.

'I can't kill you, but I can certainly kill your friends. I'd advise you not to move, Sparrow.'

Osric lifted his hands and something began, some invisible struggle I couldn't perceive. Magic passed between them and Jonah managed to draw breath, now free of Galia's clutches. But there were two of the Mad Ones and only one Osric, and he had done so much already. I could see his strength fading with every second that passed.

I ran at them, taking advantage of Osric's attack. Dren's hand flicked but he couldn't touch me and as I reached the warder I managed to slash my knife through his neck. To my dismay, the wound gushed red and then simply closed over. Dren smiled. 'No wound I can't heal, pet. So do your worst.'

Shit. Alright, no wounds. But if I could cut Dren's heart out, then surely he couldn't heal *that*. Except as I attacked him my knives glanced off something very un-flesh like — it was as though he'd covered the two of them in a fine sheen of what seemed like iron. I couldn't get at him, and he turned his power back to fighting Osric.

I backed away, thinking quickly. Osric was clever, forcing them to use all of their power and drain themselves dry. It was the only thing that might kill them. Jonah and Inga, plus a couple of the warders from the prison and the red-haired girl who'd been trying to heal me added their magic to Osric's, hammering Dren and Galia with pressure.

Galia's eyes darted up and a bolt of lightning struck one of our warders, killing her instantly. Another split the cobblestones beneath their feet, disrupting their magic long enough for Dren to flick the head from a man's body with nothing more than his wrist.

I circled around behind them. It didn't matter that I was invulnerable if they were too. As I struggled to think I saw Inga go down hard, eyes open and glassy. She'd been sapped of all life, by the look of her.

Despair filled me. This wasn't meant to happen. I'd had a plan: people weren't meant to be dying. But Penn wasn't here, and so pieces of me were disintegrating, turning to ash. Buildings were burning and I couldn't tell if the flames were real or not. It was all over, and falling, and the blood from my stomach was spreading from my center out and out and out and as I watched, utterly powerless to stop it, Jonah fell to his knees, and his eyes found mine, and he said through the blood in his mouth, 'Tell my sister I love her best of all,' on a whisper, on a breath, and then he was dead. I could see the life go from him, the buzzing lights of fireflies rising and coiling out of his chest with unbearable loveliness.

A guttural moan left me, turned to a scream of rage. I ran at Dren and Galia, stabbing ferociously at anything I could reach but I couldn't get through this fucking shield, this twisted magic, not even when I dropped my blades and went at them with my hands and my teeth, so savage I couldn't breathe, compelled entirely by a dark loathing, an endless endless fury. I wanted only blood, nothing else, but I couldn't get at it.

'Izzy!' a voice called.

Relief eclipsed all. I stumbled back from them, was caught and dragged even further by Osric. My neck twisted wildly until I spotted him, running down the palace steps, his red hair turning to flames in my mind's eyes. Why was he coming from the palace? Behind him was the Viper, but she wasn't attacking him or stopping him. She was running *with* him.

'Penn,' I sighed.

'It's alright, I'm here now,' he said. And then he turned his eyes to his parents.

FALCO

I allowed myself ten seconds to watch Isadora sprint for the wall – a moment to marvel as she stormed those ladders and carved her way alone through every single warder as not one of us had been able to do all night long. Then I turned to the fight raging around me. My horse was rearing in fear and I rushed to his side, gentling him with a hand and then swinging onto his saddle.

'Easy, boy,' I murmured, wishing for Radha and then shutting that thought away. I turned him and drew my left sword – someone had managed to remove Isadora's knife from my right arm, but the limb was now useless. My eyes scanned and took in the situation.

Both Ava's left flank and Ambrose's right was being thrown about by the attacking warders, their huge bursts of physical power cutting paths through our defense. The berserkers exploded into the fray, each of them aiming directly for a warder and trying to endure the pressure bolts that slammed into their big bodies. I watched as King Thorne smashed his axe through a warder's skull, and the resulting burst of power sent everyone within a radius of a hundred metres careening into the air. That was one though. One warder out of dozens.

Ambrose was hacking and slicing with his strange arm blades, annihilating those around him, but there was still so many more of the enemy crowding towards him. Ava flew low on Migliori, firing arrows at the warders, none of which found their marks, but she was pulling the warders' focus to her, giving the soldiers on the ground some relief from the bolts of heavy magic.

I searched for Finn, who was on her knees, eyes rolled back in her head, conjuring whatever wards she needed to. They hadn't started working yet and I didn't know if she had the strength for it – not while maintaining the veil too.

We couldn't keep this up.

That was when the gate behind me slid an inch or two and someone shouted, 'Courtesy of the Sparrow!'

I ordered foot soldiers to open it wide. 'Fall back!' I screamed to the troops. 'Behind the wall!'

My fighters flooded back through the gates – I intended to turn the tables and lock the enemy out. But the warders intensified their attack, seeing that intent. Kicking my horse forward, I thundered through the oncoming sea of sprinting soldiers, striking down any who weren't mine.

Ambrose felled a man and glanced up at me as I rode by. 'Get everyone behind the wall!' I ordered him and he nodded, ordering his flank to fall back.

But the berserkers weren't going anywhere except forwards into this incredibly uneven fight.

'Thorne!' I shouted. 'Get your men into the city!'

He was blood-soaked and mad-eyed as he ignored me, wading forwards through bodies to where a warder was squeezing the life out of several of Isadora's soldiers at once. I witnessed the slaughterman storm the warder, lift him like a ragdoll and shake him until his neck snapped. He threw the corpse away like a piece of rubbish. And he laughed.

'Thorne!'

He heard me at last, peering around until he spotted me.

'We've taken the wall. Get your men behind it.'

'No walls for us, lad,' he called, grinning fiendishly. 'Not till this is done.'

I shook my head – he was going to get his men killed. Before I could argue, something caught my eye.

A warder sent a torrent of wind through the air and slammed it straight into a woman on a pegasis. Ava had been flying overheard, firing arrows into the fray below, but as the wind caught her she was catapulted off Migliori. My lungs caught. It was too high. She couldn't survive a fall like that. I kicked my horse forwards but there were too many people between us and I'd never make it –

Something flashed fluidly through the air, mane and tail and wings streaming behind like the end of a shooting star. It moved so fast that it dipped through the air in time to catch Ava as she fell.

I didn't wait to see who was riding the unknown pegasis, but turned to the warder who'd sent that wind. Lutius.

Find your fury. Find your outrage. This was where it lived, inside this man. Kicking my horse through the berserkers, I screamed his name. His head snapped upwards and he saw me across the distance. Though he was far, I could still make out the flash of his teeth that meant the bastard was smiling.

I would enjoy this.

An invisible fist smashed me off my horse and into the ground. My right side scraped hard, skin raw. I was up and running at him, dodging another blow from his mind and spinning around a third. As I reached him he battered me with pain, dropping me to my knees.

Lutius laughed. 'I've wanted to do this for years, you spoilt, cowardly brat.'

I rose to my feet despite the pressure slamming my body. 'You should have been the hardest to fool,' I told him, 'but you were the easiest, Lutius. Because you see the worst in everyone, and you hate them for it.'

He sent weight crushing into me and I hit the ground again, cracking ribs and my elbow, twisting both my ankles. Pain made everything tremble, but I got back to my feet. I could see King Thorne approaching to help. 'Stay back!' I ordered him, and something in my voice made him stop. His eyes were red as the blood that drenched him, but as he looked between Lutius and me, he nodded once.

I swallowed, straightening my shoulders even though it hurt. To Lutius I said, 'Keep going. Throw all you can at me. You can use that corrupt magic of yours to batter my body to pieces, but you cannot get inside my mind or my soul, and you will never stop me from getting back up.'

Something flickered through his faded gaze. Something disconcerted, something surprised. He'd only ever known Feckless. He started again, smashing me with wind and earth. I hit the ground again and again, battered in the maelstrom, but each time he paused

I climbed slowly to my feet and went for him again – I would never stop.

And as this became slowly, steadily clear to him, I felt a shift in his attacks. I felt them weaken, felt them lose their aim and focus.

I smiled. He had begun to fear me.

Barely able to lift my sword, I walked forwards, one step at a time, until I stood directly before him. He lifted his hands and I felt nothing but a breeze against my face. 'For betraying your country and handing it to dangerous, mad criminals, your life is forfeit, Lutius.'

'And who is going to take it for you, Feckless?' he snapped. 'You've spent a lifetime letting everyone around you pay the price for your inabilities, for your inactivity, for your complete lack of responsibility. You're a child in a man's body, a frightened little boy who never had the courage to grow up. So who will bear *this* burden for you?'

'No one,' I promised. 'I bear my own burdens now.' And then I cut off his head with one huge swing of my sword.

'*Now!*' Finn screamed abruptly.

I twisted towards her: she looked like a goddess come from the sky, her skin blue, eyes white, the air around her throbbing with the sheer force of her magic. Every warder tried to attack her, but they were suddenly powerless; she had filled them with fear just as she had once filled me with joy. Thorne gave a wild howl and roared for his berserkers to finish the job. They set to cutting down every one of the impotent warders and I knew the battle was over.

But Lutius was the first creature I had ever killed. And no matter how deserved or how necessary, the feel of this death left a mark on my heart I knew I would never entirely heal from. I understood, for the first time, the kind of weight Isadora must carry with her every day, and as I realised this I knew something else: I couldn't let her be the one to kill the Mad Ones. That was my responsibility.

So even though my body was bruised and battered, some of it broken, I hauled myself back onto my horse and I rode as fast as I had ever ridden back to my city.

AVA

My first thought when I opened my eyes was that I had died.

Because I was lying across the spine of a flying pegasis that was not Migliori, and I was in the arms of a person with long, black hair, golden eyes and dimples when he smiled.

'Sorry I'm late, petal,' Avery said. 'I had a long way to come.'

Chapter 36

ISADORA

The Mad Ones stole emotion. They fed off it. But Penn created it.

As his peculiar brand of power reached out and took hold of their souls, Dren and Galia were filled with terror. They fought it, sent waves of their own magic at their son, but he was stronger than even I'd imagined and with sheer force of will he stopped them from gaining control of his mind.

Dren was clutching one of my knives and staggering for his son. I cracked him hard over the back of the skull and he dropped, unconscious. So Penn only had to deal with his mother. Galia was utterly distraught, sinking to her knees under the tumult of fear.

'Penn,' she wept, 'all I ever cared about was *you*. Your safety. We came back for you. My boy.' She was really sobbing now, the words tearing from her with a raw kind of honesty I hadn't expected. 'I love you,' she gasped desperately. 'Only you, just you, my son, my boy. Penn. I'm so sorry. We'll leave. Go far from here and never come back. I won't . . . *I need to protect you*. It's all that's ever mattered.'

As Penn stared at his mother while she writhed in fear, I saw tears fill his eyes and make steady tracks down his cheeks. 'I can feel your love,' he told her in a whisper. 'And I'm the sorrier for it. The sorrier for it. The sorrier for it.'

Pity twisted my heart for the wretchedness of it.

'I always loved it when you did that,' Galia whispered. 'And the counting. Do you still count, my love? My favourite sound in the world.'

Penn closed his eyes.

I noticed, too late, that Dren was no longer unconscious. He flicked a wrist and smashed Penn over the head with a blunt fist of magic.

Penn hit the ground woozily, but before I could get to his side Galia gave a terrible scream of rage. *'How dare you?'*

She rose and snatched the heart of her husband, wrenching it out through his chest.

'Ma!' Penn cried, shocked.

Her enraged gaze found her son. *'No one harms you.'*

Penn closed his eyes and regained control of her. The second he coated her in fear, her face twisted out of its fury and into something pathetic. Moaning, she sank to her knees and begged: *'Please.'*

I was already moving to her. Galia was too powerful to contain for long and she had already proved that she couldn't be imprisoned, but I didn't want Penn to do this. He shouldn't have to. So I snaked my arm around Galia's neck, placing my dagger at her throat.

'Don't!' Penn shouted. 'Izzy, I have her!'

I shook my head. *They will hate you for being ruthless, but they will be alive because of it.*

'Give me my power back, Penn,' Galia was shouting. 'Please – she'll kill me!'

Penn was trembling with fatigue, his skin pale as death. He sank gracefully onto one knee. 'I have her. I have her. I have her,' he chanted under his breath, draining her further and further.

I swallowed. *Do it.* I had to do it. This sweet boy could not be allowed to kill his mother and I had throbbing Marks on my arm.

'Hold on, hold on, hold on,' he begged me, and then the woman in my arms was begging too, and it was a nightmare, it was all the ugliness inside me begging as well, begging me not to do this. What would I be afterwards? *It's just one more,* I told myself, screamed it within my heart. One out of so many. How could it possibly make a difference?

Only it would. It had already. I could feel it, this swelling tide.

She is the reason you are even capable of killing her! She had done this to me, made me like this, she and all her kind. It was her warder magic that bound my cage and taught me to kill.

They are not the bars of your cage.

The words found me and slipped inside, and suddenly I knew. He was right. Dren and Galia weren't the bars of my cage, nor were warders of any kind. *I* was the bars of my cage; I made them with blades and blood and I strengthened them every time I took a life.

'Let her go, Isadora,' a voice said, and I wrenched Galia around to see Falco. He was bruised and bloody and moved with pain, but he was here.

'She has to die,' I breathed. Didn't they understand? Didn't *anyone*? 'She's too dangerous, Falco.'

He said again, 'Let her go. I'm going to do it this time.' He came closer, holding my frantic gaze and I could hardly breathe, could hardly see, except I could hear his voice and the calm of it soothed something violent in my chest. 'I'm going to do it, my love. You don't have to. You're free.'

And I was. I was abruptly, *finally* free of the cage. I didn't *have* to do anything.

My arms dropped and my daggers hit the cobblestones. Everything crumbled around me and my eyes lifted to the sky, the endless open sky, not a roof or a cage but an opening that stretched on and on forever. I took a deep, endless breath of air, the first air my lungs had ever breathed, and my soul reached up and out as it never had before.

On either side of my spine unfurled a set of magnificent wings, the tawny wings of sparrows, stretching out and out and out.

'*Hold on hold on hold on hold –*' Penn was whispering over and over and then he wasn't. His voice cut off.

When I looked down it wasn't to see Falco's sword in her heart. It was to see that he'd been too late. She was already dead, skin rotten and shrivelled, utterly drained of power by her son, a gentle boy filled with numbers and empathy. A boy now lying on the ground without a soul of his own.

So I stopped caring about pain or the need to tether myself to my body. I stopped caring about lucidity, or control.

I would fly and let the rest fall away.

My wings lifted me into the air, taking me higher. High enough to meet the endless sky, free at last.

PENN

The world is made of numbers. I see every one of them. I *feel* every one. Some numbers fit inside others, some form patterns, some are breakable and others aren't. Numbers are infinite and I count them because they make sense of the noise of people's feelings. The hum. A sort of buzzing, one that gets inside me and makes it hard to breathe. Their hearts flutter or their minds whirl and they give off the hum and it saturates me. They forget how much they feel, but I don't.

I can count anything.

The 6 soldiers who found me on my way to the city wall and took me to the dungeons instead. 43 minutes in this prison cell, waiting for the world to die. The 43 minutes that I am late. The 6 bars over the window, the 1 slim moon in the sky. The 13 screams from beyond the window. The deaths I will be responsible for because I couldn't get to where I said I would be.

And then. 1 Viper at the cage, setting me free.

'I've shed my skin. Would that you could, too, Penn. It might see you through this nightmare.'

But I don't need another skin. I just need more time.

I'm 43 minutes and 4 seconds late as I sprint from the prison cell in the bowels of the world. And during those 43 minutes my friends could have been killed 100 times over. If they have been, it will be my fault, my burden to bear. Because it will have been my 2 parents who struck the killing blows.

*

Even within the maelstrom there are plenty of things to count, even as I use the humming buzzing noise to do what I have never done: to make someone frightened.

The steps it took to get here, to this broken street: 913.

The number of breaths Jonah has taken since I arrived: 0.

The number of times I have felt my mother's hatred: 100. Multiplied by her fear: 1,000. And again by her greed: 1,000,000.

The number of times I have felt her love: 1, just now.

In my body there are 2 eyes, 10 fingers, 10 toes and 2 lungs. There is 1 mind, 1 soul, and 1 heart.

But it is 1 heart filled with numbers, each number with a name of their own, a heart of their own. These are the only things I can't count: the good people in this world. They are numberless.

CHAPTER 37

★

Count the seconds now. Count the moments that pass as she grows wearier, as she grows older. She is heavy with the weight of greed, the burden of magic. She gave in to that burden long ago, let it crush her into something small, small, too small for a soul to fit inside. So I'll count the seconds until she is free, until I can use the strangeness of fear to release what hides within her. And I'll count the seconds until I go, too. I'll count until I can't count anymore, can't count all of my favourite things, like Finn's stories or Jonah's jokes or Isadora's words. I'll just keep counting and the numbers will fill me up and quiet the buzzing, and they'll be gentle and sweet and they'll fill my 1 single heart to bursting.

Chapter 37

Finn

I sat on the steps of the palace, watching as their bodies were gathered up and carried away. I'd come here to this city to get them both out safely, and now they lay before me, dead. My body felt almost as dead as theirs. My heart felt worse.

I couldn't follow them into the void because I was doing everything in my power to keep it closed, to keep the sea of dead from pushing through and flooding us all. I was so weary, and not strong enough to close it properly.

Not from this side.

Someone sat beside me and I recognised his smell. Falco put his arms around me and kissed my temple, holding me close. He didn't say anything, and for that I was grateful. Together we watched Ambrose and his brother lift first Penn and then Jonah into their arms, the boys so tiny in those big, cradling hands. The Pirenti kings looked up at us, waiting for Falco's nod before turning to carry them away.

A sound came from nearby, a hideous wail. I didn't realise until Falco pulled me tight against his body that the sound had come from me, from inside me. I ruptured into violent sobs and fell against him. I couldn't breathe, couldn't bear it. Rested my head in his lap and stared up at the blue sky. 'Shh,' he whispered, stroking my face and hair.

But there was a tug that wouldn't stop tugging, a scratch and scrape and pull pull *pull*. 'They have to go back,' I whispered. 'They're already going. Find Thorne. Find him *now*. He must say goodbye to his father. I'll try to hold it.'

'Finn –'

'*Hurry.*'

I lay on the warm steps for what felt a long while. I could hear voices and footsteps all around, but I stayed still, watching the clouds and holding the veil closed with every ounce of strength I could muster.

I thought of my brothers and ached.

When it occurred to me I sat up dizzily and made my way into the grounds, to somewhere I might watch without being seen. The grass was itchy under my skin but I had no strength to stand. With my back against the wall, I waited. And I realised I should stop thinking about my brothers and start thinking about my husband.

Osric was wrong when he said we needed control over the magic to stop it from corrupting us. It wasn't about having or losing control. It was about making peace with the magic. Only then could we have not its corruption or its obedience, but harmony with it and with ourselves. Shame I'd realised this so late. I'd always been a bit slow on the uptake. But if I could somehow make Os understand the truth, he might make a difference to the warders of our future. And that, I knew, would make some of this worthwhile.

THORNE

Dawn came and the gaping dark receded from beneath me. I understood that by tying me to this tree my father had saved my life, in more ways than one. Even my beast understood. I had no more anger left, only a tired kind of peace with my role in this. And worry. A gnawing worry for my family out there.

At least I had Ma and my cousins safely here with me. They sat gathered around, keeping me company while we waited. Howl had his muzzle resting in my lap and hadn't moved all night. Sadie was chatty as usual and Ella was preoccupied with whatever Da had told her. Ma treated my wound as best she could and I felt less feverish as the morning wore on. Erik returned from the ridge to say that the battle was over and by the looks of it we had won. I asked desperately after Finn but he hadn't been able to make out individual faces. When Ma was satisfied I could walk they untied me and we started the journey to the city.

Struggling to keep up, I told Erik to take the girls ahead to find their parents. Ma hung back with me, dawdling slowly through the sun. I could only take very slow, unsteady steps. We skirted the battle remnants, of course, not wanting Ella and Sadie to see the macabre remains. But I squinted at them, sick curiosity filling me.

Erik and the girls were already inside when someone on horseback burst out of the gate and galloped towards us. I pushed Ma behind me, but saw that it was Falco. Riding to a panting halt, he swung out of the saddle. 'Quickly,' he said. 'The veil's pulling them back through.'

It took me less than a moment to understand. 'Take Ma,' I said.

'You take her.'

'The horse won't carry my weight and hers,' I snapped. 'Take her and hurry.'

'Thorne,' my mother said to me then, in a voice unlike any I had heard her use. 'Get on that horse and say goodbye to your father.'

'Oh, Ma,' I breathed, my eyes growing hot.

'Go. I'll be behind you.' Roselyn's eyes were dry, her expression resolute.

Hating myself, I mounted Falco's horse and kicked it for the gate. It was chaos inside the city. Wounded and dead were being carried on stretchers. The streets were crowded. I navigated my way through it all, heading for the palace.

He was coming down the front steps as I reached the bottom and started up them. 'Falco said —'

He barrelled into me, wrapping me in his embrace. He smelled of blood and death, but also of love. 'I'm so proud of you, my boy.' His voice trembled and he had to clear his throat. 'I'm proud to be your da.'

I swallowed, meeting his eyes and nodding. *I'm proud to be your son,* were the words in my heart, but what came out instead was, 'Ma's coming.'

Da kissed me on both cheeks and grinned, giving a little shake of his head as though he couldn't quite believe the sight of me. 'You're nothing like me, are you, kid?' he laughed. Then he was off down the steps, racing through the crowded streets to his wife.

ROSELYN

I wished for quicker feet, but I was so slow. I wished for more time, but I could feel it running out. I wished for the streets to clear, for the people to move, for magic of my own, and none of that happened.

But when I wished for you, there you were.

Sometimes the most precious wishes came true.

You were taller than everyone else, so I saw you from far away. 'Rose!' you shouted, searching for me.

I pushed and shoved, trying to get through the crowd, and Falco was yelling at everyone to move, pulling me over and around things, catching me when I tripped, but it was so busy and you were so far, my darling.

I wished to reach you, to touch you one last time, and so I did. You saw me and you came so fast and you were smiling, and reaching for me, and I for you, and our fingers touched, just the tips, and then you were gone.

I stood still in the busy street, jostled and brushed by everyone who moved around me. Falco spoke but I didn't hear him. I lowered my face and closed my eyes, and as I held my fingertips to my lips, kissing you one last time, I smiled.

Chapter 38

Ava

He was very, very real. So real I could feel his heart pounding through his shirt and mine. He was warm, and the softness of his long hair kept brushing against my neck and my jaw and my cheeks. He angled down into Sancia, finding a square not so crowded to land his pegasis, and I stumbled off and as far from him as I could get.

'Ava.'

His voice. I felt utterly mad. Couldn't stop shaking, was dizzy enough to vomit. He touched me and I wrenched away, spinning so I could shove him from me. *'Don't.'*

He raised his hands in surrender and simply stood there, gazing at me. I couldn't even look at him. Something was ripping inside me.

'Come on, petal,' he said. 'I'm not going to bite.'

I shook my head, moving further away, turning my back to him. How could this . . .? Rationally I knew it must be real, knew he must be real – Finn had opened the veil, after all – but I couldn't grasp onto it, couldn't make it fit within the person I had become, the woman I was. The loss of him made up such a part of me, of my life. Sometimes I felt like it *was* me, all anyone saw when they looked at me. The half-walker.

In the middle of the square was a stone fountain without any water. I sank onto the edge of it, my legs wobbly, and rested my head in my hands. I felt him sit beside me, leaving a good distance between us. And then he started talking to me, his words and his voice just as I remembered.

'I enjoyed your wedding day, but I thought Ambrose was a bit plain in his white tunic. Blue would have been handsome with his eyes. If

436

it had been our wedding day I would have gone for something more flamboyant. I liked your coronation too – who knew you'd been born to be a queen?' He laughed a little. I'd forgotten how obsessed with clothing he was. I'd forgotten a lot, I realised with horror. 'I like break-fasts in the morning with the four of you, and I like the stories that are told at night. But my favourite,' he went on softly, 'was when the girls were born. That's always my favourite. I go back to it again and again so I can look at the happiness in your eyes, my girl.'

'Stop,' I whispered. 'Please stop.'

He did stop, and we sat quietly.

'I don't understand,' I said eventually, face still in my palms. I couldn't look at him. 'Is this some kind of cruel trick?'

'It's just . . . a glimpse, I suppose. A chance.'

'For what?'

'For . . . some words. Some looks. A touch, maybe. Or just this. Being close. I've imagined it for twenty-three years, so I'm happy with anything, really.'

I couldn't do it. I walked to the alley that opened off the square and slipped down it, pressing my back to the warm stone of the building. Closing my eyes, I willed myself to wake.

And then I heard it. 'Ma?'

'Ma!'

'Hang on, she's here somewhere.'

The voices broke off and I tilted my head to watch, feeling so far away that I could have been watching from another world. Migliori led Ambrose and Ella and Sadie into the square, where they stopped in surprise to see not me, but a young man sitting on the edge of a fountain. He looked so beautiful and so young, sitting there in the sun.

'Who's that?' Sadie asked loudly.

I watched him stand and smile this smile, gods, such a joyful smile. Such a loving smile. And then I was watching Ambrose cross to him and take him in his arms, wrapping those stumps around him and lifting him off the ground with a wild rumble of laughter. The smaller man laughed too, returning the embrace and then wriggling out of it to lunge at the girls and kiss them frantically, making them hysterical with giggles.

'This is Avery,' I heard my husband say, and the squeals they let out then were so ecstatic that I started to cry.

Sinking to a crouch against the wall, I buried my face once more and wept. I wept for all the time lost, for all the memories he'd seen without being able to share, and for this. For the love that somehow existed in two children and a man who'd never met him. It felt bigger than me, bigger than this, than everything.

And then I heard Ella say with sudden, panicked understanding, 'Fal said the veil was closing, Da.'

Footsteps came to me. I heard him crouch, felt his handless wrists reach to brush against my back and hair. They were awkward, his touch blunt and clumsy, and I wept for this, too, unable to look at him either.

'Darling,' he said, 'time's running out.'

'I can't.'

'Why not?'

'How am I meant to . . .? I can't. It will kill me.'

'It won't.'

'Oh, *stop*. You don't know. You can't possibly. *He's not real and the woman I was when I loved him isn't real*. Not anymore. I can't afford for her to be.'

There was a silence, and then he said, 'Stand up.'

'Ambro—'

'Stand up and spend a moment with your mate, because this is a miracle. People don't get this. Nobody gets this.'

I looked at him angrily. Ambrose straightened and gazed down at me. 'I married no coward.'

As he gathered the girls to one side I remained frozen. Because if I . . . if I felt this, and he left again, then what . . . what would that do to the way I got through the days? How could I recover twice?

He appeared in the mouth of the alley and I made myself look at him. I looked at him, and I saw him, really saw him. The boy I first glimpsed in a boat out at sea, the one who turned me into a fighter, made me see what mattered in life. The boy who kissed me first, made love to me first, proposed to me first, planned to spend the rest of his life with me first. I had all my firsts with this man, this young, charming, flippant creature, this smiling creature, this laughing joking sarcastic impatient obnoxious generous creature. This was a man who died for his people, who was killed doing something foolish and brave and whose eyes had turned gold for me as he died.

'Avery,' I said, reaching for him, everything collapsing within. No walls remained, not even the skeletons of walls.

He was here with me, in my arms, his lips finding mine at last and I was wide open, my heart his. 'I never kissed you enough,' I whispered. 'I never had enough of your laughs. I never got the life we planned, but I got a different life, one without you, and you got no life, you just got to watch mine. And that's not fair.' Here it was, flooding from me in a wave of guilt. I had a perfect, wonderful life, and he had nothing. He had the eternal loneliness of watching that life and not being able to share it. He deserved so much more. 'I'm sorry. I'm so sorry.'

'I love you,' Avery said urgently, holding my face and hair and cheeks. 'I love you and I love your husband and your children. I love every moment of your life, I love it like it's mine. You don't understand how empty it would be there without your happiness. Even if I wanted to, I couldn't stop – you keep me there by the veil. Your love, petal, and Ambrose's, too, it holds me close always.'

My hands trembled from clutching him so tightly. I exhaled in a rush. 'I'm not a petal anymore. I'm nothing like one.'

'You're better,' Avery said, kissing me again.

He was so real in my hands, against my mouth. He felt warm and alive and he tasted like my childhood, like my adolescence and my memories of first becoming a woman. He tasted like the fish we caught and tasted off each other's bodies, and he tasted of the salt in our tears.

And then he tasted of nothing, no longer warm and alive because he was gone again, leaving nothing but the echo in my ears of his last word, my name on his lips.

I stood a long moment, gathering my courage and letting grief trickle away. And then I walked out into the sunlight to sit beside my family. They gathered me between them, all three managing to hold me. Ella's lips were on my cheek, Sadie's hands were squeezing my fingers, and as I turned my face to Ambrose he rested his forehead gently on mine.

'Don't cry, Mama,' Sadie urged.

'It's alright,' I whispered, feeling my husband's breath tickle my lips. 'I'm only crying because I'm so lucky. One person oughtn't get to be so lucky.'

THORNE

I ran through the hallways of the palace, through the enormous main hall with its high ceilings and marble floors. I ran up flights of stairs, through pungently smelling kitchens and dusty libraries. I checked the roof, I checked the dungeons. I looked and looked because her brothers were both dead and I couldn't find her and it was striking fear in my chest. Something felt intrinsically wrong inside me, a pounding dread, and my eyes were burning gold and wouldn't shift.

'She was here,' Falco said. 'Not long past. She sent me for you.'

'Then where?' I demanded. 'I have looked.'

'Calm down, brother,' he told me. 'We'll find her.' He said nothing of Isadora, who had also disappeared, but I got the sense that he knew his Sparrow didn't want to be found.

I took off, heading for the grounds, but this time I took the balcony and so I spotted her. Finn was sitting on the railing, her legs dangling over, light wind picking up her yellow hair. I gave a huge sigh of relief. The dread eased a little, but lingered. Something still felt wrong. 'There you are.'

She looked over her shoulder and smiled at me, a glorious smile. Her eyes were as gold as mine. 'Hello, beasty-boy.'

'What are you doing?' I crossed to stand beside her. The ocean crashed below, glittering in the sunlight. She was sitting perilously close to the edge, but I wouldn't chide her. *Finn of Limontae*, she'd say, *does not fall.*

'Waiting for you.'

I swallowed; my heart was enormously heavy. 'I'm so –' I cleared my throat. 'I'm so sorry, darling. For Jonah and for Penn. It is . . . unbearable.'

She didn't say anything, just watched the water. I had never known her not to speak, so I waited.

'How long will you love me?' Finn asked finally.

'Always.'

'And how long will you live after I'm gone?'

'Finn –'

'How long?'

I took a breath. 'As long as I'm able.'

She smiled again. 'Did you see him? And say goodbye?'

I nodded.

'It's been worth it, then. Just to have him here once more. And Avery, I think. I think the last was Avery.'

'What's been worth it?'

'And if he hadn't been here to tie you to the tree you wouldn't have made it through. I know that much.'

'What's been worth it?'

Finn turned to look at me properly, and she was smiling still but there were tears in her eyes and they were scaring me cold. 'I keep going and getting myself killed. One of these times it was bound to stick.'

And it occurred to me in a rush that I hadn't touched her.

That dread in my guts – it had known. My golden eyes had known. As I reached for her face my fingers went straight through her. A sound left me, a low groan, and I had to catch myself on the balcony. 'Come back,' I gasped. 'Come back.'

Finn shook her head gently. 'I shouldn't have tried to bring anyone through. We live and we die, and that's as it should be. I've had three births already – I need no fourth.'

'*I need you,*' I said. 'Either you come back or I follow you. *That's* as it should be.'

'Thorne. If you love me –'

'*If?*'

'*Because* you love me, you will live. You will *live*, and it will be such a life. Precious and rare and full.'

But that wasn't my life. Not anymore. Life was abruptly too long. Impossibly long. It stretched out unendurably before me, filled only with loneliness.

'No,' she murmured, 'life is a blink. Less than. I can see it now.' Her legs swung back and forth. 'Don't tell anyone yet. Leave it a while. Let them . . . be.'

441

Grief made a shell of me, a husk. I didn't care about anyone else. My beast was howling and howling and *howling* within. He would never stop.

Then my wife turned to me and smiled again, and I could see the freckles on her nose as she whispered, 'It's beautiful here, Thorne. It's filled with the most beautiful music. Shh . . . if you close your eyes and listen, I'll show it to you.'

And so I did, and she did. Through the deep binding between our souls, the one that would never break, not even in death, I heard the soft humming voices of the dead, and it was. It was extraordinary. It was the meaning of it all. It was love.

CHAPTER 39

FALCO

'They're all dead,' I said. 'Every single warder who tried to take this country from me. All but one.'

Gwendolyn the Viper was sitting inside the dungeon cell as I addressed her through the bars. She looked tired and sad. She didn't look much like a warder.

'Why should you live, Viper?'

'I shouldn't.'

I considered her. 'You saved us, in the cages. And again, freeing Penn.'

'Not enough,' she murmured. 'It wasn't enough.'

'We never feel as though it's enough, but sometimes it is. For helping us at great risk to yourself, you're free, Gwendolyn. Penn would have wanted that.'

She looked shocked. 'No, Majesty. I don't trust myself.'

'Then I shall trust you, and that will be enough.'

'She means her magic,' Osric told me from the base of the stairs. He'd been following me everywhere since the battle, intent on protecting me.

'I know what she means.'

'You should ban it,' Gwendolyn said. 'Ban all of it.'

I frowned, glancing between them. 'I'll not ban something that is born into people. That would be a crime. Instead I will trust in the strength of their spirits, and I will help guide them to kindness.'

I unlocked the cell, but Gwendolyn didn't walk from it. She knelt low and pressed her forehead to my feet.

Outside the dungeons I told Osric I needed to be alone, and I walked up through my palace to the room that had been mine, and before that my parents'. They had loved each other in this room, without being bonded, and they had died here on the same day, together, without being bonded.

I'd had Dren and Galia's belongings removed so now the room was bare. I sat on the balcony and watched the stars. I thought of my nation and felt exhausted by what lay ahead. I was sure, though. In my heart I was sure about what needed to be done, and there was comfort in that, at least.

It was Thorne who eventually found me. He pulled a chair beside mine and sat with me, watching the sky quietly.

'When do you leave?' I asked.

'Tomorrow morning. We need to get the girls home, and Ambrose is determined to rectify Vjort.'

'What will he do with it?'

'Clear it out. He told me last night that he doesn't want a single soul left inside its walls. That it will be forbidden to enter – at least until the memory of the violence there doesn't taint it anymore.'

'He's really going to change things, isn't he?'

'He says that by not putting our faith in kindness, we let it die.'

I smiled, thinking it very like what I had come to believe about the warders. 'I should find Finn and tell her how much she annoys me before she goes.'

Thorne laughed a little, but it was just a breath, really. 'She . . . went ahead. You might not see her for a while.'

'Oh. How is she?' I asked.

He shrugged. Looked at me. 'She loves you. She said to tell you.'

'And I her.'

Thorne smiled and nodded as though that was right. 'It's the girls you should be more worried about. They're already weeping at the thought of saying goodbye to you.'

I was dreading it myself.

'What will you do here?' he asked. 'The city . . . it smells of grief and pain.'

I closed my eyes. Felt his hand on my shoulder, then on the back of my neck. 'I'll just do my best to help it heal.'

'Falco, you know that if you call me, I will be here. Any time, and always.' There was something fierce in his eyes as I met them. 'There are very few people left in this world that I care so deeply for. You know that, don't you? Call me and I will come.'

I smiled, and was astonished to feel my eyes shifting to match his pale blue. 'Thank you, brother. The same goes for you. But I've never had to do this alone before. Isn't it about time I tried?'

There were unshed tears in his eyes. 'No, Falco. No. It's not about doing things alone. Nobody should have to do things alone. It's about *people*, and family, and love –'

'Okay, yes,' I said quickly, pulling him into a hug. 'You're right. So tell me what's wrong.'

'Nothing,' he murmured, but he held me tight for a long time.

'Gods almighty,' I said after a while. 'Do the berserkers know their king is such a softy?'

'Shut it,' he growled.

'*Now* you're sounding more like your da.'

He laughed.

'What a man, huh? Think your ma will marry me, now he's gone a second time?'

'You're an idiot.'

'So I'm told.'

★

Later I crept into the bedroom I'd had Ella and Sadie settled into. They were sleeping in the same bed, while Roselyn and Erik slept in chairs by the door. I didn't know exactly what that poor group had gone through together, but they clearly didn't want to be parted.

I sat on the edge of the bed, shoving Sadie over so I could lie beside them.

'Ow! *Fal*.'

'Move over then, fatty.'

She grumbled but moved aside. Ella reached over her and took my hand. 'Told you.'

'What?'

'That you were a chrysalis.'

The three of us stayed like that until morning. It was the best sleep I'd had in weeks. In the morning I kissed them goodbye, thanked Ava and Ambrose as profusely as I possibly could, and then I waved as their carriages rattled out of sight.

Osric and Brathe were at either side of me on the steps. I hadn't expected Brathe to be here, so soon after losing Inga, but he was and I was grateful.

'Let's get to work, boys,' I said. 'We have a country to rebuild.'

'Should we not wait for the Sparrow, Majesty?' Brathe asked. 'She will want her people taken care of, and a say in the ruling of Kaya, surely?'

I shook my head, my heart aching. 'Her people are our people. We are one, and so we will act as such. All who fought for the Sparrow are welcome here, or welcome to return to what remains of their forest. And as for Isadora, I don't think we'll be seeing her for a while.'

'Why, Majesty?'

I smiled, eyes lifting to the sky. 'Because she's free.'

EPILOGUE

ROSELYN

I am a long way away when news reaches us in the north of Emperor Falco's announcement. I am 'as far north as any man or woman can wander, are they not made of ice themselves', as Erik puts it.

The castle where the hirðmenn grew up sits perched on a jagged sea cliff. The icebergs in the water are blue with cold, and the sky dances violet and green some nights. It is just as he described it in his stories, or perhaps more beautiful. We sit and watch these lights together often, drinking wine and speaking softly, just as we are when Erik's sister delivers the announcement. One year from the day Falco reclaimed his throne and began to rebuild his nation. One year from the day Erik changed my life.

After Falco had crawled into bed with Ella and Sadie that night, Erik and I crept out, sure of their safety while the surprisingly capable Emperor of Kaya watched over them. We found ourselves in a dark corridor, much like the one in Vjort where it all began.

'Can I escort you to your room, Lady?' he'd asked me, and I'd nodded.

With our feet clipping against the marble – what a strange building, made of odd smooth stone – we reached the room I'd been put in for my stay in Sancia. The Pirenti folk were leaving in the morning, and though I felt bad for thinking it, I would be glad to leave this city with all its sadness. Poor darling Finn had lost both her brothers, and I hadn't known that night that she too had been lost.

We reached the door to my room and paused. 'Goodnight,' I said.

'Lady Roselyn,' Erik stalled me, 'I must ask you something.'

I waited, thinking obsessively as I had been of those last moments with Thorne, and the look in his eyes as our fingers touched.

'Would it please you to have me as your servant?'

I blinked. 'Pardon?'

'I . . . have a hole in my heart, of your very making, Lady. I must beg you to take me as your guard, for my life is yours and I shall follow you to the world's end.'

My skin burst into flames. But through that shock I understood that this was guilt given voice. 'Erik,' I said, 'you owe me nothing. *Please* believe that. I could never . . . never ask you to give up your life.'

He shook his head, his black eyes feverish. 'And you must believe that I had no life before you.'

My eyelids slammed shut. I shook my head – this was too much. He didn't know what he was saying, didn't know how disloyal even this conversation made me feel – even the *thought* of such a conversation.

'Forgive me,' he said in that deep, melodious voice.

'Guilt is no reason to change your life.'

'It is not guilt that moves me, Lady,' he murmured.

'Erik . . . I cannot . . . I have nothing to offer.'

'Then I shall make you a vow,' Erik said. 'I will never ask of you anything, Lady. *Never*. But I will follow and serve and protect. Because that is what you deserve, what your courage has earned. That and more.'

And in that dark corridor I simply hadn't known what to do except nod. From then on he followed me, stayed silently by my side, a shadow, a presence, his gentle kindness a deep and lasting comfort. I no longer felt so alone, and if I experienced guilt or disloyalty I hushed it by reminding myself that this man simply wanted to protect what he hadn't protected one night so long ago. And surely Thorne couldn't begrudge me this simple company, in a world so cold?

Now Erik and I sit in the far, far north, watching the glorious lights in the sky. The chill of the air makes me think, of course, of my husband. My thoughts never stray too far from my nieces, either, and we will return to them soon, Erik and me. We will return to my son, who has lost the greatest thing one can lose and yet still carries on. We will go back to him, because closeness is what matters, but I wanted to see where Erik came from, and how he came to be so sweet. His sisters live here with their husbands and have all turned out to be as kind as my guard.

Leerie, his youngest sister, is the one speaking Falco's announcement now. '"Choice", his Majesty has proclaimed in response to his decision, "is the most important thing in this world".' Her eyes are lit with curiosity.

'Thank you, love,' Erik says to her as she rushes off to share the news with the rest of the castle. He turns to me, smiling a little. 'He has turned out to be a worthy husband for you after all, if you change your mind, Lady.'

I blush and shake my head, then realise he is joking.

'Will we leave in the morning? I imagine you must be eager to get home to the fortress after news like this.'

I am distracted by the purple in the sky — just like the purple of Ava's eyes. Belatedly, I remember to reply. 'I'm not sure I'm ready to leave yet, Erik.' Affairs of politics have never been part of my life, nor do I wish them to be.

'As you wish, Lady.'

The words open something within me that has long been closed. I ask, unsure why, 'Am I intruding in your home, Erik? Would you have brought me here had I not asked?'

His mouth falls open. 'Intruding? No, Lady. No. I . . . have wished to bring you to my home since the first time I told you of it, back in a misty valley filled with wild horses.'

My heart starts pounding. 'But that was . . . that was before Vjort.'

'Aye.'

'You're confused, Erik. *After* Vjort was when you decided to offer your life to me.'

He smiles, and in this glowing light his strange face tattoos look beautiful. 'No, Lady,' Erik says softly, 'I am not confused.'

I shake my head, turning from him.

'Would you like me to explain?' he asks. 'I mostly get the feeling you don't wish me to speak the truth, content to remain in your memories.'

'I am.'

'Very well. Forgive me.'

449

I warn myself not to speak, but speak I do. 'What is the explanation?'

He hesitates. 'It's just . . . that I love you. Since the light of a campfire and your hair so red within it. Since then and always. I will love you, from afar, until the day I die, without needing or wanting or asking for anything in return.'

I stare at the black water, moving colours reflected on its surface. I think of the veil and my husband beyond it, and I think of the night spent learning that the protection of those I love is a greater purpose than grief or misery or being a wife. I think of the love in my heart, so much love, for my husband and son, for my brother and sister-in-law, for my nieces. I think of all this love and I realise there is still space enough for more. There is always space for more. And my husband would never begrudge me that.

I look at Erik and say, 'Thank you. It is a privilege to be loved by you, Erik.'

His eyes fall shut and he shakes his head. 'My Lady . . .'

I don't say anything more, and nor does he, but my heart whispers: *Perhaps one day.*

AMBROSE

The tasks that become impossible without hands are innumerable. The troubles in my life have increased a thousandfold. Simplicities become complex. Easy becomes difficult. I rely so much on other people, when once I was utterly independent. There is very little dignity left. I wake in the night *certain* I still have hands, that I can feel them and use them. So often I reach to pick something up, only to knock it over with a clumsy stump instead.

The things I can do without my hands are far fewer, but I think they mean more. They are worth more, because they take so much more effort.

Things like eating, drinking and dressing. Things like holding my wife, and touching her. Like helping my daughters saddle and care for their ponies. Things like facing my enemies and demanding not their fear, but their respect.

I am forty-six years old, and I have reigned longer than any Pirenti ruler has in the recorded history of the world. Before my mother, the throne was a bloody place, quickly won and lost by king after king after king. A man was lucky to survive a handful of years on that throne. And I used to believe that my longevity was because I was a man that none could kill. Because I fought and defeated all who threatened my power, protecting my family and my rule.

But here is what I know now. Here is what my family has helped me learn.

I am the longest reigning King of Pirenti not because I can make my people fear me, but because I have made them love me.

Laws are changing. Death penalties no longer exist. I am gathering a panel of people who can decide together what kind of punishment befits a crime – such decisions should not fall to one person. Vjort holds no souls and no sway over us anymore. Its barracks have been abolished, its soldiers dispersed across the country where they can't feed off each other's prejudices and violence. They have been given other jobs, peaceful jobs because we have no war to fight, no battles to win.

Nothing so important is ever easy, but because of my hands I have come to see easy as lazy. I will see a change before I die, of that I am determined. And when anyone asks me why I am doing this, I simply say that my wife inspired me to be brave enough to be the first of a kind.

AVA

In Ella and Sadie's room we have built a kind of annex around the window so that Ella can sleep within it, the cold air from outside keeping her temperature down during the night, while Sadie is kept warm. It was the only way to keep them in the same room, for they refused to be parted.

After hearing the news of Falco's announcement, I follow the steps up and up to my daughters' room, that I might climb into the annex and huddle beside them. They've turned it into a cosy fort, its walls hung with thin gossamer material and the ever-present moths. Usually they giggle and whisper and tell stories until Sadie gets too cold and then goes to her own bed, but tonight I find them silent.

'What's wrong?' I ask, squeezing my body into the small space left to me.

'Nothing,' Sadie says.

'We miss Rose and Erik,' Ella explains.

I sigh, stroking their hair. 'They won't always be north. They'd never be parted from you for long.'

'Ma, I have to tell you something,' Ella says, voice barely more than a whisper. Sadie shakes her head, looking out the window.

'Okay,' I say, concerned.

'I'm wolven.'

I frown, searching her pretty face.

'And it means you might hate me, because it makes me open the window.'

'*Hate* you? Ella –'

'I always open the window.' She starts crying and it scares me to my core. 'I opened it that night and that's why it happened. That's how he found her.'

'Who?'

'Aunt Rose,' Sadie murmurs.

'I opened the window,' Ella cries, pressing her face to my chest.

I shook my head, holding her tight. 'No, my darling. *No.* That is not your fault. You must never blame yourself for the actions of others, nor think that anything you do could deserve violence or cruelty. Sometimes people hurt each other, for any number of reasons, but that will *never* be your responsibility to bear.'

'How do we stop them?'

'With generosity and kindness and courage. Is that not what your Aunt Rose believes?'

They nod.

'She loves you both so much. We all do. Never think I could hate you, darling, no matter what you do or what you are. *Never.*'

'Even if I hurt people one day?'

I frown, stroking her face. It scares me that she thinks it a possibility. But the answer is obvious and true. 'Even then,' I tell my daughters, knowing that one of them will never be like other people. She will be different, her life more dangerous for it. But I will die to make this world the kind of place that doesn't harm those who are different. I'll die before I let my daughter be treated as another young girl was.

A girl born different, with hair and skin so ashen she was brutalised into a creature who didn't understand love. Not until it was taught to her. My daughters will not need to be taught love – they will know it, always.

THORNE

I am lying on a rock in a sea cave, thinking about the day we won Sancia back from the warders. I think of it often. In this moment I am reliving a conversation, because that is what I mostly do now. Relive things that have happened in the past. I think I am reliving this particular memory because I just received a courier message from Ambrose calling me home to discuss the Emperor of Kaya's new decree.

My mind wanders first to that very same Emperor, and how proud I am of him. What he has managed to do in one year is vast. The city has been rebuilt and restructured, and every soul who was loyal to the Sparrow is now also loyal to Falco, if only for his tireless efforts to integrate them into society and his impassioned loyalty to their leader, Isadora. My thoughts wander from that to rest on the farewell with my father, and to my mother's passage north, almost to the ice itself, with a gentle hirðmenn. And, last, it wanders to the conversation I had with my uncle that day a year ago, after the dust settled and we were alone in the kitchens.

'What was he like?' I asked. Avery.

Ambrose thought about it, balancing a piece of cheese on one of his stumps and then tossing it rather expertly into his mouth. 'Hmm . . .' he mumbled around his mouthful. 'Warm. Good-natured. Bit cocky. Very loving.'

'Sounds perfect.'

'He was.' Ambrose smiled. 'He really was.'

'Did it feel . . . How did it feel?'

'It felt like I'd known him all my life. Like he was my best friend and my brother and my lover all at once.'

I didn't really know what to say to that, so I stayed quiet, watching my uncle.

'How are you doing, boy?' Ambrose asked.

'Well, thank you,' I replied, because I did not yet *know*.

'Did it help to meet your da?' he pressed, knowing how much I had struggled with Da's identity throughout my childhood.

I nodded. 'Very much. I get it now. What you meant about loyalty.'

Ambrose nodded.

'I'm sorry . . . that you didn't get to say goodbye.'

'That's alright, mate. He and I know everything we might say to each other. He's good like that. Always seems to understand things better than you expect him to – better than anyone else does, too.'

'Aye,' I said, thinking of how deeply he had changed my life. I cleared my throat, unsure how to say what I needed to next. 'I love him. Unexpectedly, I love him. But, Ambrose . . . you know that when it comes to fathers . . .' I hesitated, then met his eyes. 'I wanted to tell you. You're the one who has been my father, and I love you as one. Always.'

His eyes widened, absurdly touched. 'Thorne.' He sighed. 'My boy. You're a son to me. I'm so proud of you.' He cuffed me over the head with his wrist. 'Now get. That wife of yours is going to need you very much.'

'That wife of yours,' a voice says now, interrupting my thoughts, 'is actually extremely bored.'

I sit up on my rock, resting my elbows on raised knees.

Finn is perched on a huge round boulder, while Jonah and Penn frolic on either side. I watch as the boys leap for the ropes and start racing each other along the course named so long ago as the Siren Nights. They swing wildly from one rope to the next, precariously hanging over the waves of the ocean cave. Finn doesn't watch their antics, her eyes fixed instead on me.

'Did you hear me, beasty-boy?'

'Yes.'

'Then get going. Ambrose wants you. Your life awaits. Shoo.'

I lie back on the rock and stare at the stalactites hanging from the roof of the cave. This was where I saw her for the second time, what feels an age ago. I glimpsed her first in a crowded city square, and then followed my house servant Winn here one night to discover the twins from the Cliffs of Limontae were running an illegal betting and rope hanging-climbing-swinging-jumping-or-whatever-it-was night. I'd thought her reckless and selfish that night. I was right about one half of that.

'Thorne,' she scolds now.

'Leave him, Finn!' Jonah shouts mid-swing. 'Let him be.'

She folds her arms stubbornly. 'Let him be to spend his life with ghosts?'

'I like that he can see us!' Penn chirps cheerfully, arriving back on the rocks first and doing a nimble victory dance. 'Nobody else can!'

I flash Finn a smug look and she rolls her eyes. 'Don't encourage him, Penn.'

It doesn't matter where I go or what I do anyway. The three of them come with me. Sometimes Da does too, but I think he spends a lot of time with Ma and Ambrose as well, even if they don't know it.

Suddenly Finn is atop me, yellow cat eyes gazing down. I can't feel her – I can never feel her. And worse, so much worse, I can no longer smell her. 'Do you have somewhere better to be?' I inquire.

'No, but you do.'

'This is my home,' I say. She's always on about me and my life, about living it better than I am but I don't let it bother me anymore. I live in the Cliffs of Limontae with Alexi, and I spend most of my time fishing or repairing the houses of the folk who live around me, or telling Alexi what his dead children have been saying about him behind his back. Ambrose, Ava and Ma take turns visiting me with Ella and Sadie – they're as well loved here as I am. Falco comes a fair bit too, when he has the time, and I visit him in Sancia a lot.

I don't go to Pirenti. Pirenti is where the gaping dark waits. The violence and the ice. The man I became in Vjort haunts Pirenti. He is cast in the shadow of the great looming mountain. Here I am free of him, and I get to be in the place where Finn and Jonah and Penn grew up, with sand and sea and cliff. What more could a man want? Apart from being able to touch his wife, of course. Apart from being able to smell her.

Penn asks me constantly about Isadora, as if he hasn't been privy to the exact same information as me. No one has seen or heard from her in a year. Falco doesn't speak of her, and he doesn't look for her either.

Not as far as I know. I can't imagine what he feels for her. All I know is that if anyone dares call her a traitor, they find themselves in very deep trouble.

'Thorne,' Finn says to me now. I sit up and she moves with me, straddling my lap though I can't feel her there. 'You two,' she says to her brothers. 'Go away.'

'*You* go away!' Jonah replies. 'We're climbing!'

Penn grabs him and they both vanish.

I meet her yellow eyes. 'This isn't good,' she says.

Oh, gods, I want to kiss her.

'I've run out of patience with your moping. So here's what's going to happen. You're going to stand up and leave this cave, and then you're going to ride north into your homeland, where you belong, and you're going to resume your job as prince. It isn't the same there now. Ambrose is changing it and you should be helping him. Depending on duties and such, you're also going to go north into the ice to spend some time with your berserkers. It'll be good for you to get back to the beast for a while. Alright? Okay, good.'

I say nothing.

She motions to me like I'm a dog. 'Come on, boy. There's a good boy, up you get.'

I can't help laughing.

Finn grins. 'There you are.'

My eyes trace her face. 'I just want to touch you.'

'You did,' she says, settling onto my lap. She moves her fingers over my face, not quite touching. 'And I just touched you, too. I touched your eyelids and your nose, and now I'm running my fingers over your lips.'

It aches, my whole body aches with missing her.

'Stand up, my love,' she whispers. 'You're more than me and our bond, and you're certainly more than this cave. So stand up and take the first step.'

Does she mean the first step in leaving her behind? Because I won't do that.

'No,' she replies. 'The first step towards whatever new life is waiting for you.'

'I can't do it without you. I need you to stay.'

'But for how long?' she asks sadly.

'I don't know,' I answer her. 'But longer. Stay longer.'

And she says, 'Of course, darling. I'll stay as long as you need.'

So I stand and leave the rock and the cave, and I start the journey north. Finn stays with me the whole way, and though we both know she won't be able to stay with me forever, I hold onto her now for as long as I can, and it's her smile and her eyes and her jokes and sarcasm that fight back the gaping dark so I can return home to where I belong: in the ice.

FALCO

Choice, I've told my people, *is the most important thing.*

I half believe that. I definitely believe in choice as a right and a necessity. But I also believe in other things. Like kindness. Generosity. Peace.

And honesty.

I believe in being who you are, whatever that might be. And if you don't know what that is, then I believe in not concerning yourself with it so much that it twists you up and gets you believing that identity is the most important thing. It's not. Identity means nothing, less than nothing. It's just something that masks truth and essence and heart. You don't need to name it or worry about it. You just need to *be*.

I've decided something in the last year: I would like to be something new. Not one of my masks or versions. Not none of them or all of them, but something else. Something that is little bits of all those versions, but also new things as well.

The new thing I'd most like to be is quiet. I never thought I'd miss the quiet of our cages, hanging side by side, but I do. So I will try to be that, but if I'm not I won't worry about it either. I'm going to just be. And now that I have spent a year rectifying some of my twenty-five year reign, I can do that.

When I was a boy I had a ma and da. I had two older brothers and one little sister. They had names and spirits, souls and smiles and gazes and words and thoughts and breaths and *lives*. I was a person who was loved. Drenched in love, a luxurious, absurd embarrassment of it.

Time and the greed of men changed that. *I* changed that. I am drenched in love once more, and this time I have earned it. Not just the love of my new family, but of a whole nation. They have forgiven me so generously that I am endlessly humbled by the human spirit. I will never forget my first family, but I will enjoy the second, because there is no one, not even a feckless Emperor, who doesn't deserve that.

I go to Elias and Sara's house a lot, and sometimes, when I can convince them out of their shyness, they come to dine with me at the palace. Wes and Anders come too.

I have been working very hard towards an end, using every skill I kept hidden, every piece of knowledge or wisdom I held secret. And when I made my announcement to my city there was an overwhelming cry of support, one that stretched throughout the world. I stood on my balcony, with the city of Sancia gathered in the rebuilt streets below, and I looked down at it all. I remembered Jonah and Penn and Finn dying there on that street, and so remembering I made my announcement.

'Greetings, Kayans!'

A cheer went up, and I smiled, enjoying the sensation of simply looking down at them without a blindfold.

'We have been through a terrible tragedy. It will live in our history as a time of darkness and loss. For that I can never make redress. I will remain responsible for this time, I will carry the burden of it always, just as I will carry the burden of the man I was.' I paused, gazing at their faces, thousands of them. They were quiet, every one of them listening. 'I was not the man you deserved as a ruler,' I said. 'I was a weak man, a cowardly one. One unworthy of you. But hear this. The woman I love believes in choice above all else and has inspired me to make a decision. To make a change. Throughout the history of Kaya we have been ruled by royal blood. Five decades ago we introduced a second ruler, one decided by the people who would rule alongside royal blood.'

I took a breath. 'I am henceforth abolishing royalty. From now on both rulers of Kaya will be elected by you. Merit will reign. The people will rule the people. I am no longer your Emperor.'

A gasp went up, a sound of collective shock. Voices rose in shouts and cries and cheers. There was a wall of noise and movement, and

I stood listening and watching it all. Quillane proved the best Empress Kaya had seen in a long time, and she'd been born in poverty, raised in the Cliffs of Limontae. She was chosen because of her passion and her knowledge, her cleverness and discipline. She'd been everything I wasn't. Kaya needed more rulers like her.

*

So now the elections are underway. Fifteen candidates have put their hands up and been sponsored by their communities, more than half of them from the Sparrow's realms. They are passionate and hard-working, and I feel inspired by them all – I feel excited by our nation.

Meanwhile, I sleep and dream of wings. I wake and think of sparrows. I eat and drink and breathe. I am.

But I am also waiting. Until I, too, am free.

ISADORA

In dreams we will find each other.

I dream of him each night, and each morning I wake to realise he's not really here.

It started with Penn's death.

I drowned in that moment. I don't remember where I stumbled to, but it was away. Falco let me go, and my last memory of him is of turning to realise he was watching me, his eyes gold.

My feet carried me away, the wound in my stomach tearing further and drenching me in blood. I'd been wrapped in a dream of flight, unaware of what was happening around me. In the real world, the two people I came across were so ludicrously coincidental that it made me wonder about fate, yet again.

Ryan, from the palace, with whom I had shared my humiliation. And the girl. The girl I saved from the dozen warders, the one who begged me to run with her, the one who said she'd never forget. Her name was Lila, and amazingly, Ryan was her husband. She recognised me before he did, gasping in horror, trying to lift me, begging him to help her. *I know her*, he'd said, and she had replied, *So do I, so help me, you muppet!*

I must have told them to take me to the house I'd been living in. The one on the very edge of the coastline, where Falco and I made love for the first time. Ryan and Lila cared for me, hiding me, and before anyone could come looking for me I bid them take me to wherever they lived.

And so it turned out that I was taken aboard a boat and sailed out to sea. There I recovered, on the lapping of the waves I had always feared. They lulled me to sleep each night and woke me each morning. I dreamed and sleepwalked and I couldn't always control it, but Ryan and Lila took turns watching me while I slept in case I moved to throw myself overboard in the night.

I learnt how to sail the boat. I healed. Neither Lila nor Ryan spoke to me overmuch, understanding that I needed quiet. I found it easy to be sweet and gentle with them. I found kindness easy, for the first time. And I had what I most wanted: solitude. A place away from other people, away from weapons and violence and those who wanted to harm me. I wept most nights with the relief of it. Of not needing my daggers. And I didn't know how I would ever go back, now that I'd been freed.

*

Ryan comes to sit with me tonight, hauling in his fishing net and casting dubious glances at me. 'I met him once, you know.'

I don't ask who – it's obvious.

'He was surprising. So surprising I didn't realise who he was until he tried to save you.'

I nod a little, not sure what he wants me to say.

'You know everyone's talking about what he's done.'

I smile: does he think I have some telepathic way of learning information from way out at sea?

'We had a message,' he says. 'The Emperor of Kaya has made a decree – one that will go down in history.'

'Don't tell me,' I say quickly. I don't think I can hear it. Hearing about him makes me want him too badly, makes me seriously consider going back to him. And that's foolish because I'm nothing now, I'm not any of the things he fell in love with. I'm not strong or determined or able to protect him. I can't fight, or kill, or lucid dream. I can't even use my daggers.

So I just fish, and watch the stars.

'You and Lila aren't bonded,' I say, which is meant as a question.

Ryan shakes his head. 'No.'

'Does that not . . . concern you?'

'Why would it?'

'What happens when you meet your mates?'

He shrugs a little, hauling the nets up and up and up. 'We won't love each other any less.'

'It's powerful magic,' I warn.

Ryan smiles. 'Yeah. But it's natural, right? Not forced, like the warder stuff. The bond's part of us.'

I shake my head. He doesn't get it.

'It is,' he insists. 'I know enough people to see – if it happens to us it's not going to make us feel pain. It's not about that. It's about love.'

I place my cheek against the wood of the boat. My heart is beating too quickly and I must slow it. On this ocean I survive by not recalling. I can't recall how badly my plan failed, how many people died for that failure. I can't recall Penn and Jonah. I can't think of Falco. He isn't mine. Not as I am now. My dreams envelop me until I can't escape them, and he's in all of them, always.

I sit with my cheek to the wood until morning, when I realise we are angling back towards shore. 'Supplies?' I ask Lila as she darts past me to angle the masts. She doesn't meet my eyes.

'Lila.'

She stops. Turns to me and takes a breath. 'I owe you my life. I'll do anything for you, Iz. Anything. Even if you don't want me to.' Then she dashes off.

And I am left watching a small dinghy row out from the palace dock, closer and closer and closer.

My body is frozen as he draws near and then climbs up the rigging. His hair is still short, though not as short as I cut it. His nose is still crooked, I see, as he hoists himself up onto the deck and turns to face me. His eyes are still crystal, bright in the morning sunlight.

'Hello, little Sparrow,' he says warmly. I close my eyes and hear him move near. 'Did they warn you?'

I shake my head.

'I'm sorry. I didn't mean to surprise you.'

'How did you know?'

'I've always known exactly where you are,' he says. 'I dream it.'

'But you didn't come.'

'I've been waiting,' Falco says.

'For what?'

'For you. To find yourself again. To recover, heal. To be alone, to have quiet. To just . . . be free of it all.'

'And you?'

'I've been getting things ready.'

'For what?'

'To leave.'

I stare at him, not understanding. His lovely face in the morning light is so dear to me I can hardly stop myself from reaching for him.

'All I want,' Falco says, 'is away. I want the horizon and new worlds, and to sail as far as I can. I want discovery, I want quiet. And you, my love. I want you most of all.'

The breath catches in my chest. 'I'm not who you think I am. Who I was.'

'Then I'll love whoever you are.'

I clench my trembling hands.

'Pain isn't cumulative,' he murmurs with a shrug. 'Whatever we've been through can be left behind on that shore if we choose.'

With his words comes a lovely truth; he keeps setting me free, again and again, to see these truths. No magic is as powerful as forgiveness. There is nothing Falco can do to me, or I to him, that we can't heal from. And this is because no magic, no hatred, no cage can ever be as immense as real love, chosen freely.

'All I need to know is if you love me in return,' he says, 'because if you don't . . . or if you need to be alone now, I understand. I'll give you whatever you need, Iz.'

I realise I have never told him, never spoken a single word of affection in all our time together. I open my mouth, but nothing comes out. I am lost for words, empty of them. His eyes are so gentle as he waits.

In my heart I feel the truth. *Whatever is left of me loves whatever is left of you. And when we become more, I will love you more. And more. And more again. Because you are my choice, my only choice.*

But if there was ever a soul born without the gift of a smooth tongue, it was me. Nothing comes from my mouth; I'm unequal to the task of giving him what he deserves. I nod, trying to let him see it in my eyes, just trying to *give* him something, anything . . .

And Falco smiles like he can feel it all the way through his body, like he knows. Like the single nod is enough.

I close my eyes and turn my face up, feeling the warmth of the sun upon it. Slow, dreamlike sweetness fills my heart. 'I don't know dreaming from waking anymore,' I whisper.

I hear his footsteps on the wood and feel his nearness.

'Am I dreaming still? I must be.'

Falco's lips brush mine. 'Then don't wake up.'

About the Author

Charlotte has been writing from a young age, and had her first novel published at 17. She is now the author of nine published novels, including the epic fantasy series 'The Chronicles Of Kaya' and the romantic dystopian series 'The Cure'. She is just as passionate about writing for film and television, and has a Graduate Diploma and a Master's Degree in Screenwriting from the Australian Film, Television and Radio School. Her television pilot script 'Fury' won the Australian Writer's Guild Award for Best Unproduced Screenplay and was a Grand Finalist in the International Emmys Sir Peter Ustinov Award for Television Scriptwriting. She currently lives and writes in a creaky old haunted house in Sydney.

Acknowledgments

I'd like to thank everyone on the team at Random House Australia for believing in this series, and for their incredible part in getting it to readers. A special thank you to Beverley Cousins, my publisher, and Lex Hirst, my wonderful editor. This has been an amazing journey, from start to finish, and you've made it a real pleasure.

A big thank you to my first agent Sophie Hamley, for your patience, persistence and kindness.

Thank you to my family for being so endlessly supportive, for believing in me and putting up with me in the throes of creative angst. Thank you especially to my mum, for reading every single draft and always being generous, excited and insightful.

And last, thank you to the readers, for being so passionate. The Chronicles of Kaya was an enormous undertaking, a true labour of love, and though I'm sad to say goodbye to it, I'm so excited to be handing this world and its characters over to you.

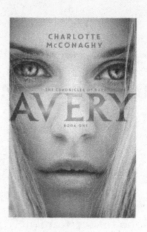

AVERY

The people of Kaya die in pairs. When one lover dies, the other does too. So it has been for thousands of years – until Ava.

For although her bondmate, Avery, has been murdered and Ava's soul has been torn in two, she is the only one who has ever been strong enough to cling to life. Vowing revenge upon the barbarian queen of Pirenti, Ava's plan is interrupted when she is captured by the deadly prince of her enemies.

Prince Ambrose has been brought up to kill and hate. But when he takes charge of a strangely captivating Kayan prisoner and is forced to survive with her on a dangerous island, he must reconsider all he holds true . . .

In a violent country like Pirenti, where emotion is scorned as a weakness, can he find the strength to fight for the person he loves . . . even when she's his vengeful enemy?

The first book in the Chronicles of Kaya, Avery *is a sweeping, romantic fantasy novel about loss and identity, and finding the courage to love against all odds.*

Available in print and ebook now!

THORNE

Lovers in Kaya have always died together, bonded in death as in life. But rumours of a cure are rife. A team of young Kayans will be sent on a quest to find the answer - for the very nature of love is at stake.

The beautiful but reckless Finn has never shied away from danger, and ending the bond means more to her than anyone knows. This adventure sounds thrilling, but Finn has always been willing to risk too much, and for the first time she has something – or someone – to lose.

Crown Prince Thorne, in the neighbouring land of Pirenti, has grown up rejecting the legacy of his father's blood, keeping caged the beast that lies dormant within. But the moment he sets eyes on the wild girl from the Kayan cliffs, his usual caution is thrown to the wind.

As the world crumbles around them, can Finn and Thorne cast off the shadows to find a love stronger than either imagined? Or is their true challenge to embrace the darkness within?

Continuing the epic series that began with Avery, Thorne *is a story of courage, sacrifice and forbidden love.*

Available in print and ebook now!